The Home for
WAR
ORPHANS

JENNA NESS
The Home for
WAR
ORPHANS

bookouture

Published by Bookouture in 2025

An imprint of Storyfire Ltd.
Carmelite House
50 Victoria Embankment
London EC4Y 0DZ

www.bookouture.com

The authorised representative in the EEA is Hachette Ireland
8 Castlecourt Centre
Dublin 15 D15 XTP3
Ireland
(email: info@hbgi.ie)

ISBN: 978-1-83618-448-5
eBook ISBN: 978-1-83618-447-8

To Kate Hewitt,
who lights candles instead of cursing the dark.

PROLOGUE

"You'll take care of her?" I whispered, nearly choking on the words. Squeezing my eyes shut, I could see the fragile veins of my lids, blood red against the sun. I forced them open. "You'll love her like your own?"

The farmer nodded. "As our own daughter, *mademoiselle*. I promise you." His sinewy arm tightened over his wife's shoulders. "We'll never forget this gift you've given us, will we, Violette?"

His wife, holding my newborn baby in her arms, just stared at me silently, her expression wavering between gratitude for the child I'd just given her and disgust that I could abandon her to strangers.

I had no choice. Couldn't she see that? I blinked fast, feeling dizzy, my body clammy and cold beneath my wrinkled dress in the warm summer air.

Swallowing hard, I reached out one last time to stroke my child's soft dark hair in the sunshine, looking down at her sweet, tiny face. She was yawning now, sleepy. For four weeks, I'd known the sharp joy and sharp anguish of being with her every moment. But I had to give her the family she deserved. Now—now or never.

But oh, that four weeks! I'd seen so much change just in that short time. Her cheeks had started to plump out, and her eyes learned to focus, lingering adoringly on my face as she nursed, her tiny hand tenderly against my breast. For the last month, lost in my love for her, I'd felt twisted like a limp, wet rag, wrung out between longing, grief and fear. Now I saw her in another woman's arms, wearing her soft baby dress, wrapped in a blanket I'd purchased yesterday in Paris. All pretty. All new.

The farmer and his wife waited.

Heart pounding, I took a deep breath and forced the words from my lips.

"Goodbye," I choked out. *Adieu*, not *au revoir*.

My baby's luminous eyes looked back at me, her forehead furrowed as if asking a question. *The* question. My legs trembled. I wanted to fall to my knees, to cling to her. To tell her I was sorry, that I was making a mistake. Tell her I'd never let her go and I'd kill anyone who tried to take her from me. Even this childless middle-aged couple with their well-kept farmhouse and flower-filled garden.

But I didn't. Instead, with another hard breath, I turned away.

I stumbled slowly over the flagstone path, going faster through the soft green grass, the asphalt of the road, the soft carpet of the train. It was unthinkable that I'd walk away from my baby, so I forced myself to run, faster and faster, until I was dizzy, until I was lost, until my heart exploded.

She could never know the truth about me.

Or about herself.

1

MARGOT

JUNE 1940

I pushed at the crowd with increasing desperation. *"Excusez-moi, madame, monsieur."* But no one moved an inch to let me pass, even as they saw the crying baby in my arms.

The southbound train whistled shrilly above the packed platform of the Gare de Lyon. The men around me muttered desperate curses, pressing forward. But there was nowhere to go. The train sitting on the tracks was already bursting, packed with hot, panting passengers like livestock headed to market. Young French soldiers stood nearby, futilely ordering people against pushing towards the train. But as they were unwilling to actually shoot, it was impossible to stop us.

Fear had spread through Paris, more terrifying than any contagion. The impossible had happened. The Nazis were at the gates of our city.

Clutching the crying six-month-old, I tried to push a few steps through the crowd, glancing up again at the bright-blue June sky. I dreaded a sudden scream of firebombs, the rat-a-tat of machine guns. We'd all heard the distant howl of Stukas in the sky. We were all afraid.

For the last year, our leaders had assured us we were perfectly safe. The Germans would never actually invade France; if they did, they'd be stopped dead at the impregnable fortifications of the Maginot Line; if they weren't, then this so-called *drôle du guerre* would end in quick Nazi defeat, a good laugh, then a celebratory dinner at a café, perhaps a cassoulet and red wine polished off by an enjoyable cigarette.

Instead, after eight months of eerie quiet since war was declared last September, the Nazis had struck with brutal force four weeks ago. Bypassing the Maginot Line entirely, they'd rammed straight through Luxembourg, the Netherlands and Belgium in a lightning-fast war that seemed superhuman, with tanks that gripped the earth, demon soldiers who fought without sleep, and planes that flew like howling devils, burning cities into fiery hell.

One by one, those other governments had surrendered rather than risk their cities being wiped off the face of the earth like Rotterdam. Our own government, which had smugly promised Paris would never be at risk, had fled the city two days ago, vanishing like ghosts, leaving the rest of us to find our own way to survive.

Or not.

I swallowed, trying to inch forward on the platform as baby Sophie struggled in my arms, her sobs falling to a hiccup, then a low pathetic moan. It was all I could do not to start wailing myself. I'd been her main caregiver since she'd been left on St. Agnes's doorstep in January, just a few weeks old. There had also been a tearstained letter, which Sister Helen had carefully saved, telling us the baby's name was Sophie, and that her poor parents were too impoverished to keep her but hoped to someday return to claim her when the world treated them better.

As if the parents were the victim, instead of the baby! I was indignant at the thought. What kind of mother would give up her child? No woman with a soul.

Baby Sophie whimpered in my arms, snot running down her nose from her recent cold. I looked down at her, my heart aching. It didn't seem fair that her parents could simply have her back now, after a single pleading letter to Sister Helen. Not fair. Not right.

But I wanted Sophie safe more than I wanted the parents punished. I looked frantically around the train platform.

"Monsieur Cleeton!" I called, but my voice was swallowed up by the noise.

Had I arrived at the Gare de Lyon too late? I should have been here an hour ago, but I'd been delayed helping Lucie. Then I'd discovered taxis had evaporated from Paris, forcing me to take the Métro, which was chaotic and crowded and ended abruptly one stop early. I'd had to run for fifteen minutes in the warm June sun, jostling Sophie with every lurching step.

Now, panicky people pressed in on every side. We all knew this train might be the last to leave Paris. Its passengers might be the last to escape the Germans. The last to live at all.

"Monsieur Cleeton!" I cried again, knowing it was useless— I'd never be heard by anyone on the train. Wretchedly, I held the crying baby above my head. My arms shook, and the strap of my leather bag dug painfully into my shoulder. With a burst of fear, I yelled, "John Cleeton!"

There was nothing—and then an answering cry.

"Here!"

I turned wildly, trying to see over people's heads as the baby squirmed and gasped, her face red. "Where?"

"Over here!" A flash of a window caught my eye. I saw a frantically waving white handkerchief through one of the half-open train windows.

The train whistled again, more shrilly than before. The

conductor started shouting for the crowds to pull back or risk getting run over. The train was about to depart.

Cradling Sophie back against my chest, I shoved through the crowd, kicking, shouting, even using my elbow against a man's middle when he wouldn't move. Finally, I managed to get close to the train window as the sound of the engine rose with the steam beneath it.

"Mr. Cleeton," I panted.

"Miss Vashon." John Cleeton looked down at me with a mixture of panic and relief. "I was starting to worry."

"How did you even get a place on the train?"

"I bribed a porter. I've been here since midnight." The American looked past me eagerly. "Miss Taylor?"

My cheeks grew hot. "Sister Helen said to thank you. But she heard a rumor the army's burning petrol rather than leave it for the Germans, and we need every liter we can get for our journey..."

"Ah." The light in his dark eyes fell.

I felt bad for him. John Cleeton was very old, probably in his mid-fifties, but still handsome, with salt-and-pepper hair and broad shoulders. He always made sure to bring candy or little toys when he visited St. Agnes's. It was clear he was madly in love with Sister Helen, while she didn't care two figs about him, except as a benefactor to the orphanage.

"Of course," he murmured. "I wish you all safe journey."

"Thank you for taking Sophie with you," I blurted out. "Most men wouldn't have done it."

He tried to smile. "You know I'd do anything for her."

I wasn't sure if he was talking about the baby or Helen Taylor. I glanced at Sophie. "She's mostly over her cold. The bag has everything you'll need." I wiped the line of snot off her cheek with the bottom of my shirt, then glanced towards the train carriage door. The shallow steps were already packed with grim-eyed people clinging to whatever they could. "But how do I get on board?"

"You can't." John Cleeton reached his hands through the window. "Give the child here."

Steam hissed against the tracks as I stared up at him in dismay. "Through the window?"

"It's the only chance."

Looking at that window, which slid only half-open from the top, I sucked in my breath. How could I make the baby fit through such a small space? It wasn't safe.

But I had to. I looked at Sophie's face, her big eyes and dark hair, and my heart clenched. Sophie, the sweet baby I'd loved for months, waking up at night to feed and change her, holding her in my lap as I studied history and did math sums in the afternoon. I loved her as I loved no one else, except Lucie. And she'd be much better off reaching Marseille in a single day's journey, to be safely reunited with her parents there—whether or not they deserved her—than waiting to escape Paris with the rest of us, driving the hot, dusty road on a slow, dangerous route already clogged with refugees and army trucks.

"All right." Trembling, I pulled the bag from my shoulder, which held her papers and clothes and milk, and pushed it through the window.

The man had barely taken it before the train gave a rough lurch forward.

"Hurry!" he gasped.

I lifted the baby towards the window, but it wasn't easy as the train was moving now, albeit slowly. "Here—" Walking forward, my body pressed against the train to avoid the crowded platform, I angled her small body horizontally, to shove her inside as he reached out. "Don't drop her!"

The train jolted, and for one horrible moment his large hands closed on air. Then he caught Sophie before her small head could bang against the window's metal frame and he pulled her inside.

I had a single image of the broad-shouldered man cradling the baby in his arms, against his sleek gray suit, his head bowed as he stared in shock, before the train's speed exceeded my own and they were gone.

I found myself blocked by crowds of people standing still, all of us bleakly watching the train disappear. I was still panting for breath, my body covered in sweat beneath my striped shirt and loose trousers.

Sophie was safe now. A lump rose in my throat as the train vanished. As long as the Germans didn't bomb the tracks, she was safe.

At least, safer than the rest of us.

2

MARGOT

Half the crowd melted away after the train was gone, leaving maybe two hundred *désespérés* still slouched over luggage, praying for another train. But the tracks were now empty, except for the bitter stench of worry and despair.

Slinking out past wide-eyed, fidgeting soldiers barely older than I was, I hurried north on the rue de Lyon, avoiding the subterranean chaos of the Métro. I couldn't stop hearing Sophie's wails in the stranger's arms on the hot, packed train.

The air was heavy and strange, though the sky was crystal blue and the summer air soft as a caress. I wondered what chlorine or nerve gas would feel like. *Taste* like. The Nazis hadn't used chemical weapons yet, but that didn't mean they wouldn't. Old Berthe had told us stories about Yperite used in the Great War, falling softly through the air to annihilate skin and asphyxiate lungs. A million Frenchmen had died, an entire generation, including her son.

I took another breath, and my nose twitched as something itchy hit the back of my throat. I tasted smoke, like burning fuel.

I waited to see if I'd collapse and die, and a moment later, when I hadn't, I looked down at my heavy, clunky old shoes that had once belonged to Berthe's great-nephew. He'd apparently been around St. Agnes's a lot last summer, while I was away in the country working as an au pair. By the time I'd returned to Paris last September, at the start of the war, he'd joined the army—I wiggled my toes—but he'd forgotten his old shoes.

Still, leaving my summer job in Boulins, the place I'd been so happy and independent, had felt unbearable, a sacrifice that still broke my heart—

Not for long. My soul sang. Soon I'd return to Boulins. The plan was that Sister Helen would leave me there on their way to Marseille. Perhaps we'd be there as soon as tomorrow, if the roads weren't too bad. In the middle of war, after nearly all my life spent in an orphanage, the arrangement seemed too good to be true.

As long as we could get there. As long as we didn't die in Paris first.

With a deep breath, I pushed myself forward in my ridiculous big shoes. Step, step, step. Clonk, clonk, clonk.

The sound echoed strangely in the quiet. The place de la Bastille, normally bustling, was empty, eerie on such a beautiful June day. The tall column of bronze and marble, crowned by the gold winged spirit representing freedom, was half buried in sandbags at the base, not much protection if the Germans really wanted to bomb it. Pausing, I looked up at the joyful gilded figure holding an upraised flame; at the star above his head. The statue always made the little girls giggle. Without exception, Noémie would take her thumb out of her mouth to plaintively ask why the nude figure's *maman* didn't make him wear underclothes, at the very least.

I jumped when I heard the distant dull thunder of explosions. Looking up from the monument, I saw a trail of thick black smoke rising malevolently over the blue rooftops. I could smell it, too.

Nervously, I hurried up the deserted boulevard lining the

eastern edge of the Marais. The normally bustling shops and stores were shuttered, desolate. I saw no one, not even a cat lazing in the sun. I tried not to imagine a Nazi soldier waiting behind every shuttered newspaper kiosk.

The richest Parisians had long since left the city, taking chauffeured cars to their estates in the south amid the first whiff of war last autumn. Over the last few months, as the Nazis began their invasion in earnest, the French bourgeoisie, both *haute* and *petite*, packed up their Peugeots and Renaults with wives and children and fled, too.

Only the desperate were left in Paris now, those too poor, too sick, too old to leave. Or too young, like the orphans of St. Agnes's.

I gasped when I heard a smash of glass, chiming shards collapsing in discordant music. Behind me on the deserted corner, three scrawny young men, pale as vampires, were climbing out through the broken window of a closed *café-tabac*, their arms full of cigarettes and liquor. My lips parted. French soldiers? *Deserters*.

One of the soldiers saw me. His face was in shadow, but the whites of his eyes sharpened. "Hey—you—"

Shivering, I turned sharply left, running through the winding streets of the Marais until I reached the rue Froissart. At the tiny alleyway of the rue des Orphelines, half hidden beneath the shadows of a wisteria-covered arch, I doubled over to catch my breath, looking behind me like Lot's wife.

But I saw nothing, just the closed shops of the rue Froissart, the slender street deserted as everything else. Of course the soldier hadn't followed me. Why had I felt such terror? Fear of the Nazis was poisoning the very air. And yet, I almost cried in relief to be safe on my own little street.

The rue des Orphelines was so tiny that calling it an alley seemed too grand a description. Once, this corner of Paris belonged to Benedictine nuns, with fields and gardens as far as the eye could see. The first foundation stone of that convent had been placed by a broken-hearted widow who'd devoted her life to charity, in part because she was kind and good, and in part to avoid being forced into a loveless marriage by her uncle, Cardinal Richelieu. She'd succeeded so brilliantly at being a benefactress that the king eventually made her a duchess in her own right, and she'd been allowed to remain husbandless as she wished. Which is exactly how Sister Helen says such stories would always end, if the world rewarded virtue as it should.

But who knows how much of that story is true?

I looked up the slender cobblestoned alley towards St. Agnes's. Officially, it was the Refuge Sainte Agnès pour Orphelines et Filles Abandonnées. As an unfunny joke, Lucie and I called it the Bin for Unwanted Girls.

The duchess's convent had been demolished long ago. This ramshackle three-story house, built in 1640, was all that remained from those days.

Once, St. Agnes's had been the most esteemed school for female orphans in Paris and maybe even all of Europe. St. Agnes orphans had grown to be exceptional women for the age: doctors, artists, and scientists, as well as secretaries and teachers.

But at the turn of the century, the duchess's endowment had finally been depleted. Funded only by charitable donations, St. Agnes's had gradually fallen into disrepair. The building now looked its age, with leaded windows, old timbers sagging on one side and additional rooms shoved on *n'import comment* over successive centuries. Sister Helen herself had only somewhat improved the look by adding pink paint—now peeling—which peeked out from behind the ivy and wisteria that had since twisted up the walls. And thanks to Mr. Cleeton, we now had modern plumbing, with hot and cold running water.

Surrounded by green trees and a shady garden behind the gates, it was the only remaining building in the little alley now tucked behind newer, grander streets built after the Revolution.

The orphanage had long passed from church hands to private charities, but lost and orphaned girls had always been so obviously well cared for, even bloodthirsty *révolutionnaires* hadn't had the heart to tear it down.

Most of our neighbors were kind, but a few starchy residents on those "new" streets loathed us. They loathed Sister Helen, too. They might have respected her more if she'd been a nun, but *Sister* was a courtesy title she'd been given while nursing for the Red Cross on French battlefields two decades before. An American, a mere *nurse*, now the headmistress of a hardscrabble home for female orphans, was far less impressive, the sort of person one might admire at a distance but certainly wouldn't want living next door.

Until recently, twenty-six of us had called St. Agnes's home. Twenty girls, of which I was the oldest; three teachers in addition to the headmistress; Yvonne, the housekeeper; and Berthe Cochet, the elderly cook who'd lived at St. Agnes's for most of her life. We also had a part-time mechanic who lived nearby with his wife, plus a daily cleaning lady to supplement the efforts of the orphans to keep their own areas tidy.

Now, Sister Helen was our only remaining teacher. Most students had departed, too, disappearing one by one as she found foster families for them further south or west. So with baby Sophie safely on the train to Marseille, there were only eight of us left: six students plus Sister Helen and Berthe. The cook, who'd lived in Paris since her birth in 1860, sniffed that no mere Boche could ever drive her from her home.

Berthe was still stubbornly refusing to leave. Our stunned French army was supposedly regrouping to the south and hopefully would chase out the Germans soon. But who knew what would happen? No one wanted to leave Berthe behind, but in just one hour, Sister Helen, me, my sister Lucie, my nemesis Josette and three little Jewish orphans would be on the road to Marseille.

Our old German-made truck was already parked in front of St. Agnes's. Four girls were climbing over the back of the truck like ants over a picnic basket. They looked up when they saw me.

"Margot, did you do it?"

"Did you really give Sophie away, Margot?"

Stung, I walked towards them. Two of the girls stood in the back of the truck, tying a tarp between the two wooden slatted walls to create a makeshift roof, while below them, the other two packed supplies against the back of the cab.

"I didn't *give her away*," I replied irritably. "I got her a comfy first-class train ride to Marseille."

Eleven-year-old Estée Lévy and her sister Rachel, two years younger, looked at each other doubtfully on the back of the truck, as if trying not to cry.

"But... baby Sophie," Rachel said.

Their grief and uncertainty churned inside me, mixing with my own. I said firmly, "She's fine."

"Estée, be careful: you're going to drop it—*Estée*," Josette cried. Though we were only a few months apart in age, the seventeen-year-old redhead was my least favorite person. Bossy. Always finding fault with my well-laid plans.

"What are you doing with that tarp?" I asked her now.

With a sigh, Josette tossed her perfectly coiffed hair. "In case it rains. Sister Helen says we might need to sleep in the back of this truck. For maybe a week."

I snorted. "A week to drive to Marseille? That's nuts. It'll take a day, maybe two."

"Says you." Josette Dubois looked down at me with cool green eyes carefully lined with mascara and black kohl, as if she were already the starlet she aspired to be.

"And you think a tarp will keep out the rain?" I scoffed.

She froze. "You have a better idea?"

"My main idea is *your* ideas are always bad."

Josette looked at me as if she'd like to lash out with a few choice words not for children's ears. "Look, Squeaky—"

"I don't mind a little rain," interrupted Rachel, stepping between us as I ground my teeth at the hated nickname. "I think it will be nice if we get to sleep outdoors."

"Easy for you to say," Estée muttered. She pushed up her glasses and glanced down at one of her precious books, resting near her on the flatbed like a security blanket. "One drop of water warps *everything*."

Five-year-old Noémie Bonnet peeked at me as she carefully placed a small box of blankets on the flatbed. Her brown eyes were sad as she cradled her ever-present teddy bear. "Did you reawwy give Sophie away, Margot?"

Stuffing down my feelings, I reached out to ruffle her hair. "Don't worry, *ma petite*. Sophie's with Mr. Cleeton, and he knows all about babies." I tried not to think about what it would actually be like for a childless widower to tend a sick baby he barely knew on a packed, overheated train. I added quickly, "Remember how nice he is, always bringing us toys? He'll take good care of her."

The little girl brightened. "You're right."

Josette finished tying her side of the tarp, looking me over from my sweaty hair to my rumpled shirt and the dirt along the edge of my loose trousers. "So you had no problems at the station?"

I scowled, irritated her sharp eyes saw so much. Josette Dubois always acted like she was better than me, more responsible, with bigger dreams. Sister Helen, sadly, bought into her act and often left her in charge. It had been a shock to both of us that morning when the headmistress had asked me, rather than Josette, to take baby Sophie to meet John Cleeton at the train station. I'd been smugly pleased.

Until Sister Helen, before she left, also asked Lucie to find a pharmacy that wasn't closed and buy medicine for Berthe. I couldn't believe the recklessness of the request. Let my dreamy little sister wander the streets of Paris alone, in such a dangerous time? No.

Josette could have gone in her place, but then Lucie would have been left alone in charge of the three little girls, an equally worrying prospect. So I'd insisted on going with her, and by the time we'd found an open pharmacy and rushed back to St. Agnes's, it was past time for me to leave. When Josette pointed it out, I'd airily told her I'd catch a taxi—of which, of course, there turned out to be none.

But there was no way I was going to tell Josette that I'd arrived an hour late at the Gare de Lyon and had to toss baby Sophie through a train window.

"Everything was fine with the train—no trouble at all," I responded serenely. I looked around. "Is Sister Helen back?"

"She's next door." Josette pressed canned goods into shelves built against the cab wall of the flatbed after Rachel and Estée handed them to her. "Trying to convince the widow to keep an eye on our place while we're gone."

"Madame Hébert?" I said incredulously. "She's more likely to burn the orphanage down."

Wealthy widow Séverine Hébert, with her hard beady eyes and long jet-black hair, seemed to hate children in general and poor orphaned girls in particular. Her elegant five-story town-house—the nicest, biggest mansion in the whole neighborhood— sat on the north corner of our alley, facing the rue Commines. She was our only close neighbor who hadn't yet departed Paris. Probably, I thought sourly, because she figured Herr Hitler was a fine fellow and she wanted to invite him to be patron of her theater.

"Is Lucie with her?" I asked.

The older girls said nothing. Estée, looking haunted, glanced at Josette, then bit her lip. Clearly she'd been told to stay quiet.

"Where's Lucie?" I demanded.

Noémie, the youngest now baby Sophie was gone, tugged on my shirt with the chubby hand not holding her teddy bear. "Wucie's not coming," she whispered. "She says she's staying to take care of Berthe."

My blood ran cold. That sounded just like the sort of hare-brained thing my sister would want to do. I forced a smile. "But Berthe's so much better already. Now she has more medicine, even *she* will tell Lucie to go. Don't worry. We won't leave Lucie behind."

As I turned away, my smile dropped.

"You're not supposed to go to the attic," Josette called. "Sister Helen said she doesn't want you to argue—"

"*Sister Helen said*," I repeated mockingly. Did the head-mistress think I'd abandon my sister? Of course I had to talk her out of it! Grinding my teeth, I went up the steps into St. Agnes's.

The foyer was empty. The best furniture had been sold this year to pay expenses, as the charitable funding had dried up amid the war. The rest had gone to cover our travel expenses. I hurried up the rickety staircase, taking the steps two at a time. The balustrade needed repair, bald of its gilded paint, with many balusters missing. It gave the stair railing the look of yellowing teeth with gaps.

I went all the way to the top, to one of the large, mostly empty dorm rooms currently acting as a makeshift medical quarantine. I knocked, then threw open the door. Beneath the shadowy eaves, it took a moment for me to see the white-haired cook, half covered with a blanket in one of the beds. "Berthe..."

Then ice froze my throat as I saw a hulking shadow sitting beside the small bed. A shadow far too large to be my sister.

The man slowly rose to his feet, his handsome face half in darkness.

I gasped. *The deserter*. The soldier who'd smashed the window glass of the *café-tabac*. He'd followed me!

Still gripping his stolen bottle of liquor, purloined cigarettes hanging from the pocket of his army uniform, he looked me over with an insolent smile. "Lovely to see you again."

It took all my effort not to turn and flee. But I couldn't leave Berthe helpless and alone. Gripping my hands at my sides, I lifted my chin. "How did you get in here?"

His sensual lips curved as he approached me, pinning me with his dark eyes. "Through the back door."

My heart was pounding wildly. "If you come any closer, I'll scream!"

"No, you won't." After leaning back hard against the door, slamming it shut, the young man kicked his wooden chair towards me with his boot. "Sit down, Mademoiselle Vashon. And be quiet."

3

HELEN

"*C'est ridicule, madame*—your orphanage is still here," my neighbor said, quite literally looking down her nose at me. "The noise. The mess! The obscene pink color, fit for a dress—not a house!" She drew herself up. "Sell me the property. I will pay you a good price, and after you leave, none of you need ever return to Paris."

Setting my jaw, I stared up at the blue sky above Séverine Hébert's elegant belle époque townhouse. She hadn't invited me inside after her butler answered the door. Instead, the wealthy French matron, perhaps ten years older than my own age of fifty, had arrived in all her jeweled silk glory to harangue me at her doorstep.

It was a game we'd played since I'd first arrived at St. Agnes's nearly fifteen years before. An acquaintance of mine had died, and I'd come to Paris in search of her two small daughters who needed care. I'd taken them to the best girls' orphanage in the city, intending to leave them there, only to discover the place was falling apart. The elderly headmistress was dying, the money that had funded it long gone. The woman was being forced to sell the building to pay off debts and banish the twenty-odd girls to a derelict boys' orphanage on the edge of the city.

In 1925, I'd looked at three-year-old Margot and little Lucie, as well as all those other motherless girls, and I'd known I couldn't let that happen. So I'd abandoned my own plans and sunk not just my life savings but my life into keeping St. Agnes's in the same house where it had existed for centuries. The girls could learn and thrive best in the very center of Paris, as so many abandoned girls had before them. They would have an education that would give them the ability to succeed.

Madame Hébert had been none too pleased when the property had been sold to me—on the understanding that I'd continue the school—for half the price she'd offered to pay, hoping to raze the building and extend her garden.

Now, as I stood at her front door like a beggar, it was all I could do to hold back my temper. For every moment of her lecture, I could feel time ticking, smell fuel burning, hear the distant explosion of bombs. I could *feel* the approach of the German army like mad dogs howling now outside the city gates, slobbering for blood.

I'd managed to get nearly all my girls into good homes in the country where they could be fostered indefinitely, but it had all taken too long. As an American residing in France, my own government had been pushing me to leave France for a year, since the start of the war. But it had taken an enraging amount of bureaucracy to get exit and transit visas for the remaining girls in my care. I'd managed to book us passage to Portugal, where we'd board another ship. But first we had to reach Marseille.

Shaking myself, I forced my focus back to the widow Hébert, who was really enjoying herself now, building insults as only a Parisienne could, layering her barbs like pastry and custard in a millefeuille.

She sneered at all of us in turn, calling me a stupid *"bien-*

faitrice américaine" who stuck my nose where it wasn't wanted, St. Agnes's a disgusting hovel, the cheerful pink color I'd painted fit only for a house of ill repute, my orphan girls grubby little demons.

I said nothing, just watched her lips elongate every vowel. I longed to insult her in turn, to use the rumor I'd heard that she'd grown up barefoot, tending goats in a small village before she'd become an actress on the Paris stage. She'd later married the wealthy industrialist who owned the theater. One would think being an artist who'd climbed from poverty to a glittering fortune would make her compassionate.

But no.

As her onslaught continued, I longed to shake her. I longed for a cigarette. Instead, I just wrapped my arms across my chest, gripping the sleeves of my old blouse, and quietly bowed my head.

Madame Hébert was losing steam, starting to repeat herself. "Your pathetic little school should have been destroyed *long ago* and sold to me. I offered *twice the price*. It's *obscene*, this obstruction—this *corruption*. And that color! *Dégoûtant!* There should be a law... Your garden should be where I keep my *trash*..."

"All I'm asking, *madame*," I said politely, when she paused for breath, "is that you keep an eye on our place—and on Berthe. You like Berthe, don't you? You liked the pies she brought you at Christmas?"

"She's endurable enough, I suppose," she said after a pause. "First, she's a Frenchwoman born, and second"—she counted off with her fingers—"she's a servant who knows her place." The widow ran diamond-encrusted fingers through her sweeping, suspiciously dark hair. "Berthe can come and be my cook, if she doesn't object to the wages. Only after she's healthy, of course. I have no wish for illness in my house."

"Thank you," I forced myself to say through gritted teeth,

"but she wishes to remain at St. Agnes's and make sure that the Germans don't try to commandeer it."

"*Commandeer* it? That's a laugh. The Nazis are far too *efficient* to endure such a *derelict*—"

"Berthe has lived at St. Agnes's for fifty years. And for your information, *madame*, the orphanage has been here for hundreds, long before your street was even a street—"

"About time that ended." She looked at me crossly. "At least the Germans know to be quiet early on a Sunday morning, rather than making so much noise when the rest of Paris is trying to sleep."

Having to ask this unpleasant woman for a favor was too much on top of a morning spent begging the fleeing French army for their discarded fuel. I couldn't catch a full breath. My lungs hadn't been the same since pneumonia had gone through the house a few months back. Berthe was still recovering from it. "Please, Madame Hébert, if you'll just—"

"*Non*," she said firmly. "If you are all going to abandon your home and flee Paris like cowards, then do it. But don't expect me to guard what you leave behind. If the Germans take it, perhaps they'll sell it to me for a fair price."

Turning, she closed the door in my face.

For a moment, I just stood there, hands clenched at my sides. Then I stalked down the steps to turn down the half-hidden alley of the rue des Orphelines.

Four of my orphan girls were busily tying down cans inside the covered flatbed of the truck. At least, Estée and Rachel were, beneath the watchful eye of Josette, as little Noémie ran back and forth, waving her teddy bear as "he" sang little songs about journeys and girls who weren't afraid.

They all looked relieved when they saw me. Noémie threw herself into my arms, looking up. "Was she mean, Sister Hewen? The witch?"

I gave her a wavering smile, rustling her dark curly hair.

"You mustn't call her a witch, Noémie." Even if I privately agreed with the epithet. "It's not nice."

"*D'accord*," she sighed. Her chubby face beamed as she waved towards the truck grandly. "Wook what we've done!"

I looked and saw the careful packing, the stacks of food and bags along the edges of the back, against the cab and slatted wooden walls, leaving room for the girls to stretch out in the middle and sleep, if necessary. "You've done wonderfully. I knew I could count on you."

They glowed beneath the praise.

Turning to Josette, I added, "Though perhaps move the milk cans a little further from the fuel, dear. We don't want anything to spoil our food."

"Of course, Sister Helen." The seventeen-year-old moved quickly to arrange the cans. In her saddle shoes, knee-length skirt and blouse she'd sewn from a pattern, she looked like an American teenager at Schwab's, waiting to be discovered in Hollywood. It was a costume of sorts, copying pictures she'd seen in magazines.

I hid a smile. Josette would be thrilled when she learned my arrangement for her future. The others probably wouldn't be quite as pleased. It was why I hadn't told any of them my full plans yet—and I wouldn't. Not until we reached Marseille.

Josette added over her shoulder, "Why are we packing so much? Can't we buy food along the way?"

I'd heard rumors food was scarce on the road, but I didn't want to make them afraid. I said brightly, "Think of it as a picnic."

"Is that why we're bringing blankets? Even though it's summer?"

"One never knows," I said vaguely, then changed the subject. "Has Margot returned? Did Sophie make it safely on the train?"

"Yes," said Estée. "Monsieur Cleeton has her."

I exhaled. Thank heaven for that. I was grateful to John for securing a precious spot on the train and agreeing to take the baby with him.

"Yeah, Margot managed not to screw it up," Josette muttered. She tossed her shoulder-length red hair, which flipped up at the ends, as she tied it up in little pin curls with rags every night.

"She did well," I said, wondering if John had felt betrayed when he saw Margot arrive at the station instead of me.

It was better this way, I told myself. I couldn't lead him on. Not after he'd made his feelings for me too clear. I couldn't give him hope, not when my heart had been frozen to ice long ago. Ducking my head so they couldn't see my face, I picked up the remaining fuel can, lifting it to the truck to fill the tank.

Josette came down from the flatbed. "Margot and I do agree about something."

"You astonish me," I said dryly. The two girls were usually at each other's throats.

"I don't think Sophie's parents deserve to have her back. Not after they abandoned her on our doorstep."

"You read their letter. The husband was ill, out of a job, the wife already caring for four children." My lungs wouldn't quite fill. I felt a little dizzy, my shoes unsteady on the cobblestones. "Now he has a job in Toulon. With the Germans outside Paris, they're anxious to be reunited."

"I don't care." Josette's young face was utterly lacking empathy. "It's like Margot said. Any woman who'd give up her baby is a horrible, wretched, unfeeling thing."

The pink house, green trees and brown cobblestones started to spin. I stared at Josette. Her pretty features, emphasized with mascara and bright-red lipstick, turned confused, then concerned. "Sister Helen? What's wrong?"

Blackness swept the edges of my vision, making Josette's face shrink, then disappear, as my knees collapsed beneath me.

4

HELEN

The man I loved was speaking from far away, over the roar of the sea, his deep voice wistful and tender. *Helen, my darling, why won't you marry me?*

My eyelids fluttered. I fought to open them, desperate to see his face. He smiled down at me, his black eyes warm, his scarred face in dark silhouette, haloed by bright sun.

"Sister Helen?" But it was a girl's voice, anxious, guilty. The dream disappeared, and I saw a different pair of dark eyes peering down at me.

Other girls pushed forward.

"Is she all right?"

"Sister Helen!" A sob.

"Oh no. Is she dead?"

A wailing lisp. "Sister Hewen!"

Blinking, I realized I was stretched on the cobblestones, my legs crumpled painfully beneath me, the belt holding up my loose trousers cutting painfully into my middle. The back of my skull ached. What in the name of heaven...?

Abruptly, I sat up, which was a mistake because it made everything wobble, blue sky and green trees and rusty brown truck swirling and smearing, compressing the world into a hazy Impressionist painting like the ones on the walls of the Musée d'Orsay.

For a moment, I sat dizzy on the ground, my legs stuck out ahead of me, my head throbbing, my body shivering. I closed my eyes. For a few seconds, it took all my effort to get enough oxygen into my lungs and not feel like I was drowning in the warm June air.

A strong hand pressed against my back, supporting me. I looked back gratefully at Josette, who was biting her lower lip with worry.

Something soft was pushed into my hands—Noémie's teddy bear was in my lap. The five-year-old considered me. "You're better now."

It was a statement, not a question. I managed a weak smile. "I guess the witch sucked the air out of my lungs."

She giggled. "Sister Hewen! That's not nice!"

The fuel can was on its side against the cobblestones where I'd dropped it when I fainted. Luckily, the lid was tight, and I'd already poured most of the fuel into the truck's engine. We needed all the fuel we could get for the journey ahead. It hadn't been easy to wheedle it from the French army, even though they'd been burning off the reserves, leaving the air dirty and acrid, as if grief and rage had a smell. But I'd made a pleasant nuisance of myself until finally one of the soldiers had hissed, "She runs a home for orphans, Henri—for heaven's sake just let her have it."

Now, I felt foolish and weak, sprawled on the road like a debutante on a fainting couch, when there was so much to do and no time to do it. I held out my hands. "Help me up."

Josette and Estée tugged on my arms, pulling me to my feet as Noémie and Rachel pushed at my ribs—not quite as helpful, but it still made me feel their concern.

Once standing, I tried to smile, hiding the slight wheezing

sound that came with every breath. Stupid pneumonia—when would it finally be completely gone?

I hitched up my belt. I'd had to cut an ugly hole into the leather the previous week to make it tight enough. I'd never been vain about my looks, possibly because I'd never had much to speak of, and I'd been resigned to a slow, steady weight gain over the years. But in the last six months, I'd seen all that extra weight disappear. I knew I should be glad, and yet...

"What happened?" Josette asked. "Why did you faint?"

"It's nothing." I ran an unsteady hand over my eyes. "We should grab the suitcases. Where are Margot and Lucie?"

The girls glanced at each other uncomfortably.

"Lucie was upstairs with Berthe..."

"Still?" I was surprised it had taken our cook so long to talk the girl out of her wild scheme. "I hope Margot knows nothing about it?"

"She, uh..." Estée and Rachel looked at each other nervously. "We didn't mean to, but..."

"Margot's upstairs tewwing Wucie she can't stay," Noémie said.

"No!"

Josette frowned. "Why does it matter? *Ce n'est pas la mer à boire.*"

She didn't understand why I was making such a fuss, why I'd tried to keep Margot from learning about her sister's ridiculous plan to stay in Paris as Berthe's nurse.

But Lucie could be quietly stubborn; the angelic ones always were. The sixteen-year-old knew nothing about nursing, was a dreadful cook and often broke the things she tried to clean, while Berthe considered herself bulletproof at eighty and would never have allowed Lucie to stay in this falling city. She would have talked the girl down.

But Margot's involvement would mean a drawn-out argument between two teenagers who were each incredibly stubborn in their own ways.

I sighed. I really didn't have time for this.

"Finish your packing," I said. "I'll handle Lucie and Margot."

I went into the orphanage and through the front schoolroom. As always, my heart lifted as my gaze fell on the rows of tidy student desks beneath the high sculpted ceiling and sunny leaded-glass windows, as I breathed in the smell of chalk, soap and old textbooks.

Classes were half in French, half in English. There were no parents to push back against my insistence that all St. Agnes's girls be equally fluent in both, though Margot had once rolled her eyes, asking why in their likely future as secretaries or housewives, they'd find English necessary. To which I replied calmly, "Being a secretary or housewife might be more challenging than you think."

All students, except the very youngest or newest, spoke English now as readily as French. They might use an occasional British word, thanks to Miss Oglethorpe from Grimsby who'd taught a few years, but even then, they spoke with an American accent, *nom d'un nom d'un nom!*

But that was how I spoke it, so that was how I taught it. Most of the older girls spoke passable German, too, thanks to Fräulein Mueller. Josette's written German was the best, though Margot reportedly excelled her in both accent and understanding. Of course I'd never told either girl that. Their rivalry was bad enough.

Fräulein Mueller had also taught math, before she'd been forced to return to Austria last September. Miss Clarkson taught science and literature before she left in tears at Christmas, returning to California, her home state—and mine. Young Mademoiselle Aubert, a former pupil of St. Agnes's who'd taught world history and secretarial skills to the older girls, had fled south a few months ago with her Hungarian boyfriend.

The war made everyone choose sides, even those who wanted no part of it.

Would we ever be able to return? It seemed unlikely. Perhaps Nazi soldiers would soon be stomping dirt over our lovely waxed herringbone wood floors. The bookshelves held only a few dusty textbooks no one wanted. All the juicy, dog-eared novels, beloved by the children, were gone: *The Wizard of Oz, Anne of Green Gables, Les Trois Mousquetaires, Les Malheurs de Sophie*, and the roguish tales of Arsène Lupin, gentleman thief.

Wearily, I went to the schoolroom's small back closet, which I used for a private office. Kneeling in front of my old desk, I dug through the bottom drawer to find a hidden compartment locked beneath a false bottom. Inside were all our identity documents and my last secret stash of money. Next to it, sitting beneath it like a coiled snake, was a crumpled telegram and an old French service revolver I'd acquired in 1917 and kept all the rough and tumble years since, nursing civilians through the Irish and Turkish wars, the sickness and starvation of Soviet Russia when that brutal country was new. And then—

I exhaled, closing my eyes. That lonely trip to peacetime Germany in 1924 had unexpectedly been the most dangerous of all. The first time I'd shot someone.

Shaking a little, I opened the crumpled telegram. I'd received it the day after war was declared, and it still made my blood run cold.

i'm coming for you.

Crushing it in my hand, I threw it in the trash bin. Another reason we had to leave. Before he could take his revenge on anyone I loved.

I looked down at the unloaded St. Etienne 8 mm revolver tucked in its leather holster. Might be smart to take it. But I didn't want to be that person anymore. I *wasn't* that person anymore.

Leaving the revolver behind, I gathered up the money, sitting back on my knees against the hard floor as I counted the bills. So little left. All the furniture worth anything had long been sold. This money would have to be enough to get us to Marseille. I thought of the road ahead and tried not to be afraid. We had three weeks before our ship would depart—more than enough time to get there, even on a slow road crowded with refugees.

I hoped.

I rose to my feet, returned to the schoolroom and took an old road map of France from a drawer. I traced the southern road with my fingertips. I'd already memorized every stop—of the first half, at least. I'd bought the map many years ago, just so I could see the dot of the town where he lived and dream of him there, just a few hours' journey outside Paris.

We'd be passing within a few miles of La Ravelle. I might even be able to see the little hillside town from the road.

I wouldn't even turn my head, I told myself. Even if our fuel was down to fumes, even if we had nothing to eat, I'd never let myself visit the town where he lived.

He had no idea I was in France. The two of us could never meet again, not when it might cost him his happiness and peace. Besides, we hadn't seen each other in decades. Back then, I'd been a young woman, a nurse traveling the world with a heart made brittle by tragedy.

Would Jean-Luc even recognize me now, my brown hair streaked with gray, wrinkles at my eyes and throat?

No. Better to leave it all in the past. Much better.

I found an empty canvas school bag left behind by thirteen-year-old Martine Durand, a buck-toothed child with a serious passion for growing flowers, now sheltering with a good family on a Bordeaux farm. Safe, but for how long now the Nazis were outside Paris?

I stared blankly at the blackboard.

Returning to my desk, I grabbed the holstered revolver with its small pack of bullets, tucking them inside the school bag. France was at war. Whether or not I wished to fight, I might have no choice, if I wanted to protect my girls.

In the kitchen, I tucked some of my precious money and a note to Berthe inside the empty cookie jar. St. Agnes's would be in safe hands with her—or as safe as anything could be beneath Nazi rule. I left a notarized letter. If I never returned, the place was hers.

After leaving the kitchen, I slowly went up the stairs, holding the canvas bag tightly to my side. I wondered how I'd tell Margot my plans. The girl, unbeknownst to her, held a special place in my heart. I'd found her at three years old, crying beside her dead mother in a cold, dirty rented room near the Place Pigalle, with Lucie, so much smaller, wailing nearby. Margot had reached out her arms to me and changed my life.

As I walked up the second flight of stairs, I gripped the banister, wheezing a breath. Upon hearing a noise behind me, I turned to see Lucie coming up the stairs, her hands full of colorful roses and white Queen Anne's lace.

My mouth fell open. "Picking flowers?"

"I know—we don't have time," the girl said, smiling apologetically. "But it was the least I could do for Berthe. She says she's feeling almost perfect now she has her medicine, and doesn't need a nurse to feel better, just flowers from the garden."

Clever Berthe to give Lucie a mission. Sixteen but small for her age, Lucie Vashon had the innocent look of an angel, with big blue eyes and light blonde hair made golden by sunlight from the stairwell window. She was wearing a faded, too-large dress left by Mademoiselle Aubert. Unlike Josette and even Margot, Lucie never gave a thought to her appearance. She wore any old dress that was somewhat clean.

She was equal parts saintly and exasperating. Saintly because she was really, truly good to everyone; exasperating for the exact same reason. She prayed for the *Nazis*, for heaven's sake—prayed they'd see the error of their ways and stop invading people, and instead be kind and good. It was ridiculous. But part of me also suspected if Lucie ever pleaded my case to St. Peter, he might let even *me* past the pearly gates because who would be so churlish as to disappoint her?

"Have you talked to Margot?" I asked hesitantly.

"No." She looked pleased. "Is she back? She got the baby to Monsieur Cleeton?"

"Yes, all is well." I held out my hand. "I can give Berthe the flowers."

Gripping them tightly, Lucie shook her head. "I want to make sure I set them up in a place where she can see them."

"All right," I sighed. Best to just get on with it then.

As I struggled up the last stairs to the attic, she floated beside me, as if air held her up—or perhaps the uplift of pure heart and good intentions.

I knocked on the door to one of two dorm-style rooms that filled the large attic and waited for Berthe's reply, then pushed open the door.

Inside, the stout cook was propped up in one of the small beds, smiling, with more color in her wrinkled cheeks than I'd seen in months. Margot looked up from a nearby chair, her expression oddly guilty. But there was a third figure beside her...

I sucked in my breath. "Monsieur Cochet. What are you doing here?"

The dark-eyed young soldier gave a crooked smile. "I'm visiting my great-aunt. I brought a bottle of Dubonnet—you know how she loves it."

Frowning, I said slowly, "You're on leave from your regiment?"

"You could say that." Roger Cochet grinned. He was too handsome, too sure of his own charm. He glanced down at Margot. She avoided his gaze.

"Do you know each other?" I looked between them. She'd been away last summer, when he'd visited his aunt so frequently, right before he'd joined the army.

"Just a little," the young man said.

"Well enough," she muttered.

I wondered what they'd just been talking about.

"Look, Berthe!" Lucie held up the ripe roses, the colors of peaches and tomatoes and plums. After grabbing a vase from a nearby shelf, she poured some water from Berthe's glass, then brought the flowers to the nightstand. "I picked the prettiest ones for you."

"They're lovely, *ma petite*," the cook said warmly. "Come give me a kiss."

Lucie did so, glancing shyly up at the great-nephew. "*Salut*, Roger."

"*Salut*." Roger Cochet smiled at her, then looked between his great-aunt and Margot, who was now scowling silently at the floor. "So we're agreed?"

"Agreed," the elderly cook said, beaming. "Just for a day. Or at most two."

"What's this?" I asked suspiciously.

Roger Cochet grinned. "I heard the rest of you are leaving Paris. I have some... free time, so when I heard Tante Berthe was still recovering from her illness, I thought what better use of my time than to care for her?"

I didn't like the idea. Didn't trust him by half. But perhaps it was my own bias—he was just too handsome to be trusted. "That's very kind of you, Monsieur Cochet—"

"I've told you, *madame*, please call me Roger—"

"But it's truly not necessary. Berthe is very nearly well, and..." I looked to the cook for support, but she was staring at me indignantly. It was clear whatever feelings she'd had against Lucie staying did not extend to her charming great-nephew. I sighed. "But of course you are welcome to stay, if Berthe wants."

"I do." The elderly cook beamed up at Roger as if he'd hung the moon.

"Though I'm surprised that your commanding officer let you leave," I added, watching his face. "With the fighting still raging to the west."

Tilting his head, Roger spread his arms wide. "It is a surprising time."

"Indeed." A deserter. What other explanation could there be? And yet it seemed petty to judge the boy for following the example of France's head of state or even my own American government, which was ducking and weaving to avoid choosing sides in this war.

Clearing my throat, I turned to Margot and Lucie. "It's time to go."

"I'll walk you out," said Roger.

Margot rose to her feet almost violently. After a swift embrace to Berthe, she grabbed Lucie's wrist, tugging her sister from the room. Roger and I followed.

I could feel something unspoken between Roger and Margot, but I told myself I was imagining things. They barely knew each other. What secret could they possibly have?

The girls stopped at the attic's other dormitory room to collect small packed bags, which held their pared-down lives, a few toiletries and mementoes, some clothes. I could feel the cold steel of my revolver through the canvas school bag. I held it tightly against my ribs as I went downstairs into my own small bedroom.

Going past the window—which looked down on the overgrown garden with its greenery and profusion of roses—I collected my leather valise, packed with my clothes, some flimsy pictures, a few books. An old wedding ring. So little to show for a life. I'd had the valise since I fled America in 1915. I'd traveled with it through warzones, but after I'd settled in this house, I'd never thought I'd have to use it again.

Carrying the leather valise down the stairs, past the empty schoolrooms of St. Agnes's, my home for nearly fifteen years, I crushed down feelings of grief, of rage. Not now. Once the girls were safe, I promised. Once they all were safe. Then I'd let myself feel sad. Then I could be angry. Later.

I left St. Agnes's, following the young soldier and the Vashon girls. Seeing us, Josette leaped out of the back of the truck, her face joyful. "Roger! I didn't know you were here!"

Stopping, he rubbed the back of his dark hair sheepishly. "Hey, Josette. I saw you were busy with the truck, so I let myself in through the back door to visit my aunt. I didn't want to bother you."

"Bother us!" Josette tossed back her long hair with an artificial trill of a laugh. "You could never!"

Roger gave her a crooked half-smile beneath heavy-lidded black eyes. "That's good to hear."

It was strange to see Josette, usually so practical and determined in her ambition to become a famous actress, get so strange and silly, looking at him with big eyes she usually reserved for the appearances of film stars at red-carpet premieres. I suddenly recalled how often she and Roger had spoken last summer, sitting in the garden, taking walks, washing dishes together. It was horrifying to imagine the girl throwing away her personality, or perhaps even her life's ambition, for one handsome, shifty-eyed young man. But then, wasn't that often the way of things for women? How often did we exchange our dreams for the comfort and safety of a home, or to help the man we loved achieve his dreams instead?

And how often did that sacrifice lead to nothing but heartbreak?

Shoving the painful thought from my mind, I stacked my valise carefully in the back of the truck, against the cab wall, and secured it with rope beside the girls' bags and stacked cans of food. Then I stepped off the flatbed and tucked my small canvas bag carefully beneath the driver's seat. It held all the precious things I wanted no one else to see.

"Did you get my letters?" I heard Josette ask.

"Letters?" Roger said vaguely.

As I got back out of the truck, she threw me a nervous glance, as if afraid I would consider her fast for writing a boy a letter. "I just wanted to thank you, Roger. You were so encouraging when I told you about my dreams last summer. I took your advice. I changed my hair, my clothes." She looked down, brushing at her skirt with her fingertips. "Though it took me six months to earn the money peeling potatoes and washing dishes at the café... What do you think?"

Roger tilted his head, surveyed her, then gave a quick nod as he reached into his pocket for a cigarette and matches. "Very pretty."

Her cheeks turned pink as she beamed.

Without a word, Margot passed by, rolling her eyes before she climbed sullenly into the front of the truck.

It would all be fine. After today, Roger Cochet would just be a memory. Squaring my shoulders, I held my hand out to the young soldier. "Thank you for staying, Roger. It's fortunate your regiment could spare you. It takes a load off my mind to know Berthe is in your care."

"Of course." He graciously shook my hand.

Maybe I'd been too hard on him. After all, last summer he'd been notoriously broke, and yet he'd bought his great-aunt the Dubonnet and seemed to care about her. I would actually be relieved to have him looking out for Berthe.

How he'd explain his presence to the Nazis, I wasn't sure. But I trusted him to sort it out.

I turned with a cheerful smile. "Time to go."

The three youngest girls—Estée, Rachel and Noémie—were already quarreling about who got to sit with Margot in the front of the truck, with its soft leather bench seat, and who'd be stuck in the back, on the hard surface of the flatbed, with only two wood-slatted walls and a tarp to keep out the weather.

Meanwhile, Margot was stretched across the leather seat as if she owned it. Opening the driver's side door, I told her sharply, "You're traveling in back."

"What?" Margot sat up straight on the bench seat. "You said you'd teach me to drive. How do you expect me to learn if I'm stuck in the back?"

"Move," I told her.

Scowling, she snatched her bag and headed for the flatbed without a word.

I turned to the little girls. "All three of you will pack cozy next to me in front."

They cheered, Noémie waving her teddy bear as Estée and Rachel tripped over each other to claim the best places in the truck's cabin, Estée's glasses askew, Rachel's dark braids flying.

"Lucie, dear." I turned towards the wisp of a girl still standing on the cobblestones, staring disconsolately towards Berthe's attic window. "Please climb in back with Margot. You too, Josette."

With a sigh, Lucie floated towards the truck. Josette, after a lingering farewell to the young soldier, her voice pregnant with tears, backed in slowly, never looking away from him.

I was glad to get her away. And myself away before the Nazis came. Just in time. If the Germans ever learned my name, I'd likely be shot in the street. I couldn't protect my girls if I was dead.

Climbing behind the wheel, I glanced behind me through

the open cab window. Everything was in order. The flatbed had food, supplies, water, clothes—the girls had done everything I'd asked. My heart ached with pride. How smart they were, how strong.

I looked up one last time at St. Agnes's. Yes, perhaps the ramshackle medieval orphanage was as ugly as Séverine Hébert claimed. But to my eyes, it had never looked more beautiful.

Back in 1925, I'd changed my life on impulse. Since then, the school had become my home, a solace and comfort not just for orphaned and abandoned girls, but also for me. Because even at thirty-five, even at fifty, a woman could still feel lost, unwanted, unloved.

Golden light bathed the three-story house in a soft glow. I feared this would be the last time I'd ever see it. I rubbed my hand over my eyes—hard.

Then I started the engine.

5

MARGOT

This is a disaster.

I gripped the steering wheel, not letting myself blink as I tried to look everywhere at once on a road so tightly packed with refugees, I was scared one of them might hit us—or I might hit them.

An overpacked car was directly ahead, its bumper ten centimeters from ours, furniture strapped to its roof that was impossible to see over. Beside the slow row of cars, people trudged wearily on foot, dragging suitcases and children and tiny dogs. I saw an old woman pushing a wheelbarrow filled with apples and squash and lettuce, incongruously topped by a shining silver teapot.

In between the mass of walkers, there were bicycles, and even a few wooden carts pulled by tired horses, who left steaming piles of manure to be crushed into the road and get on everyone's shoes.

The last time I'd been on this road, traveling back to Paris from Boulins last September, the journey had been swift. Too swift, since I'd been fighting tears the whole time.

I'd been sad to leave the Lusignys, a wealthy family who'd

just had their first baby. I'd heard about the au pair job through
a friend of a friend of Sister Helen's. The headmistress had
been reluctant to let me live three hundred kilometers away,
even just for a summer. But I'd been determined. I'd wanted to
explore the world beyond St. Agnes's walled garden.

Last summer had exceeded my wildest dreams. Hugo and
Isabelle Lusigny, deeply in love, spent all their time reading
poetry and philosophy and holding elegant teas in their château,
surrounded by the lovely rolling acres of their inherited estate.
After a few nights of training provided by their departing
nanny, I'd been allowed to run my own schedule with the baby.
I'd loved the freedom, the trust of that.

I'd missed Lucie, of course. But after years of being crowded
into the dormitory rooms of St. Agnes's, it was glorious to have a
big luxurious room all to myself, even if it was next to the
nursery on the third floor. I ate the same dinners as the
Lusignys, prepared by a real chef hired from Paris. It was a reve-
lation to eat meals served hot, rather than cold, and chosen for
their deliciousness, rather than maximum nutritional value for
minimum price. We all loved Berthe for reasons other than her
cooking.

But more than the comfort, even more than freedom, what I
loved most in that beautiful castle was the encouragement.
Every evening when I'd brought their baby to them in the
elegant drawing room, the Lusignys had praised me to the skies:
how helpful I was, how clever, how pretty. Madame Lusigny
would add slyly that surely they must know some rich young
man who would be thrilled to snatch me up.

I'd blushed, but it was all balm to my soul. So different from
St. Agnes's, where I was just another orphan. When Hugo
Lusigny heard I was interested in law, he didn't tell me that
being a secretary was the best I could hope for. He didn't say I
was too stupid to learn, as Josette might have, or sternly say I
should work on improving my lackluster efforts at schoolwork

first, as Sister Helen might. Instead, Monsieur Lusigny told me to help myself to the dusty old law books in their private library, and then he'd mused aloud that he might know people in the courts who could help get me started, if I really wanted law as a career.

He saw me as an adult, not a child. For the first time, I could imagine a path to the future I wanted. I wouldn't be a secretary waiting hand and foot on a powerful man, and I wouldn't be a housewife, either. I'd seen too many exhausted, powerless matrons in our neighborhood, with too many children and never enough money, washing endless socks, cooking endless meals, taking endless orders—and never getting paid.

Non merci. I would be the leader of my own life. A shocking ambition for any female, to be sure, which was why I hadn't shared those dreams with anyone but the Lusignys.

For years, I'd simmered with fury at all the times Séverine Hébert had set the law on us, hoping to cause Sister Helen enough trouble that she'd sell the property. Policemen and busybody officials often showed up at St. Agnes's, to check the identity papers of foreign-born teachers, or the legality of the pink color on the house's exterior walls, or responding to "anonymous noise complaints."

It caused stress and inconvenience for the whole household —and the occasional expense of hiring lawyers when money was already tight. One day, standing in the garden as Sister Helen resignedly led yet another policeman through the rows of vegetables and roses, so he could search for the poisonous tropical snake supposedly living on the premises, as had been "reported in a tip," I'd looked up at our neighbor's top window and seen the wealthy widow holding her curtain, looking down her smug nose at us. And I'd known: someday, I'd be on the other side of that window.

Someday, I'd have a spacious flat with two bedrooms, one for me and one for Lucie, with a sleek kitchen and modern conveniences, instead of the rickety rooms and dodgy heating of St. Agnes's. In *my* house, there'd be no buckwheat crêpes or boiled eggs or dreary beef stew, light on the beef and red wine, heavy on the parsnips and turnips. No. We'd have delicious things to eat, macarons and croissants and croque-monsieur sandwiches where fresh butter and cheese melted against the tongue.

I would know all the laws, so no one could use them against us. I could be the one who sent nosy *flics* to old lady Hébert's mansion then, and wouldn't she be sorry?

Lost in these happy dreams, I'd been thrilled when the Lusignys invited me to stay past the summer. I hadn't even minded when they added sadly they could only afford to pay me half salary going forward. Everyone knows that's the way of the aristocracy—once the old money goes, nothing replaces it. But with room and board provided, I was saving every franc. It would all be fine, if I could just convince Sister Helen to let me stay there for good and allow Lucie to join me.

Then Nazi tanks rolled into Poland and ruined everything. Sister Helen insisted I return to Paris. I still didn't understand why, since she'd immediately started looking for safe foster homes in the countryside for the other orphans. Why not just let me stay in Boulins, and Lucie too?

I'd theorized at the time it was because she hated me and couldn't stand to see me happy. Lucie had disagreed, suggesting Sister Helen must have some better plan for my happiness. Josette had chimed in that she was on my side, which had surprised me until she'd finished triumphantly that she would have been delighted to never see me again.

Last month, my patience had worn out. Telling myself I'd be eighteen soon, and Sister Helen would be helpless to stop me going, I'd written to Madame Lusigny asking if Lucie and I could come stay. She wouldn't need to pay us anything. We'd earn our keep tending their baby and scrubbing their three-hundred-year-old château. Madame Lusigny had immediately written back with her lavish, looping script, begging us to come as soon as possible.

When I'd told Sister Helen, to my shock she hadn't even been angry. She'd almost seemed—relieved? She'd said Boulins was on the way to Marseille, and it would be easy to stop there.

The ways of Sister Helen were indeed mysterious. Since then, I'd stopped trying to understand her.

A loud honk pulled me out of my thoughts as another car, loaded down with furniture, nearly side-swiped our truck. I twisted the wheel hard left to avoid a rearing horse, who had been spooked by another cart's oxen. Or was I the one who'd nearly side-swiped the Renault? My knuckles were white.

"Woman driver!" the man yelled, pressing on his car horn, causing the horse to my right, who'd been starting to settle, to go crazy until the farmer calmed the animal down.

I started to toss the obnoxious man an obscene hand gesture before I caught myself with a swift sideways glance at Sister Helen. She always put such importance on manners, and I couldn't deal with another lecture. But she was leaning over me.

"*Ta gueule!*" she yelled at him rudely from the passenger seat.

The driver of the car to my left fumed, trying to pass ahead. But there was nowhere for him to go on the slender road.

People's nerves were starting to fray.

It had been six days since we'd left Paris. The cheerful attitude of some refugees at the beginning, when they'd spoken about how they'd help the war effort south of the Loire—where our army was surely regrouping—had faded beneath the relentless sweat and slow crawl of the road. The painfully slow pace south was frequently stopped by bottlenecks of broken-down wagons and cars with smashed axles, sometimes abandoned and sometimes haunted by owners waiting for help that never came. Army convoys desperately trying to travel in either direction were also stuck, no matter how much their officers shouted or how heavily they leaned on their horns.

I couldn't believe we still hadn't reached Boulins. Last summer, it had taken most of a day. Yet it had taken six times that long so far, and we still had a good ways to go. Walking was almost faster than driving. I watched as the *vieille dame* with the wheelbarrow passed us by.

Sister Helen seemed more tense every time she looked at her map, muttering about running late. It seemed strange that she thought we had a deadline to reach Marseille. Maybe she was worried about fuel and food. Or tired. Estée told me Sister Helen had fainted in Paris right before we left. But then, the pneumonia we'd all suffered over spring had hit her harder than anyone. She still seemed thin and gray-faced.

Or maybe she just didn't like living on the road. None of us did. Food and shelter were almost impossible to find, the towns already picked over by earlier waves of refugees, like empty fields devoured by locusts. The canned goods and water and fuel we'd packed in Paris, which had seemed so excessive for our journey, were mostly gone, and we'd traveled only a quarter of the way to Marseille. My body ached from sleeping in the truck, next to the other girls, trying not to hear their snores or smell the sweat on their clothes after so many hot days.

Even now, as I gripped the steering wheel, it was hard not to get distracted by the crush of smelly humanity. I hated bicycles the most because they were unpredictable, and liable to turn abruptly and blindly into my path.

"Now switch gears," Sister Helen wheezed, then: "No! You're grinding the clutch."

I'd practiced my driving all morning, and now into the afternoon, to mixed results. I shoved at the pedal with my foot, unable to push the gearshift into the right place. Panic rose in my throat. Stuck in neutral, the truck slowed down, which you wouldn't think was possible going just ten kilometers an hour.

The distance between us and the overpacked Peugeot ahead increased from ten centimeters to two meters.

I heard a shout behind us, and a moment later, a young man rode past on his bicycle, his face a snarl. "Watch it! I nearly crashed into you!"

"I'm sorry," Sister Helen called with weak smile. "She's just learning."

"Fine time to learn," he retorted hotly as he passed us. "Women drivers!"

Cheeks hot, I hunched down in my seat, staring forward as I pretended to be focused on the road, even as the engine, still stuck in neutral, slowed almost to a stop. I watched the bicyclist weave ahead of us past the cars, then disappear.

"Don't mind *him*." Sister Helen took a deep breath. "Just push it into gear."

I pressed the pedal with my foot, but the gearshift still wouldn't lock. We both flinched at the grinding sound of the engine.

"Oh for heaven's sake—" Reaching over me, Sister Helen grabbed the lever and snapped it into place, no trouble at all. I scowled, turning back towards the road, feeling mutinous. Sure, everything always worked for *her*.

I'd never thought it was possible to feel so dirty. My long dark hair felt like wool, curled and knotted in the summer heat, my skin layered with sweat and grime. I probably didn't smell too nice, either. I hadn't had a proper bath since we'd left Paris.

The hot day I'd left baby Sophie at the Gare de Lyon, I'd been shiny and clean, compared to now, after so many days with no water to wash in, and only warm water to drink. We'd managed to find a hotel room only one night and all crammed in. We'd slept in a converted schoolhouse. The other nights, we'd parked on the side of the road.

Ahead of me now, I saw people and cars and more people and cars. Behind me in the rearview mirror, I saw the same. Just a river of choked humanity—weary, grouchy, frightened people trudging from Paris and further north, clutching their paltry belongings and loved ones, a river running in one direction, except for those military convoys.

Everyone seemed desperate for leadership, to be told what to do and where to go. Soldiers searched for officers, officers searched for regiments. Mayors were left to decide whether to help the train of refugees or deny them entry to their towns; whether to encourage their own citizens to flee or try to prevent it. Every mayor decided differently.

Here, as in Paris, it was every man for himself.

Occasionally, army conveyances tried to pass through, to allow scattered regiments or matériel to the battlefronts to the north and west. The Germans hadn't bombed Paris. After it was declared an open city, they'd simply marched in and made themselves at home, hanging an enormous swastika over the Arc de Triomphe. We'd heard that morning on someone's radio that France had a new leader in absentia—the great hero of the last war, Philippe Pétain. He was very worried about all us poor refugees on the road, and said the only way to save lives and keep French honor was to seek an immediate armistice, *en effet*, to negotiate our surrender to the Nazis.

The official recognition of our country's collapse caused a low-grade hum of humiliation beneath all the road noise. It was visible in the faces of those who'd abandoned their homes and businesses to the Germans, and even more so in the wan faces of passing soldiers. French pride had been smashed, proven just as illusory as the protections of the Maginot Line.

The British would have to surrender soon. Or so everyone said. But how was it possible? France giving up not just Paris but most of our country to be ruled by the Nazis—after we'd barely bothered to fight?

Roger Cochet had been right.

I'd been so angry at his words in the attic, I'd sputtered insults. But everything he'd told me in Paris was coming true.

When, at Berthe's sickbed, he'd told me to sit down and be quiet, I'd raised my chin in defiance, gripping my hands. Then I realized he'd called me *Mademoiselle Vashon*. How would some strange thief know my name? My fists had relaxed, and I'd frowned. "Who are you?"

"Don't you recognize me?" He'd seemed amused. "We met once last year—don't you remember? I'm devastated I didn't make more of an impression."

"Um..."

"You're wearing my shoes on your feet."

I'd looked down at my clunky shoes, then in a flash I'd known. Of course. I'd felt so stupid. We'd been introduced, exchanged perhaps five words, but I'd barely noticed. I'd been distracted by bad marks Sister Helen had just given the essay I'd written about Jeanne Chauvin, the first female lawyer to plead a case before a French court. *Needs work*, Sister Helen had written. *You need better foundation in your arguments. Especially if you're interested in law*. The fact that I'd written the essay in perfect English drew no praise. My brain had been spinning with the slashes of her red pen, and the last thing I'd cared about was making small talk with some relation of Berthe's.

My cheeks had burned as I'd slowly set my hands down. "You're... you're Berthe's nephew."

He'd chuckled. "Great-nephew."

"The best in the world," the elderly cook had said fervently, taking another sip of the stolen Dubonnet he'd brought her.

Handsome and dark-haired in his army uniform, he'd given me a slightly mocking bow. "Roger Cochet, at your service."

I'd looked back at his shoes on my feet. It had suddenly felt embarrassingly... intimate. "I'm sorry," I'd stammered. I prayed my cheeks weren't a humiliating red, already knowing that wasn't a prayer that would be answered. "When I saw you at the shop—I thought you were following me—and..."

His sensual lips curved as he finished, "And you thought I was a criminal who'd just smashed a window of a *café-tabac* to steal liquor and cigarettes and was perhaps coming to vandalize you as well."

"Well, yes."

He struck a match and calmly lit his cigarette. "You thought right."

My cheeks went from hot to incandescent. "What?"

"I did steal them." He gave me a slow-rising grin, lifting an eyebrow as if to say, *What did you think I meant?* before nodding towards the cook. "She knows the provenance. I have no secrets from my aunt."

"Roger didn't steal anything—he liberated it," Berthe said, her voice a little tipsy. "Dubonnet deserves a good French belly, not the fat gullet of a filthy Boche." She drank some more. Her wrinkled cheeks, so pale in her illness, took on a rosy color, her eyes as bright as a bird's. "Roger has promised to stay with me until he's sure I'm well. Isn't that kind?"

I turned to him, wide-eyed. "But aren't you enlisted? Don't you need to return to your regiment?"

His dark eyes turned grim. "There's no point. The war is nearly over."

"How can you say that?" I'd sputtered. "Of course it's not! Our forces are regrouping south of the Loire. We'll take our stand there against the Germans, just as we did in the last war, or perhaps our colonies in Africa—"

"No." He took a long, hard draw on the cigarette, his lips pressed down at the edges. "It is over. Lebrun is on his way out. Our leaders are in shock beneath the Blitzkrieg, and think the Nazis are winning the war. They believe the Germans will go easier on us if we rush to surrender before the British."

"What!" I'd been horrified enough at our government's

abandonment of Paris, but to that point, no one had been talking about surrender—merely French retreat, in order to regroup and fight from a better position. *Reculer, pour mieux sauter.* "Surrender? Are you crazy?"

"I hear things. I have eyes."

"How dare you suggest we'd ever be such cowards!"

"Think what you want." He stubbed out his cigarette in his empty glass. "But I'm not sticking around in the army, waiting to become a German prisoner of war. For one, it doesn't suit my interests, and for two, the Brits might not surrender so quickly."

"What's your plan then?"

"I told you. To take care of my own."

"You mean you're willing to live here off your great-aunt, now you've deserted our army and stolen from your own countrymen." I tossed my head hotly. "You're a sorry excuse for a man, Roger Cochet."

"Margot, oh la la," exclaimed Berthe from her sickbed.

Roger eyed me, then said quietly, "In my battalion's last retreat from Paris, my company was separated from our commanding officer. We waited for hours, but he never returned. No one came to take his place. So the way I figure it" —he gave me a crooked smile—"the army deserted *me*."

"A fine attitude."

His smile lifted to a grin. "I took personal leave to walk into Paris and check on my great-aunt. Once she's well, assuming I cannot convince her to leave the city—"

"*Eh bien*, no army in the world could convince me of that," Berthe said stoutly behind him.

Roger's dark eyes seared mine. "After our surrender is announced, I hope there will be someone who still wants to defy these monsters. And that's where I'm going to go. I'll take a boat from Brittany to Britain if I must."

I shook my head impatiently. "If you want to fight, you should be heading south to the Loire. That's where the army will make its stand. Come with us, Roger! You'll see—you can still help our army!"

He looked down at my hand. In my eagerness, I'd placed it on his. With an intake of breath, I pulled away.

"There is no French army," he said simply.

"But—" I helplessly tried to think of a way to convince him he was wrong. "France will never surrender, never!"

"It's already done." He stepped closer, looking down at me. "You won't betray me, will you, Margot?" He shook his head with a crooked smile. "I fear your Sister Helen would not allow me to remain in this house if she knew..."

"That you're a deserter and a thief?" I'd finished. With a wry expression, he'd nodded.

I'd known I *should* tell. It would serve him right, and perhaps she had a right to know, this being her house and all. And a moment later, Sister Helen had burst into the attic, giving me the perfect opportunity. But a tattletale was almost as bad as a deserter. Looking from Roger to Berthe, I just hadn't been able to do it. So I'd kept quiet.

Now, as I gripped the steering wheel, I thought of the young man's dark eyes, his charming grin. I wondered if he was still in Paris, taking care of his adoring great-aunt.

I still couldn't believe he'd been so right. And I'd been so wrong.

"What's going on?" Josette's pinched face appeared in the small slide-window between the truck's cab and the flatbed, where the other girls were holding books, stretched out beneath the shade of the tarp. "We're turning black and blue from all the lurching and stopping. Are you *trying* to kill us?"

I opened my mouth for a sharp retort, but Sister Helen got there first.

"I'm sorry," she said soothingly. "But Margot's getting better."

"I hope so." Her gaze on me was scornful. "She couldn't get worse."

Sister Helen changed the subject. "How is class going?"

Josette's expression became stern. "It's satisfactory, except Rachel is being a dunce in arithmetic."

"I am not!" piped Rachel's indignant voice. "I got the answers right. Lucie's the one who got them wrong!"

"Oh dear, I'm afraid I might have," said Lucie.

To distract the girls on the journey, and make better use of time as our truck crawled slowly down the road, Sister Helen had assigned Josette the task of being "teacher" to the younger four girls. Lucie bore it well, but the others were less pleased.

Sister Helen sighed. "Both of you should try the problems again and compare answers with Estée."

"I can't help them," Estée complained. "How can I concentrate, when Noémie keeps hitting me in the head with her bear."

"Nounours is bored," the five-year-old said unrepentantly.

"Sort it out, girls," said Sister Helen wearily, and she closed the window a little harder than necessary before turning to me. "All right. Try changing gears again."

"There's no point."

"Try."

I shook my head. "I'll go sit in back and watch the girls while you drive."

Sister Helen set her jaw. "And what happens if I get sick? Who will drive?"

"I'm not worried. You'd find a way to take care of us even if you were dead," I said lightly.

I expected my teasing to make her relax. Instead, her shoulders grew more tense. "What if we need to start driving in two shifts, night and day?"

"Why would we do that?"

She looked at me narrowly. "I never knew you to back away

from a fight, Margot Vashon. Are you going to let the little gears of this truck defeat you?"

I knew she was baiting me but couldn't resist.

"*Fine*," I bit out. "Show me again."

It took another hour of practice and more curses from people around us, maybe even one or two from my own lips, but I finally figured out how to do it. Soon, it was smooth. No more grinding.

Relief coursed through me. "I've got it now."

Sister Helen leaned back in the worn leather seat, looking out the passenger window. "Yes."

My smile slipped away. I felt oddly let down. What had I been thinking? Of course Sister Helen wouldn't praise me. She never had, and never would. The other girls, yes. Just not me. There'd always been something about me she found defective. Inadequate. Unworthy.

I concentrated on my driving, moving slowly and carefully along with the mass of refugees. Stop, slow, stop. Honestly. We were barely keeping up with the old man in a hat, laboriously propelling his white-haired wife in a pushcart as he puffed on his pipe.

"Six days out of Paris and we've not even gone two hundred kilometers," I grumbled. "At this rate, it'll be another *three days* before we reach Boulins."

Sister Helen's fingers drummed against the truck's window ledge. "We'll get Lucie there in two."

"How can you be sure?"

"Because I want to reach Marseille a few days after that."

I glanced at her out the corner of my eye. "Why are you so worried about it?"

"Because..." She hesitated, biting her lip as she looked away. "Just because."

"Wait." I frowned. "You said *Lucie* would reach Boulins."

"So?"

I gave an awkward laugh. "Did you forget me? I'm going to live there with her."

"No," she said in a low voice, her eyes not meeting mine. "I didn't forget you."

Gripping the steering wheel, I risked a longer glance.

I'd always thought of Sister Helen as matronly and plain. Neat and tidy, yes, but practical. She never wore lipstick. Her clothes were serviceable and worn; today she wore a brownish-red blouse and wide dark slacks, with sensible shoes. Her gray-streaked brown hair was pulled back in a chignon that made her cheekbones look sharp.

No. It wasn't just the chignon. She'd lost weight the last few months. From her illness? From stress?

"Margot!" she cried, bracing her arms against the front dashboard.

I turned and gasped, swerving to avoid the blackened, burned-out car in the middle of the road. Around it, the earth itself was black, splattered, hollowed out. I exhaled, focusing on not hitting the cars and pedestrians tight around us.

The first time I'd seen a charred car resting in a blackened hole in the road, just a day outside Paris, I'd goggled at it, trying to imagine what kind of accident or engine fire could have caused that. Bewildered, I'd asked Sister Helen, "What do you think could have happened to it?"

"It was bombed," she'd said quietly.

We'd passed eight other burned-out cars in the days since. We hadn't been attacked by German planes on our journey, but I'd heard whispered tales of Stukas spitting bullets on the refugee road like dark clouds expelling raindrops. Committing murder. Lavishly. Gleefully.

Though our government had abandoned Paris, I knew fighting still continued in the southwest as the Nazis pressed their last advantage. Sometimes at night, trying to sleep, I could hear distant thunder that wasn't thunder at all.

I was relieved there were no charred figures inside this car at least. A few days before, we'd had to shield the little girls' eyes from that horror, as no one had come to take the bodies. They'd just been... left there.

What was the world coming to? I shivered.

"I don't understand how the Nazis can attack this road." I gripped the wheel. "It's just for refugees. Old people! Children!"

"The Germans don't care." Drumming her fingers against the sill, even more restlessly than before, Sister Helen turned to me. "And the road isn't just refugees. Remember?"

I thought of the army trucks I'd seen, the chaos of soldiers trying to travel north and south. If the Germans were bombing to the south, perhaps they'd reached the Loire. Then how would we fight back? Especially if Pétain, France's new leader, no longer believed we should?

It's already done, Roger had told me in the attic. I felt a chill.

"But," I said helplessly, "it's not *fair*."

"There is no fair." Sister Helen looked at me in the dusty cab of the truck. "If you ever see a plane in the sky, Margot... don't wait to see what country it belongs to. Just grab the girls and run."

6

MARGOT

The campfire crackled red, scattering embers like fireflies in the night. Like many other travelers, we'd found a spot to sleep on the flattened grass lining the road, between open fields and deep shadows of forested hills. We were in luck: an earlier refugee had obligingly left a sloppily dug firepit, with a bit of half-burned wood, even, to get us started.

I tried not to think of those bombed-out cars as I watched the fire slowly whittle the wood to ash.

Noémie was in my lap, huddled against me sleepily, clutching her teddy bear with both hands. Lucie was sleeping on a blanket between Sister Helen and me, in front of the fire.

Josette and the young Lévy sisters had settled in for the night in the flatbed of our truck, parked nearby, where they preferred to sleep with their pillows and blankets and no risk of rising damp or, as Josette had added with a shudder, "snakes or bears or spiders." They'd stayed awake for the first hour of darkness, playing the mournful game of *What do you miss most?*

They missed the other orphans, of course, as we all did. They wondered about the new lives of Martine and Yvette and Anne-Marie and all the rest now scattered like stars across farms and small towns of the French countryside. Noémie hoped Berthe was all better now and baby Sophie was happily drinking fresh milk in John Cleeton's villa in Marseille.

"She's probably already with her new family," Rachel had pointed out.

"We were her new family." Estée could be a stickler for semantics. "Baby Sophie's with her old family. Her *real* family."

"*We* were her real family," Josette had said, her voice tight.

"Do you remember the books we used to read to her...?" And Estée had started reminiscing rapturously about every book in the orphanage's old library, even the encyclopedias and musty old novels no one else bothered with, before the collection had been divided amongst the orphans and the valuable books sold. Estée would have willingly read the phone book, I think, or stared at upside-down pages in Swahili, rather than face life without the comfort of a book.

So perhaps it was no wonder that, three days out of Paris, when the eleven-year-old had continued to wear the exact same shabby, navy-blue collared dress after being told repeatedly to change clothes, we'd discovered Estée had packed her travel bag only with books. When Sister Helen started lecturing her, the girl had been indignant.

"But, Sister Helen, you said to bring only the essentials."

That had caught the headmistress off guard, her mouth open. A moment later, she'd started laughing until she cried.

After wearing her same dress day and night, Estée smelled of old sweat. Everything she wore, down to the socks in her buckled shoes, was a muddled brown-gray, in spite of half-hearted attempts to wash herself in passing streams. Even her glasses were smudged with dirt. Rachel and Noémie had quarreled hourly over who was stuck sitting next to her in the truck. To keep the peace, I'd lent her my only clean socks and dress, which hung limply over her skinny frame as I'd helped wash her clothes. Estée didn't care about clothes, just books.

Her nine-year-old sister Rachel, on the other hand, thought books were the bane of her existence. They forced her to be trapped in boring, stuffy classrooms when she yearned to be outdoors. Rachel worried about the garden we'd left behind. What if Berthe couldn't properly maintain the vegetables? What if the ailing cook let the aphids run rampant over the roses? What if the widowed lady next door invited the Nazis to stomp over our pretty violets and tender green strawberries with their jackboots?

"Roger won't let them," Josette had reassured her. "You mustn't worry, Rachel. Roger will keep everything safe." Her voice had softened. "He's so brave, so wise. So strong..."

Ugh. She'd continued for a while in that vein, but I'd closed my ears before her sickeningly sweet words about Roger Cochet could ruin my digestion. No need to wonder what *Josette* missed most.

They'd finally dropped to sleep an hour ago. Our campsite was twenty meters off the road, tucked between other weary families trying to rest. Even though it was midnight, I could see the road was still busy, with some refugees holding lamps, others using only the light of the moon and still others driving vehicles with a single headlight, darkened to blue per the orders of the war department. Along the trampled fields and vineyards, there were campfires and bonfires sending sparks above the black forest, up to the dark velvety sky strewn with coldly glittering stars.

As Noémie yawned, I rose and gently carried her to the back of the truck to join the others, tucking her and her teddy Nounours together on their blanket between slumbering Josette and Estée. After returning to the fire, I sat back down on my own blanket, willing myself to relax. We were safe here. It was time to rest. In this moment, the night seemed almost peaceful.

Though not for everyone. A middle-aged couple walked past, shouting, "Amélie! Amélie?" The man turned to us as they trudged in the reddish light. "Please, *madame, mademoiselle,* have you seen a young girl? Dark-haired, five years old?"

"Traveling alone?" I blurted out, aghast.

Sister Helen was already shaking her head. "No, *monsieur.* I am sorry."

The man continued desperately, as if in a dream, "Soldiers offered to give our daughter a ride on an army truck heading south—it seemed a godsend—but we never arranged where to meet—"

"It just happened so fast," the woman sobbed, covering her face with her hands. "One moment she was in our arms—then she was gone."

"I am sorry indeed," Sister Helen repeated, looking between them. "I'll pray you find your daughter soon."

The couple moved on, walking and wailing through the night. As they disappeared into the darkness beyond the next fire, we looked at each other.

"How awful," Sister Helen said quietly. She pulled a small silver flask from her pocket and took a quick gulp, then gasped. "Losing a child."

Her voice seemed to shake a little. I was surprised that she had such empathy, or maybe she was just exhausted.

"They should have kept a better eye on her," I replied. But it was pure bravado, whistling past a graveyard. It scared me how easy it would be, in a topsy-turvy world at war, to lose someone. One instant of inattention, or simply bad luck, and someone could be lost forever.

I looked up at the distant farmhouse on a low hill. The windows glowed warmly. I wondered how all these farms and villages felt to have northern strangers rampaging through their fields and vineyards. This stomped-on, picked-over grass was now useless for anything but ground to sleep on—or campfires.

Luckily for the farmers, the grapes were still in flowering season, but people had damaged the vines. Every field we passed seemed picked clean, skeletal trees in the orchards left bony and bare, strawberries and melons and artichokes and asparagus devoured as if by a Biblical plague.

I glanced east, on the other side of the road, but that was little comfort. Above the dark, fathomless forest, on a sharp crag, a ruined medieval castle was ghostly in the moonlight. I thought of the lost little girl. Those charred figures in the burned-out car.

Skeletons and ghosts were all around us.

Unsettled, I pulled my blanket a little closer to Lucie and Sister Helen amid the warm light of the fire.

"You did a good job," Sister Helen told me abruptly. "With dinner. Making the fire. Driving. All of it." She paused. "Thank you."

I gaped at her. I couldn't have been more astonished than if she'd slapped me in the face.

It was true I'd figured out how to spark two rocks a few days ago, unlike Josette, who'd never managed it even after trying twenty times, or Lucie, who'd only succeeded in gashing a bloody nick into her wrist. Tonight, when we pulled the truck to the side of the road after dark, Helen had seemed exhausted from her turn driving, so I'd taken over preparation of our simple dinner, warming up several cans of stew directly in the flames, then passing them to the girls along with bruised apples and the rationed amount of water.

"Um. You're welcome." I didn't know what else to say. I watched Sister Helen take another gulp from the flask. "What's that?"

"Brandy."

Brandy was nothing to be alarmed about, a dainty drink for old ladies. And yet it made me uneasy. As much as I pushed against Sister Helen's stern strength, it was disconcerting to imagine her ill or needing liquid courage of any kind.

On second thought, liquid courage was a fine idea. "Can I have some?"

"No." She took another drink. I'd never seen her consume spirits, not even something so mild as brandy. I nearly choked on my water when she pulled out a pack of cigarettes from her jacket pocket.

"You smoke?"

"I quit." Lighting the end of the cigarette in the fire, she held it out, examining it in the red light. "When I came to St. Agnes's." Her lips curved up humorously as she glanced at the blue cigarette box. "The headmistress of an orphanage couldn't smoke. I had to quit. If I wanted to be a different person."

I watched as she exhaled a puff of smoke slowly, sighing in pleasure. I envied how her shoulders relaxed. "Why would you?"

"Why would I what?"

"Why would you want to be a different person?"

"Because..." Her hazel eyes were sad as she stared into the flickering red fire. "I wanted to be someone better. I'd always wanted that, even before I left home."

She'd never spoken to me like this—never. As if I were a grown woman, not a child at constant risk of disappointing her. Afraid to break the spell, I breathed, "You mean when you left America? To become a nurse on the battlefields of la Grande Guerre?"

Silence, broken only by road noise, refugees camped nearby calling out to each other, the soft roar of distant engines, the close crackle of the fire.

Her voice was soft. "I left California because my child died. My husband. My fault. I joined the war because I deserved to pay for it. I've never stopped paying."

I stared at her. Was she drunk? Was this a dream? Her words were so quiet I almost wondered if I'd imagined them.

She'd had a family?

No, impossible. For nearly fifteen years, since my first memory of her rescuing me from my mother's deathbed, I'd seen Helen Taylor as a strict headmistress, plus maybe a nurse on some ancient battlefield. I'd never imagined her as a wife—or a mother. I'd assumed she'd never loved anyone. I'd assumed she was someone who could not be hurt.

I realized I preferred thinking of her that way.

"I'm so sorry about your family," I said haltingly. "But... why would you blame yourself?"

"Doesn't matter." Helen looked up at me, then shook the ash off her cigarette with an unconvincing smile. "It was long ago. But now I'm going back, it's just..." She took another quick drag of smoke. "A lot to face."

"Going back?" I was confused. "Where?"

Helen gave a quick, worried glance towards the back of the truck. "I haven't told them yet. Once we reach Marseille, I've booked passage on a ship. I've found good homes willing to take the girls. It's not safe to be Jewish in this war."

"It's not safe for anyone," I said, but inside, I was reeling. It was true we'd all read about the awful persecution of Jews in Germany. It was why so many had fled to France, though they weren't getting treated particularly well here now, either. Every European country had refused to give them citizenship, leaving them virtually stateless and unable to get passports. Lately, even French-born Jews were increasingly regarded with suspicion, as if they were aliens in their own country. Now that the Nazis were sweeping across France, I could understand why Helen was worried. "So it wasn't that you just couldn't find foster homes for Estée, Rachel and Noémie? You always intended to take them out of France?"

She nodded. "Josette, too."

"Josette? Why? She's a foundling. There's no record that her parents were Jewish."

Helen's gaze shifted away. Then, almost as if she were

deliberately changing the subject, she added, "I never seriously looked for a home for Lucie because you found one you liked for her, at the Lusignys'."

I was immediately distracted by mention of Lucie. It made sense, but... I frowned. I'd only written Isabelle Lusigny last month. For the eight months before that, though Helen had casually mentioned a few possible foster families for Lucie—families who could only take one child, which of course we'd refused—she'd never once lifted a finger to look for a foster home for me. Why?

I knew for sure my sister and I weren't Jewish. I could still remember a priest speaking at my mother's lonely funeral. And unlike Estée, Rachel and Noémie, who'd been routinely escorted to synagogue by a local Jewish family, Lucie and I had dutifully attended Mass our whole lives.

But so had Josette. I started to ask about her again but was diverted by a more urgent personal question.

"Is that why you never looked for a foster home for me? Because you always figured I'd go to the Lusignys'?"

Helen looked at me, then shrugged. "You've always had a mind of your own."

Which wasn't really an answer. Maybe she hadn't bothered about me because I was close to eighteen, and she trusted me to handle myself. Or maybe it was because she just didn't care about me very much?

A lump rose in my throat. "Where will you take the girls?"

Helen exhaled another puff of smoke. "California." Giving a wan smile, she shook the ash off her cigarette. "Near Los Angeles. My old hometown."

I was dumbfounded. Everyone knew it was nearly impossible for anyone but Americans to go to America these days. "How did you get visas for the girls?"

More silence, then she reluctantly said, "Some people owe

me a favor. But it could still fall apart. So not a word," she warned, glancing at the truck.

"I won't say anything."

"I mean it, Margot. Not even to Josette. Not even if she makes you mad."

"What do you take me for?" I said indignantly, then at her raised eyebrow, I sighed. "I promise," I said, a little grumpily. I looked down at my hands; saw they were clasped tightly.

America.

Sister Helen had spoken very rarely of her homeland. I'd heard about something called peanut butter she'd liked eating on packaged, sliced bread as a child. We knew she'd grown up in California, apprenticed as a nurse, that she'd grown up fluent in French because of her Louisiana Cajun parents.

"Josette will be ecstatic," I said.

"She'll stay with Miss Clarkson while she finishes her last year of high school." Helen gave a crooked grin. "Right near Hollywood."

"Hollywood," I breathed. Josette would lose her mind. Most of what I imagined about American life came from the cinema: Fred Astaire in a dapper tuxedo and Ginger Rogers in a frothy dress, swirling through glamorous Manhattan; William Powell, Myrna Loy and their snazzy dog Asta investigating crimes in New York City; and very recently, Judy Garland in a blue dress being carried off in a tornado from black-and-white Kansas to colorful Oz.

There was also the America of newsreels, an unimaginably big country that kept stubbornly and inexplicably refusing to help Britain and France win this war. Coquettish America just teased us with glimpses of its army, navy and war matériel like a can-can dancer flirtatiously offering peeks of her knickers beneath her skirts before giggling and disappearing backstage. Many Frenchmen felt bitter about it.

What was the country really like?

Suddenly, my long-held dream to work as an au pair in Boulins, reading dusty law books in the château, shone a little less brightly.

"All the girls have homes?" I asked.

She stubbed out her cigarette in the dark earth. "Noémie will be in San Diego. Estée and Rachel will be together in Santa Monica."

Leaving Lucie and me behind. I felt a strange twist inside. "When will you return to France?"

She hesitated. "I'm not sure. The war..."

Her voice trailed off, and cold seeped through my bones. She was never coming back. Shivering, I looked down at my little sister, curled up in a blanket, facing towards Helen, as if our headmistress was her source of warmth and safety, not the fire. Hadn't I said for years that I was sick of Sister Helen's lectures, her bossiness, her constant disapproval? Hadn't I been eager to leave her and the orphanage behind?

Now I'd finally be getting what I wanted. But as that sank in, I felt a chill all over my body. I took a deep breath.

"The war," I agreed woodenly.

It wasn't that I begrudged the other girls their chance for safety, not at all. I didn't even begrudge them America.

And yet...

For years, I'd chafed under Sister Helen's restrictions, her orders. I'd rebelled and raged against her, even over small, sensible rules like no sweets until after supper or lights out by nine. I'd dreamed of the day I'd finally be free.

But now, with my eighteenth birthday just a week and a half away, I didn't feel liberated. I felt abandoned. I'd already lost my parents, my home, my adoptive sisters, my city. Sister Helen, for all her flaws, had protected us. Guided us. How many times had she said that finding Lucie and me, crying at the deathbed of our widowed mother, had utterly changed the course of her life?

But now, when I least expected it, Sister Helen was abandoning us. As if she'd never cared about Lucie or me at all.

7

HELEN

Seeing Margot's face fall as we sat together between the dark forest and the flickering lights of the road, I wished I hadn't told her about America. But it was inevitable. She'd have to know everything soon, and I was feeling too tired to hold it all inside. The fiercely regimented self-control of my last decade and a half was starting to fray.

How else to explain why I'd insulted the driver who'd been rude about Margot's driving? Why I'd started drinking the medicinal brandy I'd brought for emergencies? Why I'd smoked a cigarette from the stale old pack of forgotten Gauloises our gardener had left beneath the driver's seat?

The forbidden cigarette had brought a rush of relief, of pleasure—then shame. It wasn't the example I wanted to set for Margot.

Glancing towards the back of the truck, I saw the dark shape of the little girls and Josette, peacefully sleeping. The June night had grown cool. Lucie was stretched on the hard ground near me, wrapped up in her blanket, wispy blonde tendrils of hair strewn over pale eyebrows. Sleeping, she looked even more like an angel than she did awake. She was a sweet girl, idealistic, caring more about others—children, animals, the elderly—than herself.

How on earth would I convince Margot to abandon her in Boulins?

"Well. We'll miss you, Helen." Margot gave me a crooked smile, then turned quickly towards the fire. "I hope you'll all be happy in America."

My eyebrows rose when I realized she'd called me simply "Helen," as if we were equals. But perhaps she had that right. I'd let down my guard enough to tell her about my husband and child. They'd died decades ago, but the guilt and pain were still fresh as yesterday. Back then, I'd thought if I dedicated my life to helping others, I'd forget. I'd forgive. Instead, I'd veered from one tragic mistake to the next. Would anything ever free me from the past?

I'd confided the whole truth to only one living person, and that had been long ago.

Perhaps that had been another mistake, never letting myself get close to anyone since then. Maybe I could have told John Cleeton everything.

John had always looked out for us, since he'd arrived in Paris a few years ago as a heartbroken widower. He'd stumbled over two of our younger orphans who were lost in the crooked alleys of the Marais after they'd wandered a little too far from the rue des Orphelines. He'd brought them back to St. Agnes's, and we'd invited him to stay for dinner to thank him. It had been a fast friendship. After all, he was an American, too: a former rancher from Texas, who'd lost his wife to a lingering illness. He was a bit older than I was, old enough to know how hard life could be, that sometimes choices were neither perfect nor easy. And that people weren't, either.

The night before he'd left Paris with baby Sophie, if I'd told him the truth about my past, he might have understood why I could never offer him anything but friendship. Why I hadn't shown up at the train station. Why I'd come up with an excuse to send Margot instead.

I focused on the girl in the firelight.

Was Margot Vashon pretty? I wasn't impartial enough to judge. But she had an interesting face, with big brown eyes, heart-shaped lips often mutinously pressed together, and a stubborn little beak for a nose. Her face matched her character, her frequent certainty that she alone knew the right path. Her long, thick dark hair, which she was unable to comb through without difficulty and often called the bane of her existence, had on our journey come to look like a rat's nest, falling over the shoulders of her striped Breton shirt. She wore trousers, as she was often too impatient to take the Métro or even walk—she'd run. Even the red scarf around her neck was for practical purposes, to tie up her hair when it annoyed her, as so many things could.

Especially me.

Margot's eyes suddenly widened with alarm at something behind me. I turned as a man intruded into the circle of our firelight.

The stranger held up his hands as if in surrender, his face friendly. "*Bonsoir, mesdames.*"

I gave a brief nod. "*Monsieur.*"

"You see, we're neighbors." Smiling, he nodded towards a car parked a little down the edge of the road, in shadow. "My family is parked over there."

"A pleasure to make your acquaintance." But as I smiled and nodded, I was thinking of the service revolver I'd left in the canvas bag beneath the driver's seat of the truck. My main worry had been about keeping it hidden from the girls, not about having it close to hand. Stupid—so stupid. Still smiling, I said, "How can I help you, *monsieur*?"

The man rubbed the back of his dirty dark hair sheepishly.

"Well, the thing is, it's taken so much longer than we thought since we left Amiens. We were behind you on the road today, saw your extra fuel cans and wondered," he swallowed, then said in a rush, "if you could spare a little fuel. To help us reach Vichy."

"*Non.* I'm sorry," I said apologetically. "We are running low ourselves."

His gaze shifted towards the back of our nearby truck, where the fuel cans, all but one now empty, were tucked in the shadows behind the sleeping children. "I can pay."

"I'm truly sorry, *monsieur*, but as I said, I cannot help you."

His eyes narrowed. "You cannot be so heartless. I have children too, *madame*. We're already out of food and water." He tightened his hands at his sides, forcing a strained smile over his unshaven face as he wheedled, "But if you'll just share a little of what you have, we can reach my sister's house—"

"No," I said.

Margot looked tense. Lucie was now awake, blinking between us in sleepy confusion.

I rose to my feet, backing towards the truck. "I wish you a good evening, *monsieur*."

Shame flashed in his eyes, then rage. "How is it right that you keep it all to yourself?" He glared at me. "I was going to pay you, but you don't deserve it. I'm just going to take it—"

But as he started towards the truck, I'd already reached the front door. Reaching beneath the seat, I yanked out the revolver, letting the leather holster fall to the ground.

The man gasped when he saw the gun's cold steel shining in my hand. But he wasn't half as surprised as Margot and Lucie.

I said evenly, "Don't make me do something I'll regret my girls having to see, *monsieur*."

Grinding his teeth, the man held up his hands and backed away towards his own car, cursing me with vile insults in a low voice, fury in his eyes. He turned and disappeared from our small circle of firelight, presumably in search of an easier victim.

"What just happened?" said Lucie, staring after him. "Why couldn't we just share our fuel?"

"Where," Margot breathed, "did you get that gun?"

I exhaled, feeling limp as the adrenaline wore off. I closed my eyes. My knees were trembling. It had been a long time since I'd threatened anyone. I'd hoped it would never be necessary again.

"Helen?"

"Sister Helen?"

I forced myself to breathe until the only stars I could see were the actual ones in the sky. I turned to them, trying to appear calm. "I couldn't give him our fuel, Lucie dear, because we need it ourselves."

"But surely just a little—"

"If we give any away, we'll soon be begging for fuel, too. It'll be a miracle if we have enough." I turned to Margot. "Look."

Standing close to the blood-red fire for light, I swung open the chamber of the revolver. Margot stared down at it. Then she understood.

"It wasn't loaded," she said slowly.

I flinched at the reminder of my stupidity. I'd gone soft living in Paris for so long, and it showed.

"After this," I said grimly, "it will be. And I want you to know how to use it. Just in case." With the revolver still unloaded, I showed her how to cock the hammer, had her practice holding it in her hand.

"Must I too?" Lucie sounded reluctant.

"No, my dear, you're too young. But I'll show Josette tomorrow."

Margot's face fell a little. She'd clearly looked forward to having something to lord over her rival. I sighed.

I picked up the leather holster, opened the flap and pulled

out the ammunition, then showed her how to load the six cartridges. "Treat this weapon carefully. Never use it unless your life is in danger. And never let the little girls even see it. Promise."

"I promise," Margot said solemnly. Then she frowned. "But why would I have to use it? Wouldn't you just do it?"

"Just in case." I saw her open her lips to ask *Just in case what?* I stopped her with, "One never knows." I didn't want to admit what I feared, even to myself. I attached the holstered revolver to the back of my belt, pulling my loose blouse over the top so it couldn't be seen. "Now, both of you go get some rest. I'll keep watch the rest of the night."

The girls looked at each other.

"Now," I said sharply.

Lucie obediently sank back onto her blanket and closed her eyes. Margot lingered.

"I could take a turn keeping watch, Helen. Give you a chance to sleep."

There were circles under her eyes, and her shoulders were weary. But still, she took responsibility. I was proud of her. And touched. "Thank you, Margot. I appreciate it, I do. But you'll help me most by being well rested tomorrow."

Reluctantly, she spread out her own blanket and curled up next to Lucie. Sleep seemed more elusive for her. She tossed for an hour before she finally was still.

I watched over them, pacing restlessly through the night.

La Ravelle was close now. I could almost see it, at the top of distant hills to the south. In my imagination, I saw every detail, exactly as the medieval town had been that cold January day I'd finally come to find him, to tell him I'd made a mistake, to beg for his love and agree to be his wife. But discovered I was too late.

Gray sunrise peeked slowly through the cool air, lightening the black sky into the color of steel. Shivering, I stoked the fire for breakfast, along with the watered-down coffee I sorely needed before we would continue our journey.

I needed to be strong today. We'd be driving right past the town where he lived. I wouldn't let myself stop. I wouldn't let myself even look. I'd hold tight to the steering wheel, and soon La Ravelle would be behind me forever.

Get thee behind me, I thought.

We weren't the only ones stretching and starting to move in the gray-and-pink dawn. The road was already growing busier with pedestrians and vehicles and bicycles, as those who'd slept overnight in the fields returned, hoping to hurry ahead of those still at rest. An army truck honked loudly.

"Ow. What's all that noise?" Josette complained, sticking her head out from our truck. Her hair, which she'd carefully washed yesterday afternoon in a passing stream, was now tied in the rags she used for pin curls.

"It's like music compared to your snoring," Margot called from her blanket near the fire. "It blasted my ears all night, even this far away."

The redhead blushed angrily. "You should talk! When—"

"Help the little ones get dressed, girls," I told them quickly. "Let's get on the road as soon as—"

I cut off when I saw something out the corner of my vision. Turning, I narrowed my eyes, staring hard at the gray northern sky.

What had I seen? There was nothing to that horizon but distant Paris. Paris and Nazis. Nothing except the palest silver sky turning the faintest blue in the cool fresh morning. Nothing except...

Black dots like birds in the distance. I heard a low buzz, something between the roll of thunder and the patter of soft rain. I sucked in my breath, whirling back.

"Get the girls!" I cried to Josette. "Lucie! Get up!"

"What?" Lucie yawned, stretching as she sat up. Margot and Josette looked at each other, uncomprehending.

"The girls are still tired," Josette ventured. "Couldn't we give them just a little—?"

"Now!" I shouted, rushing towards the truck.

Josette looked startled, and even Lucie rose anxiously to her feet beside Margot.

I pointed. "Look!"

Then they saw it. Those distant black birds weren't birds at all.

Behind us, on the road from the north, were approaching clouds of smoke. I heard faraway screams, the rat-a-tat of machine guns. Planes coming closer, rushing towards us...

Around us, other refugees started to scream, to run in every direction. But where was safe?

Gasping, Margot followed me to the truck. She and Josette helped me scoop up the three little girls, dragging them off the flatbed in their wrinkled nightgowns as they sleepily protested. The planes were drawing closer. My wide, terrified eyes caught Margot's.

"Forest," she said.

I glanced towards the sheltering darkness of the trees some twenty yards away and nodded.

"Don't wanna get up," yawned Rachel. Josette lifted her in her arms as Margot grabbed Estée's hand.

"Hurry," I begged, cradling Noémie.

"Nounours," she cried, reaching behind her as I ran across the grass, and I knew she'd dropped her precious teddy, the only remnant of her dead mother. I didn't even look back.

We ran, but before we could reach the forest, we heard panicked cries, rising thick as morning mist from rich moist earth. I heard a frenetic howl through the air as a bomb was dropped, then exploded against the road with a sickening crack of metal and the screams of men. Seconds later, I heard the deafening roar of the German Stuka above us, the crackle of gunfire hard on our heels, the drumming of bullets slamming against the dirt and grass.

The girls raced ahead, Josette holding Rachel's hand, Margot Estée's, Lucie beside them. I'd almost reached the forest when I heard shots howl like demons past my ear. Noémie stiffened in my arms as her spine contorted. She screamed in pain, but I kept running jaggedly for the dark shelter of the forest.

We reached the safety of the cool dark trees, Noémie still screaming in my arms. As the roar of the plane abated, Rachel and Estée cried out with fear.

"Was she hit?" Josette gasped, coming close to me beneath the dark trees. Margot and Lucie instinctively cuddled the young Lévy sisters, keeping them from rushing towards their playmate. The five-year-old was covered in blood.

"It's all right, sweetheart," I told Noémie. I knew how to pretend to be calm and strong. I gently placed the little girl on the soft, mossy forest floor. "What hurts?"

"My—arm," the little girl sobbed, gripping the bloody spot on her forearm with her other hand. "*Maman*," she cried, hiccupping in blind sobs. "*Maman*."

The other girls looked at each other with anguish. Noémie's mother had died a year and a half before on a Paris street, after throwing her young daughter clear of the car that would have hit them both. As bystanders shouted for a doctor, for the police, Noémie, unharmed, had sat beside the twisted metal of the car in confusion, holding her mother's hand as the woman bled her life away on the cobblestones of the rue Lepic.

Josette looked around. "Where's Nounours?"

"Dropped on the grass."

Before I'd finished speaking, Margot started to turn. "I'll go—"

"Wait," I gasped, grabbing her wrist. "Until we're sure the plane's not coming back."

"Nounours," Noémie moaned now, switching the focus of her need.

"Anyone else hurt?" I looked around. At the shake of heads, I turned my full attention back to Noémie. Running my hands over her swiftly, I confirmed she had just the one injury. I ripped the ragged, bloodstained sleeve off her nightgown, then whispered a prayer of gratitude when I saw the bullet had gone straight through, just grazing her. But still, the wound would need disinfectant, and plenty of it, on this grimy road, with no running water, and with new dust kicked up every mile, flavored with manure, both equine and human, along with a good measure of engine grease and oil.

Margot knelt to look Noémie in the eye. "We'll get your teddy bear, *ma petite*. Don't you worry."

"He's safe," Lucie added gently, rubbing the girl's shoulder. "Keeping watch. Protecting us."

I looked for the cleanest bandage I could find, but there was nothing. Even our clothes were dirty. Finally, in desperation, I held out my hand to Josette. The redhead quickly pulled the cotton cloth ties from her hair and handed them to me. Not ideal bandages, but they'd have to do for now. I soothed, "It'll be all right, Noémie. I promise."

The girl's crying lessened as I smoothed out the cotton strips, tied several together and wrapped them snugly around her bullet wound to stop the bleeding. She looked up at me with big, tearstained eyes in the dappled shade of the forest, sucking two fingers for comfort.

Once the makeshift bandage was fastened, I rose to my feet. "We need to go back to the truck for my medical bag. Noémie, hold up your arm. Like this."

Smiling, I lifted my arm ninety degrees, as if it were a game. The little girl imitated me, wincing. My smile broadened. "Well done, brave girl. Now, do you need Margot to carry you? Or will you walk?"

"Walk," she responded stoutly, but as I helped her to her feet, she looked towards where she'd dropped her stuffed bear and added falteringly, "But Nounours wants me to carry him."

"Of course." Holding a finger to my lips, I tilted my head, listening. I heard people moaning and crying, shouting and cursing. I heard car engines coming to life, the road starting up again. But nothing in the sky. The plane had disappeared to torment and strafe the roads further south.

"It's safe," I told the girls, and holding Noémie's hand, we ventured slowly out of the forest, the others following us.

Padding across the crushed grass towards the road, we saw the army truck stopped some distance up away, men pulling soldiers from the damaged vehicle.

Close to us, I saw families weeping over loved ones who were injured or dead, car engines smoking, supplies smashed and scattered. I wondered if I should go around with my medical bag, try to offer assistance. My gaze rested briefly on Margot. Could I leave the girls all in her care? How would they react if I left them alone for an hour? How would she? I didn't know what to do.

First, I needed fabric for a sling...

Rachel picked up a bruised apple that had tumbled across the grass from a nearby tree. "Look, Sister." She held it up. The fruit had been split clean through by a bullet hole. Looking through it with one eye, she giggled. "Just like Noémie's arm." Then her face fell as she looked at my shirt. "Sister Helen..."

"Don't be mean, Rachel," Josette snapped, picking up the teddy bear, tattered as usual but apparently unhurt by the Nazi plane. She handed the stuffed animal to Noémie, who clutched it tightly with her good arm, then turned her face up to me.

"Nounours says you must carry us both," she said with dignity.

Still staring at me, Rachel nudged her sister, and Estée's eyes went wide in turn.

"Sister Helen," Estée gasped.

Ignoring them, I smiled down at Noémie. "Now, let's see about a sling—"

But as I started to pick her up, I felt a sharp sting in my abdomen that made me flinch, but I ignored that, too, distracted by something moving in the corner of my eye. I turned my head.

Some ten meters away, a man was rummaging in the flatbed of our truck, still parked in the grass where we'd camped the night before.

"Stop!" I cried.

He looked up. It was the same man who'd cursed us, his expression now twisted with defiance and guilt. Holding a fuel can, he hopped from the end of our truck and rushed towards a car already waiting in the road, engine running. The car's back trunk was open, stuffed with our food and supplies. Including my medical bag.

"Stop! Thief!" I screamed, reaching behind my back for my revolver. But the man was already throwing himself into the front passenger seat of his car, clutching the fuel can to his chest. The haggard woman at the wheel pressed her foot on the gas, and the car lurched forward, knocking the trunk shut, ducking and weaving dangerously down the crowded road. Through the back window, I saw the solemn faces of young children staring back at me.

My fingers trembled on the holster. Then I dropped my arm.

"Why don't you shoot them?" Margot cried.

Closing my eyes, struggling to fight my rising panic and grief and anger, I whispered, "There's children."

"But they took our food. Our fuel!"

"Maybe we'll still be all right..."

But even as I spoke the words, I knew we wouldn't be. We'd only had that one full gas can left. Swallowing hard, I looked at the six girls staring at me. I felt another sharp pain in my side. I felt like I was going to faint. I felt...

"Helen, you're bleeding," Margot said, her voice suddenly scared.

All the girls were now staring at my side, just above my right hip. I looked down. I touched my wine-colored blouse. My palm came away covered in blood.

"Oh," I said mildly. "I've been shot."

And I fell to my knees.

8

HELEN

Margot was at the wheel, since I couldn't drive. We'd shouted across the road for a doctor, and when no one came to help, the girls had managed to pull me into the soft leather seat of the cab. It had taken fifteen minutes to drive half a mile in the increasing traffic, in a small single-lane column of cars that passed the slower pedestrian, horse and bicycle traffic, around blackened cars, injured people and the broken hollows of the road where bombs had landed, recently or previously.

Gripping the wheel, Margot threw me anxious glances. "According to the map, the next town is close, just a bit off the main road. It will have a hospital, I promise."

"It won't," I whispered. "The town's too small."

A hard shiver racked my body. I blinked hard to keep myself from passing out. The bullet from the German Stuka had entered my body just above my right hip. It was still inside me. Somewhere between my intestines and my liver.

"The town might have a hospital—how do you know?" Her knuckles were white. She glanced at the dog-eared road map spread out between us on the bench seat. "You don't even know which town I'm talking about—"

"La Ravelle." Speaking the name out loud sucked the remaining breath out of my lungs. Tears stung my eyes. I'd promised myself. I'd sworn it by everything holy.

Margot looked at me, terrified by those tears. I'd never cried in front of the girls—not once. "There will be a doctor. Surely the town's big enough for that, or it wouldn't be on the map."

"No," I whispered, though I knew she was right. There was indeed a doctor in La Ravelle. I repeated helplessly, "No."

But our supplies had been ransacked. The extra fuel cans were gone, along with my medical kit and most of our food and water. There were some small mercies. The thief hadn't had time to bother with our suitcases or bags. We still had our clothes and Estée's books. I had our identity papers and our small stash of money. But what use were those, without food or fuel?

With Josette's help, I'd managed to wrap some pajama pants around my blouse to slow the bleeding. But red continued to seep from the wound, and I could only imagine what the bullet was doing inside me. What it might have hit. What time I might have left.

Tilting my head back, I breathed through my mouth and nose, ignoring the dark spots over my vision, the slanted streaks of light through the morning drizzle now shimmering over people and cars and trampled green fields along the southbound road. I could lean back because Margot had whisked the revolver back into the canvas bag beneath the seat without drawing any attention.

With effort, I glanced towards the back window of the cab. The little girls, along with Josette and Lucie, were huddled together beneath the waxed canvas tarp slung over the wooden slats as a weak roof. Rain was dripping off the edges, and wind was whipping it towards them.

I didn't have their visas yet. How could I help them if I was dead?

"Helen," Margot begged. "*Please* let me look for a doctor."

I flashed hot, then cold. La Ravelle. Was it fate? The place I'd most hungered to see, the temptation I'd fought to deny, and now in a monkey's-paw twist of fate, I'd arrive on his doorstep injured, with six children in tow, filthy and begging for his help.

What choice did I have?

Leaning my head back, I breathed in resignation, "La Ravelle."

"*Dieu merci*," the girl whispered. A few moments later, she turned the wheel, steering the truck away from the crowded slowness of the main thoroughfare to a slender road past a small sign: *La Ravelle, 3 km*.

In the distance, past the sea of vineyards, I could see a picturesque medieval town clinging to a hilltop, a ruined castle at one end, a church bell tower at the other. La Ravelle. His town. I closed my eyes, crossing my hands over my pounding heart. I'd been here once before, in 1922—arriving from Greece just in time to see Jean-Luc at the door of that stone church, kissing his beautiful young bride beneath joyful scatters of rice over the snow.

Pain caught in my throat. For a moment, I seriously wondered if I would have actually preferred to die than to see him again. Especially like this.

But the girls.

An ache filled my throat as I stared up at the town, watching it get larger and larger like a lady in a tumbrel might have regarded an approaching guillotine.

I remembered La Ravelle, barely bigger than a village, as achingly beautiful that January day, with its medieval timbered buildings and small main square sparkling white, sunshine glistening like diamonds against the snow. I remembered the laughing, pretty bride in her white lace dress, eyes shining with love beneath the wind swirling her long veil, her hands full of red roses. And the handsome, older, dark-haired groom smiling down at her.

It had cut my heart out.

I held my breath as Margot drove us into the town...

But La Ravelle was no longer a place of dreams. In the gloomy rain, the small winding streets were now crowded with trash. Refugees overflowed from every tavern and inn, camping in the park or sleeping in cars. Even the town square, so wretchedly beautiful that long-ago winter's day, was nothing like I remembered. It was filled with gray people, some standing and talking together angrily, others slumped on the wet ground, unmoving beneath the gray rain.

"Where can I find a doctor?" Margot said out loud, more to herself than me, as she looked right and left, driving slowly. She peered anxiously at the town hall as we passed the square. "I'll ask the *maire*?"

"Go to—a building painted blue." Unless he'd changed it. Maybe he'd changed it after all these years. Holding my breath, I pointed down the slender main street. "Turn left at the corner."

"Where?"

My body shook. I whispered, "There."

Around the corner, I saw the three-story house he'd described to me so lovingly in Greece, the house I'd seen only once in reality but still haunted my dreams. The house that could have been my home.

"How did you know?" She glanced at me doubtfully, then pulled the truck in front of the blue house. There were no other cars parked along the slender winding street. That seemed odd, but I didn't have time to worry about it. Margot turned off the engine.

"Where's the hospital?" Josette's pinched face appeared in the cab's window.

"Helen said a doctor lives in the blue house."

Josette disappeared. A moment later, she was opening my passenger door, holding out her hands to help me down. Her voice was gentle. "Lean on me, Sister Helen."

As I stumbled out of the truck, Margot was suddenly at my other side. "We've got you."

Walking was difficult, and I was glad to have their sturdy shoulders supporting me.

As I approached the white door of the blue house—blue like the Aegean Sea where we'd once kissed on rocky shores—I felt like I was floating, like I was in one of my recurring dreams where I came here not as myself, with all my flaws, but had been transformed into his sweet young bride, innocent and perfect.

I trembled. "This is a mistake," I whispered. "I can't."

But the girls were relentless. They held me up on both sides, and I had no ability to turn and flee.

Leaning forward, Margot knocked on the door. We waited. She knocked again, harder.

"Doctor, are you there? Please help us!" she cried. "A woman's been shot!"

Inside, there was a low thud of footsteps, then the door swung open.

A stranger stood framed in the doorway, a man with salt-and-pepper hair, scarred on one cheek with wrinkles around his black eyes, trim and broad-shouldered, wearing a white coat. Then I blinked, and in that blink, my memories filled in the cracks, and I saw him. The same man I remembered from nearly two decades before. The man I'd promised myself I'd never see again. The only man I'd ever loved. I took a shuddering breath.

"Jean-Luc," I whispered.

9

MARGOT

The kitchen was warm and filled with sunlight, giving the wattle-and-daub walls a rosy glow. I exhaled in pleasure, breathing in the smell of beef stew bubbling on the stove, yeasty bread rising in the oven.

Was I in heaven?

I was fresh from a bath, wearing a soft clean robe over skin scrubbed clean. The younger girls had bathed last night, but by the time it was my turn, I'd already fallen asleep. The water had been lukewarm, as they had only cold running water, but Madame Ravanel had been kind enough to boil three pots of hot water on the stove to add to the fresh cold water, just for me. It had been bliss to have a proper bath, and wash all the dust and grief and fear off my skin. My hair was still wet, twisting in thick dark curls over my shoulders as I came into the kitchen, clutching clean clothes, still a little damp after being hung to dry in front of the fire earlier that morning.

Smiling, the doctor's wife looked up from stirring the pot on the wood-burning stove. "Are they dry, *ma petite?*"

I beamed back at her. "Yes. Thank you a thousand times."

"I'm sorry they weren't already dry before your bath, but

what with all the rain..." She looked at the robe with regret. "I'm sure you'll be happy to get out of that old thing."

To me, her borrowed robe was softer than the silks of Arabia. I clutched the long sleeves. "I can't thank you enough."

Her smile widened. "Tea?"

She held out a chipped mug, and I almost wanted to cry.

I stood in the middle of the sunlit kitchen, just cradling the warm mug in my hands. "You've been so kind. You and your husband both. Thank you."

Madame Ravanel snorted a laugh, her eyes suddenly merry. "I don't think anything I've done is so wonderful. It's my husband who's the hero."

"He is at that," I agreed fervently.

When we'd arrived at the blue house yesterday morning, Helen had inexplicably blurted out his first name on the doorstep, then fainted, slumping forward.

Dr. Ravanel had caught her, looking as if he'd seen a ghost. After lifting her into his strong arms, he'd carried her into his surgery, which comprised the ground level of their home, and gently lowered his unconscious patient onto the examining table, peppering us with terse questions. Who were we? Where had we come from? How had she been shot? But as Josette and I had rushed to explain, he'd barely seemed to hear us. He'd only had eyes for her.

"Helen," he'd said softly, cradling her cheek, his strong-featured face almost as pale as hers. "*Helen.*"

He cut the fabric off her torso with shears and looked grimly at the wound, then us. "When did this happen?"

"Two hours ago—"

"She's lost so much blood." A wail came from behind him. Turning, we saw Lucie with the three little girls in the front doorway. All four of them were crying, looking scared out of their minds.

Setting his jaw, the doctor went to the back staircase, calling for his wife. A pretty, plump-cheeked woman had appeared on the stairs. "Yes, my love?"

"I have a patient who's been shot by a German plane. Please take these children upstairs and give them something. Then I may need your assistance."

Cursing the Nazis under her breath, she'd herded the rest of us up the stairs. Looking back, I had one last image of Helen, unconscious with blood covering her belly, and prayed I was doing the right thing, given the man was a stranger to us.

But Helen had told me to come here. She knew him—she must, or she wouldn't have said his name the way she had. I had to trust her decision.

The doctor's wife had taken us upstairs to the comfortable, warm kitchen, where she served us thick slices of chocolate gâteau and glasses of milk before leaving to help her spouse. We were left to be hosted by her fourteen-year-old daughter, Suzanne, who told Estée that *of course* she could read all the books on their shelves, and offered the younger girls crayons and a half-used coloring book. When the little girls cried with worry for Helen, Suzanne told them stoutly that they had nothing to fear because her father was the best doctor in all of France, "which, since France has the best doctors, makes him the best in all the world."

The little girls were soon distracted, sprawling on the rug in front of the fire, coloring drawings of happy young children at play, with dogs, at home, at school. After reiterating that Helen would be all right—perfectly fine—Lucie and Josette and I returned to the kitchen table, with nothing to do but drink milk and eat cake, waiting with our hearts in our throats.

It seemed like hours later when Dr. Ravanel came back up the stairs, looking exhausted, his surgical gown smeared with blood. He looked between the three of us, then his eyes had focused on me.

"It was difficult," he said quietly. "The bullet nearly pierced the liver. She... If she'd waited much longer, it could have caused permanent damage or turned into sepsis, which she wouldn't have survived." He spoke slowly, choosing his words carefully. Dumbing down medical terms? Or trying not to scare us? He finished, "But I repaired the damage. I believe... I believe she'll be all right."

I could have embraced him. Instead, Lucie and Josette and I jumped up, hugging each other with noisy tears. The younger girls rushed in from the parlor.

"What's wrong?" demanded Estée, clutching her borrowed book.

"Why are you crying?" said Rachel, gripping crayons in both hands.

"Sister Helen is going to be all right," Josette told them, tears running down her face.

The younger girls looked at each other, unimpressed.

"You told us that already," Rachel said, and they returned to the parlor.

Josette laughed, wiping her tears. "And they believed me? I'm a better actress than I thought."

Her fingertips smudged black kohl beneath her eyes. It was the first time I'd seen her smudge her mascara on the whole journey.

It was ridiculous, really, the way she'd kept carefully curling her hair and putting on makeup while trudging the heat and dust of the southern road. Did she think some Hollywood director was going to jump out of the bushes and make her a star? If she knew her real chance for stardom was directly ahead... that she'd be going to Hollywood with Helen and the little girls, and all her dreams would soon be coming true...

Dr. Ravanel had cleared his throat. "Madame Taylor is groggy from ether, and I expect she'll sleep the rest of the day. She'll need lots of rest over the next few weeks. Where are you staying in town?"

Josette and I had looked at each other.

"We're traveling to Marseille," Josette said, her cheeks pink. "We've been sleeping by the side of the road, or in the truck."

"We could find a hotel room in La Ravelle," I suggested, but just saying the words, I heard how ridiculous they were. Even if we could find an available room in this overcrowded town, how would we pay for it?

"I see." Dr. Ravanel looked grim. He turned to the parlor doorway. "My wife told me there's someone else who's wounded? A bird with a broken wing?"

"Me." Standing up from the braided rug, Noémie held up her arm in the firelight. A moment before, she'd been focusing on her crayons but now reminded of her injury, she started to cry.

"May I see?"

She nodded. Coming forward, Dr. Ravanel gently pulled back the edges of the makeshift bandages created from Josette's cotton hair ties. He released her with a nod, one comrade to another. "You've been brave, little one. Come downstairs, and I'll clean it right up."

Noémie regarded him seriously. "Will it hurt?"

"Yes, just for a moment. Then I'll give you a lollipop. Is that a fair exchange?"

She considered, then nodded.

Pausing before he went down the stairs, he looked back at us. "You're all orphans from Paris? Helen is your headmistress?"

I noted the unconscious way Dr. Ravanel had shifted back to her first name, rather than the more formal *Madame Taylor*, and wondered how well they knew each other. And if John Cleeton, the American rancher who'd taken Sophie to Marseille, knew anything about Dr. Jean-Luc Ravanel, who lived with his wife and child in La Ravelle.

But how could he, when none of us had ever heard the man's name before?

"From St. Agnes's," Josette said. "Sister Helen wanted us away from the Nazis, so she found everyone else foster homes. We're the last ones, on our way to Marseille."

"And Boulins," said Lucie.

"*Sister* Helen." He paused. "You're not telling me," he said incredulously, "she's a nun."

"Oh, no. Some people called her that because she was a nurse, and it stuck..." Josette glanced at me, forehead furrowed. I could tell she was wondering the same questions I was.

"Has she lived in Paris long?"

"Forever," said Noémie. Lucie gave her a little cuddle.

"Not forever, but years and years," said Lucie. "Since I was a baby."

Dr. Ravanel shook his head a little, as if he could hardly believe his ears, then squared his shoulders. "Don't worry about finding a hotel, children. Madame Taylor will stay in our guest room until I'm sure she's stable." He looked at his pretty, plump wife. "My dear, surely you could manage to find places for all the girls to sleep? Just for a few weeks?"

"A few..." Madame Ravanel had looked startled, as well she should, given her husband had just volunteered her to feed and house seven extra people for weeks. Then she'd looked at Noémie, who was cradling her arm with big woeful eyes. The woman had sighed, her heart seemingly melting. "Of course they must stay."

Since then, Madame Ravanel had taken care of us as if we were her own, learning our names, hugging us without reserve. Keeping their tiny guest room for Helen as soon as she could be moved, she'd found the rest of us comfortable places to sleep in their snug little house—the three little girls on the two sofas, a chaise longue for Lucie, and Josette and me on the soft rug near the fire, cosseted by pillows and blankets. For supper, in a miracle second only to the biblical fishes and loaves, she'd magically turned the coq au vin meant for three into chicken soup to feed ten.

Putting the little girls to bed last night, including Noémie, who was proud of the new white bandage on her arm, Madame Ravanel sang them lullabies before she tucked them into their bedding on the sofas—something that brought us older girls, watching from across the room, to tears. No one, not even Sister Helen, had ever tucked us in like that. Noémie seemed to cling to her before she fell deeply asleep, holding Nounours to her heart and sucking her thumb.

Now, I looked at Madame Ravanel in the sunlit kitchen. She was petite, perhaps forty, with blonde hair tucked in a loose bun and the start of wrinkles at the corners of her blue eyes. Her forehead was sweaty from the heat as she stood at the stove in her apron and old dress, house slippers on her feet shuffling over the wood-planked floor. Her comfortingly stout figure—her waist nearly buried by her shelf-like bosom beneath the apron— just made her that much more comforting and motherly. I already adored her.

"I can't thank you enough, *madame*. You've been so kind."

"Anyone would have done it, my dear," she said serenely. She went back to stirring the beef bourguignon on the stove. "Oh, and we moved Madame Taylor upstairs while you were in the bath. Jean-Luc said she was doing well enough, and we thought she'd be more comfortable resting in the guest room than the cot downstairs."

"She's awake?" I asked eagerly. She'd been sleeping last night when I'd been allowed to peek on her downstairs. Dr. Ravanel hadn't permitted any of the other girls to see her, afraid of disturbing her rest. "Can I go see her?"

"We'll ask if she's well enough for visitors." She held out her hand. "Are you done?"

I gulped the last of the tea and gave her the mug.

In the bathroom, I changed into clean panties, socks and

brassiere, and my favorite soft shirt and trousers. I glanced at myself in the mirror, and thought of trying to comb my thick, curly, dark hair, then remembered I'd left my comb in the truck. Leaving my hair to make its own bad choices, I went into the sitting room.

Washed clothes were still strung near the fire, drying out. Nearby, Suzanne Ravanel played checkers with Josette. The Ravanels' only child, Suzanne was skinny and gawky, wearing an old blouse, skirt and bobby socks. She had big brown eyes like her father. Her dark curly hair reminded me of mine, almost impossible to control, though unlike me, the girl managed it, braiding it in two thick plaits. Big band music floated from the wireless.

The Ravanel family was loving and warm, the kind I'd always wanted, the kind I'd once yearned to run away from the orphanage and find. It felt disloyal to the girls, to Helen, even to the memory of my poor dead parents, but I still couldn't keep myself from wondering: What would it have been like to grow up in a family like this?

Madame Ravanel had mentioned she had two grown-up stepsons, the product of Dr. Ravanel's first marriage to a woman who'd died long ago, now missing on northern battle-fields. The Ravanels were suffering grief and worry of their own, and yet they still had enough heart to offer a home to strangers.

I heard the heavy creak of stairs, and the doctor appeared from downstairs, where he'd managed a steady stream of patients all day in his clinic. I followed him into the kitchen. His brown eyes looked weary, his graying dark hair disheveled, a five o'clock shadow over his jawline as he came forward to kiss his wife.

"*Zut*," she chided him, "what kind of feeble kiss was that?" She stepped back from where she'd been stirring the stew with a ladle, her plump cheeks rosy, her hair curly from steam.

He gestured awkwardly towards me. "I don't want to shock the girl."

"Is it such a shock to see a happy marriage?" she demanded, arms akimbo.

A little sheepishly, he kissed her on the lips. She sighed into his arms briefly, then straightened, turning back to the stove. "How was it today?"

"Busy."

"Did anyone pay?"

He looked down. "A few."

Madame Ravanel sighed. "And our patient upstairs?"

"I checked on her an hour ago, changed her bandage and gave her something to help her sleep."

"How is she?"

"As well as can be expected." His dark eyes looked sad. "After being shot, on top of..."

"On top of what?" I demanded.

Dr. Ravanel looked startled, as if he'd forgotten I was there. He said smoothly, "Exhaustion. Traveling through a war zone with six children, how could she not be exhausted?"

But he and his wife exchanged glances. I knew he wasn't telling me the whole story.

"Dinner's ready," Madame Ravanel said briskly. "Tell the children to wash their hands."

Five minutes later, we'd all somehow managed to pack in around the rectangular wooden kitchen table, their family of three, plus us six girls. It was snug but warm, and I relished the noise, Dr. Ravanel's low laugh as he argued about philosophy with his daughter, his wife's gentle reproach that they mustn't argue at the dinner table. The Nazis seemed a world away.

Every bit of food was served, except for the last two slices of freshly baked bread and the bottom scoop of beef stew in the big bronze pot, which were saved for Helen.

"That was delicious, my dear. As always," the doctor said,

his bowl practically licked clean, and she beamed beneath his praise. Then he slowly rose to his feet. "I suppose I should get ready."

Her smile disappeared. "You can rest tonight, surely? After keeping an eye on their truck all last night?"

He shook his head. "I would like nothing better, *ma chérie*. But there are sick patients who can't reach our clinic. That pregnant woman sleeping in the square might be in labor already. I cannot leave them to fend for themselves."

"These refugees!" She tightened her fists. "It's not enough you help them for free. Now you have to walk there! It'll be dark when you come back. It's not safe—you know it's not..."

"Nothing will happen." Dr. Ravanel put his hand gently on his wife's shoulder. "It'll all be fine."

She lowered her gaze mutinously. "Tell that to poor Bisou."

"Bisou?" Lucie said.

"Élisabeth," her husband warned.

"The terrier next door," Madame Ravanel told us. "The sweetest little thing." Her eyes darkened. "Then a few weeks ago, thieves broke in when our neighbors weren't home. And they..."

"They what?" Lucie cried.

"This isn't the best time," Dr. Ravanel said, glancing towards the three little girls at the end of the table.

Suzanne, catching her mother's glance, rose to her feet. "May we be excused, Maman?"

"Yes, my darling."

Suzanne carried her dishes to the sink, then headed into the parlor, the little girls trooping after her like she was the Pied Piper.

When they were out of earshot, her mother told us softly, "The men who broke in next door hit poor Bisou with something hard to stop her barking."

Lucie turned white as a sheet. "Did she die?"

"*Non*," said the doctor. "She's healing. But it was so unnecessary. She's just a little fluff of fur, no threat to anyone. The thieves could have tossed her in a closet. Instead, they bludgeoned her—almost as if for fun."

Lucie looked sick. She whispered, "Who would hurt a helpless little dog?"

My sister always wanted to help everyone in need, but dogs held a special place in her heart. After our favorite neighbor's sweet elderly beagle had died last year, Lucie had begged Sister Helen for a puppy. The headmistress had refused, not wanting the orphanage to have more chaos and another mouth to feed. So my sister'd had to content herself with leaving food for the birds in the garden. But the dream continued.

"And if that wasn't enough for these heartless bastards"—Madame Ravanel ground her teeth—"last week, they stole every car on our street. Including our truck!" She tossed her head in fury. "Think of it! The truck Jean-Luc uses to help the sick and dying—they just took it! And now he must walk!"

"It's good exercise," Dr. Ravanel said with an apologetic smile, trying to soften his wife's fury.

"It's ridiculous—why you must neglect your family and your health to care for people who can't pay, when the price of everything is so dear, and we're barely getting by!"

For the first time, it occurred to me there'd been very little actual beef in the bourguignon. The stew had been flavored so well, and the bread had been so delicious, I hadn't noticed. But looking around the house with sharper eyes, I saw, though the room was cozy and warm, several tiles were cracked and missing from the floor, the dining table was old and rough, the bowls chipped, the glasses mismatched. And—horror—I suddenly realized I'd only seen Jean-Luc eat a single bowl of stew, though I'd eaten two. They'd shared everything with us. I blushed guiltily.

"And now," his wife continued, "we must always lock our

doors and live in fear. While *you* must walk endless kilometers in the dark of night! What about when it turns cold and starts to snow?"

He looked at her quietly. "We'll get by, Élisabeth. We can't let it stop us doing the right thing."

"Please use our truck, Dr. Ravanel," I blurted out. "Helen won't mind."

Josette's eyebrows rose across the table at my casual use of Helen's first name. I gave her a crooked grin as if to say, *Ben oui* —that's right.

"Thank you, Margot. That's very kind," Dr. Ravanel said. "But it's good for me to get a little exercise. And better for your truck to remain here, where I can ask the neighbor boy to sit up in it all night and keep an eye on it."

"And how much will that cost?" his wife grumbled.

"We can manage."

She lifted her gaze to his pleadingly. "Stay home and get some rest."

"Tomorrow night," he promised, rubbing her shoulders. "Yves promised he'd have space in his garage by then."

Madame Ravanel refused to be mollified. "We can only hope a locked garage will stop them. Those beggars from the north have flooded our respectable town and brought crime and grief."

Josette and I, conscious of being beggars from the north ourselves, looked at each other uncomfortably. "Isn't it the Nazis who've done that?"

She straightened in her shabby wooden chair. "We haven't seen any Nazis here, just Frenchmen and Belgians and Dutch who threaten and steal and leave trash on our streets. I never thought I'd see the day!" Staring between us, she sighed, her cheeks turning red. "But that's nothing to do with you, my dears. Forgive me."

Folding his lanky form into the chair beside her, Dr.

Ravanel looked at her intently. "Refugees are just like us, Élisa-beth. It could be us next. The whole group can't be blamed for a few bad apples."

"I know," she sighed. "But it's just not right—"

"Perhaps up north, someone is taking care of Paul and Daniel, wherever they are—giving them food and shelter and hope."

His wife turned pale. "Yes." She licked her lips, blinking back tears. "Yes, you're right." Taking a deep breath, she gave him a trembling smile. "I will try to bear it more cheerfully, for their sake."

He took his wife's hand in his own and kissed it. They looked at each other, and I saw such tenderness between them that it made my heart ache. Then he glanced at us with a forced smile. "Well, it's getting late. I'm afraid I must—"

"You stayed up all night watching our truck?" Josette tilted her head, eyes wide. "And you're hiring someone to watch it tonight?"

He shrugged. "The truck and our house, too. Don't worry. You'll be quite safe."

My alarmed eyes met Josette's. All day long, with Helen recovering from surgery, and all of us sheltered and fed in this comfortable home, I'd never thought to worry about our truck, parked on this quiet, tidy street of row houses.

I said with dark humor, "I guess it's lucky most of our things were already stolen from the back of the truck."

Josette's lipstick-red mouth twisted. "Perhaps we should thank the man who did it."

Lucie, not listening, whispered aloud, "Who would hurt a dog?"

Beneath our mutual bravado, I could see my own fear in Josette's eyes. Even if the miracles continued, even if the truck wasn't stolen and Helen recovered from her bullet wound without complications—how would we continue our journey?

How would we even reach Boulins, let alone Marseille, without food or fuel?

We couldn't ask the Ravanels for more. We couldn't. It was bad enough Dr. Ravanel had stayed awake protecting our truck and the family would be spending their precious money to keep it safe again tonight. The truck was our responsibility, not his. As Madame Ravanel had said earlier, it just didn't seem right.

I thought of offering my own small stash of francs saved from working as an au pair the previous summer. But that didn't seem right, either. That pitifully small amount was all I'd have to protect Lucie and myself from any unforeseen disaster after we were on our own.

What could I do?

"Thank you for a delicious dinner, my love." Dr. Ravanel rose to his feet. "I must be off."

"Yes, thank you, Madame Ravanel," said Josette, rising in turn.

"It was delicious," I said, setting down my napkin.

"Delicious," Lucie murmured, then wandered to the kitchen window, drawing the curtain aside to look disconsolately at the street in the twilight.

Josette and I cleared the table, taking the dishes to the sink. But as I heard Dr. Ravanel say farewell to his daughter in the parlor, then go downstairs, I suddenly couldn't bear it. Wiping my wet, soapy hands, I ran downstairs after him. I caught him in the downstairs surgery, just as he was leaving.

"Wait, Dr. Ravanel. Don't hire the neighbor boy tonight," I said breathlessly. "I have a better idea."

10

MARGOT

The stairs squeaked beneath my feet as I carried Helen's dinner tray upstairs. I paused outside the closed bedroom door.

Biting my lip, I looked down at the tray, just beef broth and bread really, with water and milk to drink. Food for an invalid. There was also, unexpectedly, a pink rose in a tiny bud vase, a kind gesture from Madame Ravanel, who grew them in flower pots, as their row house had no garden.

I was about to break a promise, and I already felt guilty.

Headmistress or not, was it right for me to ask a woman who'd been shot by a Nazi plane just yesterday to help solve our current problems? Her only job should be getting well.

Maybe I wouldn't ask her. Maybe I'd just give her the tray, say some comforting words and go. I wouldn't tell her anything about where Josette, Lucie and I would be sleeping tonight. I'd figure out alone how to replenish our fuel and supplies. Maybe I could just let Helen peacefully recuperate, as I'd promised Dr. Ravanel.

Maybe not.

Biting my lip, I hesitated. Then I gave a soft knock on the door and went in. If she was still asleep...

But she wasn't. I rejoiced to see Helen's eyes were open as she rested on the small bed beneath a blanket. Turning on the lamp near the door, I said, "How are you feeling?"

She started to sit up, then stopped, wincing. Coughing a laugh, or maybe laughing a cough, she said, "Fine."

I set the tray down on her nightstand, next to her pill bottle. "Here's your dinner."

She sniffed without appetite. "What is it?"

"Beef broth. Bread." I smiled at the pink rose. "And a flower. Isn't that nice?"

"Jean-Luc," she whispered, taking the rose in her hands.

I'd never seen her smile like that—the smile of a dreamy young girl.

"Madame Ravanel did that," I clarified. "His wife. She's lovely."

Naked, raw emotion twisted her face—longing, grief, despair. She dropped the flower on the tray as if it had burned her. Turning away, she reached for the two pills and glass of water on the nightstand.

But I'd seen what I'd seen, though I still couldn't believe it.

Was Helen secretly in love with Dr. Ravanel?

Impossible, I told myself. In the first place, it was obvious they hadn't seen each other in years, maybe decades. And in the second, Helen Taylor had never shown love for anyone—not the milkman who flirted with her and brought flowers, not the elderly nobleman who'd invited her to dinner in his *hôtel particulier*. Not even American cowboy John Cleeton, who'd been so wonderfully kind to all of us, and who also was rich and not bad-looking, had managed to win her affections.

Turning away, I gave an awkward chuckle into the silence. "Madame Ravanel has taken such good care of us, you might have trouble getting the girls to leave. Noémie's wound is small —it isn't bothering her at all. The Ravanels' daughter offered Estée some old clothes. Madame Ravanel washed everything for us, heated water for our baths. She even tucked the little girls in last night"—I smiled—"and sang them lullabies."

Helen's voice was flat as she slumped back against the pillows and closed her eyes. "A better mother than me."

I stared down at her, shocked. I hadn't meant my words as a slight. Of course I hadn't.

Or had I? Any protests froze in my throat. Hadn't part of my brain been judging Helen for the fact she'd never once sang Noémie—or the rest of us—a single lullaby?

I shook the mean thought from my head. "I only meant you mustn't worry. We're in good hands." I sat at the end of her bed in the shadowy room. "Just focus on feeling better. Dr. Ravanel says you'll make a full recovery."

"Did he?" Opening her eyes the merest crack, she looked out the small, bare window. The looming night was darkening between blood red and a bruising purple. "That's good to hear."

"Why have you never mentioned him before? If you're such good friends?"

Shifting her weight in the bed gingerly, she flinched, staring down at her midsection, lumpy with bandages beneath her over-sized pajama top. "What do you mean?"

She was wearing men's pajamas. They had to be the doctor's. "You didn't want me to come to La Ravelle at first, even though you were bleeding so badly. But you told me exactly how to get to this house. You knew Dr. Ravanel's name. Were you friends when you were a nurse? Did you fall out?"

"I'm—tired, sweetheart." Her voice was soft as her eyes slid away. "Thanks for—food, but I should... rest..."

Sweetheart. She'd never called me that before. Or any of the other girls, either. Rarely, she'd called them *ma petite.* Never *sweetheart*, not in French or English. Was she hallucinating? Had she forgotten she was speaking to plain old Margot Vashon —the girl who irritated and disappointed her?

"Right. Of course. Sorry. I'll go." My words fell over each other like the hooves of a runaway horse. I rose unsteadily to my feet and started for the door. Then I stopped. "But the thing is, you should know…"

But I saw there was no point in asking either advice or permission. She'd already fallen asleep.

I moved close again and looked at her. I was accustomed to thinking of Helen Taylor as strong, hard, strict. But now, with her brown-gray hair loose over the pillow, I saw the hollows beneath her cheekbones, her pale skin, the sunken shadows beneath her closed eyes. Her breath was a soft rattle as she slept.

She wasn't impervious to pain. Not at all.

An ache lifted to my throat, and I suddenly hated myself for giving her a hard time, even just in my own mind, about some stupid lullabies. Helen had given her life, as well as her life savings, to protect and take care of us. Why had I never appreciated this? Why hadn't it been enough?

I was going to be eighteen soon. A woman grown. Rather than criticizing Helen, fighting her and expecting her to solve all our problems, it was time I took responsibility for myself.

It was time I took care of *her*.

Leaving the tray untouched beside the bed, I crept out of the room, closing the door silently behind me. I took a deep breath, suddenly fiercely glad about the plan I'd made on impulse.

I was a little frightened. But surely, since I'd convinced Dr. Ravanel, it couldn't be *that* crazy?

"It's our truck," I'd told him in the clinic an hour before. "I'll watch over it."

"You? Watch out for thieves?" With a laugh, he'd looked over my wild hair, my slender frame. "You wouldn't scare a flea!"

"Don't be so sure." Putting my hands on my hips, I'd narrowed my eyes into a fierce glare.

With a snort, he'd held up his hands in mock surrender—somewhat comical since one of his hands held a medical kit and the other a fedora. He set down his arms, his trench coat falling back over his white shirt and gray trousers. "Not bad, kid. But I'm afraid I couldn't let you sleep all night out in the street."

"Because I'm young? Or because I'm a girl?"

"Well..."

"Don't worry. I'll bring Josette and my sister, too. The three of us." When I saw he wasn't convinced, I added, "Plus a gun."

His dark eyebrows lifted. "If you think I'm giving you my hunting rifle, you're sorely mistaken. If my wife didn't skin me alive, Helen would."

I tossed my head. "You don't have to give me anything. I have my own."

"Hunting rifle?"

"Gun."

He laughed, then sobered, wide-eyed. "You're serious?"

"Come on—I'll show you." I went outside to the truck, opened the hood and pulled out the small canvas bag I'd hidden in the best place I could think of—tucked into a small hollow of the engine where the girls would never think to look. "See?"

He sucked in his breath as I held up the holster beneath the streetlight.

"I haven't seen this in a long time," he whispered, taking it and unbuttoning the holster, before pulling out the unloaded gun and turning it in his large hands. It gleamed dully in the dim light. He looked up at me. "You know how to use this?"

"Of course I do," I said primly. "Helen taught me."

His expression changed. "Did she?" He tucked the revolver back into the holster, wrapping it in the school bag, and handed it back to me with a slight bow of his head. "In that case, *mademoiselle*, I defer to you."

"You do?" I said, a little astonished. "You'll let us do it? Sleep in the truck tonight?"

"Of course." He shrugged. "If the three of you have been trained by Helen, there's really nothing more to say, is there?"

"Uh, no." I wondered if he'd change his mind if he knew I'd never actually fired a bullet. I decided not to mention it.

Putting on his fedora, Dr. Ravanel shook my hand, one soldier to another. "I'll be back a little after midnight. Hopefully it'll be quiet. We've had no break-ins this week. It's possible the thieves have already moved on to the next town." He'd given me a cheeky salute. "*Bon courage, mademoiselle*."

"See you in the morning," I'd replied a little uncertainly, then watched as he walked down the street, whistling in the darkness.

Standing outside Helen's door, I blinked away the memory. It was one thing to decide to take responsibility and another to actually take it. I needed to tell Josette and Lucie. I wondered how they'd take my plan.

"Is she well?"

Nervously, I turned to face Madame Ravanel, who'd just stepped into the hall. "Yes, just tired." Then, hesitantly, I told her the plan for tonight. The kindly woman was shocked and tried to argue, until I informed her that her husband had already approved it; after that, she reluctantly gave in. When Suzanne came up the stairs, she shared the news with her daughter brightly, as though it were all a lark—until Suzanne suggested she should join us in the adventure. She shot that idea down fast.

"I'll come check on you later," Madame Ravanel said, watching me with worried eyes as I turned to go downstairs.

I shrugged. "No need. *C'est un jeu d'enfant*." It's nothing.

I said it with more confidence than I felt.

Coming downstairs, I saw Josette coming out of the bathroom, followed by the three little girls, all of them holding toothbrushes and wearing freshly cleaned nightgowns—even Estée, though hers, borrowed from Suzanne, was slightly too long.

Josette's nightgown was the prettiest, bought just last autumn. Her shorthand and typing, unlike mine, were atrocious, a fact I never tired of pointing out to her, so she worked at a café for money to buy cosmetics and fabric. Her red hair was pressed into the large pin curls she always did at night. She looked me over anxiously. "How's Sister Helen?"

"Too tired to eat. Other than that, fine."

"Good." She relaxed a little, then frowned. "So what did you need to talk to the doctor about?"

"I'll tell you in a minute."

In the parlor, Lucie was making the girls' beds, pulling sheets and blankets over the sofas. She was wearing a nightgown, blonde hair uncombed but clean, her pale eyelashes and eyebrows setting off her big blue eyes. Assuming we found fuel and food, and the others could continue their journey to Marseille, soon it would just be the two of us in Boulins—the two of us against the world. I crossed the room and pulled her into a fierce hug.

Lucie looked at me, surprised but pleased. "What was that for?"

"Nothing." Blinking hard, I tried to smile. "I just love you, *ma sœur*."

"What is it?" She looked alarmed now. "What's wrong?"

"Nothing," I repeated. Stepping back, I smiled broadly, looking between her and Josette. "Everything is fine."

My smile seemed to terrify them. The other two looked at each other.

"Is it Sister Helen?" Lucie sucked in her breath. "She's taken a turn for the worse!"

"Is she dying?" Rachel whimpered next to her.

"Dying!" Noémie instinctively started to wail.

"No, no, no," I rushed to say, then lowered myself to one

knee and hugged the little girls in reassurance. "She's doing wonderfully. I saw her—she's doing just fine. You'll see her tomorrow."

"Then what is it?" Josette demanded.

"Something fun." Rising to my feet, I tilted my head and grinned. "The three of us are going to have a little adventure."

11

HELEN

"How can we get away?" I asked desperately.

The angles of his handsome face were rosy-orange beneath the vicious brilliance of the blaze. An ugly red slash crossed one of his cheekbones, burned into his flesh by hot twisted rebar just minutes before, when he'd reached to pull me out of the collapsed concrete building which had tumbled all around us.

Jean-Luc's jaw tightened. "Just stay close."

His hand was tight around mine, but my heart was still pounding at the narrowness of our escape. I could feel the heat of the fire through my bones as it devoured the seaside town, a ghoulish bonfire in the night.

The Greek troops had been routed, vanquished during what they'd assumed would be an easy victory; after weeks of battle, the Turks had pushed them all the way to the Black Sea. Doctors and nurses were neutral, here with the Red Cross, trying to save anyone who needed saving. When fire had broken out, we'd stayed to evacuate our last patient into the overstuffed ambulance—stayed too late. We'd be charred corpses if we waited for an ambulance to come back for us.

Desperately, Jean-Luc looked right and left, past the

destruction, past the screaming villagers. Which side had started the fire? No one knew. We just had to get out.

I looked down at his hand covering mine.

After so many years working together, it was the first time Jean-Luc had held me this way. The first time anyone had held my hand since 1915, when my husband and child died. Since I'd numbed my heart, flinging myself into the service of others in the bloodiest, cruelest parts of the world. I'd told myself I was seeking redemption. The truth was I'd wanted to die.

We'd worked well together, doctor and nurse, and after the Great War ended, Jean-Luc found it unbearable to return to his unfaithful, vicious wife, who'd told him flatly that she had no intention of giving up the lover now sleeping in their bed. And I had no desire to go back to America. So when he'd invited me to join him in other war-torn lands that needed us, caring for typhus and cholera victims amid Soviet Russia's grim famine, the injured and sick in the Anglo-Irish war, then here, in the Ottoman Empire—I'd said yes.

For the six years since we'd met, we'd tried to heal the world —and escape our own crushed souls. And we'd done more than that. In the world's roughest places, our lives were often at risk, so he'd taught me to be brave. Taught me to fight.

The stones and wooden houses of the burning Ottoman village were literally crumbling around us, raining death from above. The fierce blaze consumed the forest surrounding the village, leaving us nowhere to run, pushing us towards the wild drowning sea. But his larger hand clutched mine as he protected me with his body, pushing forward through the crowds and chaos. I felt a thaw in my iced-over heart that had nothing to do with the heat of the fire. Was it because it was finally allowed? Because he'd received the shocking telegram just last month that his estranged wife was dead, killed in a crash with her paramour?

Jean-Luc turned to face me and pointed somewhere into the darkness of the aptly named Black Sea. "See that boat?"

I saw nothing. "Yes?"

"If we can reach it, we'll live. Do you agree?"

"Yes," I said, but I didn't care where he was taking me. I only knew that right now, my heart was pounding for a reason that had nothing to do with fear.

But too late! When he'd received the telegram, he'd told me with haunted eyes that his traveling days were over. With his wife and her lover dead, Jean-Luc had to return to France to care for his two young sons. As soon as our patients were safe, he told me, and this battle was over, he would go. It had broken my heart.

Now I wondered if we'd both die here, burned alive, just when I'd decided I wanted to live...

We ran past the burning houses, felt the hot edges of the fire, heard its soft, hungry roar coming closer. When we reached the water, Jean-Luc stepped out into the cool waves. "Wait!" he cried suddenly in Greek, staring out at the darkness. Pushing me forward in the water, he said, "You must take one more..."

A gruff voice in English. "We have room only for one."

I clutched Jean-Luc's hand. "I'm not going without you."

His dark eyes were luminous as he gave me a crooked smile. "I'll find another way. You go first. Blaze the trail."

"No..." The fire at my back was hot against my skin. I felt it coming close behind me, saw our shadows black against the water that brushed our knees. "Please. Don't make me leave you. Not now..."

He stared down at me, then his eyes widened. With a ragged intake of breath, he pulled me into his arms. "How long have I wanted—" Lowering his mouth, he kissed me in front of a wall of flame. When he pulled away, he said hoarsely, "Once we're safe, you'll come to France, Léna. You'll be my wife."

"Yes," I said, though I'd sworn to never marry again. "Yes." The word felt strange on my lips and teeth, as if my mouth were filled with cotton balls. "Just don't ever leave me—"

"I'm right here."

But Jean-Luc's voice sounded different than I remembered. Weary. The air felt cooler, and the crackle and howl of the fire suddenly grew quiet. I heard the rasp of my own breath, felt the erratic pounding of my own heart.

It took effort to open my eyes. For a moment, I saw only darkness. Where was the Ottoman village? Where was the fire? For a moment, I couldn't remember where I was or how I'd gotten here.

"It's all right, Helen." His voice was low. "I'm here."

In the pale gray light from the curtainless window, I saw a plain wooden cross on the wall. The faint light lingered against the edge of his face as he sat beside the bed, wearing a plain white shirt, rolled up over his forearms, and dark trousers. Were we back in Athens, in the place where we'd been evacuated after the American ship had plucked our lifeboat from the sea? For hours, he'd floated beside the lifeboat, my hand clutching his, never letting go. We'd wept when we were saved. For one perfect night, in the simple room above an Athens taverna, we'd made love, promising each other forever, vowing to wed before we booked passage to France.

Then, when I woke up, I'd ruined everything. Haunted by guilt, I'd felt unworthy of such happiness, and told him I could never be his wife. I'd told him to go to France alone and forget about me.

Within two months, I'd realized the depths of my mistake, but by then, it was too late.

Had God answered my prayers, given me another chance, sent me back through time to Greece in 1921?

"Jean-Luc," I choked out. My throat was dry, my voice

creaky, as if I hadn't used it for days. I swallowed and reached for him. "I dreamed you left me."

He took my hand from where he sat beside the bed. "I heard you cry out. I'm here."

For a moment, I gloried in the feel of his rough hand in mine, resting on the white blanket. Then I blinked.

The blanket was wrong. Too thick. The room was wrong. Too big. And when I looked up at his face, that was wrong, too. He had gray in his hair. Crinkles at his dark, serious eyes. And the scar on his cheek had faded from an ugly red to pink.

"Were you dreaming?" He turned on the little lamp beside the bed, flooding the room with light. "We need to talk."

As I blinked in the harsh light, reality came crashing down around me. I was no longer a young nurse with a broken heart, stoically traveling the world. I was now a fifty-year-old head-mistress who'd fled Paris with my young orphan girls.

And Jean-Luc had a wife...

She's lovely. Margot's cold words echoed in my ears. *Madame Ravanel has taken such good care of us... She even tucked the little girls in last night and sang them lullabies.*

When had she told me that—an hour ago? A week? The poisonous words had ricocheted through me, more destructive than any Nazi bullet. I remembered grabbing the pills beside my bed with shaking hands...

"What time is it?"

"Almost dawn."

"How long have I been here?" I said hoarsely.

Still sitting at the end of my bed, Jean-Luc looked at me in the small light of the nightstand lamp. "You arrived the day before yesterday."

It all seemed a blur from the moment I'd set foot in the blue house in La Ravelle. I dimly remembered the agonizing pain of being helped into the clinic, the awful surgery, the hallucination of being helped up the stairs. Then afterward, strange dreams on a cloud of—well, drugs. Even now my head didn't feel quite clear.

Had I really told Margot about my husband and baby when we'd been sitting by the campfire? When I'd been drinking—and smoking? What was wrong with me?

I put my hand to my forehead. "Prognosis?"

"We got the bullet out. You're lucky it didn't hit anything important. You've had some fever. I was worried about infection. You were tossing and turning, so I left you a few sleeping pills." His eyebrows rose when he saw they were gone from the nightstand.

"I was in pain," I whispered. In pain that it hadn't been Jean-Luc but his wife who'd placed the rose on the tray.

He shook his head a little. "I'll give you some more, but be careful. They pack quite a punch."

"I noticed," I said ruefully. "They knocked me out instantly, though the effects don't last long."

"They're usually used for minor surgery, not sleeping. But my stores of medications are running low."

I prayed I hadn't said anything stupid in my earlier stupor. It felt strange now, tense, to be so polite, barely more than strangers. The last time I'd seen him, he'd wept, held me, begged me to reconsider, pleaded his eternal love for me.

No. That was Athens. The last time I'd seen him had been three months later, when I'd seen him at La Ravelle's church door, celebrating after marrying his pretty young bride.

"May I?" He gestured towards my abdomen.

I glanced down, my cheeks burning when I saw I was in men's pajamas that could only be his.

Sitting beside me on the bed, he helped prop me up against the pillows, then slowly unwrapped the bandage around my naked belly, where a spot of red had bled through, and checked the bullet-wound entrance, above my hip. I managed not to flinch as he used an antiseptic solution from his bag to clean it and applied a new bandage. When he was done, I exhaled, missing his closeness in spite of the pain it had brought.

"Don't worry," he said as he caught me looking down at the pajamas again. "My wife put those on you. She helped with the surgery, also." He nodded towards the untouched food tray on the nightstand. "Élisabeth brought up some apples and cheese, since you never touched your dinner. She helped you with the chamber pot when you couldn't walk."

I remembered a woman, kind and pretty and gentle. I suddenly hated her. I said thickly, "Please thank her for me."

"I will." Jean-Luc looked at me dispassionately, all doctor. "How are you feeling right now?"

"Fine." I remembered that tone of his voice, how he'd used it on patients in Verdun when bombs were still falling and the makeshift battlefront hospital was filled with the shrieks and groans of bleeding, limbless men. In Dublin, in Tsaritsyn, in Sakarya, whatever dangerous place we were in, wherever patients were suffering, Jean-Luc used the same calm, soothing voice he was using on me now.

"No pain?"

"My belly hurts. My hip." I used my own calm voice—the same one I'd used as his nurse and put to good use at St. Agnes's in all the years since. "My girls—"

"Safe. Well. The little ones are sleeping downstairs, the older ones slept outside."

"Outside? All night?"

"They've been keeping an eye on your truck. Don't worry—they're doing well. I just checked on them through the window and spoke to them when I came home around midnight. I think they're rather proud of themselves. No other pain?"

Why would the girls be sleeping in the truck? I'd have thought they'd had enough of it. "Just a little achy and stiff from being in bed so long."

"Your wound is still fresh. You lost a good deal of blood.

Moving too much could tear your stitches and cause injury. You know the drill. You need a few weeks of rest."

"A few...?" In a flash, I remembered Marseille, everything still left undone. "It's the twentieth of June?"

"The twenty-first, now it's almost dawn."

"The Germans—?"

"No longer on the attack," he said soothingly. "Pétain took over the government and ordered our army to stand down."

"I remember hearing he wanted an armistice—"

"If the British surrender, the war will be over. Then perhaps my boys will be found."

My heart skipped a beat.

"Paul and Daniel are missing?" I whispered.

He nodded, his face grave. His voice cracked a little as he rubbed the back of his head. "Daniel was with the army in Dunkirk. I've had no word of him since. I'm not sure about Paul. Last I heard, he was serving as an attaché to one of Reynaud's assistants. Since Pétain took over... I don't know."

I grabbed his hand. "They'll be found, Jean-Luc—I know they will."

He seemed to hold his breath, staring at our intertwined hands. "Thank you."

Then he pulled away.

Silence fell between us, regret for the massive pain of war. I wondered if he ever thought about us. If he ever regretted that.

"Helen," he said quietly, "we need to talk."

Did we? Should we?

After holding on to my secret so long, I was suddenly terrified. Of course I couldn't keep a secret of this magnitude, not here and now, as I sat in his house. Jean-Luc could see right through me, past skin and muscle and bone to the truth I'd buried so deep even I had almost forgotten.

"About what?" I croaked. Perhaps I wouldn't have to say a word. Maybe he'd known, from the moment he saw her.

Clawing his hand through his wavy dark hair, he rose to his feet, paced three steps, then back. "Helen, do you know you're sick?"

"Of course. I was shot."

"I mean your lungs." His anguished black eyes pierced my heart. "Léna, you know you're dying? Don't you?"

12

HELEN

Léna—his old nickname for me. I stared at him, holding my breath. Then I realized what he'd said.

"Dying?" I croaked.

Jean-Luc looked down at his hands. "I'm sorry. I'm just a little... I shouldn't have said it like that. It's possible it won't be fatal. But it's serious."

"*Possible* it won't be fatal?" I said faintly. I suddenly wished for those cigarettes. Where had I left them? I looked for my valise, where I'd most recently placed our money and all our documentation, carefully tucked at the bottom to be safe from prying eyes. Thankfully, it had been stowed in the front of the truck, safe from the thief who'd made off with our supplies.

Oh heavens. What happened to the old service revolver? Then I remembered Margot had hidden it in the old school bag beneath the seat, and exhaled. She'd keep an eye on it. I rubbed my hand over my eyes and whispered, "I need a cigarette."

He snorted. "That's your first reaction?"

"There's a pack in my valise. Is it still in the truck?" If the girls were out there right now, leafing through birth certificates...

With an expressive Gallic snort, Jean-Luc went to the nearby wardrobe and pulled out the leather bag, then placed it on the end of my bed. I ripped it open, then rifled through until I saw the identification papers. I exhaled. Beside it was the blue pack of Gauloises. I placed a cigarette to my trembling lips.

Jean-Luc pulled a matchbook from his pocket, lit a match and held it out to me. I put my hand over his, to keep it steady. The small flame burned between us, red against his skin, reminding me again of the fiery night we'd nearly died together.

I realized to my shock that his hands were trembling, too.

"Thank you," I mumbled, pulling away. I leaned back against the bed's headboard as smoke filled my lungs, calming me. "I quit for a long time, but…"

"War," he agreed. Our eyes locked. My heart twisted, and I wrenched my head away, exhaling a puff of smoke.

"You're mistaken in your diagnosis, Doctor. I had pneumonia this spring. It hit me hard, that's all."

"It's not the pneumonia. I've listened to your lungs."

"What then?"

He hesitated. "One possibility is—tuberculosis."

Tuberculosis. That could mean a long, slow death, simply fading away, usually over a few years. The best treatment was to move to a warm, dry climate, but often that didn't work. I met his gaze. "And the other possibility?"

Then I met his miserable gaze, and I knew.

"Lung cancer?" I breathed.

He nodded, his jaw hard.

"But—that's rare," I said desperately. Rare, and an absolute death sentence.

Jean-Luc frowned. "Not as rare as it used to be. It used to be only coal miners who'd get it, but now, in the last twenty years…" He shrugged. "There's been a huge rise in incidence. No one knows why."

I exhaled, closing my eyes. Lung cancer. I'd seen a few cases

in my time as a nurse, mostly after the war. Perhaps it had something to do with war? Mustard gas—chemical warfare? But I
hadn't been exposed that I knew of. At least not very much.

Taking another slow puff, I exhaled, to steady myself.
"Well. Either way, it doesn't matter."

"How can you say that?"

I tapped the ashes into the bowl he held out as an ashtray.
"It's triage, that's all. I can't bother with my lungs, not until we
reach Marseille."

"Yes. The girls told me you're taking them there. But why?
For all we know, the Germans might decide to help themselves
to the south, too."

"Some of the girls are Jewish. You've read how Jews are
treated in Germany?" At his grim nod, I continued, "I can't let
them fall into the Nazis' hands." I lifted my chin defiantly. "I've
booked us passage from Portugal on a ship to New York."

His jaw dropped. "New York!" He started to say something
more, then stopped himself. I wondered if he was remembering
all the times I'd proclaimed I would never, ever go back to my
home country. He swallowed, then just said, "When?"

"We leave Marseille for Portugal July first. But I'll need a
week or two to finalize the visas with the American consul
there." *Finalize* was one word for it.

Jean-Luc looked incredulous. "You paid for passage across
the Atlantic, and you don't even have American visas? Do you
know how hard they are to get?"

"I'll get them," I said firmly. "I just need time."

He stared at me, then shook his head with a low whistle. "I
should have known you'd have some insane plan." His dark eyes
gleamed. "You always could make things happen that no one
else could, even in the old days."

The warmth of his gaze poured through me like a beam of
sunlight. It tempted my frozen heart to thaw again, my body to
unfurl my limbs, to uncurl my crushed soul and come to life.

But I had to resist my feelings. He belonged to someone else now.

"Thanks," I said carelessly, looking away and taking another drag of my cigarette.

"You will go to the hospital in Marseille." I looked up, surprised by his harsh tone. He held up his hand to stave off any argument. "They'll have what La Ravelle does not. An X-ray machine, the latest equipment and methods. The best doctors..."

"You're the best doctor," I said softly.

His lips curved. "Maybe once." He gave me a crooked grin. "Now I'm just a country doctor who delivers babies and tends broken bones."

His smile squeezed my heart.

"Jean-Luc," I breathed.

For a moment, our eyes held. He took a step towards me. "Then after Marseille, you'll get a second opinion in Lisbon. You'll get an appointment with the best pulmonologist in New York."

"You're overreacting—"

"Promise me."

His dark eyes burned through my soul.

"I promise," I whispered.

"Good." He looked away. "I can't believe it, Léna. You were in France this whole time." His voice was low, layered with unspoken hurt. "All these years, I've imagined you still nursing in faraway battlefields or perhaps a married woman with children. And you were in Paris."

"I never married..." I forced a grin. "But I did end up with plenty of children." As our eyes met, my smile fell away. "I saw you, you know. I was here. On your wedding day."

Jean-Luc sank to sit on the end of the bed, shocked. "In La Ravelle?"

I gave a single unsteady nod. "A few months after you left Greece, I followed you to France."

"But—but you told me to forget you!"

"I know." I looked down at my cigarette, then gave him a crooked smile. "I arrived in time to see you and your bride leaving the church as people cheered and tossed rice. A sunny winter day. Sparkling snow."

His mouth was agape. "Why—why didn't you come talk to me?"

"The last thing I wanted to do was cause problems. I... spent time in the north of France, roved around for a few years. I got a letter from an old friend, a Scottish nurse who'd married a German after the war. He was treating her badly. I went to Munich to help her and got in a bit of trouble." Shivering at the memory, I wrapped my hands around my body. "Her husband came home early—he'd been in jail—and found us packing her things—and their baby's."

"No!"

"Afraid so." I gave a short laugh. "I had to shoot him in the leg to get them away."

"Did your friend escape?"

I nodded. "Flora made it to Scotland. She divorced him and was able to raise their daughter alone. Strange to think that the girl and her father are now on different sides of this war. No wonder the man never stopped being sore at me."

"Well, too bad for him."

"Too bad for me, too, since it was Otto Schröder."

His laugh cut off. His voice became strangled. "Hitler's friend?" At my nod, his handsome face turned pale. "You must get out of the Nazis' reach as soon as possible. Perhaps..." He considered. "Perhaps you can be well enough to travel in two weeks. The visas will just have to—"

I shook my head. "I must leave tomorrow."

"You know you'll never make it! You have to rest and heal. At least... at least a week."

As much as I hated to admit it, he was right.

"Five days," I said reluctantly. The most I could spare.

Jean-Luc sighed. He shook his head ruefully. "You always were tough. And stubborn."

"Said the pot to the kettle."

Outside the three-story house, I heard a dog barking, whining piteously. After taking a final puff of the cigarette, I stubbed it out in my water glass.

"You're happy, aren't you, Jean-Luc?" I said, not daring to meet his eyes.

He didn't answer, and shame made my cheeks hot. What right did I have to ask?

"Very happy," he said finally. "I have a wife I treasure, two grown sons and a daughter I adore. My world is small, but I take care of those I love."

Those I love. I looked down at my hands, clasped together over my blanket to hide their trembling. "I'm glad."

"And you, Helen? Are you happy?"

With effort, I forced my gaze to his. "As happy as I have any right to be."

Silence fell in the bedroom, left half in shadow by the small light of the lamp. I felt overwhelmed by memories that felt as if they'd happened yesterday, gripped by all the feelings I'd repressed for so long. Every pulse and thrum of my blood demanded I tell him the secret hanging between us. I could open my mouth, and in two seconds, Jean-Luc's peace and happiness would be shattered. I could take it all.

In the resulting chaos, would that secret make him mine again, even for a moment? Or would it destroy him, along with his family, his home and his gentle, kind wife who'd cared for me so generously, even though I was a stranger?

The silence tensed between us, then abruptly snapped. He rose to his feet with an impersonal smile.

"Well, I should let you get some rest." He glanced at the small window, at the rising gray light. "It's nearly morning."

I looked around the little bedroom, cozy but modest. This might be the last time we'd ever speak alone. I heard myself say, "Did you ever tell your wife—about us?"

"I don't keep secrets from my wife. I told Élisabeth everything the day you arrived." Jean-Luc gave a small smile. "You know what she said?"

That she hated me with savage jealousy? Because that was how I felt about her. "I couldn't guess."

"She said she owes you a debt."

"What?"

"For changing your mind about marrying me in Greece. Élisabeth was only nineteen, but she'd already been the boys' nanny for two years when I returned to France. Hortense had been too busy with her lover to..." Setting his jaw, he shook his head. "I won't speak ill of the dead. But I felt awkward and ashamed, facing my boys after so many years away. I was a stranger to them. But Élisabeth was there for us. My sons already loved her," he said simply. "It was easy for me to decide to love her, too."

So that was how it had happened. I'd always wondered. Pain squeezed my chest. "I'm glad," I forced out. "She seems like a wonderful woman."

He gave a jagged nod. "The best in the world." His eyes met mine. "But, Léna," he said in a low voice, "you must know—"

The dog who'd been barking outside suddenly gave a harsh yelp. I sat up when I heard men shouting; a girl's sudden high-pitched scream.

Lucie.

My wide eyes met Jean-Luc's. "The girls!"

He sucked in his breath. His face was hard as he turned on his heel. "Stay here."

13

MARGOT

Lucie and Josette had been none too pleased when I'd told them they had to give up sleeping in the warm firelit comfort of the Ravanels' parlor and instead spend the night in the dark street, keeping watch over our truck. Lucie had been reluctant to leave the little girls, until I'd reminded her they'd be quite safe with Madame Ravanel and Suzanne upstairs. Josette hadn't wanted to take her hair out of the pin curls.

"So don't," I'd told her. "Leave them in. It's dark. Who's going to see?"

"But..." Josette had bitten her lip, agonized with indecision. Lucie and I looked at each other, then burst into laughter.

"I don't think you need to worry about movie directors in La Ravelle," my sister told her, not unkindly.

"She's not just worried about *movie directors*," I hooted, less kindly. "She's picturing how she'd feel if Roger suddenly showed up here. He'd finally see all the work needed to maintain those Hollywood looks!"

She glared at me, hands tightening as if yearning to slap my face. I smiled back at her sweetly.

Glancing at the little girls, who were watching with big eyes from their makeshift beds near the fire, Josette tossed her pin-curled red hair. "Fine, Margot Vashon. I'll come guard the truck with you. You're going to need me because I'm twice as brave as you, and we both know it, Squeaky."

That wiped the smile from my face. One of the problems of growing up with people you dislike is that you both know each other's weak spots with deadly accuracy. She never could let me forget the cold winter night I'd screamed when something furry had brushed my cheek in my sleep. Josette had calmly turned on the dormitory light, used her water glass to trap the mouse and gently dropped it out the window into snow-covered bushes. All these years later, she still called me Squeaky sometimes.

I'd been eleven.

But the memory seemed to put Josette in good humor. She and Lucie had changed out of nightgowns into trousers, and at Madame Ravanel's suggestion, we'd borrowed bulky coats and caps left behind by Paul and Daniel Ravanel to give us a boyish appearance, at least from a distance. She'd packed us butter sandwiches, then the three of us had trooped out into the dark street carrying blankets and pillows, feeling like we were living a childhood dream of adventure.

The rain had stopped, and if the June night wasn't exactly warm, at least it wasn't freezing cold. The three of us stretched out on the flatbed of the truck, wrapped in blankets, our heads on pillows, and looked up past the holes in the tattered canvas tarp, towards stars sparkling in the dark-velvet summer night.

"I never saw stars like that in Paris," Lucie whispered.

We'd promised ourselves we'd save the sandwiches till midnight, but we grew hungry and devoured them after just thirty minutes, looking up at the stars, telling swaggering dreams of our future: Josette was going to be a movie star, "beloved and beautifully dressed"; I imagined myself to be a lawyer dealing out justice to evil-doers; Lucie wanted to run St.

Agnes's for girls, "but with a house next door for abandoned animals, and another one on the other side for elderly people. So I can help everyone."

After licking our fingers of every trace of fresh-churned butter and eating the last crumb of crusty bread, we talked boldly and felt quite grown up. Soon, we imagined ourselves guarding not just the truck, but the house, the block, La Ravelle, perhaps all of France.

Before we'd settled in the back of the truck, I'd shown Josette and Lucie the old service revolver, taken out from where I'd hidden it beneath the hood.

Josette had gasped, asked where I'd gotten it, then wanted to hold it. I'd shown her how to use it, as Helen had shown me. Josette had quickly grasped the basics and had practiced aiming the unloaded revolver at the base of the nearby streetlight, while narrowing her eyes and saying stupid things like, "Just try to come and take our truck, *espèces de voleurs!*"

My sister had been reluctant even to touch the weapon. She'd been nervous the whole time she'd held it, hadn't asked any questions and had quickly passed it back to me.

I'd carefully replaced the bullets, warning the girls not to touch it unless we were threatened with violence. They'd looked at each other wide-eyed, suitably impressed.

Since then, I'd tucked it on the back shelf against the cab so I could keep an eye on it.

Our discussion turned dreamily to what we'd be doing if we were still back in Paris.

"We'd be in our beds, asleep," Lucie said, a little longingly.

"Lights out," Josette agreed.

"Forced to bed at nine, as if we were still seven years old," I said, but my usual resentment at that situation wasn't there anymore. It almost seemed quaint now, the idea of twenty lost and unwanted girls in pinafores, studying languages and math in the ancient, ivy-covered walls of St. Agnes's, surrounded by trees, hidden in a tiny medieval alley in the middle of Paris. Girls came and did not leave until they were eighteen, off to find jobs as secretaries, or shop girls in nice department stores, or as teachers, or as wives.

No orphans had ever been adopted out—not since I was five and Josette four, and a wealthy couple had come to St. Agnes's. They'd visited again and again, treating us all to ice cream, clearly trying to choose one of us to adopt. Then they'd simply disappeared. Josette and I had both cried for weeks—she with grief and me with relief, since they hadn't stolen Lucie away. It had all caused such uproar that Helen had announced that the girls of St. Agnes's would no longer be available for childless Parisians to pick over like pieces of meat in a butcher's shop. We would be our own family.

Now, whispering softly in the darkness, Josette, Lucie and I spoke wistfully about the days I'd once despised. Awake by six, wash, breakfast (always the same: eggs, brown bread and oatmeal, except for holidays or someone's birthday, when we were allowed juice and baguette tartines with jam). Classes in three separate rooms, separated by age and skill, math and German with Fräulein Mueller, science and literature with Miss Clarkson, world history, typing and shorthand with Mademoiselle Aubert.

The smell of chalk and wax as sunlight from lead-paned windows pooled warmly on the parquet floors. The quiet scratches of pencils, dipping our pens into inkwells, writing a few lines in our blue composition books before dipping again. Scrubbing and cleaning the orphanage for hours, peeling potatoes, washing dishes. An hour for physical exercise in the garden, rain or shine, the younger girls playing noisy games of hopscotch or hide-and-seek as the rest of us played pétanque if the weather was fine—or unsuccessfully sought excuses to go inside if it wasn't.

Dinner around the long tables, wholesome and cheap, often

boiled vegetables and a bit of chicken, dessert only rarely. An hour of leisure if we were done with schoolwork, then more washing, prayers and bed. Then wake up at six to do it all again.

I'd chafed against that constricted life, finding it tedious, not to mention unfair that I should be treated exactly the same as seven-year-old Marie-Louise, only with the requirement that I sometimes tutor or help the younger girls in addition to my own tasks. I'd resented Helen's stern steadfastness, and for the last month, I'd been counting down the days until my actual life could begin in Boulins.

But our old lives—with the soft beds, the warmth and comfort with plenty to eat, and a headmistress stronger and more fearsome than any guard dog, all tucked in a magical place hidden behind the buildings of Paris—now seemed like a fairy tale.

The moon was bright in La Ravelle, the street quiet. Conversation petered off, and we yawned in the lovely night.

We were startled awake by noise. I sat up in alarm, shaking the embers of sleep from my eyes. Blinking hard, I watched as a group of four men and two women came down the street towards us, drunk and quarreling. They paused at the truck.

Standing up, I pulled Paul Ravanel's cap low over my eyes. Hoping they couldn't tell I was shaking, I growled, "Move along."

"What's this?" The first man looked between the three of us, then tilted his head.

"A fierce little pup and his friends, protecting their truck."

"That rusted thing?" another man scoffed. "I doubt it would even run."

"Get going, I said!" Tightening my hands, I glared at them. Lucie and Josette pulled down their caps and glared, too.

The men glanced at each other as if unsure whether to be insulted or amused.

"Come on, Gaston," one of the women complained. "You promised us wine."

"So I did." The man touched the forehead of his cap towards me ironically, then led the group noisily away. Josette frowned, her gaze following mine.

"They didn't seem like thieves."

"You don't even know what a thief looks like."

She snorted. "Neither do you."

She was right, which was very irritating. I hadn't liked their look—shifty and a little too bold. Or was that just my imagination playing on my fears? How did I know what a criminal looked like?

After they disappeared, I exhaled, sinking down beside the others in the truck.

"Well, thieves or not, you scared them off," Josette said. "Good job, Squeaky."

I looked at her sharply, but her expression seemed sincere.

"What if they just needed directions?" Biting her lip, Lucie looked after them, her slender face worried. "I hope we weren't rude."

We didn't let ourselves get sleepy after that. To stay awake, we spoke about movies we'd seen, books we'd read, gossip from the old neighborhood. We wondered aloud what had happened to our fellow orphans sent to foster homes in the French countryside. Did thirteen-year-old Georgette now have more cheese at her Breton farm than even she could manage to eat? Did eleven-year-old Léa, who'd always wished for brothers to climb trees with, ever return to the ground now she had four of them in Poitou?

We wished fervently for more sandwiches.

Around midnight, we'd heard footsteps trudging down the slender lane of row houses, but it was only Dr. Ravanel, returning from his rounds.

He'd peeked in the shadowy back of the truck. "Everything

all right, *les filles*? Want me to take over, so you can go sleep in the house?"

"*Mais non*," Josette had said, lifting her chin. "We're doing fine."

I was almost proud of her.

But a few hours later, my shoulders ached, and my eyelids were heavy as I yawned in the cool June night.

Streaks of waning moonlight broke through the dark lowering clouds once again threatening rain. It was no longer possible to see the stars. Even Lucie was getting grumpy, and Josette and I were sniping at each other every hour, almost like church bells calling the time. By now, all three of us were looking longingly at the blue-painted house, with its tidy windows, one glowing warmly against the night. None of us were happy to still be cold and awake and nervous, sitting in the back of the rusty old German-made farm truck.

Shaking my head hard to focus on the dark street, I said, "You two can stretch out and close your eyes. I'll keep watch."

Josette snorted. "You think I could sleep knowing you're standing over me with a gun? *You* go rest. I'll take the pistol, if you please."

"It's a revolver," I retorted. "And it's loaded. I'm not just handing it over without supervision. You'd just end up shooting yourself."

"Me? We both know I'm more careful about everything than you."

"Yes, I suppose, so careful that if someone tried to steal the truck, by the time you worked out who to shoot and how, the thief would have already driven it off into the night. No wonder, for all your talk of being a movie star, you've never tried to go to a single audition—you just keep washing dishes at a café!"

Josette stared at me, wide-eyed.

Turning, I sat on the edge of the flatbed, my feet hanging

over the side, and stared out at the dark, quiet row houses. The only noise was the distant howl of a dog and bits of trash rattling down the cobblestones, moved by a desolate breeze like tumble-weeds in a western. It didn't seem like the hotbed of crime of Madame Ravanel's fears. Though of course with the neighbor's dog bludgeoned and cars stolen off their street, it was under-standable she'd be upset. But like Dr. Ravanel had said, maybe the perpetrators were long gone?

"You are unbearable," Josette said suddenly behind me. I looked back. Her face was strained and pale beneath the tweed cap. "So greedy you must have everything you touch all for yourself. You stuff your face with our rations. You constantly demand everyone's attention. And now no one else can be trusted with your stupid gun? You only ever think of yourself."

"Don't be ridiculous," I said, stung. Did I really seem that way? I glanced towards Lucie, who'd wrapped herself in her blanket on the dry side of the flatbed, muffling her ears with the pillow.

"You think you're so superior," Josette continued in a low voice, her eyes glittering. "Bossing everyone around. Pretending you know what you're doing, even when you don't. Misleading others into believing you're special and brave. Hoping they won't notice when you make stupid, thoughtless mistakes." She snorted. "You, a lawyer? That's a laugh. Any client of yours would end up facing the guillotine—even if his only crime was a speeding ticket!"

I sucked in my breath, hurt to the core by hearing her accuse me of all the deepest weaknesses and fears that consumed me in the dark.

An evil idea grabbed my brain.

"Is that so?" My voice was calm, pleasant, as I stared idly at my fingernails. "Well, I take it back. I think you're smart to be so cautious. The one time I've ever seen you really throw yourself at something is with Roger Cochet, and that's just been painful to watch. Painful for Roger, too, who finds it impossible to be rid of you."

The redhead stood up on the flatbed, gasping, eyes white in the darkness. "Take that back!"

I snorted, remaining seated. "We both know it's true. You cling to him like a barnacle. Like a pox. Everyone feels embarrassed for you."

Her eyes blazed beneath her cap, her hair lumpy with pin curls beneath. Her hands were tight at her sides as if it was all she could do not to slap me. "I can hardly wait to dump you in Boulins so I'll never have to see you again. I'm only sorry poor Lucie will be stuck with you!"

I shrugged. "Lucie and I will be fine without you."

"And for your information, Roger is *not* trying to be rid of me. He wants to meet me in Marseille!"

"What?" I said, truly astonished.

She lifted her chin defiantly. "I gave him the address of Mr. Cleeton's villa before we left Paris. Roger said he had friends to the south, so he might come and check on me. He told me to take good care of myself. Would he have said that if he didn't care about me?"

I snorted, relaxing. "You really are the end. He was being polite, that's all. He's not coming to Marseille. And, anyway, it doesn't matter because as soon as you get there, you and Helen and the little girls are all going to—"

"Will you both please *shut up*?" Lucie said crossly, sitting up. "I'm so sick of you. Both of you." She looked between us. "Isn't it enough that we've already lost all the other girls—baby Sophie and Georgette and Léa and the rest—along with our home? Now you want to ruin our last memories of each other, too, before we part in Boulins—maybe forever?"

The two of us, chastened, hung our heads.

"Sorry, Lucie," said Josette. "I didn't mean to wake you up."

She frowned, glancing at me. "It's Margot who's the problem. She—"

"I don't want to hear it," my sister cut her off. "You're always complaining about something. If it's not being far apart from Roger—a man you barely know, by the way—it's because you ran out of your face soap, or your lip rouge melted, or you have to walk too far in those ridiculous saddle shoes, and you're afraid you're getting a blister and don't want to use a plaster—"

"A girl never knows when she might be discovered—"

"Stop!" Lucie yelled. "Don't you realize we're in a war? It's like you think you're already in a movie and the rest of us are just your audience!"

"That's not true," she protested.

"See?" I looked at Josette smugly. "Even my sister agrees—"

"And you, Margot." My sister turned on me ruthlessly. "You're older and should be wiser, but half the time, I swear Noémie has more sense than you. You pretend to care about fairness and justice, then you do the stupidest things on impulse and never admit fault or say you're sorry."

"Exactly," Josette cried.

Lucie scowled, a foreign expression on her usually angelic face. "If anyone should hold the gun for Sister Helen, it's me. Not because I'm the oldest or brightest, or good at fighting or dealing with mechanical things, but because I don't act like a spoiled child. At least I'm not a burden to poor Sister Helen. No wonder she's so exhausted. It's not just from the bullet. She must be tired of cleaning up your messes because heaven knows I am fed up with both of you!"

Silence fell in the darkness. All my defenses fell away as I considered her words. Especially coming from my little sister, of all people. Lucie was so patient and kind and always tried to see people at their best. Especially me.

So what did it mean that even she was fed up?

From the day our mother had died, even at three, I'd felt my helpless baby sister needed my protection and care. I'd never, not until right this moment, considered how Lucie might also have been taking care of me.

"Sorry, Lucie," I mumbled.

"Sorry, Lucie," Josette said.

My little sister exhaled, then turned over on her makeshift bed. "Now *goodnight*."

"Goodnight." Josette lowered her head to her pillow, too. And I was left alone with my thoughts.

I'd nearly blurted out the secret I'd promised Helen I'd keep, that Josette was going to live in America. And I hadn't done it to make her happy but hoping to hurt her, to cut her with the thought that she'd never see Roger again.

You cling to him like a barnacle, I'd told her. *Like a pox.*

A coldhearted thing to say, not even true. More than unkind —it had been cruel. So maybe she was making her interest in him plain—so what? Unlike me, Josette had no sister, nor even a brief memory of a parent. She'd been left at St. Agnes's door late on Christmas Eve in 1922, a whimpering newborn wearing only a diaper, swaddled in a blanket like the Christ child. The former headmistress had chosen her name.

I still remembered how Josette had hugged me so tight when Lucie and I had first arrived at the orphanage, like we were already friends. She'd been just a toddler, desperate for love.

I stared at Josette's sleeping form, feeling ashamed. I knew I should tell her I was sorry—that I hadn't meant what I'd said. But Lucie was right. I didn't like to say the words.

An hour later, I finally shook her awake. Her eyes flew open, growing hard when she saw me. "What do you want?"

I licked my lips, trying to think of a way to apologize. But I was the one who felt cautious now. I muttered, "It's your turn to watch."

She tossed off her blanket. "Fine."

Falling gratefully into my own blanket, I pushed my cheek against the pillow and looked up at the sky, where the canvas tarp hung limply askew. Some of the clouds had parted, but the stars were disappearing, one by one, as the black sky to the east slowly changed to slate gray. The night was nearly over. I closed my eyes, and even as I told myself I wouldn't sleep a wink, I fell straight into dreaming, something to do with the alleys of Paris turned into rivers of red wine, before I was interrupted by the shrill sound of a dog barking, then yelping in pain.

"No!" I heard Lucie say, and my eyes flew open at the same moment she screamed. "Stop it! Leave her alone!"

The flatbed bounced beneath me as she pushed off, throwing herself off the truck.

Blinking, dizzy and half asleep, I sat up just in time to see my skinny little sister running full-bore towards two hulking figures at the end of the dark street in the early gray dawn.

The fat one was holding his hands over his big fat belly, laughing. The skinny one, laughing as well, was holding an ugly metal shovel over the head of a small, cowering dog.

14

MARGOT

"Lucie, stop," I cried, but she didn't.

Josette lifted her head from her pillow, blinking, yawning. "What's happening?"

"Lucie's in trouble!"

Josette sat up straight. "What?"

"Hurry!" As I pointed down the lane towards the men threatening the dog, I lunged for the service revolver on the back shelf. But the leather holster was empty.

"She offered to take watch." Josette wiped the sleep from her eyes, pushing to her feet. "You have the gun?"

"It's gone. It must be..." We both looked past the streetlight towards the end of the dark lane, where Lucie's shadow was lost against the two shadows of men now towering over her.

With a gasp, we scrambled off the back of the truck and rushed towards her.

As we drew closer, I saw Lucie had wrapped her arms around the quivering dog, as if to protect its life with her own body. She was yelling at the top of her voice, "Don't touch her!"

"Well looky here." The skinny man holding the metal shovel leaned it back against his shoulder, glancing at his friend.

"We were sick of this ugly dog following us, begging for scraps. But now we have a new game to entertain us, don't we, Jacques?"

The fat man looked down at my baby sister, at her wispy blonde hair, which now tumbled over her shoulders, as her cap had flown off. "Seems we do indeed."

The other man grinned. "You want to play, little girl?"

But as they started to reach towards her, my sister fumbled in the pocket of Daniel Ravanel's oversized jacket, then pulled out the revolver, brandishing it in the air like David facing down two Goliaths.

"Back away," she panted, kneeling on the road, one arm wrapped around the little dog. "Or I swear..."

Both men froze, staring at the gun, gleaming in the first pink light of dawn.

Then the skinny man snorted and swung his shovel wide. He knocked the revolver out of her hand easily, sending it scuttering across the cobblestones.

"No!" Lucie cried, reaching out for it too late. But eyeing the shovel, she didn't move away from the dog.

"Sorry, little *mam'selle*." The fat man leered before he casually sauntered towards the gun. "But thanks for the—"

He stopped when he saw Josette and me.

We lunged for the revolver at the same moment.

As Josette dove low, I knew she had a better chance. Every summer, in baseball games Helen organized on field days in the open grass of the Square du Temple, she'd been St. Agnes's best slider, every time. So I adjusted my aim and, like a bullet, threw myself directly at him.

Smashing my hands against his shoulders with every bit of force I possessed, I knocked him just enough off balance. We both landed belly-first on the cobblestones with an *oof*. For a moment, I lay still, wheezing for breath.

Then I felt someone kick at my spine. I gasped in pain, rolling over.

The skinny man's head appeared over me, silhouetted against the dark sky. Words were pouring from his mouth, curses so vile, they left my ears ringing. "You think you can attack us, little girl?"

He kicked me again, this time in the belly, and I cried out, curling my knees against my striped shirt as I lay against the cold, hard stones.

A loud bang made us both flinch and look.

"Now"—Josette's voice was steady as she held the just-fired revolver in the air—"you will drop that shovel to the ground, *monsieur*, and you'll both turn around and go back where you came from, or I swear to *le bon Dieu* that my next shot will go straight through your heart."

Bold words, especially since Josette's brief practice holding the revolver hadn't involved her ever actually firing it at anything. My teeth chattered. If she tried to shoot the man, she'd likely hit *me*.

And yet. Though her cap was gone and her pin curls wildly askew, her face was resolute, and her arm did not tremble.

"So." Josette shifted her target from one man to the other. "Which of you wants to die first?"

The two men looked at each other. The skinny one muttered, "It's just a dog."

He dropped the shovel, and it clanged against the cobblestones. Lucie, her arms still protectively around the animal, flinched as the men walked away. They turned and shouted one last insult from the corner, then sullenly disappeared.

Wincing with pain, I pushed myself to my feet and rushed to my sister. "Lucie, Lucie, are you all right?"

"I'm fine," she protested as I hugged her and checked her anxiously for injury. Irritated, she pushed me away. "Get off. I'm fine." She looked down at the little dog—a dirty, starving little mongrel with big dark eyes and matted brown fur. "She's the one who needs help—she's starving and afraid. Dr. Ravanel." She looked past me in relief. "Thank heaven. Help me bring her into the clinic."

Turning my head, I saw Dr. Ravanel standing some distance away, his shoulders taut, his face astonished. He took a deep breath.

"We heard you scream and thought—" He stared down at the shovel, frowning. Then he gave a low laugh, turning to us. "You were right, Margot. You girls are tough. You handled them all on your own."

Lucie, Josette and I looked at each other. Suddenly, my body was shaking as I fully realized what had just happened, how close it had been.

"Dr. Ravanel, check Margot, they kicked her," Josette said.

"Are you all right?" Lucie demanded, looking scared.

"I'm fine." I gave Josette a glare. My belly and spine barely hurt anymore from the skinny man's feeble kicks. And I liked being praised as *tough*. I liked it very much.

"Good." My sister exhaled, then turned to him earnestly. "But, Doctor, my dog..."

"Yes." He came forward, all business. "I'm no veterinarian, but I can at least..."

He fell to his knees and spoke softly to the scared animal. I stared at them, suddenly worried.

My dog, Lucie had said. I feared she'd never give the animal up now. Another mouth to feed. I couldn't recall any household pets at the Lusignys' château in Boulins, though there was plenty of space amid their gardens and barns and fields. I told myself we'd just have to work it out.

"I don't think anything's broken, but I'll check more carefully inside." Dr. Ravanel tried to reach for the animal, but the little dog backed away. He glanced at Lucie. "Perhaps you should—?"

"Don't, Lucie," I said. "I'm sure it has fleas—"

But my sister had already gently lifted the dog and cradled it against her chest. I sighed.

Pink streaks of sunrise stretched wide across the sky, frosting the clouds orange, casting the medieval rooftops in dark silhouette as we turned back towards the blue house.

Dr. Ravanel stopped when he saw his neighbors, staring out sleepily from their windows. "Go back to bed," he called. "Everything's all right."

Then he turned and saw his wife in her nightgown, her arms folded, standing at his own door. Helen appeared like a wraith behind her, pale and weak, holding her hand against the door jamb as if she were about to fall over.

"They're all fine," he told them calmly. "A little tussle about a dog, that's all. The girls did well." He grinned back at us. "Any criminal should be frightened to meet *you* in a dark alley."

"Sister Helen." Josette came forward anxiously. "How are you feeling? Should you be up and walking?"

"I told her not to come down the stairs," Madame Ravanel sighed. "She insisted."

Helen bit her lip, her face guilty. "I had to see you were all right."

"We're fine," Josette said, clearly aching to hug her. She gingerly patted her shoulder instead. "You're the one we were worried about."

"I'm good as new," our headmistress replied, but her smile was strained. Her eyes sought me out. "Everyone is really okay?"

"Better than okay," Dr. Ravanel told her, his warm eyes smiling down at her. "You should be proud of how well you trained them."

Her forehead crinkled at the word *trained*, and she looked at me. I shrugged.

"Jean-Luc—the shovel?" Élisabeth Ravanel pointed at it.

He nodded at her grimly. "I thought of that as well. It could be the same one. I didn't touch it—just left it where he dropped it. Did you call the police?"

"Louis will be here in a few minutes."

"Good." Turning back to Helen, Dr. Ravanel said gently, "Let's get you back to bed. Josette, can you help her?"

Josette put her shoulder under Helen's arm. I saw the back tip of the revolver still hanging out of her jacket pocket.

"Let me help instead, Josette," I said loudly, giving a little elbow on her side next to the revolver. We couldn't let Helen realize the revolver had nearly gotten someone killed tonight. We'd get lectured till our ears bled.

Josette's eyes widened as she realized she still had the loaded gun casually in her pocket. She backed away, her hand covering it. "Um. Thank you, Margot. You're so very kind."

"What's wrong with you two?" Helen demanded.

Josette and I glanced at each other.

"Why, whatever do you mean?" I asked innocently.

"What could be wrong?" Josette asked in the same tone.

Helen looked between us suspiciously. "You're not fighting."

"Why would we fight?" Leaning in, Josette patted my shoulder, which conveniently hid her pocket from Helen's view. "We're sisters."

15

HELEN

"And our truck was just sitting there?" Élisabeth Ravanel said in disbelief the next afternoon.

"In the forest outside town, Louis said." Hanging up the phone, Jean-Luc turned gleefully towards the four of us sitting agog around the kitchen table. "His men caught the two of them camped out a few blocks from here, and the skinny one started singing like a canary."

Shifting in my chair, I put my hand against the pain in my side as I said breathlessly, "How did you first suspect those two men were the same thieves?"

Jean-Luc hesitated, glancing towards Lucie. "That shovel. It was the right shape for the injuries I'd seen on Bisou..."

Lucie looked up indignantly from the sink, where she was bathing Choupette for the fourth time since the little dog had come into our lives yesterday. "I'm glad the police caught them. They deserve the guillotine."

It wasn't like angelic Lucie to be so bloodthirsty. She seemed quite serious.

"Well, they're under arrest. Their camp in the woods was strewn with our neighbors' possessions. They'd already sold the other cars, but apparently our ambulance truck was too recognizable." He glanced warmly between Margot, Lucie and Josette. "You girls have my gratitude. You had the strength and presence of mind to stop them. And lead the police right to them."

"We didn't do anything." Josette and Margot looked at each other. "Lucie was the brave one."

"Oh, sweet pup," my sister crooned to the shivering dog. "My sweet, sweet darling."

Lucie wrapped the animal in a towel, lifted her from the emptying sink, then sat nearby on the floor to dry her off. As Élisabeth Ravanel rushed to scrub the sink out with lye soap, her daughter Suzanne flopped beside Lucie on the floor. One girl toweled off the dog's paws as the other brushed her damp fur—no longer matted, now soft. The muddy brown color had melted into a gentle copper.

My gaze lingered on gawky Suzanne, wearing a casual shirt and dungarees in that way of the young. The girl's dark curly hair and deep brown eyes were just like her father's.

"Those men will go to jail, won't they?" Margot demanded.

With a shiver, I looked between the two dark-haired girls, then at Jean-Luc, almost holding my breath, caught between longing and fear. How could he not see it?

He just smiled at Margot. "Yes. Definitely."

"I'm glad," Lucie said. "After what they did to the dog next door, what they tried to do to Choupette, on second thought the guillotine's too good for them!"

Jean-Luc's dark eyes met mine, and he shrugged, his lips curving in a smile just for me. There was no point in explaining to her that the two ruffians were under arrest for stealing cars and burglary. Lucie had already firmly decided on the far greater crime.

"That's wonderful news, Jean-Luc." Sink now sparkling clean, his wife moved back to the big pot of chicken soup bubbling on the stove. "Just in time, too. Now you can drive to Madame Lollard's tonight to check on her new baby, rather than walk." She hummed a happy tune. "Now that's proper French justice. I'll need to bake Louis a cake to thank him. No, four cakes—one for each of his men."

"Can I have cake, too?" asked little Noémie, peeking in from the parlor, her teddy in her arms.

"Cake?" Rachel appeared behind her, dark braids flying.

Her older sister Estée looked up from her book—she was now halfway through a borrowed copy of Les Misérables—as she called, "Did someone say cake?"

"Of course you'll all have some," Élisabeth Ravanel promised warmly. "In the meantime, wash up for lunch."

"Hooray! Lunch!" the little girls cried, rushing to wash their hands.

I watched his pretty wife—some ten years younger than I—move swiftly across her snug little kitchen, pulling fresh-baked bread from the oven, serving everyone in her dainty apron, ladling mouthwateringly fragrant soup into the bowls, starting with her husband at the other end of the table.

"Thank you, my darling," he told her, his eyes glowing with love. Catching my breath, I looked down at the floor. Then he said in a different tone: "Are you all right?"

Looking up, I found Jean-Luc frowning at me. Everyone turned to stare. I put my hand over my worn blouse, with its thick bandage over my abdomen beneath. "It was just—hurting a little."

My cheeks were burning, though it wasn't a lie.

He started to rise from the table. "Perhaps I should—"

"No," I bit out, then added less harshly, "Please don't interrupt this lovely lunch."

"This looks delicious." Josette's eyes glowed at Madame Ravanel. "I always wondered what it would feel like to have a home. I never knew my parents..."

"You poor dear," the good woman said softly and patted her thin shoulders before serving her an extra big bowl of soup.

I suddenly wondered what Josette would say if she knew the truth about her parents. She'd have to be told, sooner or later.

Later, I told myself. When I told her about America. When she asked me why it was too dangerous for her to remain in France—I'd tell her everything.

"I'm a little cold. Josette, dear"—I looked at her across the table—"would you mind running up to my room? I think I left my sweater on the bed."

"Of course, Sister Helen." Swiftly, Josette rose from the table, pausing only to give Margot a quick glare. "Don't touch my soup."

"Wouldn't dream of it," Margot responded meekly.

"Don't forget us, Maman," said Suzanne, getting up from the floor, still holding the old hairbrush she'd been using on Choupette, now filled with dog hair. "We're hungry, too."

"Wash your hands," her mother ordered, pointing towards the sink with her wooden spoon. As Suzanne reluctantly complied, the woman turned to Lucie. "I'm pouring a bowl for you. If you eat it all, *then* I might have some scraps for Choupette. But I want to see you eat your own lunch, not sneak it all to her."

"I'd rather Choupette—but all right," Lucie sighed, surrendering to a greater force. Even she was unable to resist Madame Ravanel. After tucking her dog tenderly into an old blanket beneath a pool of warm sunlight on the kitchen floor, she followed Suzanne to wash her hands.

Madame Ravanel poured soup for Margot, then reached me at the end of the table. I saw a mixture of emotions on her face, but kindness won out. "I'm glad to see you're feeling so much better, Madame Taylor, and able to join us for lunch today."

"It's so late now, you should call it dinner," her daughter pointed out, squeezing in at the table.

"Lucky for you, little miss," her mother responded tartly, "I've made enough for two meals' worth." Ladling chicken soup into my bowl, she nodded towards a small ceramic dish. "Butter's there for the bread."

"Me, too?" said Suzanne.

"Certainly not. Butter is for Madame Taylor. She needs her strength to recuperate."

"Me, too," crowed Noémie, holding up her arm to show off the tiny, healing scab there.

"I wish I could be shot," moaned her daughter, eyeing the butter.

I saw the worried glance between her parents and wondered if they were thinking of Jean-Luc's two grown sons, missing somewhere up north.

After spreading butter on my slice of fresh crusty bread, I offered it to Suzanne. "I can share."

She took it eagerly. "Oh, thank you!"

"As long as you don't give any to Lucie. She'd only feed it to the dog."

"I would not," cried Lucie, but red spots appeared high on her cheeks, which happened when she told a fib.

"Thank you, my love," Jean-Luc murmured as his wife finally sat beside him at the table. "I don't know how you manage to always make such lovely meals when our groceries are few." He took her hand and lifted it briefly to his lips. "You're a miracle."

She looked at her husband adoringly.

I watched the doctor and his wife together at the end of the table. Golden sunlight created a halo around their heads, his dark, hers light, both beginning to streak with gray. She leaned closer, and he put his arm around her. My heart twisted, and I looked away.

Nearby, their daughter, who'd already scarfed the buttered bread, was surreptitiously sneaking bits of chicken from her soup to Lucie, who then tucked it inside her napkin—then, a few minutes later, when no one was looking, fed it to Choupette. The little dog had already left her blanket to sit directly at Lucie's feet. Wherever Lucie went, Choupette had to go. The little pup looked up at her as adoringly as Élisabeth Ravanel looked at her husband.

A wave of grief and uncertainty surged through me. Since the men had attacked the dog the previous dawn, I'd tried to warn Lucie we couldn't take Choupette with us when we left here. I didn't know if the Lusignys would want a dog at their castle in Boulins, but from what Margot had told me about them, I doubted it. And I certainly couldn't take the animal with me to Marseille—or on the ship that, God willing, would take us to Portugal and thence to New York.

But all my concerns and firm directives had fallen on deaf ears. Lucie had responded with equal firmness that the warm-hearted Lusignys, of whom she'd heard so much from Margot, would surely welcome Choupette as a wonderful companion to catch rats and herd sheep, the canine companion and protector needed by all châteaux everywhere.

How she believed her dog could do these things, I wasn't sure, as since yesterday, I'd seen the animal do nothing but eat, accept pets and caresses, be repeatedly bathed to get rid of her fleas, laze in the sun and bark at strangers through the window. But Choupette was Lucie's, and Lucie was hers. So I'd let it go. Perhaps she was right. And after all, how much might Lucie need comfort—her and Margot both—once I made it clear that Lucie, and only Lucie, would remain at the château in Boulins?

Love made a person lose their reason. As a friend of the doctor had found space last night for our truck in his locked garage, just a few blocks away, all the girls had been able to sleep in the parlor. When Josette had helped me upstairs to bed, she'd rhapsodized dreamily about Roger Cochet's good qualities, all of which were as imaginary as Choupette's, as far as I could tell. The boy was kind to his great-aunt perhaps. He'd brought her a bottle of Dubonnet and sat with her while she recuperated from her illness. But that hardly made him a hero. He'd likely deserted from the army, and I assumed he'd already left St. Agnes's, probably with the money I'd left his great-aunt in his pocket.

But there was no point saying that to Josette. She was interested in romantic fantasies, not the truth. Once we reached Marseille, it wouldn't matter. Once they were apart, her romantic fantasy of him would end.

Or would it?

I looked at Jean-Luc at the end of the kitchen table, smiling at his wife, speaking to her in low tones, his dark eyes shining, and felt a punch in the belly. Even after all these years, seeing his happiness with another woman was agony. I wanted to feel glad for him. I knew only a horrible person with a dark, twisted soul could feel such grief—at his joy.

But he could have been mine. That was the thing I couldn't forget, the poison in my heart. Watching Élisabeth Ravanel bustling around their cozy home in her embroidered apron, eyes glowing over round, rosy cheeks, baking bread in her kitchen, all I'd been able to think was... *I could have been her.* This house could have been my home. I could have been the one taking care of him. I could have been the one to raise his daughter, clean his home. I could have been Madame Ravanel. With his name. In his bed.

We'd had only one night of happiness together, in that Athens hotel in 1921, just after we'd been rescued from the fire. We'd planned to wed the next morning, as soon as we could find a priest.

But I'd woken up in a cold sweat. I didn't deserve another

family after what I'd done to my husband and child. Jean-Luc deserved a better woman as his wife.

He'd spent days trying to convince me to change my mind, days he couldn't afford, with his young motherless sons waiting in France. He'd finally kissed me farewell before he'd boarded his ship, tears streaming down his cheeks as he'd whispered he'd love me forever.

When I'd discovered I was pregnant a couple of months later, that had given me the strength to claim him. I might not deserve a man like Jean-Luc, but our baby was innocent. I'd rushed to France.

Too late.

Fleeing La Ravelle after I'd seen the newlyweds, I'd rented an anonymous apartment in Paris. Shortly before the birth, a friend of a friend had told me about childless dairy farmers in Meaux, outside the city. I knew my baby could have a better life with them—far better than traveling with me to the most dangerous places of the world or being raised as the fatherless child of a broken-hearted, unmarried woman.

It had nearly killed me to give my baby away. But I'd done it —for her. I'd spent the next years trying to forget, training to fight beyond ways Jean-Luc had taught me, both to expel grief and to be strong enough to travel alone. Before I'd left Paris for Germany, an American diplomat had asked me for a small favor, to deliver a letter outside official channels. That one favor had led to another...

I'd never expected to receive a wrinkled letter from the farmer's wife, forwarded many times around the world before it had finally found me. That letter had changed my life.

"Dr. Ravanel," Margot called, breaking my reverie. "Thanks for letting me help in your clinic today. It was good to learn a little first aid."

"You weren't horrible at it." He tilted his head. "You might have a future in medicine, *ma petite*."

"A doctor?" Margot's nose curled. Her cheeks colored with pleasure at his compliment, but she shook her head. "I'm going to be a lawyer."

"A lawyer, *zut alors*," he said teasingly. "There are too many lawyers in the world already."

"I could never be a doctor. It would be too stressful to hold someone's life in my hands."

"You think you won't do that as a lawyer?" He lifted dark eyebrows. "Besides, you already do hold a life in your hands. Your own."

Margot stared at him, then blinked. "I never thought of it like that."

"You should. I'm telling you this for your own good, *mon enfant*. The happiness of your life will be determined by how much responsibility you take for it."

"I apologize for my husband," Élisabeth Ravanel said with a laugh. She looked at him lovingly. "He does like to pontificate."

"And how," Suzanne said, rolling her eyes.

"*Ah non*, was I lecturing again? Sorry." Reaching out, he took his wife's hand. "I'm glad I have you to keep my flaws in check."

She smiled. "It is your only one."

For a moment, I couldn't breathe. Shredded old lungs, scarred old heart. Soup half eaten, I pushed up from the table. "Thank you very much, Madame Ravanel—"

"Élisabeth, please."

"Élisabeth," I managed. "Lunch was—um. But I need to—start packing..."

Turning, I fled the kitchen, nearly bumping into Josette, who was coming slowly down the stairs.

"I'm sorry, Sister Helen. I didn't find your sweater." Josette's voice was low. She wouldn't meet my eyes.

"Don't worry about it." Her face was pale and strange. I frowned at her. "Is everything...?"

Jean-Luc had followed me from the kitchen. "You're still not well. You must stay and heal at least another week."

"I promised you three more days." As I turned to him, Josette slipped away. I flinched at the pain: from my wound. From staying. "Even that, I can ill afford."

He came closer in the shadowy quiet of the hallway. "Léna…"

"I should rest." I backed away, then stumbled up the stairs to the safety of the dark, quiet guest room. I wrapped my arms around my body, feeling the bandage still beneath my blouse. But it wasn't the bullet wound that hurt me most. Or my lungs that apparently were going to kill me, either fast or slowly.

Closing my eyes, I leaned back against the bedroom door. I could still see his dark eyes glowing, and all I could think of was the past we'd shared, a lifetime ago.

When I'd first met him in 1915, I'd been bruised and bloodied to my soul, no good to myself or anyone, all but dead. Wishing I *had* died, along with my husband and child, of the diphtheria I'd unknowingly brought home to them because I'd insisted on continuing work as a nurse during an epidemic against my husband's express wishes—and to his shame.

I'd been too scared to depend on Arthur's income alone, as because of his rages, he'd frequently found himself unemployed. I'd been too scared of ever being helpless and penniless like I'd been as a child.

Working beside Jean-Luc amid the danger and chaos of French battlefields, as the bombs exploded around us, always knowing each breath could be our last, I'd slowly learned to smile again. After an injured soldier had attacked me in camp, late at night when I was alone, Jean-Luc had insisted on teaching me how to fight. I had been shy at first, then gradually loved sparring with him, the physicality of it, the intimacy. He'd shown me self-defense and even taught me how to use a gun, and he'd done it with kindness—and respect.

And I'd loved him for it. Helplessly. Hopelessly. Knowing I wasn't worthy.

I jumped at a loud bang on the bedroom door, behind my head. I nearly fell over my valise, which gaped open nearby. My voice trembled as I cried, "I'm fine, Jean-Luc."

"It's Margot. Let me in."

Stepping back from the door, I wiped my eyes. "Come in."

The brunette stepped in, wearing her striped shirt and scarf and slim trousers. Her clothes were practical yet chic on her slender figure. But her dark eyes were blazing as she stepped inside the room.

"Tell me right now." She closed the door behind her and whirled on me. "What's really going on between you and Dr. Ravanel?"

16

HELEN

"Nothing," I said, shocked.

Margot sensed her advantage and plowed forward. "You're lying. Stop lying to me."

The truth trembled on my lips. How I was dying to tell someone, *anyone*, the whole awful story. But telling Margot my secret would be even worse than telling Jean-Luc. She was still just seventeen with a fiery temper. Indiscreet as she was, how could she keep such a secret? Everyone would likely know everything within the hour, from the girls to Jean-Luc and his wife and daughter. Probably the neighbors as well.

Or would they? As far as I knew, Margot hadn't said a word to Josette about my plans for America, though she must have been sorely tempted. Maybe she was changing. Amid this awful war, with me out of commission the last few days, perhaps she'd been forced to grow up.

"Tell me the truth," Margot demanded. "What's going on?"

"Nothing." I spoke the truth as an evasion. "Nothing is going on between me and Dr. Ravanel."

Observing me in the shadowy silence of the guest room, she narrowed her eyes. "I don't believe you."

"Believe what you want," I replied stiffly. "But I'm hurt if you're thinking I'd ever be involved in something immoral. Jean-Luc is a friend from long ago. I haven't spoken with him in decades. He loves his wife and would never betray her. That's it."

Tilting her head, she looked at me, considering. Then she frowned. "But I've seen the way you look at him. It's like..."

"Like what?"

"Like Estée when she sees a new book or Rachel a particularly fine flower. Like Lucie when she pets Choupette, or Josette when she's with Roger. You look at him like... like you've been waiting for him your whole life."

My throat went dry. I took a deep breath and stared at the closed door, my packed valise. We were leaving La Ravelle in just a few days. Beneath the weight of the secret I couldn't tell, I yearned to share something, anything.

What difference could it make to share just a tiny bit of the truth—to give myself that much relief, at least?

"Fine." Exhaling, I looked away. "I did love him—once." My voice was low. "Jean-Luc and I worked together during the Great War, and for a few years afterward, in other wars and plagues all over Europe. But nothing ever came of my feelings. At first because he had a wife back in France. After she died, Jean-Luc had to return home to his sons. We had one night where we both admitted we... cared for each other. He asked me to come back to France and marry him. I said yes."

"*What?*" Margot looked astonished. Was it at the thought that any man had ever proposed to me or that I'd had the stupidity to refuse him?

I gave her a weary smile. "But I changed my mind."

She goggled at me. "Why?"

"Why...?" I looked out the window. Because it had seemed disloyal to the point of cruelty for me to be happy with a new family, when my husband and son were dead. "It's a long story."

"This is why you put off Mr. Cleeton, isn't it?" As I looked at Margot in surprise, she shook her head. "We all wondered why you never give him the time of day, when that cowboy's clearly in love with you. It's because you never got over Dr. Ravanel."

My cheeks colored. "I wouldn't say *that*," I hedged. Even though it was true.

"Good. Because it's too late. Dr. Ravanel is married." The combative light in her eyes faded. "I'm sorry. Of course you know that. I'm not trying to be mean. He just asked us to be gentle with you. He said you're facing something scary and difficult—he wouldn't say what, but I know. It's going back to America, isn't it? After all these years?"

I knew Jean-Luc had been thinking about my lung disease. I was trying not to. The prospect of either tuberculosis or cancer scared me to death. "He shouldn't have said anything."

"What happened to you there? To your family? Why do you blame yourself for their deaths? Why did you never go back?"

Too many painful questions. "I'm going back now."

"Yes, but it took an army of Nazis to drive you to it. And I suspect it's more for the girls to be safe than you."

I stared at her, then licked my lips. She knew me too well.

And she also didn't know me at all.

"You know I was born in Louisiana." My words were creaky, like the gasping start of a rusted engine. "My parents were Cajun. Taylor was my married name. I was born a Beaumont."

Memories flickered through me. My mother smiling, speaking in French; my father's hand squeezing my shoulder as we waited for the train. The swampy Louisiana air as we left St. Bernard Parish, as my parents had heard rumors that the oilfields of California were desperate for workers and paid far better.

"Should we do it, *ma petite?*" they'd asked me, smiling. "Should we take the gamble and go?"

As a child, I'd felt honored, included. But of course, looking back as an adult, I knew now they'd already made the decision.

Looking away from Margot, I sank to the small bed. I'd spoken of my past only to Jean-Luc, and even that was so long ago. Sharing anything about my childhood felt foreign. I was out of practice, didn't know how.

"My father was an engineer," I said softly, then shook my head. "Perhaps not a very good one. We left for his new job in Los Angeles when I was eleven. But before we arrived... our train derailed in the California desert."

She sucked in her breath. "What?"

"My parents died in front of me." If I closed my eyes, I could still hear the screams, the wrench and crack of metal as the cars collided, the silence amid the smoke and fire. The hoarse, jagged sounds of my parents' last gasping breaths. My mother wheezing, *I have a daughter. Someone help my daughter.* I shook the memory away—hard. "I had no family, no friends there. No one knew what to do with me. I was left at the nearest orphanage."

I could still see that desiccated building outside a small desert town, sixty miles east of Los Angeles. The hot blaze of the sun, tumbleweeds rolling past the empty landscape, the flat white basin of a nearby dried-out lake. Once, it had been a resort for Los Angelenos. Now, it was abandoned and forgotten.

We children were always hungry, always thirsty, always hot—especially in the windowless "work room" where we sewed lace collars by hand for the great ladies of Beverly Hills, until the smallest girls collapsed off their chairs from heat and exhaustion.

Margot's eyes were huge in the bright sunlight of the Ravanels' guest bedroom. "Orphanage? Like St. Agnes's?"

"No," I said harshly. "The owners worked us. Starved

us." I could still remember the gaunt form of an orphaned girl a year older. It had been the scandal of her death by starvation that had pushed the nearby townsfolk to take over the orphanage. "Things got better, but I never forgot what it was like to be hungry and helpless. After I left, I trained as a nurse at the hospital and worked as hard as I could. But once I got married, my husband insisted he'd take care of me."

"Your husband." She looked bemused, as if she couldn't imagine such a creature. "What was he like?"

"Handsome. Charming." I gave a brief, bitter smile. "Arthur had a good job when we met, selling things door to door. It attracted me, how steady he was." My lips twisted. "But it didn't last. He was always getting in fights. We moved all over Los Angeles. No job ever lasted for long. He lost another job right after our baby was born. So I weaned Billy and went back to work."

"Back to work? When you had a newborn?"

I said wryly, "As shocking as it sounds now, it was even more so twenty-five years ago. But what else could I do?"

"Who took care of your baby?"

I felt the pang of her judgment, a mere echo against the roar of my own.

"A neighbor, since I couldn't trust Arthur to do it. I was trying to earn enough to take care of everyone," I whispered, then looked away. "Instead, I killed them. Both of them."

"Killed them?" she breathed. "How? No. I don't believe it. You would never hurt anyone in your care. Not like that."

I looked down at my hands, clasped in my lap. I could barely remember Arthur and Billy now, just flashes in my mind. My son's tiny hand holding my finger—or was that another child's? My husband's low laugh—or was I remembering Jean-Luc's?

"There was a diphtheria epidemic. I brought it home." My

voice was dull. The back of my throat felt dry. "I survived. Arthur and Billy—didn't."

I'd vowed to remember my husband, and the good, early days of our courtship and honeymoon, and my sweet ten-month-old baby son for the rest of my life. Standing at their graves, I'd wanted to throw myself in with them.

Now, twenty-five years later, I could no longer recall the details of their faces. It filled me with shame. But the woman I'd been then, a young wife and mother just twenty-five years old, no longer existed. The world had changed entirely since 1915—but not as much as I had.

"You mustn't blame yourself." Margot handed me a glass of water from the nightstand. I took it and drank deeply, wiping my mouth as I set down the empty glass. My throat hurt.

"I'm sorry," she said finally, sitting beside me on the neatly made bed. "I shouldn't have needled you. As a kid, I thought you had no feelings at all. I never imagined you could feel heart-break or grief."

I rubbed my eyes with a low laugh. "You thought I was just the bossy pain in the neck who kept you from staying up late and eating sweets."

Margot flashed me a quick look, then laughed sheepishly. "Yeah. I guess." She looked down at her hands. "Now I feel bad. Anyway. We'll be leaving for Boulins as soon as you're well enough." She bit her lip. "But how will we get there without food or fuel?"

I smiled, pretending confidence I didn't entirely feel. "Jean-Luc thinks he can find us some fuel. His wife promised to pack us food." Generous offers I would have refused if I could. "We'll sleep on the road. We'll be fine."

My shoulders were tight. I still had something precious I could sell, though it would hurt. And would it even be enough?

We'd find a way to get to Marseille. We *had* to.

"Thanks for everything you do for us." Margot's words startled me. She'd never expressed gratitude before. She paused, then said slowly, "I have a little money I saved from last summer. If that would help."

I knew what that money meant to her. I felt a lump in my throat. "Thank you, my dear. Let's hope it doesn't come to that."

She gave a wistful smile. "After Lucie and I are with the Lusignys..." She looked sad. "We'll never see you again, will we?"

Her voice was stilted.

This was a conversation I'd been putting off too long. But it was either tell her now, in this private moment, or give her a wretchedly unpleasant shock with Lucie and all the rest of the girls watching at the Lusignys' château.

"Margot, there's... there's something I need to ask. Before we reach Boulins." My words were slow, awkward.

Her brow furrowed. "What is it?"

I licked my lips, wheezing a little as my lungs searched for breath. "I know... I know you've been a little nervous, wondering about how you'll make your own way in the world."

"So? Who wouldn't be?" She sounded defensive.

I ran my fingertips against the texture of the blanket, not quite meeting her gaze. "What if—what if I knew of a way you could enroll directly at a university? Study properly for a real career in law, that could support you for the rest of your life?"

Margot's eyes lit up. "But..." She frowned. "There's no university in Boulins. And anyway, how would I afford to spend my days studying? I'd need a job to support us. Even living with the Lusignys, they'll expect us to pull our weight."

"There's a... job. You could work for a bit, then spend the rest of your time as a student. Only a student."

She gasped. "That would be—" Her eyes narrowed. "Would I have to work as a secretary?"

I shook my head, knowing how much she despised typing

and shorthand, even though she was good at it. "You'd be a caretaker for children. You'd find it easy."

"And the pay?"

"Excellent, for the short time you'd work."

"Room and board?"

"Included."

She rose to her feet, pacing the tiny guest room as if electricity were coursing through her body. Stopping, she said accusingly, "What's the catch?"

I took a deep breath and looked her straight in the eyes.

"You'd have to leave Lucie in Boulins and come with us to Marseille."

There. I'd said it. At least, half of it.

But that half was bad enough. She gasped in horror. "Leave my sister behind?"

"For now. Not forever." I told myself the words weren't a lie. Who knew what the future might hold? "Just for a while."

"Why couldn't I just bring her to Marseille?"

"It's impossible. The job is short-term but intensive. It may require some travel at first."

"Travel? In the middle of a war?"

"You'd be quite safe."

"How long before I could send for her?"

"Several months." It was an understatement, not a lie, I tried to convince myself. But my cheeks were burning. "Several months" might mean several years. Or never. Margot would be on the other side of the world, far from the war she'd left Lucie in.

Even with my rosy description, Margot looked doubtful. She paced, then shook her head. "I can still become a lawyer at the Lusignys'. Even if it takes a little longer, I'd rather stay with my sister."

"You'll never be more than a servant in their château. You said they're not even going to pay you?" At her troubled nod, I continued, "Once you're there, you'll be stuck. But if you come to Marseille, Margot, if you take this chance, your future will be assured. You'll be able to finish college and earn enough money to make a new life—for both of you."

She stared at me, then said, "Do you know the employer?"

My lips curved. "Quite well."

I watched from the edge of the bed as Margot paced, clawing back her dark curly hair. She stopped, then exhaled, facing me.

"All right," she said. "I'll do it."

"Good." I exhaled, nearly giddy with relief. Everything I'd said was true, more or less. She'd be able to send for Lucie eventually, in America. Maybe by then I'd be able to get her sister a visa. Maybe.

"Thank you, Helen." She clutched my hand with a nervous smile. "The truth is, I was scared at the thought of being alone after you're gone. I trust the Lusignys and loved staying there. But if I can get a good job that leads quickly to a law degree, and start a new life with Lucie that much faster... And I'm able to take care of her and pay our bills... maybe it's worth it."

"I hope so," I whispered.

She faltered, looking away. "But... how will I tell her?"

"Remind her it's just temporary. And she'll have Choupette." I felt a pang of guilt as I rose to my feet and gently put my arm around the girl's shoulders. I knew I needed to tell her the rest. I'd procrastinated too long already. But it was hard. I took a breath. "Margot..."

There was a hard knock on the door. Jean-Luc pushed in, his face grim. "Pétain's on the radio. You need to hear."

Downstairs, we listened to the wireless as the new prime minister of France, the great French hero of la Grande Guerre, listed the exact terms of our country's surrender to the Nazis, though he called it an armistice. He'd just signed a deal with Hitler.

In three days, France would be split in two. The northern and western section—more than half the country, including Paris and the entire Atlantic Coast—would be occupied by the Germans until the end of the war, which the prime minister hoped would be soon. The southern part of France would be administered by Pétain and his newly formed government from a new capital south of the demarcation line. The millions of refugees who'd fled war zones to the north were ordered to remain in place until the destroyed train tracks and bridges could be repaired. Then, repatriation could begin.

"So the war is over?" said Margot, looking around the parlor, confused. "Everything will return to normal now? The soldiers will come home?"

"They're to throw down their arms and yield to the German army. They'll be prisoners of war until the British surrender," Madame Ravanel replied, biting her lip. She glanced at her husband. "Does this mean we'll get news about Daniel and Paul?"

"I don't know," he said heavily.

"Do we even need to go to Marseille now, Sister Helen?" Estée asked, sitting on the floor with her sister and Noémie, where they'd been playing a board game.

"We're going home!" Noémie clapped her hands.

Jean-Luc's dark eyes met mine, and the old understanding flashed between us. Traveling between so many battlefields, so many countries, we'd learned to read between the lines of politicians and their lies, their omissions and half-baked hopes.

"La Ravelle is in the occupied zone," he told me grimly. "You need to get south of the line as soon as possible."

"And you, Jean-Luc. Come with us to Marseille." I gestured urgently towards Élisabeth and Suzanne. "You and your family."

He gave the crooked smile I'd always loved, the one resigned to an unpleasant truth. "La Ravelle can't survive

without a doctor. I can't abandon my neighbors. Or my sons."
His lips pressed down, but his voice was light as he said, "I must
stay and help here as I can."

I wanted to rage, to argue, to cry, to demand. But I knew
that smile. He would never leave La Ravelle, not if he believed
his duty was to stay.

"We could take your wife and daughter then," I said desperately. Even as I spoke, I had no idea how we'd travel with two
more people—or what they'd do in Marseille after we left. But I
owed Jean-Luc that much.

"Yes." He turned to his family. "Perhaps you should both—"

"No," cried his wife. "I won't leave you."

"Never, Papa," said Suzanne, hugging him tight.

He sighed, then looked at me. "You see how it is."

His voice was quiet, without judgment. But I felt it anyway.
The sharp memory how once, long ago, I'd let him leave without
me. Just as I'd left Arthur and my baby to work at the hospital.
Neither man had forgiven me, and I'd never forgiven myself.

This was the difference.

A woman could not both work and love. Because in love a
woman had to give everything, in a way no man could ever
imagine.

"Well then," I said.

"Well then," he agreed sadly.

I looked at Margot, who'd already risen to her feet, fidgeting.
"Go pack up, girls. We're leaving."

"Right now?" Josette said and looked at Margot.

"So soon?" she said.

"I wish you wouldn't go," said Suzanne unhappily, with an
eye towards Choupette, who was barking and playing with
Lucie in the hallway, chasing the red ball they'd dug up from
her old toy chest. She picked up a crumpled bit of fabric that
had fallen behind the sofa. "Is this your sweater, *madame*?"

"Yes." I took it. "I must have forgotten it when I was down here earlier—thank you, dear." I looked at Margot and Josette. "Get everyone ready."

Their shoulders sagged, then they turned towards the little girls looking up with dismay from their half-played board game. "Come now. Tidy that up."

"I'll make some meals for the road," Madame Ravanel said, turning briskly towards the kitchen. "Suzanne, give me a hand."

Jean-Luc alone didn't move. As everyone rushed around, he stood by the wireless, head bowed, his arms crossed over his broad chest. He exhaled, his dark eyes anguished as he said quietly, "Helen, I wish…"

He said no more. But just that was enough to almost destroy me.

As our eyes locked, I felt a rush of love for him, of grief and regret. I wanted to cry, to rail, to beg him to leave his family and come away with me. I wanted to tell him I deserved his loyalty, too. To tell him about our daughter.

But I knew I'd only hurt him and those he loved most. It would cause jealousy and mixed loyalties and blame. His wife and youngest daughter didn't deserve that. Neither did he.

I forced my lips into a smile. "I should go. Check on the packing." I lifted my lips into a ghastly grin. "Make sure Estée doesn't accidentally take all your books."

Jean-Luc stared at me, and my smile fell away. The telephone started ringing, as it often did, with calls from patients who needed help. "I'll phone the garage," he told me thickly. "Ask Yves to bring your truck out front."

"Thank you."

He gave a sharp, jerky nod and turned away, his lanky body and long legs stumbling into the kitchen, where I heard him answer the phone. "Dr. Ravanel."

I took a shallow breath, then a deeper one. I looked down at my blouse and slacks, clean and scented with lavender soap, which Jean-Luc's wife had washed for me. I'd lost so much weight now, even the belt barely cinched the waistband, clinging to my bony hips. I'd need to cut another hole in the leather to tighten it.

Later.

After going upstairs for my valise, I caught a glimpse of myself in the bedroom's looking glass, my pale skin, the dark hollows beneath my eyes, gaunt cheekbones, limp brown hair hanging over my shoulders. I was at least clean from yesterday's bath, but my body looked uncared for, like an abandoned, unloved old house with broken windows and peeling paint, the owners long since fled.

I grabbed my comb and yanked it hard through my hair—so hard it brought tears to my eyes—then twisted it back into a tight chignon, using the same worn pins I'd used for a decade. I stared at myself one last time, then turned away, checking the room to ensure it was tidy and I'd left nothing behind. I had my clothes in my valise, along with a few personal items, the documentation and birth certificates, a small bottle of Jean-Luc's sleeping pills, even the unloaded revolver back in its holster, minus a bullet.

I would leave no trace. Jean-Luc would go on with his family and be happy.

Coming back down the stairs with heavy steps, I held my valise with one hand, the other wrapped around my bandage against my belly, as if to keep blood from seeping out. Jean-Luc, pacing at the bottom of the stairs, came forward when he saw me, his handsome face filled with emotion.

He started to speak, then said merely, "Let me carry that."

"I can manage my own bag." I didn't look at him as I walked into the parlor. The girls were in a general state of disorder amid their packing. "Is everyone ready to go?"

"If we can't go back to Paris, Nounours wants to stay," Noémie wailed.

"Must we leave so soon?" begged Rachel. "I promised Madame Ravanel I'd repot her flowers."

"We can't go yet," cried Estée, clutching a leather-bound tome from the Ravanels' shelf. "Not until I finish reading everything."

"Please," Rachel said, looking at her sister with tears in her eyes. She turned to me desperately. "Not yet. Please."

My heart twisted for the Lévy girls. Their mother had died when Rachel was born; their father, distracted by grief, had died just months later in a factory accident. Of course they wouldn't want to leave here. It had already become more like home than the family I'd tried to make for them at St. Agnes's. I felt a lump in my throat.

"It has been a very lovely visit, hasn't it?" I said with forced cheer. "But I'm afraid we must get to Marseille."

My injury had delayed us too long. Our ship would leave in ten days—and the American visas that hopefully would be waiting there, far from the prying eyes of the embassy in Paris.

Turning to Élisabeth Ravanel, who was standing in the kitchen doorway, her lovely face shadowed, I held out my hand. "Thank you for letting us into your home, Madame Ravanel, and taking such good care of us. You are an extraordinary woman."

She hesitated, her face surprised, then shook my hand. "You are most welcome. And... I think you are extraordinary, too." Her cheeks were red as she turned away. "Suzanne—"

Her daughter came forward holding two big cardboard boxes filled with sandwiches and apples, bread and cheese, and bottles of water, too. "For the road." The teenager looked at Lucie. "There's food for Choupette, too."

Lucie took one of the boxes, then embraced her. After

Josette took the other box, Suzanne fell to her knees and wept over the little copper-colored dog, who seemed confused by the extravagant gesture but licked her face to offer comfort.

"Come, girls. Time to go."

No one was happy. Coming downstairs, crying and dragging their bags, the little girls whined about how they didn't want to go, how they hated the road, hated the truck and weren't overly fond of me at the moment, either. Lucie was distracted with her dog. Josette was lost in thoughts of her own and still wouldn't look me full in the face. Something was clearly bothering her, but that would just have to wait.

Margot, usually the first to join in any criticism of me, coaxed the girls downstairs with, "Come now, *les filles*. It's not that bad."

As Jean-Luc had promised, our truck was parked on the cobblestones in front of the blue house. I stopped at the door, letting the others go outside ahead of me. The older girls helped the younger, and Lucie's dog bounded around them all, tongue lolling. Choupette seemed delighted, as if she thought this was a fun game.

I looked back at Jean-Luc, who'd followed us to the door with his wife and daughter. "Thank you so much."

"There's extra fuel cans in the back," he said quietly, coming closer to me. "They weren't easy to find. But you'll have enough petrol to reach Marseille, if we're lucky."

We. If *we* were lucky. I took a breath, inhaling his scent of wood smoke and soap for the last time. The French often kissed each other's cheeks, saying farewell to someone dear. But I could not. Not with him. Arranging my face into a polite smile, I held out my hand.

"Thank you, Jean-Luc." My voice was courteous, but no more. "For everything."

His dark eyes burned through me, then he reached out to

shake my hand. For a split second, I felt the warmth of his palm against mine. Then it was gone.

Exhaling, I gave a stiff final nod towards Madame Ravanel and Suzanne, then turned towards my girls. "*Allons-y.*" Let's go.

Rachel was crying, Estée muttering even as she clutched the old book that Jean-Luc had told her to keep, Noémie desperately clutching her teddy. But as the older girls placed their bags in the back and gently pushed the younger ones towards their seats, they waved farewell, promising to write Suzanne endless letters.

But as I turned to follow them, Jean-Luc grabbed my hand. "You'll see a specialist when you reach Marseille," he said urgently. "Remember. You promised me."

I felt hot tears behind my eyes.

"I'll remember," I whispered, looking at him one last time, trying to memorize the features of his face, his smell, the way his broad shoulders filled the doorway, the eternity of his dark eyes.

The same dark eyes as Suzanne's.

The same dark eyes he'd given my daughter, too. I glanced back at her.

Margot looked back at me.

How had everyone not seen the resemblance at once? The same dark eyes, the same dark curly hair? The same laugh?

Beneath my glance, Margot's expression slowly changed to a frown of confusion.

"Helen?"

I whirled to face Jean-Luc, knees shaking.

Tell him. The thought went through my mind like an evil snake twisting through lush green paradise. *Tell him now.*

I fought against this last temptation with white-knuckled desperation.

If I told him, we'd be connected forever.

If I told him, the perfect, easy happiness he had with his family would end.

If I'd ever loved him, how could I do that to him?

If I'd ever loved him, how could I not?

"Goodbye," I choked out. Turning away, I stumbled down the steps to where the girls and Lucie's dog waited in the old truck.

I knew I'd never see Jean-Luc again.

17

MARGOT ·

The truck's windows were rolled down in the warm June evening. Birds were singing as I drove in the steady line of cars south, past green fields and vineyards in golden light from the sun lowering to the west.

Boulins was far too close. Traffic was moving faster, just when I most wanted it to slow down.

The crowds of refugees had lessened on the road, but against Pétain's order, many of them were now traveling back north instead of south.

I gripped the steering wheel, feeling the rattle of the truck's engine beneath the worn front seat cushion. Even after our days off in La Ravelle, as soon as I climbed back into the truck, my body remembered the feeling of traveling and didn't like it. Within minutes, my joints started to ache.

And if *I* felt bad...

I looked towards the other side of the bench seat. Since we'd left the Ravanels', Helen had stretched out uncomfortably beside me, hunched against the passenger door, silent and pale, her hand covering her closed eyes. I could hear the rasp of her quick, shallow breath over the low growl of the truck's engine and road noise. We'd only been driving an hour, and I was worried.

"Want to stop for a rest?" I asked.

Helen didn't move. "No."

For a while, there was only silence, broken by the sounds of traffic; the buzz of refugees' voices as we passed them by. The girls were in the back of the truck, playing with Lucie's dog and talking wistfully about the Ravanels.

This was all going too fast. If we could get over the Loire, we might even make Boulins before dark.

My stomach clenched.

I wondered what Marseille would be like. I still couldn't believe I'd agreed to take a job there. Was it really just sunshine and palm trees, above a sparkling turquoise sea?

Not that it mattered. Helen had mentioned my nanny job would require travel. Where would we go? Who would my employer be? Without Lucie, I'd hate every minute.

I was doing this to secure our future, I reminded myself. I'd be leaving her only temporarily, and she'd live in a beautiful castle, looked after by the kind, elegant Lusignys. She'd be fine. We'd both be fine.

But oh, how I regretted every kilometer that brought us closer to the moment of parting!

I glanced down at the map. Boulins was right on the demarcation line. That likely meant the town would be split in two—half occupied, half free. But the Lusignys' château was south of town. My sister would be on the "free" side across the river.

But still.

The thought of leaving Lucie anywhere close to the Nazis left a cold mass at the pit of my stomach. No matter how I told myself it was for a good reason, and only for a short time, it felt like a horrible betrayal. She'd have Choupette. She'd have Hugo and Isabelle Lusigny to discuss philosophy and poetry. Just for a few months. Then she'd come live with me. Whatever Helen had said, I was sure I could find a place for her while I attended university.

But Marseille was unknown—and far away. While we were coming closer to Boulins with every turn of our wheels.

Coming over a hill, I saw a shining gray river in the distant valley. "Look—the Loire!"

"Hmm," Helen responded noncommittally, so I knocked hard on the half-open window behind my head. "Girls! The Loire!"

They exclaimed in a much more satisfying fashion.

The Loire River was the safe destination everyone had spoken of since the war began, the place where we'd once imagined our army would regroup, and ultimately triumph, as in the Great War two decades before.

But the river looked forlorn, the gray water sluggish, the bridges destroyed to prevent a Nazi invasion. As we drew closer, the traffic on the road slowed, then stopped. Near the destroyed bridge, I saw a long queue of cars, trucks and pedestrians on both shores of the river, waiting for the ferry.

We sat in the line of cars for an hour, moving forward at a snail's pace. As twilight faded, the line stopped moving entirely.

"Ferry's closed for the night," a man in a nearby Renault told us. "Might as well settle in till morning."

So we did, parking right where we were on the road for the night. Leaving Helen stretched out in the front of the truck, I joined the others in the back. There wasn't enough room for all six of us to lie down, so we let the little girls stretch out.

I crushed in next to Lucie, with her little dog sleeping in her lap, and Josette, who was in some kind of sullen snit, giving everyone the silent treatment. As the three of us sat up all night, trying to sleep with our heads leaning against the side wall, she wouldn't even look at me.

Probably mooning over Roger, I thought. I'd heard her ask Madame Ravanel earlier if she could use their phone to call St.

Agnes's. The kindly woman had regretfully informed her that phone calls to Paris, normally just hugely expensive, were now impossible.

"I miss the Ravanels," I told Lucie now in a low voice, looking out at all the cars parked behind us on the moonswept road. "I miss their house."

"So warm and cozy," Lucie agreed, petting her sleeping dog. "My second-favorite place, after home."

Home. She meant St. Agnes's. I shivered. Would we ever be home again?

I stared down at the little girls curled up beneath their blankets. They'd be gone forever to America, but it wasn't too late for Lucie and me. Yes. We'd go back to Paris someday. After I got to Marseille—after I got my degree—after I was a full-fledged lawyer—after the Nazis magically disappeared.

After, after, after.

I stared at Lucie, my heart pounding. This was the moment to tell her I was going with the others to Marseille. I'd be leaving her in Boulins on her own.

But I couldn't. My lips parted, then I chickened out.

Beside me, I noticed Josette staring at nothing, her posture stiff, her jaw tight. I nudged her with my elbow.

"What's wrong with you?" I whispered. "Lost in magical dreams of Roger?"

"Shut up," she said, her voice cold and quiet. She got up and moved to the other side of the truck. I stared after her in surprise. Not only sullenly silent but unusually touchy.

I spent the rest of the night waiting for the right moment, the right courage, to explain to my sister that I'd be leaving her in Boulins on her own.

But I never did. I fell asleep sitting up, and only woke as dawn rose pink and soft over the valley, as the car honked behind us.

"Traffic's starting to move up front," the driver called. "Ferry must have started again."

"Right. Thank you." Wiping the sleep from my eyes, I climbed back into the driver's seat. Helen was still stretched out over the front seat. She stiffly moved her feet back to give me a place to sit.

"Doing all right?" I asked, worried about the way her hands wrapped around her middle.

She gave me a small smile. "Just fine, *ma petite*."

When it was time to move, I started the engine, drove the truck forward a bit on the road, then turned it off again as the ferry left with its load of vehicles. We burned through fuel at an alarming pace all morning, starting and stopping. The sun was high in the sky before we reached the dock, where a rusted barge waited, captained by a disreputable white-haired elf of a man. He demanded an exorbitant price to ferry us, far more money than I had. He snorted at the francs I offered. "Not nearly enough."

For a moment, I thought we'd have to give up the whole thing, and live permanently on this riverbank. Then Helen unexpectedly reached into her valise and pulled out a gold ring with a diamond which I'd never seen her wear. "What if we add this?"

My throat tightened as I realized she'd given him her wedding ring.

"That will suffice," the ferry captain said, snatching up both francs and ring.

I wondered what it had cost Helen to part with her memento. I shivered, remembering what she'd told me about her husband and baby boy. What would that even do to a person, to lose everyone she loved? And it had happened to her not just once but three times. With her parents. With Dr. Ravanel.

Whatever she'd said, it was clear to me she still had feelings for him. I wondered why she'd broken their engagement so long ago. How awful it must have been, to make a single mistake that still haunted her, even now.

As our truck was ferried over the Loire, the barge packed cheek by jowl with cars and pedestrians, Helen remained inside the truck, resting, as Josette stonily kept an eye on the little girls in the back. But Lucie leaped out, weaving through the crowded deck to let her dog stretch her legs. I followed them to the barge's railing.

Dappled sunlight had broken through the clouds. It was playing across the water, silver and gold against the waves, glowing warmly over little villages on distant green hills.

I took a deep breath. I'd get no better chance than this.

"Lucie, we need to talk."

Her oversized dress gave her the look of a waifish ghost as she smiled at her dog, watching the wag of her tail. "About what?"

"It's serious."

Lowering to one knee, she fed Choupette the saved half of her own sandwich from breakfast that morning and glanced up at me chidingly. "It's always serious with you lately. You should spend more time with Choupette. She's such a happy little soul. You'll—"

I sighed. "Lucie."

She rose, her forehead furrowed. "What?"

"We should arrive at the Lusignys' in a few hours..."

"I know."

"But something's come up. I mean, it's changed. I'm not..." I took a deep breath. "I'm not going to stay there with you."

"What do you mean, not stay?" She patted my shoulder consolingly. "Don't be nervous. They liked you before. They'll like you again."

There was no other way to get through it but blurt it out.

"Helen said there's a job for me in Marseille that would give me the ability to go to university."

Lucie frowned. "In Marseille?"

The ferry was already approaching the southern shore. I didn't have much time. "I need a real career, Lucie, so I can support us. We can't depend on the Lusignys forever."

"You're the one who told me how wonderful they are—and that they encouraged your idea to become a lawyer."

"They are wonderful, but..." I shook my head. "We'll need money, not just room and board. The sooner I'm a lawyer, the safer we'll be. And Helen won't be around to help us."

"She and the littles will just be in Marseille, won't they? That's not so very far."

Lucie didn't know they'd all be in America. I licked my lips. "We need to find a way to start our own lives." I thought of Helen, working as a nurse against her husband's wishes, and squared my shoulders. "This temporary nanny job will pay enough to support me at school."

I glanced back at our truck parked between other cars. When she'd left her own orphanage at my age, Helen had been smart. She'd focused on becoming a nurse and earning enough money so she'd never be helpless and poor again.

The question hit me. So why had Helen abruptly given up being a nurse in 1925, and given up her independence and entire life savings to take over an ailing Parisian orphanage? Yes, she'd been worried about Lucie and me, the newly orphaned daughters of her old friend. But still. She'd sold her old wedding ring, probably her last possession of any value, just to get us ferried across the Loire.

Taking responsibility for needy, penniless children: what a strange choice for a woman who'd been so determined to never be broke. I thought I'd known Helen Taylor. Now I felt I didn't understand her at all.

"But," Lucie whimpered, "I don't want to stay in Boulins without you."

I turned to her, feeling the soft morning breeze on my face. "I'll send for you in Marseille as soon as I can."

"How long?"

"Months."

"Months!" she cried.

"Weeks," I improvised, vowing, "I'll be such a good nanny that my employer will soon agree to let you come stay with us. In the meantime, you'll be well cared for with the Lusignys."

My sister's big blue eyes shone with unshed tears. "But—"

"Plus, you'll have Choupette."

Lucie looked down at her little copper-colored mutt, who smiled back at her, panting, tongue lolling. "I... I suppose." She bit her lip. "How will I reach you? Where will you be staying in Marseille?"

"I don't have the address yet, but I think we'll be staying first at John Cleeton's villa. The Villa del Mar. As soon as I know the name and address of my new employer, I'll write." I gripped her hand. "You'll be safe at the Lusignys'. We just have to be separated a short while, but it will be worth it. I promise."

"All... all right." She looked down, tried to smile. "Like you said. It's only for a little while. And I have Choupette."

I knew she was being brave. That hurt even more than if she'd yelled and complained.

As the ferry reached the shore, we reboarded our truck. Helen took one look at Lucie and me and said she was feeling quite well enough to drive, if Josette would sit next to her with the map. My sister and I could sit together with the little girls in back for the final stretch to Boulins.

As Helen drove us off the ferry to the shore, past all the pedestrians and cars waiting on this side to go north, I sat in the back of the truck, petting Choupette and explaining to the three little girls that I'd be going to Marseille with them. As Noémie,

Estée and Rachel cheered and hugged me, I looked at Lucie's wan shoulders and tried not to cry, pretending to be strong so she wouldn't start crying, too.

Again, the traffic on the road seemed to go faster, and faster still, just when I wanted everything to slow down.

I was startled when I saw a Nazi truck drive past us on the road, casual as you please, flying that nasty blood-red flag with that spider cross over a circle of bone. Then another one. But I guess it's true that people can get used to anything because within hours, I no longer noticed them, blending in with the weary French. They didn't bother us; we didn't bother them.

The fighting was over. No more fear of bombing or being shot. Our own armies were surrendering themselves as prisoners of war. German soldiers just nodded at us pleasantly as they passed and kept going wherever they were going.

We arrived at the edges of Boulins in late afternoon. As we drove through the prosperous town, I noticed a checkpoint being built near the intact bridge. German soldiers were busily putting up a new guardhouse, while a few others worked on a fence nearby. We slowed nervously, but the bored-looking soldiers ignored us.

The demarcation line wasn't even official yet. We still had two days before the split would be actively enforced, and yet preparations had already begun. Once we'd passed through, I shivered, glad to have the occupied zone behind us.

A few kilometers outside the city, we reached the Lusignys' wrought-iron gate. Our old truck drove slowly up the long, slender road laced with tall green trees, passing cattle in the golden afternoon sun, flipping their tails as they placidly ate grass. When we came over the vista, we saw pink flowers blooming near the ivy-covered white château with its dark blue roof.

"Is that where I'm going to live?" Lucie breathed, wide-eyed.

"A real castle!" hollered Rachel.

"It's something out of a fairy tale," breathed Estée.

"You're a wucky dog, Choupette," Noémie chortled, scratching the animal's ears.

"It's... very beautiful." Lucie tried to look pleased, but she cradled her little dog close, her blue eyes haunted. I felt an ache in my throat.

After piling out of the truck near the grand front door, we rang the doorbell. I expected the prim white-haired housekeeper I remembered from last summer. Instead, Madame Lusigny herself answered the door, a toddler whining at her feet.

"Oh, thank the good Lord above. I expected you a week ago," she added reproachfully.

Isabelle Lusigny had dark circles beneath her eyes, her brown hair disheveled, her elegant dress wrinkled and unkempt, stretched tight over her pregnant belly. The big diamonds she'd always had in her pierced ears were gone, leaving her earlobes forlorn.

The toddler yanked on her hem, chanting, "Maman... Maman... Maman..."

She flinched and looked us over with a weary smile. Her smile froze when she saw Lucie's dog, but she said only, "Come in."

Madame Lusigny led us into the front sitting room, which seemed emptier than I remembered—and dirtier. As she motioned for us all to sit down on the two antique sofas, both rather careworn, no one came to serve little cakes and tea, as I'd been greeted with last summer. I wondered what had happened to the household servants. I looked around the empty bookshelves, the blank spots on the walls, squares of darker-colored wallpaper where paintings had once been.

"Oh," she said awkwardly, following my gaze. "We've been

doing some redecorating. We're realized that knick-knacks are so—bourgeois."

"Your house is lovely," said Helen tranquilly, sitting beside me.

"Where's Madame Petit?" I ventured. "And Armand, and the rest?"

"Scarpered off as soon as times got tight." Her expression hardened. "There's no loyalty in the peasant class anymore."

I managed not to flinch. Out the corner of my eye, I saw Estée and Rachel flash each other looks at the word *peasant*.

Hugo Lusigny sauntered in. "Welcome, girls. Glad you could..." His voice trailed off when he saw the dog in Lucie's lap. He glanced at his wife, but she was too busy with their child to notice. "Glad you could finally make it."

He was a short man, with thinning hair and expansive belly beneath his vest. I noticed the gold pocket watch he'd loved to show off was missing from his vest pocket. He was followed by a younger man I didn't recognize.

"I don't think you ever met my brother Rémy?" Madame Lusigny said, struggling with her young son, who'd been hitting her to get her attention. Picking him up wearily into her lap, she said, "Rémy's been staying with us since he left the army."

"A pleasure," her brother said, giving us a sweeping bow. He was well dressed, polite, smiling. Perfectly respectable. So why did something about him seem a little... off?

Baring his teeth into an ingratiating smile, he looked at each of us in turn. His gaze seemed to linger on Lucie.

"Mademoiselle Vashon." Monsieur Lusigny lounged in a chair across from us. "Still hoping to become a lawyer?"

"Yes, indeed, *monsieur*," I replied, smiling. Leaning forward on the crowded sofa, I looked at the plump toddler in his wife's arms, trying to ignore the way he was now playing patty-cake with her face. "Auguste has grown big. Such a handsome boy!"

"Yes." She gave a weary nod, struggling to hold my gaze beneath the pushing palms of her son. "I was happy to get your letter. To be honest, Margot, I can use the help. Our last servant left weeks ago, and as you can see"—she glanced down at the swell of her belly—"we're expecting another baby. And I don't know how I'll..."

"Isabelle's having a hard time," her husband agreed, leaning back comfortably in his chair. "I'm afraid she's overwhelmed by everything."

She gasped a laugh that sounded a little crazed. "Half the servants left when the war began. The rest left when we couldn't afford to pay them anymore."

"It's hard to find good help," her brother said, turning from Lucie to look me over slowly. My cheeks burned beneath his intrusive gaze.

"Isabelle's not much of a cook," sighed Hugo Lusigny. "Or skilled at cleaning, either. The place is a mess." He looked sadly around the sitting room, from the empty spots on the walls, to the bare shelves, to the dirty carpet. "The clutter and noise are starting to distract me from my study of philosophy, so I'm glad you and your sister are here to help her."

I'd liked him fine last summer, as he'd often praised me and treated me as if I had great intellectual potential. Now I felt annoyed. It seemed rather unfair that he expected his wife to single-handedly care for their child and do the work of ten servants, then complained about her sub-par cooking and inability to keep the rooms clean enough for his enjoyment in peacefully reading Sartre or Voltaire. I forced another smile.

"Madame Lusigny, *monsieur*, I'd like to introduce my sister, Lucie Vashon."

My sister patted her dog. "And this is Choupette."

The Lusignys looked at each other with alarm. Though the pup had grown less skinny and quivered less after days of Lucie's extravagant love, she'd never be pretty, with her too-short nose and squinty eyes.

"You never said anything in your letter about a dog." He gave a theatrical sneeze. "Dogs and I, we don't—" He sneezed again.

"I'm so sorry, *madame, monsieur*," said Helen apologetically. "I'm afraid Lucie adopted her on the road."

"Some thieves wanted to smoosh her with a shovel," chimed in Rachel. "We saved her."

"You'll be glad of a sheepdog surely?" Lucie said eagerly. "A good ratter?"

The couple looked at each other.

Monsieur Lusigny demanded, "Has your dog been trained for that?"

"Uh..." As enthusiastic as she was, my sister couldn't outright lie. "She's the sweetest, most loyal dog ever. You'll love her. I've just started training her." She set the pup down on the dirty rug. "Sit, Choupette."

The dog looked up at her, panting, her tongue lolling out. Still standing, she gave her tail a tentative wag.

"Sit," Lucie said with increasing desperation. Choupette tilted her head quizzically, clearly confused. "Uh, she'll get it. You'll see."

"Well. That's as may be." Sniffing, Monsieur Lusigny shook his head. "Dog'll have to sleep in the stable."

"With horses?" Lucie blurted out in dismay.

I could see a vein pulse in his thick neck. "Horses are gone."

"Choupette wouldn't like to be in the cold barn alone, separated from me—"

Hugo Lusigny's jaw stuck out, and knowing his stubborn, pugilistic streak when someone was being "unreasonable," I suddenly feared this was about to fall apart. I turned desperately to my sister.

"Just for a little while," I begged. "Give Madame and Monsieur Lusigny time to get used to the idea of a dog."

Lucie stared at me.

"Well, all right," she said slowly, and I knew what a huge concession that was for her. She turned to the couple. "But soon you'll see what a good pup she is, and you'll—"

"We have a room for you both upstairs," Madame Lusigny said. "Right next to the nursery. The same room you liked, Margot."

"I always loved that room," I said. "But I'm afraid it's only my sister who can stay. I must go on to Marseille."

"Only your—sister?" Isabelle Lusigny looked doubtfully from me, sturdy and dark-haired and a known quantity, to pale, ethereal Lucie with a dog at her feet.

"Lucie's wonderful with children," I rushed to say. "You'll adore her."

"I hope so," she said, struggling with her toddler, who was now staring at the dog and pushing at his mother to get loose. She turned to Lucie. "Could you watch him the rest of the evening then bathe him and put him to bed? I feel like I haven't slept in days..."

"I can help you with my nephew tonight, Mademoiselle Lucie," said Rémy, smiling. "If you want."

"No," Hugo said sharply, looking at his brother-in-law. "Isabelle will help her."

His wife sighed, her shoulders slumping a little.

I looked around the château's dingy front room. It was nothing like I remembered. Nothing like I'd dreamed it would be.

Everything had changed. The lack of money brought the Lusignys' characters into different focus. Would my sister be expected to work night and day, doing what no single person could? Who would watch out for her, make sure no one took advantage of her?

My gaze sharpened on Madame Lusigny's brother. He'd stepped a little closer to Lucie, and her dog suddenly stiffened and let out a low growl. Even Choupette didn't like it here.

Madame Lusigny, too, stiffened, staring at the dog. "Is he growling? The beast must definitely stay in the barn. Not fit for human company—or safe for our innocent baby."

She threw her arms around the toddler, only to have him slap back in irritation, still reaching out his chubby hands towards the dog. When I'd left last summer, baby Auguste had been colicky but, other than that, a sweet little thing. Now he seemed as sour and entitled as his father.

"Well," that man said jovially, rising to his feet, "I'll let you say your farewells before Isabelle shows you to your room, Mademoiselle Lucie. I'm sure you'll both want to get started on dinner."

I suddenly wasn't sure I wanted to leave Lucie here. *She'll be fine*, I told myself firmly. What could happen? It was a castle in beautiful fields, in the free zone of France. I'd loved it here. Why wouldn't she?

But I didn't want to be parted from her. And worse, I felt fear. Something vague.

I was being silly. It was just for a month or two.

Rising to my feet, I murmured, "Thank you, *madame, messieurs*." I nodded politely in turn. "We'll get Lucie's things."

Helen, Josette, Estée, Rachel and Noémie followed Lucie and me out of the sitting room, down the hall and out the over-sized door of the château. Everyone's shoulders slumped. Even Choupette seemed depressed.

Reaching into the back of the truck, I picked up Lucie's bag. I tried my best to infuse good cheer into my voice. "I'll come upstairs with you. Help you get settled in."

"No." My sister's face was strangely calm as she took the bag. "You should all just go. It will be easier."

The rest of us looked at each other.

"We don't have to rush away," Helen said gently. "We can stay for a few hours, at least—perhaps spend the night in Boulins, until we know you're comfortable."

Lucie shook her head. "Stretching it out will only make it harder."

Squaring her shoulders, she looked down at Choupette, who looked up at her.

"Lucie," I choked out, my heart in my throat.

She gave me a smile, her lower lip trembling. "The sooner you get to Marseille, the sooner you can send for me—right?"

"Right," I said, feeling wretched.

One by one, the girls went to Lucie to say farewell. Even Noémie's teddy hugged her, as tears poured down the little girl's face.

"I don't want you to weave, Wucie. I don't."

"I don't want to leave you either, *ma petite.*" Lucie looked older than her sixteen years as she hugged the little girl back. She smiled tenderly. "But sometimes in life, in war, we must be brave. Can you be brave for me, Noémie? You and Nounours, too?"

Sniffling, the little girl wiped her eyes and nodded. Estée and Rachel joined in the hug, followed by Josette, who was openly weeping. Helen wrapped her arms around all of them.

Only I stood apart. When the others stepped away from her, wiping their eyes, they told Lucie brightly how lucky she was, what an adventure this would be. But they said it differently now—now that they'd actually seen the truth inside the castle.

It was unbearable. I looked at Helen pleadingly. She knew without words what I was asking her and shook her head. We couldn't bring Lucie with us.

I moved forward and hugged my sister fiercely, then pulled back to look at her face. I wanted to memorize every detail, the color of her eyes, the way she was struggling to smile through her tears.

"It'll be lovely," she said. "An adventure."

She was just repeating the words others had said. I nodded, wiping my eyes, trying to smile.

"Take care of yourself," I said hoarsely. "I'll send for you as soon as I can."

"I know." Lucie gripped my hand as if she never wanted to let me go.

This was a mistake. I couldn't leave her. I couldn't...

I felt a catch at my heart as her hand released mine; the sudden choking fear I'd never see her again.

Turning away, Lucie lifted her small bag over her shoulder, then went inside the Lusignys' castle, her little dog trotting sadly after her. She didn't look back.

18

MARGOT

I was still barely holding it together a few hours later. As twilight started to fall, as I parked the truck in the little town of Ganteaux, near the square.

I'd talked Helen out of staying the night in Boulins. I wanted to reach Marseille as soon as possible. But as I turned off the engine, my heart hurt so much I put my hand over my ribs, trying to hold in the pain radiating through my body.

I'd left her. My little sister. My only family.

Glancing at me silently, Helen opened the rusted passenger door with a creak, then slammed it closed behind her. Sitting motionless in the driver's seat, I took another breath and listened to the noises around me—the mournful call of birds, the girls talking to Helen in the back. I heard Noémie moaning, "Wucie... Choupette..." and it seemed its own kind of plaintive cry, joining the sob of birds over the day's lost light.

I didn't realize how long I'd been sitting there blankly until I heard the wrench of my door and saw Josette looking up at me. Her eyes were sympathetic beneath her mascara, and even her carefully coiffed red hair seemed subdued as she said quietly, "Can I help, Margot?"

I shook my head, wiping my eyes. "I'm being silly."

"Yes. Silly." Whatever had upset Josette earlier seemed forgotten. Her voice was gentle, and as our eyes met, I saw my grief mirrored in her own.

I tried to smile. "She's safe with the Lusignys. Safe and warm. You saw the house."

"A real castle," Josette said.

We looked at each other, loudly leaving the rest unsaid.

"Anyway," I said weakly, "I'll send for her soon in Marseille. Once I'm there for good."

"We'll all be there to welcome her."

"You won't because—" I cut myself off. It was nuts that Helen was still keeping America a secret. It didn't seem right. It would utterly change their lives.

I suddenly wondered what other secrets Helen might be keeping.

"Because what?" Josette said, her brow furrowed. "Of course we'll be in Marseille. Where else would we be?"

I looked away. "Nothing. I didn't mean a thing."

"Josette," Helen called from the curb with the girls. "Is she...?"

The redhead held up an apologetic finger, then turned back to me. "Come on, Margot," she said gently. "Let's go see if the *maire* has a place for us to sleep. I smell hot food."

Normally, I would have been excited by that. Since we'd left Paris, there had been precious few towns who'd actively tried to welcome us. Many ignored us, and a few had barred refugees altogether. Repeating to myself that Lucie would be fine with the Lusignys, absolutely fine, I forced my legs to slide out of the driver's seat, leaning back heavily to close the door.

We were directed by the mayor and his wife to take refuge in the nearby *lycée*, and assured that our truck was in no danger of being stolen here, and all the cars would be guarded, in any case.

Inside the modern brick school, we found a large gymnasium, set up with rows of cots, about half of which were filled with people. We were fed hot soup and bread at long tables in the cafeteria.

I ate mechanically, tasting nothing. Afterward, we were each given a blanket and pillow, and directed to our cots to settle in for the night. I numbly lay down, with the two youngest girls on the cots beside me.

But I couldn't sleep. I stared up at the high ceiling, feeling claustrophobic in the warm, stifling air of the gymnasium, in spite of all the windows open in an attempt to create a crossbreeze. I listened to Noémie's soft snoring, and the coughs and whispered prayers of strangers in the darkness around us.

Lucie.

My closest friend, the companion of my whole life.

My earliest memory was the thready sound of her hungry wail, from a crib or perhaps a cardboard box or wardrobe drawer in the darkness, as I'd gripped our mother's cold hand. Maman had been face-first on the bed when Helen had found us in a tiny room in the Place Pigalle. I could barely remember Violette Vashon now, beyond the scent of rose water and sad blue eyes. She'd had pale-blonde hair just like Lucie's.

I'd been trying to wake up Maman so she'd feed the baby. Worrying about that baby had been the central core of my life.

I hated myself for leaving her alone in Boulins.

The early dawn sky was steel gray outside the gymnasium's windows as I rose from my cot.

"Helen." I shook her shoulder in the darkness. "I made a mistake."

She jumped, then sat up in her cot, frowning. "Margot? What time is it?"

"I never should have left Lucie. We have to go back."

"Go—back?"

"It's just a few hours' drive," I pleaded. "Please—"

"No," she said very quietly, so as not to wake anyone. "I'm sorry, but no. Even if we could spare the time—what would she do in Marseille?"

"I'll figure something out." I wiped my eyes fiercely. "I'll convince my employer to give her a job, too, or maybe Mr. Cleeton would let her stay. His villa is big enough, isn't it?"

She shook her head sorrowfully. "It's a rental. John's planning to sail on the same ship we are."

I exhaled. "Then I'll find something else. I can't leave her."

"I thought you trusted the Lusignys."

"I do—I did—but it was different last summer. I was happy there, but... everything's changed. No servants, no money. They're falling apart. And..." I stopped short of mentioning my misgivings about Rémy. As my sister herself would point out, it was unkind to slander a total stranger. "I know I could manage there, but—you know how she is."

Helen bowed her head. I didn't need to explain about Lucie's idealistic, impractical ways, how she sometimes floated through life on clouds of dreams of a world of goodness and peace.

"I'm sorry," she said. "It's done. We can't spend six hours going back to Boulins and returning again. Lucie must stay where she is. For now."

"No." Sitting back on my haunches next to the cot, I folded my arms. "If you won't help, I'll go back alone."

"Alone?" She stared at me. "What are you talking about?"

"I'll hitchhike. Walk." I tossed my head with more bravado than I felt. "Get a ride back north with one of those helpful German convoys."

Helen's eyes were wide with horror. I waited, shivering, half expecting her to say *Farewell then, and good luck.* After all, she and the girls had a ship to catch.

Instead, she did something worse. She took a deep breath.

"Lucie's not really your sister," she said quietly.

I drew back. "What are you talking about? Of course she is. I remember our mother and hearing Lucie cry..."

"You were three years old." Her voice was barely a whisper. "They adopted you as a newborn. Claude Vashon wasn't able to give Violette children due to his injuries in the war. Lucie was her only natural child."

It wasn't enough she was claiming my sister wasn't my sister, now my parents weren't my parents? My mouth fell open.

"You're lying," I whispered hotly.

She looked at me. "When have you ever known me to lie?"

"You've lied to the girls for weeks about America," I retorted. Nearby, Noémie flopped over on her cot, snoring softly. I lowered my voice. "Who knows what other secrets you're keeping?"

Something changed in Helen's face, and she blushed.

I'd always known Helen Taylor to be an honest person—painfully so—but seeing that blush, I knew I was right. She was keeping something from me.

"How did you know I was adopted?" I said slowly. "Did my mother tell you?"

She looked away. On the other side of the gymnasium, a few people were starting to stir in the early morning, village women bringing out muesli and bread and milk. I could smell coffee brewing. "I told you. I knew her."

"You were friends."

"Not... exactly." Helen hesitated. "I met them once, on their farm outside Paris. She and her husband were unable to have children, so they adopted you. But after her husband died, the farm failed. She wrote me, asking for help, but I didn't get her letter for almost a year. By the time it reached me, she was working as a prostitute in Paris. That's how she got pregnant with Lucie."

Something ugly rose in my soul. "You're saying my mother

was a—?" I couldn't say the word. "And my sister was the product of that?" My face was burning as I rose to my feet, clutching my hands into fists. "You'd say anything, wouldn't you, just to prevent any delay to reaching Marseille? Even the most terrible lies about the people I love most in the world. I was starting to admire you, Helen, but—but—you have no soul!"

I turned and fled.

"Margot," she cried. "Wait!"

I stopped, wiping my eyes.

Helen rose from her cot. Nearby, Josette and Rachel were awake now, sitting up in bewilderment. From across the cavernous gymnasium, I felt the eyes of other refugees, strangers.

She came close to me, her face resigned. "I just remembered. I forgot to give Lucie her identity papers before we left."

"What are you saying?"

"She might find it hard to travel. The Germans are getting organized. Once they start with their bureaucracy, there's no telling where it will end. She'll need her papers."

"But she's in the free zone—"

"It might not matter." Helen stared at me. "All right," she said. "We'll go get her. Just don't blame me when she's stuck in Marseille—"

I threw my arms around her with a sob. Helen pulled me into a tight hug, whispering nonsensical words of comfort. A moment later, she was joined by Josette and all the other girls hugging me as well.

"What happened?" Estée demanded. "Why are you crying?"

"We're going to get Lucie," I told her, and the girls cheered.

"And Choupette?" Noémie yelled happily.

"Of course." I smiled through a sheen of tears.

We dressed and packed up quickly. The good people of Ganteaux even gave us bottles of water and a small amount of petrol as we left—just a few liters but welcome—and wished us well on our journey.

"We're all in this together. On this side of the demarcation line," the volunteer said, beaming at us, "France can continue as always."

We climbed back in the truck and returned north on the same road we'd driven the previous night. The morning air was fresh and clear, and I knew we were doing the right thing. My heart became lighter with every kilometer.

As Helen drove, I sat in the back, entertaining the little girls with stories of how surprised Lucie would be to see us, increasingly improbable tales of her leaping to the top blue roof of the château, and Choupette flying halfway to the moon, that had them rollicking with laughter. The journey was easy, and everyone was in good spirits at the thought of soon having Lucie and her little dog back with us.

The happy mood lasted all the way until Boulins. Seeing the castle in the distance, I felt suddenly anxious.

"Drive faster," I begged Helen. Her eyebrows rose, but she pressed down harder on the acceleration as we flew past the long, slender road framed by trees.

I told myself I had no reason to feel anxious. We'd reach the Lusignys' house and find my sister washing dishes or scrubbing laundry or chasing little Auguste through the garden as Choupette barked happily after them in the sunshine. I had no reason to worry. No reason at all.

The truck had barely slowed down in front of the château before I jumped out and rushed to the tall front door, shouting for Lucie, ringing the doorbell five times. I looked towards the garden, up at the windows. All empty. I didn't even hear the sound of barking.

Hugo Lusigny finally appeared at the door in wrinkled pajamas, holding his pipe in his hand, with an irritable expression.

"I'm here for Lucie." I looked behind him eagerly. "I'm sorry, *monsieur*, but we've realized my sister is needed in Marseille. Can you get her, please?"

"No."

I blinked. "No?"

"We're not sure where she is," he said heavily, clawing back his wispy hair.

I drew back. "What do you mean?"

His troubled eyes met mine, his round face hollow above his five o'clock shadow. "Your sister disappeared from the château sometime during the night."

19

HELEN

"Disappeared?" Margot gasped, standing at the door of the château. "What are you *talking* about? She can't disappear! Lucie's a person, not a ghost!"

"*Ouais*, but... we... we just can't find her." Hugo Lusigny sucked on his pipe. "We think she and that dog must have... run away."

"Run away?" Margot's hands tightened, as if she was yearning to give him a hard shake. Her dark eyebrows lowered furiously. "What did you do?"

"Do?" He staggered back a step, his pipe falling out of his mouth. He picked it up off the smudged marble floor. "Nothing!"

But there was something shifty in his eyes.

"Monsieur Lusigny!" she cried again. "*Where is my sister?*"

He looked haunted, the sunlight shining off his balding, sweaty pate. "I swear to you, I do not know!"

"*Monsieur.*" I stepped between them calmly. "I see you are upset. If you would like, we can help search your house and gardens."

"Uh..." He glanced behind him, and I saw the shadow of his

wife, looking a little ghostly herself, standing at the base of the sweeping staircase. She shook her head. He turned back to me. "I'm not sure..."

"Don't worry," I assured him pleasantly, pushing inside. "We'll be very careful."

I stepped into the shadowy foyer, beneath the ancient chandelier with its dull, broken crystals. My old leather shoes echoed against the dirty black-and-white checkered floor as I gestured for the girls to follow.

"Madame... Taylor, is it?" His wife came forward, her face pale. "The Vashon girl is not here, I tell you. We called for her this morning. We looked everywhere. She is gone. So there is no point—"

"We'll just make sure, shall we?" I kept my smile firmly in place. "Now. When did you see her last?"

"Last night after dinner," Hugo Lusigny said, looking uncomfortable at the invasion of orphans of various sizes, now glaring at him, except for Noémie, who looked like she was about to cry. "It was abominable—the pork was still raw on the inside, the dessert fairly burned..."

"We did our best," his wife said crossly.

"So Lucie helped with dinner." I could recognize the signs of the girl's cooking. There was a reason Berthe never let Lucie anywhere near the kitchen. "Then she joined you for dinner?"

"She..." Red circles formed on the woman's pale cheeks. "She took her plate outside to the barn. I think she was worried about her dog..."

"She wanted to feed it to her dog, more like," her husband muttered.

"And after that?" I asked.

The couple looked at each other. He shrugged. "I went to my study to review my notes on Rousseau. I must have fallen asleep in my chair because the next thing I knew, Isabelle was shaking me awake, demanding to know if I'd seen the girl.

Which I hadn't." He huffed with a flare of nostril. "A damned nuisance start to finish."

Margot looked as if she'd like to slug him. I gave her a warning glance.

"Madame Lusigny? You haven't seen Lucie since dinner?"

"N-No."

But she wouldn't meet my gaze. I stared at her for a long moment.

"All right, girls," I said, turning to them briskly. "Let's do a search."

"Like we did for Fräulein Mueller every time she lost her glasses?"

"Yes. Exactly." I clapped my hands. "We'll search each part of this castle. Stick together, stay within earshot. But whoever finds Lucie first—or even finds a clue—gets a prize." Estée and Rachel eyed each other competitively, bracing themselves like sprinters at the starting line. "Ready? Go!"

"Lucie, Lucie!" Shouting her name, the two girls took off through the foyer, Noémie toddling unsteadily behind them with her teddy bear, shouting at them to wait. Margot, Josette and I followed, searching more methodically through one grand salon after another, the Lusignys trailing after us, protesting that Lucie had never been in this room or that. We looked anyway, shouting her name.

The castle was even more dusty and forlorn than I'd thought. In some of the large, high-ceilinged rooms, there was no furniture at all, and one entire wing was just closed off. We passed cavernous open-mouthed fireplaces in cavernous empty rooms, and it was as if each gaping maw had devoured every stick of decoration and comfort.

Hugo Lusigny accompanied his wife for only a few rooms, until we reached his study. This chamber, with its wood paneling, leather chairs and large oak desk, was still very comfortable, with shelves full of leather-bound books and two expensive-looking oil paintings depicting dogs and horses. As we passed through it, he watched us like a hawk, warning us not to touch anything, sputtering that he'd never allowed Lucie in here, that children weren't allowed at all, "nor ladies, either."

I looked more carefully but saw nothing suspicious, no trace of Lucie.

Margot's face was filled with guilt and despair as we went through each room. "It wasn't like this last summer," she kept whispering. "It wasn't."

"We'll find her," Josette said, patting the girl's shoulder. "Don't worry, Margot. We'll find her."

We went up the sweeping stairs, searched the large bedrooms, and found more evidence of disrepair and neglect, but nothing more.

"Where is the nursery?" I asked.

Isabelle Lusigny looked resigned as she pointed at the ceiling.

We trooped up another set of stairs, these far less grand, clearly meant for housemaids, not duchesses. Margot led us to the room she'd stayed in last summer.

Situated next to the nursery, the small bedroom could have been lovely, with its single bed, tiny fireplace and single picture window overlooking the green sweep of the estate, from the gardens to the distant hills. Instead, it seemed dusty and smelled faintly of mildew. Nothing of Lucie was visible. The bed hadn't even been slept in. The coverlet was tucked carefully around the pillow.

Margot turned back to us wide-eyed. "I'm the one who makes a bed like that." She turned to Madame Lusigny in disbelief. "You didn't change the linens after a year?"

"Why should I?" she said defensively. "They were clean, weren't they?"

Pushing on the adjacent door, I peeked into the darkened nursery. I expected to hear the soft breaths of a sleeping child, since he hadn't been importuning his mother. But the crib was empty. "Madame Lusigny, where is your baby?"

Her gaze shifted. "He's... uh, with my brother."

Ah, I thought, looking at the nervous twitch of the woman's shoulders, the slant of her eyes towards the window. *Ah*.

But knowing that the secret she was hiding involved her brother didn't bring me relief. To the contrary. As I caught my breath, I could hear the wheeze of my lungs. I felt a lingering sharp ache in my side.

"Where is Monsieur Rémy?" I gave a polite smile. "I would very much like to speak with him."

"He's... uh... outside. Playing with Auguste in the garden."

Clapping my hands, I called, "Come, girls! Back downstairs?"

"There's more rooms up here you haven't seen yet," Madame Lusigny said. "All the staff rooms, and an entire floor of attics upstairs. If you'd like to—"

"No. Girls?"

"Did you find her?" Rachel appeared in the door, her dark braids flying. She sighed when I shook my head.

"Let's go look outside."

"All right." By now, the little girls were starting to droop, Noémie muttering about *so—many—stairs*.

They brightened after we stepped out of the shadowy château, back into the sunshine.

"Which way to the garden?" I asked, waiting until she reluctantly pointed.

"But, Madame Taylor, m-my brother knows nothing—it is impossible that he knows anything," Isabelle Lusigny stammered, following us as we crunched over the gravel driveway.

"Doesn't hurt to ask," I said, not slowing down. My insides were churning as we walked through the overgrown grass towards the garden. Behind me, I could hear the little girls playing leapfrog in their short dresses and bobby socks, giggling when they felt the long grass swish against their bare legs.

The ornamental garden was even more neglected than the castle. The pond was thick with algae, the flowers quivering beneath the bullying triumph of towering weeds. The topiaries stretched out into the sky, no longer revealing any hint of a civilized shape.

We found Isabelle's young brother sitting disconsolately at a bench placed at the center of an overgrown maze, staring at nothing as his toddler nephew gleefully yanked flowers out of the ground. The young man rose to his feet, startled, when he saw us.

"Monsieur Lusigny," I began.

"Moreau," he corrected, frowning at his sister, who quickly lifted her child into her arms. "What are you—?"

"We're here for my sister," Margot blurted out. "Have you seen her?"

"Oh, is she missing?" His dark eyes shifted away. He cupped one hand over his forearm, and I saw the bandage beneath the sleeve.

I surged forward and grabbed his arm. Before he could react, I yanked back the fabric and bandage in a single movement.

"What? How dare you, *madame!*" he cried, drawing back his injured arm. But it was too late. I'd already seen the ugly red punctures that had broken his skin.

"A dog bite." My eyes pierced his. "Choupette bit you?"

The girls gasped, looking at each other. Choupette had patiently put up with endless brushing and baths and tight hugs. One afternoon in La Ravelle, Noémie had even dressed her in some of Suzanne's baby clothes and made the dog sit beside her teddy bear at a pretend tea party. Choupette had borne it all without complaint.

We stared accusingly at Rémy Moreau.

"Choupette wouldn't bite someone," said Estée.

"Not without reason," said Josette.

"She's the sweetest little dog in the world," said Rachel.

Margot came forward in the little clearing of the overgrown hedge maze, her hands gripped into fists, her face like thunder. "What did you do?"

"Me?" Rémy cried, backing away from her, though he was six inches taller. "Nothing! I tried to help your sister. When Hugo started criticizing the dinner, she picked up her plate and ran off. She seemed sad." He licked his lips, his short forehead sweating beneath his waxy dark hair. "So I followed her to the barn and tried to comfort her. To make her feel at home..."

"Rémy." His sister's face was so pale it looked almost corpselike as she looked at him beneath the harsh daylight. "You didn't..." She swallowed. "You promised us never again..."

"I barely touched her! I only put my arm around her shoulders, that's all—the sort of gesture a priest might do in full view of his congregation. And then the dog just bit me out of the blue!"

"Oh!" Isabelle Lusigny rushed towards him. "When I think of everything it took to get you out of trouble last time! All the money! The maid. The greengrocer's daughter! Both of them just fourteen! Each time, we had to pay off the family, the police. Even the army didn't want you after that. You said it was an accident, you weren't at fault, they seduced you. You promised it would never happen again!"

"I didn't do anything—I told you!" he said peevishly. "I followed the Vashon girl to the barn, put my arm around her, told her everything was going to be all right—and her wretched dog bit me! Then they both ran off! How am I to blame?" He looked around wildly. "I'm the victim here!"

His sister stared at him, then slapped his face.

Rémy Moreau put his hand on his unshaven cheek, astonished as he stared down at her with big eyes.

Isabelle Lusigny's eyes were wet with tears as she turned back to Margot. "I'm sorry," she choked out. "I told myself he deserved my trust. I told myself I was wrong to worry..."

Margot's forehead crumpled. She turned away. "Let's check the barn." Her voice was thick with unshed tears. "Maybe Lucie left something behind."

We left the brother and sister with her whining toddler in the center of the maze, following Margot without a word, all of us glancing at each other with worry.

I believed Rémy Moreau's story, as far as it went. Whatever he'd intended with Lucie, he hadn't gotten far, not with Choupette there to guard her. But that wouldn't help us find her now. If anything, it only made it more certain that she'd left the Lusignys' land entirely and disappeared to—where?

We found the barn empty, just abandoned horse stalls, old hay and rusted tools. Dappled golden sunlight shone through the broken slats of the barn, illuminating dust motes and little bits of hay floating through the air.

"We never found her bag," Josette said suddenly. "It must be with her. That's good, isn't it?"

"She doesn't have much. Just her clothes and a few francs." Margot's head was bowed.

Guilt went through me. "And I still have her identification papers. She won't get far."

Josette seemed to flinch at my mention of the papers, and I knew she must be thinking the same thing I was: even with my heart breaking over Jean-Luc and my bullet wound aching, how could I have been so stupid as to forget?

All morning on our journey here, my brain had been scrambling to think of how on earth I could possibly manage to take Lucie to America, along with the others. The exit visa. Booking passage on two different ships that were likely already filled to the rafters. And most impossible of all: that American visa. How could I ever convince them? Would this be the last straw?

I'd been so worried, I'd never imagined an even more desperate problem might be waiting for me here at the château.

We left the barn and stood on the gravel circular driveway, blinking in the soft afternoon light. Around us, green fields were bathed in gold, and the castle towered over us, like something out of a fairy tale. All the little girls were crying.

"Wucie," Noémie wailed. She unconsciously rubbed the scab on her arm from the German bullet.

"Did she really run away?" Rachel cried.

"Where could she have run to?" Wiping her tears, Estée pushed up her glasses, clearly trying to calm herself. "We have to think. How can we find her?"

Margot, Josette and I looked at each other. We, too, were trying to be calm. But I could see they were as terrified as I was. The prospect of Lucie lost, on the road... I thought of all those missing children we'd heard of during the exodus from Paris. Who knew what could happen? Who knew if she'd ever be found?

If she'd survive?

She could be hurt, starving. She could be attacked. I thought of the two ruffians in La Ravelle who'd wanted to murder her dog just for sport.

Margot looked up at the château, gleaming white and blue in the sun. From outside, it still looked elegant, serene, powerful, the symbol of a societal order that had lasted hundreds of years. "I can't believe I thought this was a happy place—and safe. I don't know what I—" She shook her head, then glanced at the nearest window and told Josette grimly, "Grab some rocks."

To my shock, the redhead nodded and started looking along the edge of the driveway.

"Here's one," said Noémie and obligingly held up a rock bigger than her hand.

With a gasp, I snatched it from the five-year-old's palm and dropped it back to the ground. I stepped between them and the house.

"Girls, smashing windows won't help anything. We need to find Lucie. Before she's really lost."

That was so obviously true that the girls stopped looking for rocks and stared at me anxiously.

"But how?" Margot choked out, her dark eyes filled with grief and guilt.

"She probably went looking for us. She might already be south—is it possible we passed her on the road?"

"I didn't see her—but I wasn't looking," Josette said.

"Me either," said Margot, chewing her lower lip furiously, and I knew she was likely kicking herself for spending that morning entertaining the girls with stories rather than keeping her eyes on the road. But how could she have known?

"As far as she knew, we were planning to stay in Boulins last night," Josette said suddenly. "Maybe she went north, back into town looking for us?"

"Let's go to the town square and see if she's there or left us a message," I said firmly, with more confidence than I felt.

I took the wheel this time because Margot was in no state. Ignoring the twinges of pain I felt whenever I turned my torso, I drove back the three kilometers to the center of Boulins. The new Nazi checkpoint getting built at the river bridge was nearly finished. As the official date of the armistice wouldn't begin till tomorrow, I hoped they'd just ignore us, as they had yesterday. But this time we were waved down by a German soldier.

"*Bonjour, madame*," he said in heavily accented French. He did not smile.

"*Bonjour.*"

"Where are you going?" He glanced back through the wooden slats of the truck. "You and your children?"

"We are going to pick up my daughter in town."

"Your daughter?" He looked again at all the girls—dark-haired, red-haired, they looked nothing alike. With a shrug, he stepped back. "*Bonne journée, madame*."

"*Bonne journée*."

He waved us forward. Sweating a little, I drove on.

The Boulins town hall seemed desolate, no one offering food or shelter. Townsfolk passing on the street glared at us with hard, suspicious eyes. We parked in front of the police station on the town square. I told the girls, "Wait here."

"But I want to come," Margot said.

"It will be a madhouse," I said firmly. "Better just I go in."

"I'm not just going to sit here."

"Let her help," said Josette.

"Fine." I pointed towards the community boards posted outside the town hall. "Go see if she left a note. But stay right there. Keep one eye on the truck. And don't follow me."

We were now in enemy territory, and there was a powerful German officer who likely walked with a limp because of me. I couldn't risk any of the girls blurting out my name or asking loud questions if I used a pseudonym. Otto Schröder was a foreign propaganda minister; he was assuredly in France. And if he could find me, he'd kill me—and perhaps everyone I loved, for good measure.

Be careful, his former wife had written from Scotland years before. *Otto's never forgiven me. But he hates you even more.*

Perhaps that explained the terse telegram I'd received from the Nazi officer right after war was declared last September. It simply said: *I'm coming for you.*

He'd addressed the telegram to me at St. Agnes's, rue des Orphelines, care of the American embassy in Paris.

Otto Schröder knew where I lived. He knew who I loved.

We needed to get out of occupied France as soon as possible.

The police station was nearly deserted. No Germans. What

a stroke of luck. At this late hour, I saw only a single French policeman on duty.

"Missing girl?" he replied irritably. He shoved a paper across his desk, not bothering to look up. "Fill this out."

I took the official paper, which had spaces to fill in for the missing person's name, last whereabouts and so on. "If I do, you'll help us look for her?"

He gave a low snort. Still not bothering to look at me, he pointed to a nearby desk with his pen. I saw stacks of filled-out papers clearly just gathering dust.

Any dreams I had of a team of policemen searching up and down the streets of Boulins and all the surrounding environs for Lucie crashed. I hesitated to write down my name in a French police report—or the address of John's villa in Marseille. What if Otto Schröder or the Gestapo came looking?

But that worry was dwarfed by my fear for the sweetly naïve, kind-hearted sixteen-year-old. Telling myself that Lucie was already listed in government records as an orphan of St. Agnes's, I wrote down my name and gave St. Agnes's as our address. In the unlikely event the French police found her, I prayed Berthe would find a way to contact us.

Choking back tears, I dropped the paper back on his desk. The policeman didn't look up as I left.

"What did he say?" Josette said eagerly when I came out of the station.

I wiped my eyes. "They can't help us."

Margot and the little girls were already searching the many messages posted outside the town hall in faded writing on crumpled, wind-rattled papers. There were more written in chalk on the sidewalk. Each plea was more pitiable than the last.

Missing for ten days our beloved son Jean, age 6, given to soldiers in a truck heading south near the town of…

Looking for our great-aunt Mireille Latour, age 91, separated with her push-chair near bridge of...

Child found, age 2, parents and name unknown. Please contact in order to...

Many of them were dated days or even weeks before, the chalk half smudged with new messages written over it, the papers fluttering desolately in the soft summer wind. Every loss now was ours. Every lost child was Lucie.

My heart ached.

"What do we do?" Margot whispered, staggering back, her dark eyes filled with tears. It was plain that she'd hoped Lucie would be found here simply waiting, dog at her feet.

Josette squeezed her shoulder. "Don't worry. If she's here, we'll find her."

We spent the next few hours asking everywhere, at little hotels, at schools, anywhere refugees seemed to be. We spoke to the *maire*, asked at every church—of which there were more than a few, in a town of twenty thousand people. We pushed through till sunset was a memory. Then we ate dinner on a grassy hillside, above the moonlit river, silently eating bread and cheese and apples from the bag Élisabeth Ravanel had made for us. I kept an eye on the time on my cheap little watch. At 11 p.m., we were out of time. We couldn't risk getting trapped in Nazi territory.

"What do we do now?" Margot asked, her lovely young face filled with despair.

I had a sudden happy thought. "Lucie knew we were going south, right? Does she have Mr. Cleeton's address in Marseille?"

"She knows the name of his villa." Margot wiped her eyes. "So?"

I exhaled and gave my first real smile of the day.

"So," I said cheerfully, "Lucie would have no reason to walk three kilometers north into Boulins to leave us a message, not when she knows we're desperate to head south. She likely just went straight to the main road, knowing we'd catch her up."

"Then why didn't we see her on the road when we drove back to the Lusignys'?"

"Like Josette said, none of us were looking then. Or maybe she hadn't caught up to the main road yet. Maybe she found a place to sleep last night and she started walking late. She doesn't have a map. But she's smart. She'll find the main road."

"You really think so?" Margot asked miserably.

"Sister Helen is right. And don't worry, Margot—Lucie is stronger than she looks." Josette's expression was gentle. She gave a low laugh. "How many times did we think she needed to be babied and protected, then she'd manage to steamroll us and get her own way?"

"Choupette," I murmured as an example.

The little girls giggled as Margot gave a choked laugh. "Lots."

"Lucie might look like a helpless angel," Josette said firmly, "but she's tough. You'll see."

"Plus, she has her dog to protect her," Estée said stoutly.

"Listen to Josette." I threw the redhead a grateful glance. She was being unusually kind to Margot, and I appreciated it. "We'll get back on the main road and head south. We'll check every town for messages and keep an eagle eye. Shouldn't be hard to notice a lone blonde girl walking with a dog, once we're careful to look. We'll find her."

With a deep breath, Margot nodded, and we all climbed back into the truck.

As we drove away from the Boulins town square, our little group seemed unusually quiet. We were just six now. I missed Lucie and even, somewhat to my surprise, her dog. I hadn't fully realized till now how much joy and energy they brought us. I glanced at the tight shadows on Margot's face and wondered what it was costing her to remain calm.

When we went back through the checkpoint, the same German soldier came over with a flashlight, his expression a little sour.

"*Madame*. Again." He glanced in back. "You did not find your daughter?"

He'd counted the number of children in my truck? "There was a miscommunication," I said carefully. "She must be at a friend's south of the river."

He looked at me, unsmiling. "I assume you have identification papers for all these children."

I felt a chill. I tried not to show it and only smiled. "No, I'm afraid not, *monsieur*. We just left home, and I didn't think it would be necessary, as we were only driving across town."

He glanced back. "Your license plate says Paris."

"We've been staying with friends here the last few weeks." I paused, then added timidly, "I beg your pardon, *monsieur*, but the new rules—I thought they didn't begin until tomorrow?"

"It's past midnight."

"Midnight? But..." I looked back at my watch. It said 11.15 p.m.

"We've changed French time. Your country now has the honor of being in the same time zone as the Reich." The German soldier stared at me, then set his jaw. "I will let you through, *madame*. But next time, you must have identity papers. For all of you. Do you understand?"

"Of course." I smiled widely. "Thank you for being concerned for our safety, *monsieur*. *Merci, bonsoir*."

I gripped the steering wheel as I drove away.

Margot looked at me. "Why didn't you just show him our papers?"

"I didn't want to take the risk." I couldn't tell her about my past, both because it would scare her—and because it scared me.

The main southern road was easy now, in the middle of the night when only the most determined refugees were traveling in defiance of Pétain's orders to remain in place. Some were hurrying back north to their own homes in the occupied zone, Nazis or not, while others continued to flee German rule in spite of all our government's assurances of safety, heading south towards the Mediterranean in blind hope of escape.

We peeled the blue film off our truck's headlights for brighter illumination, and did our best to scour the fields and forests, looking carefully at every passing figure in the moonlight. We drove for only an hour, until we were well out of sight of the demarcation line, and I could breathe again. Then I pulled over to the side of the road, and we all did our best to sleep—trusting that if Lucie and Choupette walked by our truck, they would wake us.

But over the next few days, in spite of our best efforts, we never saw any sign of Lucie's slight figure or her scrawny copper dog. Margot sat forward in the passenger seat, straining to look right and left, peering into every passing car and truck, examining every rock and bush from her window. Josette and the girls did the same in the back, and so did I as I drove. But it was no use.

Traveling so slowly, stopping in every little town, we'd gone only three hundred kilometers—nearly two hundred miles. Even after twenty-five years away from America, my brain often still thought in miles, not kilometers. Strange how permanent a childhood could be.

We'd already dodged a few German military trucks traveling through our supposedly "neutral" sovereign French territory. Broken-down vehicles still littered the road, along with the detritus of beloved, sentimental, expensive items which had probably been dragged all the way across France, only to be discarded here. It was startling to see a grandfather clock standing lonely amid the sunflowers. A wheelchair left askew in the dirt on the side of the road. An oil painting of someone's aristocratic ancestor sneering haughtily from a gilded frame crushing a row of lavender.

We slept in a kindly farmer's barn one night; on the pews of a church the next. Each town welcomed us differently—some of them gave us food and a bit of fuel, others only scowls and hard words. Some greeted us with warmth, others not at all.

Everywhere we went, Margot seemed possessed by a demon, focused on finding Lucie. She barely seemed to eat or sleep. In even the smallest village, she would scour the boards for messages. As I drove the truck, Margot would roll down her window and shout at people walking nearby, "Excuse me, have you seen a skinny blonde girl? With a small dog? I'm looking for my sister!"

My sister, my sister. She went out of her way to use those words, especially when I was in earshot. She clearly hadn't forgiven me for telling her they were not related by blood. Telling her had been necessary, but I still regretted the savage pain of the truth. I loved Lucie Vashon. I wanted my girls to be safe and happy—all of them. But now... what would become of them?

Occasionally, as she said *my sister*, she'd flash me an accusing glance. She would have happily blamed me for everything. But I knew she really blamed herself. And it was eating away at her.

As we traveled further south, the scent of the wind seemed to change, along with the architecture. The wattle-and-daub houses of the north turned to thick, squat stone bastides, or stucco with red tile, or whitewashed farmhouses with blue shutters, covered by pink bougainvillea. The rolling green forests of the Auvergne blended with lavender fields and vineyards. Estée clapped her hands the first time we passed a bright, happy field of sunflowers.

But the road itself was neither bright nor happy. This was

our third day of looking, but there was still no sign of Lucie. Margot was growing gaunter and more frantic by the hour. As we passed yet another abandoned car on the side of the road, its doors hanging open, the wheels at a strange angle that suggested a broken axle, I heard a strange rattle in our own truck's engine and shivered to my bones. I told myself fear was playing tricks on my mind.

Our truck just had to hold on long enough to find Lucie and reach Marseille. After that, we'd have no need of it.

No. Then a whole new set of problems would begin...

We could see cragged mountains in the distance when we stopped for a lunch of stale bread and cheese, a picnic spread on a blanket on the grassy hillside. The air was soft, warm, smelling of lavender. I tried to make the lunch festive to cheer the downcast girls and hoped no one would notice we didn't seem to have quite enough bread or cheese, and the three apples that went to the little girls were wrinkled and bruised, with no apples at all for the adults.

Adults. When had I started thinking of Margot and Josette that way?

Sitting on the blanket, I stared at the lavender fields across the dust and noise of the road. There, the fields were green and soft purple, swaying like ocean waves beneath the hand of the wind. Behind us, I heard birds singing in the dappled sunlight.

You know you're dying? Don't you?

I blinked fast, my throat constricting, even as I tried to take another deep breath, to prove to myself that Jean-Luc's diagnosis was wrong. I couldn't have tuberculosis. Couldn't have lung cancer.

But I felt an ominous crackle inside my lungs.

"Hey! Hey there! Madame Taylor!"

We all looked sharply towards the man's low, deep voice. Margot, who'd scarfed down her bread and cheese, choking it down with a swig of water, was already up and pacing, gritting her teeth with impatience over the slowness of the rest of us to finish.

She stopped when she saw the young man on the road, leaning against a rickety bike, smiling up at us on the hillside.

"You all make a pretty picture," he called to us teasingly.

Josette gasped, looking as if she might faint. "Roger!" she cried and raced down the hill, the little girls stumbling after her with happy cries to embrace Roger Cochet, our cook's young nephew.

I felt less pleased. He'd found us, tracing us from Paris all the way to northern Provence. Turning up like a bad penny.

I'd known many dangerous men over the years I'd worked as a nurse: soldiers, power-mad bureaucrats, young wild rebels. Handsome *gauchos* in South America, during that time I'd promised the US government I'd never talk about. But men like Roger were the most dangerous of all—too charming for their own good. How on earth had he found us?

"What's *he* doing here?" Margot muttered, her arms folded tightly. She'd hung back on the hillside.

I shrugged, rising to my feet. Maybe I was being too harsh. Roger Cochet was still young. Time would tell what sort of man he'd turn out to be. But as I heard the soft squealing laughter from Josette, as she hugged him again and again, I couldn't help myself from wishing he was a thousand miles away.

It took Roger a moment to be free of her arms. "*Bonsoir, les filles.*" He laughed, then, sobering, he bowed his head towards me. "Madame."

"*Bonsoir,*" I said a little sourly. "What a coincidence you found us."

"A lucky chance at last." He beamed. "I thought you'd be in Marseille by now." His eyes lingered on Margot. "I've been looking for you constantly since I left Paris."

I cleared my throat. "You left Berthe?"

He nodded. "When I left her, she was well. Though none too pleased when Germans moved into the house—"

"Germans! At St. Agnes's!" The girls looked at each other in dismay.

"A German officer for some reason alighted on the place, though there were empty houses in better neighborhoods that are far nicer. Most of the high command has billeted at the Hôtel Raphael." Roger looked at me. "You told my great-aunt that if you never returned, St. Agnes's was hers?"

"So?"

"That explains it." He sighed. "Tante Berthe insisted she must remain on the premises, to make sure they didn't burn the place down, and I could not talk her out of it. But she told me I'd better go, so I wasn't sent to work in Germany or tossed in the nearest prisoner of war camp."

"You fled the orphanage, leaving your elderly aunt to fend off the Nazis on her own?" I said sharply.

He gave me a strange look. I had the grace to blush. After all, hadn't I done the same?

Softening my uncharitable words with a smile, I turned and started tidying up the picnic. "You came so far on a bicycle, Monsieur Cochet. I'm glad you made it safely."

"Oh, a bicycle, before that a ride in someone's car, before that walking... You know how it is." He shrugged, confident in his charm. "I'm delighted I found you." His eyes returned to Margot. "Glad to see you all are well."

"We're *not* well," Margot snapped. "My sister is missing." She stopped short, biting her lip. "You—you didn't see Lucie on your way from Boulins?"

"Missing! That's awful." He shook his head. "No, I'm sorry."

"It's a sign, Margot," Josette told her, patting her shoulder. "If Roger found us, Lucie can too." She turned back to the dark-haired young man eagerly. "How long did it take you to get here from Paris? What news of the city? Where are you going now?"

Overwhelmed by her questions, he answered only one. "Um... Marseille?"

"Would you like to ride with us?"

Stroking his chin, which seemed smooth enough that he'd barely need a shave, he said in visible relief, "I would at that. Thank you, Josette. My legs are getting so sore on the bicycle I think I've started going backward."

Her pretty face sparkled, her red hair and makeup perfect, as always. "We have plenty of room, don't we, Sister Helen?"

Hiding a scowl, I demurred, "Once we find Lucie, I'm not sure we'll..."

"We'll make room." Josette and the other girls were already helping him lift his bike into the back of the truck.

Margot's irritated gaze met mine. I had one ally, at least.

"Yay! Roger!" Rachel cried, taking his hand. "Sit in the back and tell us more of your stories."

"Which story?" he responded, amused.

"Any," Josette murmured dreamily. "We love them all."

"I'm not giving him my space if we sleep in the back," Margot grumbled as the two of us carried the blankets back down the hill.

But Roger had overheard. "I don't mind sharing space." He winked at her, and Margot rolled her eyes. Thank goodness at least *she* seemed immune to his charm.

She turned back to me impatiently. "Let's go, let's go."

I nodded with a quick shallow breath. She climbed in the front cab with me, as the other girls eagerly joined Roger and his bicycle in the back. Josette leaned close against him.

But I'd seen the way he looked at Margot. As I started the engine, I could feel trouble coming.

Lowering clouds darkened the sky as we continued down the road. Unless the Nazis had changed the French calendar as well as the time, it was June 27. At this pace, we'd reach Marseille just days before the departure of our ship. We had just enough fuel. I still had some money left. If we found more food and water on the way—and nothing else went wrong…

It's all going to be fine, I told myself, in the same firm way Jean-Luc told hysterical bleeding patients to calm down and let themselves be treated. In three days, two if we were lucky, we'd be in Marseille, where I prayed we'd find Lucie waiting for us at John Cleeton's villa. Maybe she'd hitched a ride. Maybe she'd arrived already.

Once there, though, we'd have a whole new set of problems. What would we do with Lucie if she was there? What would we do if she was not? How many American visas could be secured? What if I couldn't get them in time? What if…

I stared at the road ahead.

You know you're dying? Don't you?

20

MARGOT

"He's so charming. So wise. He knows so much."

Squeezing my eyes shut, I flopped over on my cot, trying to shut out Josette's soft whisper in the cloisters of the darkened abbey, trying to block out my rage and fear and grief so I could sleep. I needed to rest so I could look for my sister tomorrow. But it was impossible while listening to Josette's endless dreamy dribble-drabble about Roger.

"Are you in love, Josette?" Estée's voice was awed, with the wide-eyed acceptance of an eleven-year-old who fervently believed in romantic fairy tales. I ground my teeth.

It was bad enough that after dinner, when it had started to rain, the three little girls had clamored to sit beside Helen in the dry comfort of the cab, and I'd been forced to sit in the back of the truck for two hours with Josette and Roger. The canvas tarp had finally started to disintegrate, and soft drizzle had pooled over the flatbed as I'd watched Josette, usually bullishly head-strong in her opinions, disintegrate, too—into a vapid would-be coquette, simpering and touching Roger's arm, asking him again how he'd been so smart to know he should walk away from his regiment when his commanding officer disappeared, how he knew so much about the world, how his arms were so muscled and strong, etc. etc. It all made me gag.

If Roger was uncomfortable with her hero worship, he hadn't shown it. Instead, he'd answered her questions, explained the provenance of his deep insights and kept sneaking little glances at me, as if he'd expected at any moment, I, too, might join the Roger Cochet Fan Club. Ugh.

When traffic slowed on the road in the next town, forcing Helen to drive the truck at a snail's pace, I'd hopped down and walked in the misty drizzle, my big shoes getting wet in the puddles on the road. It was easier that way, to ask everyone we passed about my sister.

I was the one who'd insisted we keep going, even after the late summer twilight had turned violet, long after the little girls had fallen asleep in the front cab and even Josette was complaining and wanting supper. Finally, Helen pointed out it was getting too dark to see, with the fading blur of our one headlight (the other had burned out), and if I kept walking I might get hit by a passing car, which would do Lucie no good at all. With ill grace, I'd agreed to stop at the next town and sleep.

"Besides," Helen added, "you never know—we might find Lucie there."

Her words cheered me, especially when I saw the moonswept village surrounding the stark grandeur of an old Romanesque abbey on the hill, beneath the dappled moonlight of heavy dark clouds. It did look like the kind of whimsical place my sister would seek out for shelter. We went to the *maire* in the town square, and I crossed my fingers, holding my breath as I asked them the same question I asked everyone.

But we found nothing—no Lucie, no note. No one had seen a blonde girl traveling alone with a little copper-haired dog. We were directed to the abbey on the hill for food and shelter, but she wasn't there, either.

At least the nuns offered us a comfortable place to sleep in their cloister overlooking the abbey courtyard. They also insisted that Roger, as a man, must sleep separately in the outlying grange, with other refugee men. Small favors. And they'd fed us well—a beef-and-bean cassoulet, a southern dish I'd never tried before. It had been served hot, satisfying after so many hours in the cold summer drizzle. But I hadn't let myself enjoy it. How could I, until Lucie was found?

"Roger says he has friends in Marseille. Soldiers who left the army before the armistice, like he did. Patriots." Josette's voice. "De Gaulle's calling on all good Frenchmen who still want to fight to join him in England. Roger says he might go..."

"He's so brave," sighed Rachel in the darkness.

Pulling my pillow over my head to block them out, I tossed on my cot, pulling the thin borrowed blanket tighter, trying to get comfortable. Trying to force my body to sleep.

"Oh yes, he is. Not just brave but so smart. Roger has all kinds of plans to..."

It was no use. Teeth clenched, I pushed the pillow aside. My eyes opened wide in the dark, and I stared up at the shadowy stone ceiling above us as I breathed the warm night air. I looked past the columns of the cloister to the dark greenery of the courtyard garden.

How could Josette be so lovesick over Roger at a time like this? Lucie was missing. Was she somewhere safe or sleeping out in the night? Was she suffering—in pain—*scared*?

Pushing the blanket aside, I abruptly sat up, the pillow falling to the stone floor. We'd all slept in our clothes, as it was a public space, and anyway I'd insisted, so we could leave all the sooner in the morning. My heart was pounding. I couldn't hold myself still.

"I'm going for a walk," I whispered to Helen, who'd settled into a nearby cot. Her eyes were closed, but I knew she wasn't sleeping. I could tell by the uneven wheeze of her breath.

"Don't go far," she said, not opening her eyes but not trying to stop me. I wondered if she'd stuffed her ears with cotton, to be able to endure Josette's romantic yammering.

I walked back through the cloisters, crossed through the courtyard, unlocked the wooden door that led outside and went out into the night. The abbey bell started its sonorous ring for midnight prayers, echoing plaintively into the night like a funeral bell. *I toll for thee*. I shivered.

It was official—June 28.

I was eighteen years old. A woman grown.

Outside the abbey were more shadowy gardens. I took a deep breath of lavender and cypress, and looked up at the abbey's spire, sharp against the moon. I heard the hooting of an owl from the forest, the distant howl of a wolf. The rain was over, the clouds lifted; the night was warm, and I could see the stars twinkling coldly down.

Lucie. She'd been my one thought, day and night, since we'd left her with those wretched Lusignys—and Rémy Moreau, who deserved far more than a slap for scaring her. Though I'd tried to blame Helen, I knew it was my fault. I hated myself for abandoning her. For thinking, even for a moment, it was the right thing to do.

Every time I tried to eat, I'd wonder if she was starving somewhere, and food tasted like ash in my mouth. I was almost afraid to sleep, since the nightmare I'd had while sleeping in a barn two nights ago, of Lucie lying on a bed of rocks, beneath the rain, trapped in a ravine, starving as the panicked echo of her dog's barking slowly faded. I was haunted by ghosts of what might be.

The ghost she might already be.

Lucie's not really your sister. Helen's words were still a dagger in my heart, no matter how many times I told myself she'd been lying, that she just hadn't wanted the inconvenience of returning to Boulins.

But it was true Lucie and I looked nothing alike. Strangers

had occasionally commented on it, their eyes sliding between us: Lucie pale and blue-eyed, a slender waif with wispy blonde hair; me six inches taller and sturdy, with dark curly hair, dark eyes, dark brows. Lucie floated; I could lift heavy things and run for kilometers. Our temperaments were even more different.

So? I raged in my heart. *It doesn't mean a thing.*

And yet...

No matter how many times I told myself Helen had lied, I couldn't quite believe it. For all her sins of omission, I'd never known her to outright lie. And if it wasn't a lie, that must mean it was... true?

No. I took a shuddering breath, pacing in the darkness. I heard the wind rustle through the trees, dead leaves crackling beneath my feet. I'd already lost too much. I'd lost my sister somewhere to the backroads of France. I couldn't let Helen's words take the comfort of our bond away, too.

Not just my sister but everything that made me *me*. Because if I was really adopted, if I wasn't the orphaned daughter of Claude and Violette Vashon, dairy farmers from Meaux, then who was I?

"Margot?" Roger's husky voice.

Wiping my eyes, I turned guardedly, making sure my expression gave nothing away. But he still somehow knew.

His smile disappeared. "What's wrong?"

"I just hate wasting time." I stared at the grass beneath his old shoes still on my feet. The soles remained damp from rain puddles on the road and were starting to wear thin. "We never should have come here. We should have kept driving through the night. There's enough moonlight."

"You agreed to stop."

"Because..."

"Because you thought your sister might be here."

I turned away. When I spoke, my voice was muffled with unshed tears. "What are you doing out here, Roger?"

He came a step towards me in the dark garden, beneath the stark shadows of the old stone abbey. "I couldn't sleep in the grange. All those men snoring and sweating in the heat, plus the old smelter still smells like sulfur." He rolled his eyes. "Like the entrance to Dante's Inferno. I thought I'd go for a walk." He hesitated. "Actually, I've been standing outside the abbey for an hour. Trying to decide whether I could convince the nuns to let me check on you."

He was looking at me with odd intensity. I shifted my feet. "It's not quiet in the cloisters, either."

"Women don't snore surely?" he said lightly.

"Snoring would be an improvement. It's Josette. She won't shut up about you." I glared at him in the moonlight. "You should stop encouraging her."

His eyebrows lifted. "Encouraging her?" He sounded incredulous. "How?"

"By letting her hang on your every word. She thinks you're some kind of hero, and you let her believe that. We both know that's not true."

I thought I saw a flash of hurt in his eyes before he gave me a crooked smile. "You know me better, eh?"

"Yes." I folded my arms, looking down at the river, shining in the moonlit valley. "From the moment I saw you pilfering liquor and cigarettes from the *café-tabac* in Paris."

"As Tante Berthe explained, I was liberating them..." His expression sobered as he came closer. "I might surprise you someday, Margot. If you'd just give me half a chance."

I faced him straight on. "Surprise me how?"

Roger lifted his chin. "I've decided I'm—I'm going to fight. To find others who don't want to surrender." He looked at me earnestly. "Did you hear about the radio address from de Gaulle?"

It was all I could do not to roll my eyes. "I heard Josette mention it. So you're off to England, are you?"

He flinched a little at my tone but said only, "No one knew de Gaulle's name before now. He was a nobody, the new under-secretary of defense, but when our government gave up, he fled to Britain with Churchill rather than surrender. De Gaulle is calling for all free men to resist the Nazis. And for his courage, Pétain has labeled him a traitor." His lips twisted at the name of our new prime minister. "But once I'm in Marseille, maybe I can catch a ship to Lisbon. And from there, I hope, to London…"

"So you're off to save la France," I said sardonically. "You're going to sacrifice your life and be a big hero." Snorting, I shook my head. "Josette might believe that story."

"But you don't."

"No." But my heart hurt a little, and I knew my bitterness wasn't really targeted at Roger. It was at myself, for abandoning my sister so I could go to university and become a lawyer.

I hated myself. Which meant I hated everyone.

Roger came closer in the dark garden outside the abbey, almost close enough to touch. "You really don't like me, do you?"

"Why should I?"

He said quietly. "You see through my act. That's what Josette loves, by the way, not me. But you're different. You see right through me. You see who I really am."

Something in his expression made me catch my breath. He was too handsome, too strong, too close. I felt a strange tension sizzling through my body, but I said nothing.

Roger looked down at his hands. "I deserted the army. I've done things against the law. I've been selfish my whole life. I don't want to be that man anymore, Margot." He took a deep breath. "And since last year, when we met, I haven't been able to stop thinking about you. Your haunting eyes. Your beauty. But it's more. You truly don't care what anyone else thinks, as long as you're true to yourself. It's a rare quality."

His fingertips touched the dark curls tumbling over my shoulders. Our eyes held in the moonlight.

I trembled. I couldn't let him come any closer. I didn't know why. I just suddenly knew if I did, my life would change.

His gaze dropped to my lips. "You make me want to be more…"

"I should go." I turned and fled, racing back through the wooden gate, which I relocked with shaking hands before returning to the safety of the cloisters where all the women were sleeping. Josette and Rachel were silent now, aside from deep breathing and an occasional quiet snore. But my heart was pounding. I carried with me the image of his handsome face, the yearning in his dark eyes.

Wordlessly, I picked up my pillow and blanket and climbed back into my cot. In the silent night beside the shadowy courtyard, even as I told myself I wouldn't be able to sleep, I closed my eyes and fell into a dreamless slumber, the deepest and hardest I'd had for days.

Good thing, too.

The next morning, after being reunited with Roger—I greeted him coldly—we'd barely traveled forty kilometers through sunlit lavender fields and vineyards before the traffic on the main road started to slow. Then it stopped altogether, and we found ourselves at a standstill on the main road, with nothing but parked cars ahead and behind. *Again*.

"There must be an accident," Helen said, fretting, as she struggled to look ahead. She flinched every time she moved, and I could tell she was in pain from sitting upright in the cab for too many days. Her breathing was hoarse, too. Sitting beside her, I glanced back through the window.

"Looks like there's a Nazi convoy way behind us, trying to get through." I grinned, smacking my lips. "Just as stuck as the rest of us."

She flinched again, twisting to look behind us. She seemed

to hunch down whenever Nazis passed by, but maybe it was my imagination. The Germans we'd met so far had been polite to us —other than invading and pillaging our country—and I couldn't imagine any reason they'd take particular interest in a middle-aged American headmistress. America was still neutral in the war.

Helen peered at the map, stretching it out over the steering wheel. Our truck hadn't moved for ten minutes. "We need to get off this main road."

"But what if Lucie's walking just ahead—"

"Margot." Helen looked at me. "You must know Marseille's our best chance now."

I stared at her, then sighed, giving up the forlorn hope. We were so far south of Boulins, even I was forced to admit it was a laughable fantasy that Lucie could have hiked ahead of us on foot. Far more likely that someone had given her a ride south. We had to pray she was waiting for us at John Cleeton's villa in Marseille.

Helen placed her finger on the map. "We can cut through here."

I looked down at the spot doubtfully. We were lucky she'd thought to bring a map from Paris—most people didn't own one, so hardly any refugees risked taking side routes off the main road.

And yet... I frowned at the amorphous green blob on the map marked *Luberon*. There were precious few towns inside the mountainous wilderness, and only a few roads. "Are there enough details on the map?"

"We'll figure it out. Here." Her face had turned pale. "I think... you'd better drive for a while. I need to... stretch out..."

The fact that she'd make such an admission made me worry. She seemed hobbled by exhaustion, barely able to catch her breath as she went to stretch out in the back of the truck with Roger and the little girls to look after her. Climbing into the driver's seat in her place, I bit my lip. Surely Helen's injury should have been well on its way to healing by now, shouldn't it? But she still moved stiffly, often wheezing for breath.

I heard startled voices from the back of the truck when Helen appeared. Roger, who'd never ventured any opinion about our route before, actually tried to argue with her that we shouldn't go into the Luberon but should remain on the main road.

"Traffic will start moving soon," he pleaded. "We don't want to be stuck in the mountains with winding dirt roads."

Even exhausted, Helen put him in his place. "It'll be slower but more direct. Besides," she added bitterly, "this main road is crawling with Nazis. I'm sick of the sight of them."

"I guess I'm your navigator now," Josette said brightly, climbing into the passenger seat beside me. Amid my roiling anxiety about Helen, her forced cheerfulness seemed unbearable, and so did her frequent mournful glances towards the back of the truck. *Nom d'un chien*, was the girl unable to cope without Roger for even a few hours?

Grinding my teeth, I started the engine. "Just tell me where to go."

For a moment, she looked tempted to say something rude, but she only replied, "Let's get off the main road." She picked up the map, then looked up and down for a full minute before she finally proclaimed, pointing, "Take that side road."

It was the only visible exit from where we were parked on the main road. I barely kept myself from rolling my eyes. It had taken her a full minute to see something so obvious?

But it got worse. So much worse.

By early afternoon, we'd gotten lost several times in the cragged hills and valleys of the Luberon, amid the olive groves and cedar forests. Once, we turned on to a road that became a tiny goat track that twisted up the limestone canyon, forcing us to laboriously turn the truck around to double back; another time, I followed her directions perfectly only to realize we'd just spent an hour breathing dust over a rocky hill and ended up in the same place where we'd started. I was getting cross. I wished we'd gone through Avignon. I heartily wanted to kill her.

"Haven't we already gone through this town?" I demanded as we drove along the slender cobblestoned main road of yet another picturesque village. "Josette, are we going in circles again?"

"Um... let me check."

"*Josette.*"

"Uh..." She was frowning, staring at the map. "Give me a minute."

Same honey-colored village church, same stone houses with sloping tile roofs surrounded by forest and a vineyard; same scant shops and cafés. It looked perhaps a little bigger than the last lonely village, but was it actually the same one?

"We're lost again," I accused.

"No," she snapped, turning the map upside down.

As we drove through the village, I saw a lonely Nazi truck parked near a tiny police station, across the street from a bar with a black cat on the sign. I exhaled, relaxing as I saw the village's name above the small building of the *maire*. "Caraillon. New town."

"Told you," she said, visibly relieved. She pointed at the map. "Caraillon."

But still—Nazis in the Luberon's wilderness? I wondered how far we'd have to get before we stopped seeing German trucks. Though officially the lower part of France was independent and neutral, and not the vassal of Germany, everyone knew the Nazis now ruled Paris and the rest of France, and most of Europe, really. And now even here we saw the plain evidence of Germans at liberty.

Past the tiny, sleepy town of Caraillon, we reached a fork in the road.

"Which way?" I asked.

"Uh." Josette held the map one way, then the other. "I'm not sure." She peered out her window, tilting her head to try to see past the tall white limestone cliff that pressed against the road to the right like a towering wall. "Are we going east or west?"

"Are you serious?" I looked at her, wide-eyed. "We're going south, you idiot."

"I know that," she snapped, "but I'm not sure how far we—"

"I don't know why you bother navigating." Seething, I snatched the wrinkled map away. "*Noémie* would be better at it."

"Hey!"

Ignoring her, I gritted my teeth and placed the wrinkled map over the steering wheel. "I'll do it myself."

"Fine. It wasn't my idea," said Josette huffily. "I never claimed to be any good at reading maps."

I looked over the green blob on the map, but embarrassingly I couldn't make head or tails of it either. Though there was no way I'd admit this to Josette.

"Well?" she demanded.

Peeling my eyes away from the map, I peered ahead to look at the fork in the road. The winding, thin canyon road headed south, while the other went towards the forested mountains to the east.

Hearing Helen and the girls laughing with Roger, Josette glanced at the back window longingly. "Now, if you don't need me..."

"Honestly, can't you survive without his company for five minutes?" I demanded. "It's getting ridiculous."

"Roger is special," she said defensively, tossing her perfect red waves. "If you had any imagination or romance in your soul, you'd see it."

His dark eyes shimmering in the moonlight. *You're different. You see right through me. You see who I really am.*

I could have wiped the smug look off Josette's face if I'd told her. But something stopped me. Last night still seemed like a dream. I didn't want to make it real.

Setting my jaw, I turned away. "You're the most pigheaded girl who ever lived."

"Roger was the first to tell me I was pretty enough to be a movie star. He said I could do anything I wanted in life. Can you imagine anything so sweet? And the way he takes care of his great-aunt…"

"You mean by ignoring her," I said over the lump in my throat, "then occasionally stealing her a bottle of liquor?"

"I told you, he did more than that! You're being mean!"

I stared at her incredulously. "And you're being stupid."

"*Stupid!*" She glared at me. "You're just jealous because *for once* someone likes me more than you. You're so selfish! You can't bear it if someone else gets any attention!"

I sucked in my breath, whirling my head to face her. The map I'd been holding with my wrist crumpled and fell to the floor of the cab as the steering wheel twisted and the truck jerked to the right. "That's it! I can hardly wait until you're in America, so I never have to see your face again—"

The truck exploded.

We were lifted off the ground and propelled forward. As Josette gasped, I twisted the steering wheel in desperation, but it did no good. I had no control. From the back, the little girls screamed, Helen cried out and I heard the low, desperate baritone of Roger's voice, telling them to hold on to something, *hold on.*

The truck slammed hard into the solid limestone cliff to our right, then spun around, dragging us away from the road. With a sickening wobble, we started to tip over, then slammed into a hollow recess of the cliff. The truck fell back to the ground, still upright.

But we'd landed at a strange angle, hidden from view of the road. I panted for breath and looked at Josette, who was doing the same. Her terrified eyes met mine.

"Are you all right?" I managed.

Wide-eyed, she nodded. We both got out and rushed to the back.

Estée, Rachel and Noémie were all crying, pressed against the back of the cab, with Helen cradling them together and Roger protecting all of them with his wide arms, his hands tight against the slats of the walls.

"Is anyone hurt?" I cried. If I'd accidentally hurt them, on top of Lucie...

Roger lowered his arms stiffly. I saw red marks slashed across his hands, where he'd gripped the wooden slats to keep Helen and the girls from flying out of the back during the truck's spin. He looked down at them. "Everyone all right?"

Helen nodded, rubbing the back of her neck, checking the little girls for injury. "Everyone safe?"

"Ow," Noémie complained, now she could move again. "Estée stepped on my foot." She bashed the eleven-year-old with her teddy bear, which after weeks of travel now looked dusty and worn, the stitching of its mouth loose, one of its eyes missing.

"You elbowed me," the girl retorted, adjusting her glasses. "Then screamed like a baby right in my ear."

"I'm not a baby." Noémie's lower lip stuck out. "*You* are."

"Watch your big fat mouth."

"They're fine," Helen said in relief. As she wiped her eyes, her hand seemed to tremble. She looked at Roger. "Will you help me down?"

A moment later, we were all standing on terra firma,

surveying the truck glumly. The problem was easy to diagnose. A tire had blown.

"We just need a new tire, that's all." Josette looked at Helen. "It's not that hard... right?"

Helen didn't answer. Staring at the exploded rubber, she stiffly got down on one knee, rubbing her hand over the shredded tread, as if she could magically heal it with her touch. "I... I don't..."

"Maybe we could just walk to Marseille?" suggested Estée hopefully.

That question was answered, alas, by a quick consult of the map.

"It's a hundred kilometers, at least. Sixty miles." Helen put her hands on her forehead. "We only have three days." She gave a laugh that sounded almost hysterical. "We're not going to make it."

I'd never heard her sound so helpless, so defeated. In all the years I'd resented Helen for her bossiness, wishing she could be cut down a peg or two, I'd never imagined the reality could be so awful.

Kneeling, Roger glanced beneath the truck. I saw a flash of concern over his face as he rose, swiftly masked as he turned to Helen with a relaxed, confident smile.

"As Josette said, we need a new tire. Shouldn't be too hard. I worked as a mechanic in the army. Didn't we just go through a village?"

"Caraillon," Josette murmured.

He nodded. "I'll bike back and see if I can buy one."

"Oh? Just like that?" I retorted. "Don't you know there's a war on? Hundreds of refugees have probably gone through here. We're not going to find a spare tire just waiting. Even if there were, how would we pay for it?"

Roger shrugged, pulling a box of cigarettes from his pocket.

"So I'll steal one. We passed a truck similar to ours in the last town. I bet their tires would fit."

"You want to steal someone's tire?" Rachel said, eyes wide.

"Not *someone's*." I stared at Roger, my blood turning to ice. "The *Nazis*. That truck in the last village was German-made, too. An Opel, like ours."

"No," Helen breathed.

"You wouldn't dare," Josette said.

Roger's smile widened to a grin, a twinkle in his eye. "How hard could it be?"

21

MARGOT

Roger's plan was simple, he said. Foolproof. He'd "liberate" a wheel off the Nazi truck while the soldiers were distracted.

"Distracted by what?" Helen asked sharply.

He smiled. "Men forget everything when there's a pretty girl around. Especially *young* men," he added almost pompously, from his elderly perch of twenty-two. He looked between Josette and me. "The whole world knows that French girls are the prettiest and most charming of all."

Josette blushed beneath his praise, and even I had to fight not to feel flattered. Then she looked at me, and I looked at her, and I could see we were sharing the same thought: neither of us thought the other had any such charms of enticement. I wasn't too thrilled by the idea of trying to flirt with a German, either.

"Have my girls distract Nazi soldiers?" Helen stiffened. "Are you out of your mind? There must be another way."

He tilted his head. "Such as?"

"We find a used tire to buy from someone, anyone. I have a little money left." She reached into her valise and pulled out the pitifully small number of francs, which she held out to him. "Surely someone needs money!"

Shaking his head, Roger gently closed her hand over the bills. "Margot is right." He glanced at me. "Even on this backroad, many refugees have surely picked it clean—whatever our wartime authorities hadn't already taken. You know how hard it's been all year to find any tires or engine parts. Even if we found a tire for sale, it would be at ten times the regular price. You don't have enough money."

Helen's shoulders slumped. "Fine," she said in resignation. "But if we must steal, it can't be from Nazi soldiers."

"You'd rather steal from good Frenchmen, who are struggling just like us?" Josette said indignantly.

"She has a point," I said.

With a deep breath, Helen tried to square her shoulders, as if her injuries weren't still paining her. She wheezed softly, "If it must be the Germans, then... then I will be the one to distract them."

Roger bit his lip. "Madame Helen, forgive me, but—you would remind them only of their mothers. They would not wish to spend time talking to you, for fear you meant to upbraid them or ask them to take out the garbage. I'm sorry. It must be Josette and Margot."

She stared at him, then looked down, holding her hands over her injured body. Looking up again, she stuck out her jaw. "*Non.* I won't risk it. That is my final decision."

I put my hands on my hips. "It's not for you to decide. We're not children anymore."

"You're wrong. You—" She stopped with an intake of breath, covering her mouth with her hands. "Margot. It's the twenty-eighth. You're eighteen today."

"Eighteen!" Josette exclaimed a little enviously.

"*Bon anniversaire!*"

"Happy birthday, Margot."

Estée, Rachel and Noémie clustered around me, hugging me. I smiled at them, though I felt no joy in my heart.

"So I'm all grown up." I made my voice cheerful. "And I'm going to help Roger get a tire. So we get to Lucie in Marseille."

"But the danger."

"It's not that dangerous, really." Glancing at Roger, I added, "You know what you're doing, don't you?"

He caught the mood I was trying to project. "Absolutely. I've done this a million times and haven't been caught yet."

Looking at him, Helen managed a ghost of a smile. "You've stolen spare tires off the back of Nazi trucks a million times?"

"Not exactly that, but the method is the same. Don't worry. I'll take no unnecessary risks. The girls will just talk to them briefly, smile a little and I'll whisk away a tire before they have time to blink. Then we're back on the road."

"And you'll carry the tire all this way? Caraillon is at least three miles back."

"I'm stronger than I look," he said solemnly. He grinned. "I'll just roll it."

"We can do this, Helen," I implored. "Please, just trust us."

"Well..." She looked full of misgivings, then helplessly spread her arms. Since we were so determined, what could she do?

"Put this on." Josette handed me one of her dresses, which even I had to admit was far prettier than my usual striped shirts and trousers. I quickly pulled it over my head in the scant privacy behind the truck. When I came back around, she was holding a small mirror, refreshing her own makeup, her hair and dress perfect as always.

"Well?" I said with a clumsy curtsey. "Will I do?"

"Hmm." Narrowing her eyes, she carefully put red lipstick on my lips, then smeared a little color onto my pale cheeks before finishing off my *maquillage* with a puff of powder over my nose. She looked at my wild dark hair, then shook her head with a sigh. "*Zut*, even I cannot fix that."

As I twisted my red scarf into a headband to tame it back,

Roger looked between us with a low whistle. "Wow. They won't even know what hit 'em."

My cheeks turned hot beneath his scrutiny, and I lowered my gaze to study my clunky scuffled shoes. I said to Josette, "I don't suppose you have any pretty shoes?"

"You know your feet are too fat, even if I wanted to," she replied, adding, "Don't stretch my dress out," before she lifted her face into a smile and walked towards Roger.

"Are you both sure about this?" Helen said, looking between us unhappily as the three younger girls exclaimed over the shocking spectacle of me in a dress.

"You look like Cinderella!" Rachel said.

"I want a new dress," Noémie sighed.

Josette and I looked at each other.

"We can do this, Helen," I said confidently.

"We can," Josette echoed.

Helen took a deep breath. There were tears in her eyes as she embraced us both. She even kissed the top of my head, shocking me a little, before she looked me straight in the eyes. "Be careful." Her voice caught. "Come back as soon as you can."

"Nothing to worry about. We'll be right back," Roger said cheerfully, as if we were running down to the *épicerie* for a bottle of milk.

And the three of us left, Roger pushing his bike, walking around the curve of the cliff that hid the truck in a hollow recess. We started north along the canyon road, avoiding the occasional cars and puddles of mud from last night's rain.

"I'll bike on ahead of you," Roger said a few moments later. "If anyone sees you from now on, you should appear to be two girls alone. Did you see where the truck was? Across the street from the bar with the cat sign?"

"I saw it," I said.

"What do we do once we get there? Just, um"—Josette's

cheeks turned pink—"go up and flirt with any Nazi soldier who's nearby?"

"More or less." Roger grinned, then his smile faded. "Don't worry. I'll be hiding nearby, even if you don't see me. It's why I want to get there first. Try to distract the soldiers for ten minutes."

"How?" I huffed.

He smiled. "Just go and talk to them. Suggest they take you inside the bar for a drink."

Josette was so shocked she briefly stopped walking. "Inside the bar?"

"Is that a problem?"

She looked at him, then started walking again. "No. No problem."

"*Bon courage, mes amies.*" He looked at each of us, then quickened his pace and disappeared up the road with his long stride.

Josette and I walked in silence.

"What did you mean earlier?" she said after a while.

"What?"

"Right before the tire blew. You said something about me going to America. I don't understand. Was it some kind of taunt? You think I'm stupid for dreaming of Hollywood?"

"Just forget about it," I said, not meeting her gaze. I was ashamed I'd said anything, after I'd promised Helen so faithfully I wouldn't. I mumbled, "Sorry."

Josette exhaled. "In that case, I'm sorry, too. I shouldn't have called you selfish. You're not. At least... not always."

"Thanks," I said dryly.

We passed a field of brilliant red poppies bobbing their heads in the sunshine. *In Flanders Fields...* I shivered, afraid for my sister, afraid for everyone in Europe. So many had died in the last war. How many would die in this one?

I walked faster. "We just have to do this, right?"

"Yeah, but…" She faltered. "What do I know about flirting?"

"Not much, considering what I've seen with Roger."

"Hey!"

"Sorry. The truth is, I don't know anything, either. I've never flirted in my life." I gave her a crooked grin. "Hopefully it's like Roger said. French girls are the most charming in the world. We just have to hope it's in our blood."

"I guess so," she said doubtfully.

All too quickly, we reached the slender cobblestoned lane through the village in the valley surrounded by cedar- and pine-covered hills. There were perhaps a hundred honey-stone houses, squat with blue shutters, covered with bright bougainvillea, all huddling together, snug beneath the church bell tower, like placid sheep tended by a shepherd.

Parked in front of a tiny police station, we saw the military truck, with that hideous spider-and-blood flag. A single skinny soldier stood nearby, pacing disconsolately. He stopped to light a cigarette.

Just one German soldier? Only one?

As promised, Roger was nowhere to be seen. I felt Josette hesitate, looking around. I felt her nervousness and fear. What if we couldn't do it? What if the soldier figured out what we were doing and we all ended up in jail—or worse?

Yet what choice did we have except to be brave?

Tossing my hair, I arranged my face into what I hoped was a beguiling smile and went forward. "Excuse me, *monsieur*, might I trouble you for a cigarette?"

The young soldier, who seemed barely older than we were, looked up, startled. Seeing Josette and me crossing the street towards him, he blushed a little and said in German, "*Es tut mir leid, Fräulein, aber ich spreche leider kein Französisch.*"

"May I please have a cigarette?" I answered in German, still smiling, since he didn't speak French. No, why would he? Not at all necessary in conquering a country. My German was rusty, since it had been nearly a year since Fräulein Mueller returned to Austria, but I hoped still serviceable.

His face lit up. "You speak German."

Josette and I shrugged and smiled.

"Of course we've learned the most important language in the world," she said in the same language, which I thought was laying it on rather thick—and also showing off, since her marks in German had always been better than mine. But only because she was better at giving teachers the answers they wanted.

The boy beamed at us. "*Bitte*," he said, offering us each a German cigarette out of his pack, then using his lighter on them, one by one.

I took a long drag, smiling with what I hoped were come-hither eyes. The effect was slightly ruined when Josette, who'd never smoked before, choked on her first inhalation, coughing, her face red. The German soldier and I grinned at each other as I patted Josette's back.

"It's her first cigarette," I told him, lifting an eyebrow. "So tell your friends. You gave a French girl her first time."

His blush deepened, and for a moment, he appeared tongue-tied. He finally said in a flustered voice, "Yes. Um. I will."

Josette's face looked a little green, but she bravely attempted a second drag of the cigarette, which went better. She managed a watery smile.

I peeked up at him through my lashes like I'd seen Mireille Balin do on the silver screen. "Where are you from, soldier?"

"Regensburg." His Adam's apple seemed to travel up and down his throat. "In Bavaria."

"First time in France?"

"Uh... yes."

"Then you perhaps have never tried, uh"—I scrambled to remember—"*pastrie*."

"Pastis," said Josette, as if it was the same word I'd mangled.

Luckily, the soldier didn't seem to notice. She smiled at him, holding her cigarette, letting it burn, no longer trying to smoke it. "It's what we drink here in the south."

"Not to be missed," I agreed and took another smooth puff of my own cigarette, to remind her there were some things I could still do better. The truth was I'd only smoked maybe ten cigarettes my whole life, all during a three-month stint last year when I'd washed dishes at a restaurant to buy Christmas gifts for the girls. The skin on my hands had peeled and turned red, but it was still preferable to secretarial work. "You're just waiting here?"

He nodded towards the tiny police station. "My commanding officer needed to place a call back to Paris. Plus, we are a little lost since we left the main road," he confessed and immediately looked abashed, as well he should be because it was probably a treason punishable by death for a German soldier to ever admit to being lost.

"Sorry to hear it," I said, smiling, as if I couldn't imagine the feeling. "We were just going to that bar"—I nodded across the street—"to get a glass of pastis. If you'd like to join us."

"Oh..." He looked back at the little bar, with its black-cat sign and the name, La Bête Noire. Then he glanced towards the tiny station, where, one could only imagine, his superior and his compatriots were on the phone with Hitler himself, likely planning all kinds of diabolical machinations against the innocent French populace. "I'm not supposed to leave my post..."

"Such a shame. Isn't it, Helyette?" I said sweetly.

She glared at the atrocious pseudonym, then matched my smile. "A real shame, Albertine," she agreed. She allowed her shoulders to sag in disappointment, at just the right angle to show the merest flash of cleavage at her neckline, which I grudgingly had to admit was a brilliant maneuver.

His eyes lingered. The cigarette fell out of his mouth.

Embarrassed, he stepped on it to put it out, as if he'd dropped it intentionally, and glanced at his watch.

"My commanding officer said they'd be in there another hour. I suppose"—he looked right and left—"if we just went in for a quick drink, it wouldn't hurt anything. This village seems like it's full of good, honest Frenchmen."

I smiled, looking at him as if he were the most handsome, interesting thing in the world. A look I guessed this pale skinny boy hadn't seen since he'd crossed the Low Countries into France. Probably not much back in Regensburg, either. "*Wunderbar.*"

"But very quick."

"Of course. Our little peace meeting, yes? To promote the friendship of both our countries?"

"Yes." He seemed clearly relieved to frame it in a way that didn't mean dereliction of duty. He held out his two arms. "*Meine Fräulein?*"

We each took an arm and went into the bar.

It was dark inside, with the window shutters closed against the sunlight. There were six small empty tables and only one customer—an elderly man, muttering to himself at the other end of the bar. He ignored us as we sat down and seemed to be in intense conversation with his own empty glass.

The barman, with dark middle-parted hair and a sweeping mustache, was startled to see two French girls on the arms of a Boche, casual as you please. He was respectful to the soldier, but his mustache shook as he muttered things to Josette and me in French that would have been humiliating if true. I pretended not to hear.

"*Bonjour, monsieur.* Three small glasses of pastis, if you please." I held my breath, hoping the soldier would offer to pay. We'd never thought to ask Helen for money. Fortunately, he quickly set Reichsmark coins on the bar, which the barman had no choice but to accept.

The pastis tasted like licorice, quite horrible. If the barman had spat into our drinks, it could only have improved the taste. I only choked down a few sips. Josette, for her part, was for once the stunning actress she always claimed to be. Polishing off her small glass, she smacked her lips and proclaimed it delicious.

The soldier took a few sips before his mouth tightened like a prune. He looked again at his watch. "Now perhaps we should—"

"What's your name, soldier?" Josette interrupted.

"W-Werner Brunner."

"What are you doing in this part of France, Werner?" I fluttered my eyelashes. "Let me guess. A secret mission?"

He flashed us a look, then puffed out his chest. "On our way to Marseille. Seeking an enemy of the Reich."

"An enemy? Who?" I asked, trying to stretch out the conversation.

He shrugged. "It's not my place to question. If my superiors say she is, she is."

Josette and I glanced at each other. "*She?*"

His Adam's apple bobbed nervously. "I've said too much. You two are going to my head," he added with a weak smile. "I should..."

"Care for another drink?" Josette said.

Werner shook his head. His glass was still half full. He sighed, his teeth chattering as he glanced at the door. "The truth is, I should probably—"

Josette leaned forward, cleavage-first, putting her hand on his arm. "Tell us about Regensburg," she purred.

We did our best to push the limping conversation along, but eight minutes was all we could manage before he looked again at his watch and rose to his feet, clearly fearing his commanding officer.

"So," Werner Brunner said casually as we walked back into

the sunlight, "we're driving to Marseille, as I said. But I'd be happy to see you again if you—"

Then he stopped, eyes wide. We stopped too.

His military truck was *gone*, Nazi flag and all.

"What—?" The soldier stared across the street at the empty spot in front of the mayor's office where it had been parked. He looked all around, as if the truck might perhaps be hidden under a bush or behind a tree. Then he whirled towards us, suspicion in his eyes.

"Is something wrong, Werner?" Josette asked, channeling Lucie's angelic innocence.

He looked at her, and for a moment, he was uncertain. Then he turned to me.

The moment he saw my guilty face, the jig was up. I could feel fire in my cheeks. My feet were already backing away.

"*Schnell, kommt her!*" The young soldier ran inside the police station, shouting, "*Helft mir!*"

Josette grabbed my arm in a panic, dragging me down the lane and around the houses at the corner. We heard the noise of an engine, and the Nazi truck suddenly roared behind us.

Roger thrust his head out of the driver's-side window. "Get in!"

22

HELEN

The sun was hot. I watched the little girls play in the grass and dirt in the quiet, hidden hollow of the limestone cliff, tucked away from the gravel road. I could hear an occasional car drive by. For the last hour, the girls had played hopscotch over lines and squares traced in the dirt.

But the distraction was starting to wane. Estée was looking bored and yet didn't seek out her small dusty pile of books, perhaps because she'd read them too many times. Noémie, giving up, flopped down desolately on a patch of fragrant wild lavender, crushed by the earlier spinout of the truck when the tire had exploded. Even Rachel was starting to wilt, her leaps more like shuffles now, and she'd given up trying to get the others to play with her.

I was trying not to think about Margot and Josette, and their valiant—foolhardy?—effort with Roger Cochet to steal a tire in the village. Why had I agreed to it? How could I have let it happen?

I should have been the one risking my life stealing a tire, instead of the one left behind tending the children. I should have found a plan that didn't threaten any of my girls. I still couldn't think of such a plan, but surely...

I took a deep breath; tried to ignore the slight wheeze.

"Why are we still going to Marseille, Sister Helen?" Rachel had come over to stand beside me, her face tired. "If the war is over, can't we just go back home?"

Stroking back her long dark hair, I hugged her sadly. "I wish the war was over. But it's not. You're just not safe in France."

"But—" Her dark eyes looked up at me, a little bewildered. "Isn't Marseille in France?" She scratched her head. "Do I have my geography wrong?" She turned to her sister. "Estée, isn't Marseille in France?"

"Of course." Estée sat at the end of the truck, swinging her feet. "'La Marseillaise' comes from there, silly."

I felt a small chubby hand in mine. Looking down, I saw Noémie, who confided, "I don't mind travewing, but Nounours is tired of it."

I tried to smile at them. "Don't you like picnics and fun? Isn't this a nice break to be out in the fresh air, compared to writing compositions and doing sums in a stuffy classroom?"

"I'd rather be home," said Rachel.

"With the lending library down the street," said Estée.

"Tending my garden," said her sister.

"Sleeping in my own bed," added Noémie.

"Eating Madame Cochet's *poulet et frites*," sighed Estée.

"I miss home." Noémie started to cry, and the sight of the three little girls' pitiable faces was more than I could bear. My lungs felt tight, my bullet wound still dully aching, though it had scabbed over beneath one of the small clean bandages Jean-Luc had given me.

Jean-Luc. I suddenly wanted to cry with them. I'd lost him forever now, even the dream of him.

And now I was scared I'd lose Margot and Josette, as well as

Lucie and her little dog. Where were they? Were they in danger?

Amid the soft sunshine, I breathed in the scent of cedar and lavender and scrub pine. The sky was a brilliant blue above the limestone cliffs. The very beauty of the landscape seemed cruel.

We needed a diversion—all of us.

Snapping my spine straight, I grabbed a blanket and spread it on the grass in the shade of the rusted truck. "Come sit with me, and I'll tell you a secret. Something good."

Noémie stopped crying, her eyes bright, her thumb in her mouth. She curled next to me on the blanket. The Lévy sisters came and sat near me on the soft grass.

"A secret!"

"A happy surprise?"

"It's a present," guessed Noémie.

You shouldn't tell them yet, a voice warned. *Don't promise anything until you have the American visas in hand. It's not guaranteed until then.*

But we needed something better to distract us than hopscotch. We needed *hope*.

"It's a present of sorts..." Leaning forward, I whispered, "After we get to Marseille, all of us are going to board a ship. We'll stop in Portugal..."

"Portugal?" The girls looked at each other.

I smiled. "Then we're going to America."

The thumb popped out of Noémie's mouth, her eyes wide. "America?"

"And even better. No more orphanages. You'll have your own home, where you'll be loved by your own families who want to take care of you."

Three sets of astonished eyes.

"A family," whispered Rachel.

It was a relief. I'd been hatching plans for this for nearly a year, from the moment the Nazis had driven their tanks into

Poland. Blinking fast to hide my tears, I nodded, smiling. "Yes. The three of you will be safe and loved with new families, far away from war."

"We'll take a ship to America?" Noémie asked.

I nodded. "It'll *chug-chug-chug*"—I demonstrated the movement with my hands—"across the ocean, and then we'll take the train."

"We'll speak English all the time there?" said Estée with a little trepidation.

"Yes. But that won't be hard, not for bright girls like you. You're used to it, anyway, with all the English at school, aren't you?"

"I'm scared," said Noémie, her eyes big as she clutched her teddy. "I don't want to go to America."

"There's nothing to be scared of." I hugged her close. "I'll help you settle into your new home. You'll go with Nounours, Noémie, to a pretty city called San Diego, right by the ocean, where you'll be adopted into a large family with three older sisters, in a big lovely house with a backyard and a sweet little dog."

"Three sisters to play with?" breathed Noémie. "And a dog?"

I nodded. "You're all going to be adopted."

For years, the word *adopted* had been forbidden at our orphanage. I'd refused to allow childless Parisians to shop for potential daughters at St. Agnes's, in part because I feared losing Margot, but also because it caused such pain every time a child was rejected or ignored.

Now, it was like magic. The girls were rapt.

"Adopted," Rachel breathed.

I turned to Rachel and Estée. They'd had a hard childhood before they'd come to St. Agnes's, their parents dying within months of each other after Rachel's birth, passed around distant family, treated as burdens no one wanted. I took a deep breath.

"Estée and Rachel, you'll be adopted by a mom and dad who've always longed to have two such smart, kind daughters. They live in a sunny town by the beach not too far from Noémie, in a town called Santa Monica. You'll have two cats, a playground nearby and a synagogue just around the corner. You won't have to attend with a neighbor, like you did in Paris. You'll go with your own family. Doesn't that sound wonderful?"

The three of them looked at each other.

"They—they really want to be our parents?" asked Rachel uncertainly.

"Yes." I felt a lump in my throat. I'd found their new families through old contacts in California, friends of friends, doctors and nurses of the hospital I'd trained in. "And you must all be brave and encourage Josette. She doesn't know yet, but she'll be living in Los Angeles with Miss Clarkson."

"Miss Clarkson!" They smiled at mention of the former St. Agnes's teacher who'd returned to America six months before. Then Estée's face grew wistful.

"But... will we have friends?" She bit her lip. "Will people like us in America?"

"Of course they will," I whispered over the lump in my throat, hugging them. "Who could do anything but love you?"

Estée pulled away, her dark eyes haunted through her glasses. "But what about you, Sister Helen? Where will you live?"

My throat was aching so painfully now I no longer had space to feel anything wrong with my dodgy lungs or my scabby bullet wound. "I'll take you to your new homes, and make sure you're all settled and happy. Then I will write, and I'll always be with you in my heart. And so proud of you."

"But—where will you go?"

Yes, where? I hadn't lied to Margot when I'd told her about a job. I'd planned to pay her a salary to help me ferry the girls across the sea, and then I'd find work as a nurse in

Los Angeles, while Margot attended college nearby. But what
if Lucie wasn't found? Or what if she was, but I was one visa
short?

I couldn't imagine a world where I had to leave my daughter
behind. Never again.

Unless Jean-Luc was right and I had lung cancer. Then I'd
soon travel to a place Margot couldn't follow. My only hope
would be to at least get all the girls to safety before I died.

No. I put my hand to my forehead. I mustn't think that way.
If I had tuberculosis, I at least had a chance of a few more years.
I could go back to the dry desert of my youth—or maybe to
Arizona...

"What is America like?" asked Rachel.

"Wiw we meet Shirwey Temple and Rin Tin Tin?" asked
Noémie.

We were interrupted in our quiet spot by the sound of a
loud engine. We barely had time to scramble to our feet before a
big army truck barreled around the edge of the boulder and slid
to a hasty stop in the dirt. We gasped as Roger, Margot and
Josette tumbled out of it, laughing, wild-eyed with exhilaration
as they turned to us in triumph.

"Sister Helen, you wouldn't believe it—"

"I was about to kill Roger—"

"B-But what is this?" I stammered. "You were supposed to
bring a tire, not a whole truck! Is that...?"

"We managed to get the flag off," Margot said gleefully. "It
wasn't easy."

"There wasn't a spare. We're going to take one of the
wheels. We'd better do it fast." Roger, rummaging in the back of
the stolen truck, resurfaced with a box of tools and a jack—but
not before I saw him tucking something else secretively in his
jacket pocket. I wondered what he'd found in the stolen truck
that he'd decided not to tell us about.

"You stole a truck from the Nazis," I breathed.

"The key was still in the ignition, and I decided it was faster to take the whole thing. Especially since I needed tools, too."

"Josette and I flirted with the guard." Margot was beaming. It was the first time I'd seen her look happy since Lucie disappeared. "It was easy. You did a good job, Josette."

"You mean when I nearly vomited trying to smoke a cigarette?" They grinned at each other like best friends, laughing. "It was awful. I don't know how you managed to look so good."

"Then both of us trying to keep a straight face as we drank that horrible pastis—"

"I didn't think it was so bad, but I almost lost it when we came outside to discover the truck gone!"

"You could have warned us," Margot accused Roger. "I wondered if you'd deserted us, and we were about to be hauled off to jail!"

"How could I warn you?" Roger placed the jack, using it to lift the truck before kneeling by the wheel. "I didn't know I was going to do it myself. But they'll start looking for us. So we'd better hurry..." He pointed at a wrench. "Hand me that."

Josette leaped in front of Margot to give it to him. Margot's lips twisted a little. Amusement? Annoyance?

I turned back to Roger. "Do you know what the Nazis will do if they get a hold of you?"

He shrugged, using his weight to remove the bolts. "They never saw my face."

A chill went down my spine. "But that soldier saw the girls."

"He has no proof they did anything but flirt." He glanced back at them. "Does he?"

Margot shook her head. "He was already in the station when we ran away."

His eyes twinkled. "You did amazingly, both of you—"

"Do you have any idea of the danger you've put us in?" My voice was shrill in my own ears.

The three of them stared at me, shocked.

I ran my hand over my sweaty forehead, thinking of the oceans of dead and eviscerated soldiers and civilians I'd seen in the Great War. The killings I'd seen in Soviet Russia and Turkey and South America in the years afterward, for far less provocation than stealing a military truck. "You have no idea what you've done."

"I've been a soldier in a wartime army, *madame*." Roger rose to his feet with icy politeness. "Forgive me, but I believe I understand far better than you." Brushing the dirt and dust off his hands on his trousers, he glanced at Margot and Josette. "I could use some help."

The two silently helped Roger pull the solidly made wheel off the German truck, then roll it towards our own rusted vehicle. He exchanged the good Nazi wheel for our own useless one.

"Now"—he pushed the wheel with our shredded tire back towards the Nazi truck—"we'll put our old one on theirs."

But his voice was restrained. Their joy had fled. My panicked criticism had melted away their pride and camaraderie.

I'd had bravado when I'd been young, too. I remembered the thrill when Jean-Luc and I had just managed something impossibly dangerous, like performing life-changing surgery under heavy fire. Or the things I'd done afterward, in Germany, when I'd helped Flora escape her abusive marriage. In South America, after I'd lost both Jean-Luc and our child, and barely cared if I lived or died, I'd done my government a favor— because why not? Recklessness, stupidity, risk… that feeling of being truly alive.

"Why are you replacing the wheel on the Germans' truck?" Josette frowned. "Why bother?"

Roger sat back on his haunches, looking sweaty and handsome and capable. "They'll find their truck eventually—I trust that much about German efficiency—and I want them to think it was just stolen by some kids on a joyride until the tire blew. That way they won't think to look for a different truck with a stolen tire. I hope." He focused, quickly screwing the bolts to attach the ruined wheel, then rose to his feet. "Ready?"

I quietly herded the little girls into the back of our own truck once more. I still couldn't bring myself to say *sorry* or even *thank you*. Not until we were away and I knew for sure that their Nazi escapade wouldn't be the end of all of us.

I knew I was being churlish. Roger's plan had worked. If not for him and Margot and Josette, we wouldn't be getting back on the road right now. Why wasn't I grateful? Why was I so angry? So—afraid?

It wasn't just because I felt marginalized, left out of the mission for being too old, too *motherly*. It was more than that.

Stealing the truck, risking that added attention, was even more dangerous than Roger realized.

"Margot, Josette," Rachel cried suddenly, clapping her hands. "Wait till you hear what Sister Helen told us!"

"We're not going to stay in Marseille," Estée said eagerly. "We're getting families, all of us, and—"

"We should get going," I said hastily. "I'll drive. Josette, come sit with me."

The redhead tossed me a pleading glance. "I'm really not any good at navigating..."

"She's horrible," Margot affirmed. "I can navigate for you."

"No. I want Josette," I insisted. When they stared at me, I added in a gentler tone, "The only way to improve is through practice."

They nodded. That sounded more like what they expected from me.

But for once, I wasn't worried about improving anyone's character. I needed to tell Josette about the plans for America before the little girls blurted it out. And more.

It was past time for Josette to know the truth—about everything.

Climbing into the driver's seat, I tried to ignore the pain twisting through my body. My half-healed bullet wound still hurt, and I ached all over—from exhaustion, from traveling hard at fifty, from whatever was wrong with my lungs.

Josette climbed into the passenger seat with slumped shoulders. Behind us, we could hear the girls chattering happily to Roger and Margot. I closed the window between us. "Don't worry about them."

She looked down disconsolately at the wrinkled, dirty map.

I started the engine. "We need to get towards a city, so we can hide in the traffic. Out here on this country road, we're sitting ducks."

Josette looked at me, startled. "But we took their truck. They'll be stuck in Caraillon, at least for a while. They won't bother chasing us…"

"Don't count on it," I said grimly. Though the Germans we'd seen in the unoccupied zone generally seemed under orders to be polite in their invasion of France—unlike how they'd treated the unfortunate citizens of the Low Countries and Poland—I doubted they'd show much kindness to any civilians who'd outright stolen military property. And Otto Schröder was already looking for me.

Leaving the stolen German truck in the hidden recess of the cliff, I drove carefully around the boulder, looking right and left to make sure the coast was clear. I saw no one in either direction, so I pulled our truck onto the slender gravel road. The new tire seemed fine, causing just a slight list to the left and shudder of the axle, with the other three tires nearly bald in comparison.

"Now. Look at the map and tell me where to go."

"Well…" Josette hesitated, then peered at the map. "In a few kilometers, a road will branch off right that leads towards a busier road. But we'd have to drive east, instead of south. We could lose ourselves in traffic sooner, but it would add time getting to Marseille..."

"We'd better just do it," I said, glancing behind me.

I drove as fast as was safe on a thin road weaving up and down and all around pine- and scrub-covered crags, dodging the occasional horse and cart, and once even a farmer drawing cattle down to summer pasture. I went around the animals carefully, then increased speed as much as I could, with five people sitting in the open back of the truck.

Josette pointed at a dirt road, barely visible between trees. "Turn there."

"You sure?"

"I'm sure."

I turned the wheel, and as we left the gravel road behind, I stepped on the gas. But once we were some distance from the purloined Nazi truck, I glanced at her out the corner of my eye.

"Josette, we need to talk."

"About what?" Distracted by Roger's and Margot's laughter, she twisted to look in the cab window behind us.

"I just told the little girls that once we reach Marseille... I'm taking them to America."

Josette whirled to face me, her eyes wide. "America!"

She couldn't have looked more shocked if I'd said we were going to the moon. I nodded. "I've arranged passage through Portugal, and we should"—*should*—"have visas waiting for us at the consulate in Marseille." I gave a cheerful smile. "We're going to have a new life. In a new country."

She looked like she was going to cry. "But, Sister Helen, it's so far away!"

"I know."

"What will I do in Marseille without you?" Her voice was sad. "Unless"—she looked at me sideways—"there's a job waiting for me too? Like Margot's?"

Her eyes were oddly watchful. I hadn't lied to Margot about

the job—not exactly—but my cheeks went hot. Suddenly, like the Lady of Shalott, I was sick of all the shadows.

"You're coming to America, too," I told her, gripping the steering wheel.

Her mouth fell open, and a mixture of emotions crossed her face. "But—but why?"

I glanced at her. "This past year, I found out who your parents were."

Josette's face was strained as I told her who'd left her at the orphanage door on Christmas Eve in 1922, and why. The wild scrub-covered hills of the Luberon flew by, beneath a wide blue sky laced with puffy white clouds.

Afterward, she was so pale and stricken, her lipstick looked like a slash of blood against her skin, her hair tumbling like fire over her shoulders.

"All this time I've wondered," she breathed. "I dreamed about who my parents could be. Thought up good reasons why they didn't keep me. Now…"

"Now?"

She turned away. "I wish I didn't know."

"Josette…" I put my hand on her shoulder, desperate to offer reassurance.

She pulled away, wrapping her arms forlornly over her ribs. "Forget it."

"You'll be safe in America—"

Whirling, she glared at me. "You want me to *run away*? To abandon France when it needs me most? To leave *Roger*!"

Caught off guard, I flailed, "A boy you barely know…"

She shook her head fiercely. "I'm not going!"

My hands tightened on the steering wheel. I remembered how idealistic I'd been at her age, dreaming of a happier future. I'd convinced myself Arthur Taylor, the charming, handsome salesman who brought supplies to the hospital where I worked, was a romantic paragon with endless good qualities. But we'd barely known each other when we'd wed.

No wonder our marriage had been nothing like I'd expected. Arthur had been disappointed, too—bitter that I wasn't a sweet, traditional little woman who could make him straighten up and become a big success, just by believing in him enough. But when I went back to nursing for pay after Billy was born, it made my lack of confidence in him clear.

Then they'd died. And Arthur had won our argument forever. He'd been right. I was—would always be—wrong.

I'd left for Europe on the current of a different dream—of giving my life up to the service of helping others in the war. Then I'd discovered that reality was nothing like the patriotic posters showing a beautiful, calm, gentle nurse virtuously tending the wounded and sick. War was a vast nightmare of mud and blood.

The point was, you couldn't fight a romantic dream with reason and sense. You could only fight it with a different dream.

I glanced at Josette out the corner of my eye. "You'll be living with Miss Clarkson until you graduate high school."

"Miss Clarkson?" Her eyes lifted. Then she shrugged with deliberate indifference. "No thanks. She was never my favorite teacher."

But I knew I held the winning card. "I didn't tell you where." I paused, then delivered the ace up my sleeve. "You'll live in Los Angeles. Near Hollywood."

I heard her intake of breath; saw the flash of unwilling excitement in her eyes.

Then she sat back with a shrug. "I don't care about Hollywood anymore. It doesn't matter. Not like true love."

Oh dear.

"You'd go to high school for a year, by the ocean, amid sunshine and palm trees," I tried. "Maybe you'd go to a soda fountain with your friends and get discovered like that starlet in your movie magazine. What was her name?"

"Lana Turner," she said flatly.

"Yes. Her." I increased the speed of the truck. The mountains were getting a little less wild, the fields smoothing out.

Josette glanced at me sharply. "You're taking Margot to America, too, aren't you? That's why you wanted her to leave Lucie behind. You only wanted Margot."

My lips parted in shock. "You... What makes you say...?"

"I thought so." She gave me a hard look. "When are you going to tell her?"

My mouth went dry. "Tell her?"

Her eyes cut through me. "That she's your daughter."

My heart hammered in my chest. I turned to look forward as we bounced over rivulets in the road. I heard the engine give a rattling sound, then suddenly a hard knock that made me jump.

But the knock was from the window behind the cab. Margot's face appeared. "Can you slow down over the bumps? We're bouncing so hard back here our tailbones are starting to fracture."

"There it is!" Josette said suddenly, and looking, I saw a busy road ahead, clogged with traffic. I hadn't realized till right now how worried she'd been about her directions. She flashed Margot a triumphant look. "I took us to the exact right place. On the first try."

"Even a broken clock is right twice a day," Margot said, unimpressed, and closed the window.

"Josette." I turned to the girl anxiously. "Whatever you think you know, you won't..."

"Don't worry." She looked at me sideways. "I won't tell Margot anything. And don't tell anyone about me, either," she added sharply.

"I won't. But, Josette, about America—"

"I'm done talking," she said and rolled down the passenger window.

As we merged onto the main road, where traffic was busy but at least moving steadily, I fell silent, deciding to give her some time to come to terms with everything.

I wondered how she'd known about Margot. How had I given it away? And if Josette knew... could Margot have figured it out, too?

No. Impossible. She would have said something. But she was focusing only on finding Lucie.

I slid open the cab window. Roger was telling the little girls outlandish stories of his life in the French army. But as soon as we hit the main road, even though Margot must have known it was hopeless, she started shouting questions at everyone we passed, whether the other person was walking, driving a car, riding a bike or sitting on a horse.

"Have you seen a blonde girl? With a copper-colored dog?"

"You're wasting your time," I called to her, but she didn't seem to hear. As we traveled down the congested road, she kept at it for hours, until her voice started to crack with strain. Hoarsely, she yelled the question at a family packed into a beat-up sedan that was passing slowly in the other direction.

The father peered at Margot, pushing up his glasses as he slowed. "Yes, about five kilometers back. You a relative?"

I gasped, pressing on the brakes.

"You saw a blonde girl?" Margot repeated, stupefied. "With a dog?"

"I think so," the man said, looking at his wife for confirmation.

She leaned over her husband in the car. "A blonde girl walking with a group. A dog was wandering all over, getting in the way of traffic. Big red dog."

"Almost ran him over," complained the husband.

"Lucie!" Margot breathed. Clasping her hands together, she

looked at me through the cab window, then at Roger in the back of the truck. She looked beautiful in her joy, her lovely dark eyes sparkling, sunshine casting a halo on the long dark hair falling over her shoulders.

"You found her." Roger's voice was full of tenderness and admiration. Josette shifted mutinously in the seat beside me.

"*Donc, les filles*—we'll have Lucie back with us within the hour!" As the little girls cheered in reply, Margot's face appeared in the cab window. "Drive faster!"

"I can't, not without plowing into the car in front of us," I pointed out.

She tried to look down the road. "She should be just ahead."

I heard a louder rattle in the engine, or was I imagining it? We just had to make it a little further, I told myself, gripping the steering wheel as if to give it strength. Just to Marseille. The words were like a drumbeat in my head. *Just to Marseille.*

"Look." Josette pointed, sitting up straight beside me.

I followed her gaze. Just ahead, between a steady stream of cars and an open field of sunflowers, a small, ragtag group of people walked along the side of the road. I saw the slender shadow of a girl. A large dog bounding around them. "Margot! Look!"

"You see her?" Her eager face reappeared in the window. "Slow down! Let me out!"

I saw her intention, but before I could pull over, she flung herself out the back of the truck and fell to one knee. She staggered up, her knee scraped and bloody, then galloped down the road.

"Lucie!" Margot screamed, waving her arms. "We're here. Lucie!"

23

HELEN

I'd barely turned off the truck's engine before Roger rushed past, following Margot down the side of the road. Getting out of the driver's seat, I saw the little girls climbing down from the flatbed. As Estée helped Noémie down, Rachel tripped on the gravel. When the eleven-year-old turned to help her sister, Noémie stumbled off after Roger and Margot, heedless of the steep incline on the side of the road—or the danger from the steady car traffic.

"Josette!" I cried. "Grab her!"

Josette jumped down from the passenger seat and flung herself at Noémie, dragging the little girl safely back.

"Ow," the five-year-old complained. "Why'd you grab me?"

"I didn't want you to get hurt!"

"You're the one hurting me!" Noémie said indignantly.

I felt breathless as I gathered up the three young children. As I wheezed to catch my breath, Josette looked at me with silent worry. I wondered when I'd have to tell them about my lung illness—and the grim prognosis. Tuberculosis was the best-case scenario...

Later, I told myself. *In Marseille, once we're safe. Or maybe on the ship. Or maybe in Los Angeles. Once they have others to look after them.*

I suddenly wished I had someone else to look after all of us. I thought longingly of John Cleeton. The widowed Texas rancher had been so kind, so devoted, to all of us. And I'd barely given him a civil word for it.

Yet another mistake to regret. It made me tired thinking of all the mistakes I'd made in my life.

I glanced down the road. "Is it really Lucie?"

"It has to be," Josette said, brushing the dirt off her pretty dress. She followed my gaze. "I can hardly wait to..."

Her voice trailed off. And that's when I saw it, too. That dog was too large. With a glossy red coat. Not copper.

But Margot was already reaching eagerly for the blonde girl's shoulder. "Lucie!"

The girl turned, and it was clear even from this distance that it was a stranger. This girl was too old, her face too long, plus she wore glasses. She looked startled, irritated. She spoke quietly with Margot for several seconds, then, with a shrug, turned away.

As the small group continued walking south, the dog bounding around them, Margot stood disconsolately by the side of the road, her shoulders sagging. Then she covered her face with a sob.

Roger pulled her into his arms, and she cried against his chest in front of the sunflower field. My heart broke for her. For all of us.

"Everybody back in the truck," I said.

"But what about Lucie?" Rachel clamored.

"There was a mistake," Josette said quietly, ruffling the girl's dark hair. "It's not Lucie."

"What?"

The little girls looked at each other in dismay.

"Not Wucie?"

After herding them back into the truck, I turned back to Josette. The redhead was staring disconsolately towards Margot and Roger. He still had one arm strung over the brunette's shoulders as the two walked slowly back towards the truck. Margot's eyes were downcast, her shoulders sagging, her walk the shuffle of someone much older.

Josette squared her shoulders, tightening her hands at her sides. I could see what it cost her to cast her jealousy aside and show compassion instead.

"Margot," she said gently. "I'm so sorry."

"Leave me alone," Margot snapped and pulled away from Roger, too.

I held out my arms, expecting her to reject me, too. But Margot's expression crumpled, tears falling down her cheeks as she came to me with a sob.

"I'm so sorry," I whispered, stroking her back. "So very sorry. Come sit up front with me."

She wiped her eyes angrily. "What's the point? We're never going to find her."

"Please, *ma petite*. I need your help."

Her eyes shimmered with pain, but pushing up the sleeves of the dress she'd borrowed from Josette, now wrinkled and dingy, she took a deep breath, and nodded.

"Don't worry. I'm sure Lucie's waiting for us in Marseille— you'll see." Josette patted her shoulder with a big smile, clearly happy at the prospect of sitting beside Roger again. Catching my disapproving eye, the redhead rearranged her face to look suitably sorrowful, then went to help Roger lift the little girls into the back of the truck.

I hobbled back to the driver's side door. I'd wanted Margot close to me so I could try to comfort her, to offer hope. But also to finally be done with shadows. I needed to tell her about America. Tell her all of it.

But I hadn't lied when I'd said I needed help. My lungs

were aching. I had to catch my breath before I climbed back into the driver's seat. Even after I sat down, for a moment, my vision went gray, and I saw spots, like stars in the night. I wondered if I should ask Margot to take the wheel. I took another breath, and another.

Climbing beside me on the bench seat, Margot gave a hysterical, tearful laugh. "I'm never going to see her again, am I?"

"You don't know that," I said soothingly. "You must have hope you'll see your sister again."

She glared at me. "You don't care about Lucie. You tried to convince me she wasn't even my sister."

Her voice was accusing, but I saw the grief in her eyes, and I knew I wasn't the one she really blamed for Lucie's loss. "Everything's going to be all right."

And maybe it would be. My vision righted itself, and I started the engine.

As the summer sun started to lower to the west, Margot stared out the passenger window at the passing landscape of lavender fields and Romanesque stone churches, ancient-looking farmhouses, olive groves and scrubby pine trees. The horizon turned pink and orange over the steady traffic on the road.

I looked at her. I needed to tell her. And yet I was afraid.

"We'll need to stop soon," I said finally. "Get some supper, find a place to sleep."

"It doesn't matter," she said dully.

Silence fell. I heard the twitter of birds, that low, disturbing rattle in the engine I was trying to ignore, the off-tempo wheeze of my breath.

"Or," I said carefully, "we could just push on. We're making good time. We might be able to make it to Marseille by midnight." I paused. "Lucie could be waiting at John's villa."

Margot looked at me. "You don't really believe that."

"I don't know why not." At this point, it was our only hope. "She's resourceful. Stubborn. Maybe she and Choupette got a ride. Maybe she's been at the villa for days, tapping her foot and worrying about us."

Margot's expression changed into a small, unwilling smile as her despair slightly released its hold. "Maybe."

"John told me about his villa. It sounds very nice. She's probably eating ice cream, walking Choupette as she window-shops along La Canebière. I'm sure John would spoil them both."

"John Cleeton is a good guy." She used the French term— *un mec bien*. She tilted her head, considering me. "You should give him a chance."

I blushed a little. Had she read my earlier thoughts? "What are you talking about?"

"Has he told you he's in love with you?"

You know how I feel, don't you? I could still hear John's voice the night before we'd left Paris. He'd come to St. Agnes's at my request, and I'd asked him to take baby Sophie to her family, if he managed to get a seat on the train. He'd readily agreed, but then, as we'd stood alone in the shadowy foyer of the orphanage, long after the girls and Berthe were asleep, his gaze had fallen to my lips. "Helen... you must know I'd do anything for you."

I'd almost let him kiss me. Then I'd pulled away. "I'm too old for romance, John."

He'd looked incredulous. "That's ridiculous—"

"It's late. I'll see you at the Gare de Lyon in the morning." I'd practically shoved him out the door.

The next morning, I'd sent Margot with baby Sophie in my place. That had been the reward for all his devotion.

But how could any man ever claim my heart, when it had been lost long ago to Jean-Luc? Even after all hope had been lost for years, decades, I'd been true to his memory.

And yet...

For a moment, I felt wistful, picturing John's steady face, his salt-and-pepper hair, his broad shoulders. The strength of his hand when he'd briefly taken mine.

But it was too late to change my mind. Besides, John Cleeton, handsome, wealthy and kind, deserved better than a broken-down woman like me.

Staring at the road, I told Margot, "I chose an independent life long ago."

"That's not true."

I nearly jerked the wheel, turning to face her. "What?"

She looked at me steadily. "You quit being independent the day you came to St. Agnes's."

My mouth opened. Nothing came out.

She pressed her advantage. "You said after being hungry as a child, you'd vowed to work and always have your own money. You'd defied your husband rather than risk being poor and helpless again." She tilted her head. "Then you gave up your job, your life savings, and your freedom to stay in Paris and be headmistress of a bunch of orphan girls. As an unpaid volunteer." She looked at me. "Why?"

I caught my breath. I longed to tell her the real reason.

But after everything I'd gone through with Josette, I suddenly couldn't find the strength to tell any more painful truths today. Especially to my daughter, who mattered more than anyone in the world. When I told her, she would hate me.

Just thinking of it, my body started shaking.

In the back of the truck, I heard the muffled sound of Roger entertaining the girls with a silly song, Josette's melodic voice joining in with the chorus.

I'd tell Margot everything in Marseille, I decided. After we knew about Lucie. When we had more privacy and time.

"I told you. I... knew your mother," I said carefully. "After she died, I took you and Lucie to St. Agnes's because I'd heard it was the best girls' orphanage in Paris. But the old headmistress was dying. The endowment was depleted. The property was going to be sold, and the girls moved into an overcrowded orphanage outside the city. I looked at all of you and I... I just couldn't bear for you to endure what I lived through. So I took all the money I had and bought the property, and became headmistress." I swerved, dodging a pothole. "It was just supposed to be temporary, until I could find someone better. But..."

"But you never found anyone better."

I glanced at her, then nodded.

"I never found anyone who cared more," I said quietly.

My hands were trembling. She was right: I had almost no money left. All the money I'd saved from working hard over my lifetime, including the money from selling my husband's house, was gone. I'd sold the orphanage's furniture to arrange second-class passage over the Atlantic, and I'd have to cable friends after we arrived in New York for our train fare to California.

I was running short on time, too. Our ship would leave July 1, leaving almost no time to finalize the documentation, or to blackmail my contact in Washington if the consul tried to renege on the promised visas. We'd already been through so much. It was chilling to think our biggest difficulties might still lie ahead.

What would happen if Lucie wasn't waiting for us in Marseille? I'd have to somehow convince Margot to board that ship and escort the other girls to safety, while I remained in France to find Lucie Vashon.

I'd have to find the strength...

As I drove, listening to the low rattle of the engine—the hollow sound of a dying breath—I started coughing. Except this time, when I pulled my hand away from my mouth, my fingertips were red.

I wiped my hand against my blouse, glad the fabric was dark. Glad Margot was too distracted to see.

As the truck bumped along the road, past more pine trees and green fields, the rattling engine started to clunk more loudly. The sun was starting to lower towards the western horizon, the shadows turning long, malevolent. The clunking sound built sharply, accusingly. The engine gave a loud metallic clang, then gasped and gave out.

My lungs were doing the same. I couldn't stop coughing.

"What's happening?" Margot asked in alarm.

As smoke rose from the truck's hood, blocking my view, I managed to pull us to the side of the road. I tried to start the engine again, but it wouldn't turn over. The truck had finally given up, like all the other ruined vehicles we'd seen abandoned along the roads since we'd left Paris. Passing those, I'd always whispered a silent prayer that it wouldn't happen to us. Now it had. And we were still seventy kilometers—over forty miles—from Marseille.

Gripped by coughing, I leaned my head against the steering wheel, desperate to get air into my lungs.

"Helen?" I heard Margot's panicked voice beside me. Then: "Josette! Roger! Come quickly!"

My door was wrenched open.

"What's wrong?"

"Sister Helen—"

But as I tried to turn towards the faraway voices, they faded, and I fell off the driver's seat—falling, falling, before it all went black.

24

MARGOT

I'd let myself be happy. That was my mistake.

After we stole the German truck, I'd felt a strange elation, as if Roger and Josette and I were a team, our own tiny private army exacting revenge: taking at least a truck in exchange for our nation.

The news that a blonde girl with a reddish dog had been seen walking south had brought me even greater joy. I'd nearly kissed Roger when I heard. Not that I cared about him. I'd just been so *happy*.

I should have known disaster was around the corner. The bitter disappointment of seeing a stranger's face instead of Lucie's had been crushing.

Now I was losing *Helen*?

"Madame?" Roger leaped forward, catching our headmistress as she fell head-first, eyes closed, out of the driver's seat, towards the gravel on the side of the road. Cars continued to roar past, dangerously close to the open door. "Madame Taylor! Can you hear me?"

"What's wrong with Sister Hewen?" Noémie wailed.

"Is she dead?" whimpered Estée.

"Don't be stupid," Josette snapped. But her expression was terrified. Our eyes met and, without speaking, we helped Roger pull Helen away from the smoking engine of our truck to the other side, away from the road. We set her down gently against the soft grass.

Helen's face was ashen, her body unmoving.

"Is she breathing?" I whispered.

Roger put his ear to her mouth, then shook her head. "I can't tell."

Josette reached into her dress pocket, then pushed her powder compact towards him. "Use this."

His dark eyes lifted, and he placed the mirror against Helen's pale lips. We held our breath in silence. I could hear the plaintive call of birds somewhere in the darkening sky.

Helen couldn't be dead. I thought of how cruel I'd been, taking out all my own guilt and regret and fear over Lucie on her. Quarreling with her. Thinking the worst. All my years of just being a bad kid wanting to stay up late instead of doing my math homework, of sneering at my secretarial courses, of speaking French when she wanted me to speak English and vice versa.

It was just supposed to be temporary, until I could find someone better... I never found anyone who cared more.

After a decade traveling the world, nursing the wounded and sick through battlefields and pandemics, Helen Taylor could have spent her hard-earned nest egg being comfortable in America, investing in the stock market, becoming a woman of means.

Instead, she'd spent every penny to take care of us. And not just her money. Her time. Her heart. She'd made St. Agnes's a home, and when the Nazis had threatened Paris, she'd found every child a new family.

Helen might have tempted me away from the Lusignys' with that job in Marseille, but she wasn't the one who'd decided to leave Lucie behind. I'd made that choice. Just me. How could I have blamed her?

I stared down at her closed eyes, clutching her hand. "Please wake up, Helen," I whispered. "Please."

I nearly wept when, a moment later, a soft sigh came from her lips, and her eyes fluttered open. Finding all of us hovering over her, and herself lying on the ground, Helen's expression changed to alarm. "What happened?"

"The engine broke down," Roger said. "You managed to pull the truck off the road. Then you fainted."

"Oh." She struggled to sit up. "Help me—"

"Careful. Take your time."

"Girls—" Helen looked anxiously from me to Josette and the three little girls. "Is everyone all right?"

Typical that upon waking from a dead faint she immediately was worried about everyone else. "We're fine." I lifted my head. "But..."

We all turned towards the broken truck, smoke curling from the hood.

"Can you fix it?" With a shuddering breath, she clasped her hands. She'd never been a big fan of Roger, but in this moment, she seemed almost like she was praying to him.

He looked uncertain. "I'll see."

He grabbed the purloined Nazi toolbox from the back, then opened the hood. After waiting for the smoke to dissipate, he poked around the engine, his expression grim, before looking beneath the truck, touching his fingers along a tire that was raised slightly from the ground. Then he turned to us with a sigh.

"The engine needs more work than I can do. But we're lucky that it died when it did. The axle looks about to give out, which could have caused even more trouble. And the three old tires are all so worn, they're all about to explode, too." He bowed his head. "Even if we were in Paris, even if there were no war shortages, I'm not sure this truck could be fixed." He looked at her regretfully. "I'm afraid, *madame*, there is nothing to be done now but walk."

Walk! We looked at each other in horror, thinking of all the poor devils we'd seen trudging on various roads, burdened by their belongings, without the shelter or supplies a vehicle could provide. Now the St. Agnes truck would join the long-stretching cemetery of dead and abandoned cars.

Still looking pale where she sat in the grass, Helen pointed towards the truck. "Margot—brandy?"

Hurrying to the truck's cab, I returned with her little silver flask. She took a long gulp and coughed. Handing it back, she wiped her mouth. I took a little bracing sip as Roger held out both hands.

"Are you well enough to stand, *madame*?"

Helen nodded and allowed him to pull her up.

"But we can't possibly walk to Marseille," Josette protested, holding the wrinkled, crumpled road map one way, then the other. "The children could never make it, and..." She looked with trepidation at Helen. Leaning against Roger, our head-mistress was wheezing with every breath.

"We will because we must." Roger looked down at Helen. "We'll pack what we can. Only take what's most important."

"We could go to Aix-en-Provence," Josette suggested. "It's perhaps twenty kilometers. There's a hospital."

"No." Helen's voice trembled. "Please. Marseille. We have to catch that ship. We're running out of time."

Roger turned. "Margot?"

I took a deep breath. Every muscle in my body wanted to take Helen to Aix-en-Provence, a city big enough to have a good hospital, where she could see a doctor. But her eyes begged me. Then I followed her gaze to the little girls, who were all unusually quiet, their faces scared.

I gave a sharp nod. "Marseille."

"But, Margot!" Josette argued.

"We can make it." Keeping my voice calm, I turned to Estée. "We'll help you younger ones carry your bags."

The girl looked at me incredulously through her glasses. "I'm eleven. I'll carry my own bag."

"Me, too," Rachel said stoutly.

"And me," Noémie said.

I smiled at them. "Good girls."

Thirty minutes later, we'd picked over the truck like it was the carcass of a dead animal, consolidated bags, and used clothes to create slings around the bodies of the adults to carry food and bottles of water plus Helen's valise and the small flask of emergency brandy. Estée was in charge of keeping the youngest girls close, so they didn't wander close to the cars and farm wagons rumbling past us on the busy road.

Roger, Josette and I would carry what we could in our hands and on our backs. Roger carried twice as much as we did, including his clothes and Helen's, the leather holster with the old revolver and several heavy bottles of water.

Weighed down with clothes and blankets, Josette looked at him with big adoring eyes. "You're so strong."

"Don't forget the map," he told her. Then he turned to Helen. "Do you know where we're going in Marseille?"

"I marked the route to John's villa on the map. It's in Saint-Victor, by the old port."

"Don't worry. We'll get there." Roger looked down at her almost tenderly. It made a pretty picture, the handsome young man supporting Helen as if she were his own mother. Then he lifted a cheeky dark eyebrow. "Are you up for walking, *madame*? I am glad to carry you, but I'd like to know in advance so I can rearrange my bags."

She drew herself up with dignity. "You definitely will not carry me."

But I saw her tremble and snatched the map from Josette.

"There's a town ten kilometers ahead." I glanced at the sun, sighing into twilight. "We can find a good place to stop for the night. Maybe find a doctor."

"Sounds—good." Her breathing was hard. "Roger and Josette, go on ahead. Estée, you and the girls go with them."

No one moved. We all just stared at her with worry.

Rolling her eyes, she waved them on impatiently. "Go on. I mean it. Margot will help me at my own pace."

Silently, we started walking down the edge of the road past fields of flowers and vineyards.

I held Helen's arm, acting as her support, but the two of us soon fell behind the rest. I tried to fit my brain around the idea of plodding like this for the next two days. I could feel every painful step of her fragile gait as she flinched. It was all I could do not to grab her arm and force it round my shoulders so I could try to carry her myself.

"Relax, Margot." Helen's lips twitched in a grotesque smile as she glanced at me in the reddish light. "I'm dying. So there's nothing to worry about."

I waited for the punchline. Finally I said, "It's not a very funny joke."

Her smile fled. "I suppose it's not. I just wanted to tell you that you don't need to worry. Because the truth is, there's nothing to be done. Jean-Luc... he said I may have lung cancer. Which is fatal." She shrugged. "Nothing to be done."

I stared at her, unable to breathe.

"B-But," I stammered, "you had pneumonia, that's all. You're just taking a while to get better... And then the bullet from the German plane..." My heart was hammering strangely. "You can't be *dying*."

"Well, if you want to be technical, everyone alive is dying, but yes. It's also possible I just have tuberculosis. I'll need to get X-rays. See a specialist. Unlikely to find in the next village, but perhaps Marseille."

No wonder she'd seemed so weak, fainting and wheezing for breath for the weeks of our journey, and even before, in Paris. I kicked myself for not noticing sooner. "Why didn't you tell us?"

Her smile was rueful. "I didn't want to see it myself, until Jean-Luc told me. After we left La Ravelle, I didn't see the point of worrying everyone." There were tears swimming in her eyes. "I'm sorry about Lucie. I never imagined..." She took a gulp of air. "I'm sorry."

"It's my fault." I looked down at my feet in the passing headlights, dusty big shoes on the uneven gravel along the road. I looked at the dark shadows of Josette, Roger and the rest ahead. "I shouldn't have left her, especially not after I met Rémy Moreau. I never trusted him." My throat caught. "I should have insisted from the beginning that she come with us to Marseille. You've done your best to take care of us all for so long. I had only one person to take care of, and I let her down."

We walked in silence. Every time she started to say something, she hesitated and fell silent again—or coughed. In the distance, we could see the lights of a small village twinkling in the deepening twilight.

"Margot," she said finally. "There's something you should know about Marseille. Something I've been scared to tell you."

"What?"

Her eyes shifted to her valise on my shoulder. She took a breath. "I got you a ticket on the ship. To come with us to America."

"America! Why?" I paused, then demanded, "Were my parents Jewish, too?"

Now she was the one to look away. "No."

"How do you know? You said Claude and Violette Vashon adopted me. Do you know anything about my—"

"I know because—because I know." She stumbled. I caught

her but not before her knee hit the ground. She was gasping for breath, her face white.

"Roger! Josette!" I screamed. I turned back to her. "I'm sorry," I begged her. "Please don't talk. Just keep up your strength."

"You have to come with us," she gasped. "You must."

"Do you have a ticket for Lucie, too?"

She suddenly avoided my gaze. "I—we'll talk later."

I knew what that meant. And there was no way I'd ever leave Lucie behind, not even to help the little girls, not even if Helen begged me. I set my jaw. "I'm not going."

"Please, Margot—you must—" she breathed as the others started hurrying towards us.

"Why? Why would I?"

Helen exhaled, closing her eyes.

"You're my daughter, Margot."

25

MARGOT

Standing by the side of the road, I stared at Helen in shock, my mouth agape. A whirlwind tore through my brain, swirling questions in disbelief.

But Roger was suddenly there, Josette and the little girls closely behind.

"What's happened?" He swooped in, lifting Helen with his strong arms. "*Madame?* Did you faint?"

"Almost," I said numbly, when she didn't answer. "She stumbled and fell. I think she's delirious. She's saying—crazy things."

Helen's lashes fluttered. Her eyes met mine. Her expression was sober, even scared, in her pale, anguished face. And I knew she wasn't crazy or delirious at all. She'd told me the truth.

I was her daughter.

Roger set his jaw. "That settles it. I'm carrying her."

I saw Josette's alarm—and Helen's too—as they both weakly started to argue (that it was impossible, in Josette's case; that it was unnecessary, in Helen's). Beside them, the little girls started to quarrel and fight. Everyone was tired and hungry, tired of rough travel, tired of the Nazis, tired of car trouble, tired of the weary journey most of all.

"Do you all need some help?"

A stranger's voice, friendly and loud, with *l'accent marseillais*.

Turning, we saw an elderly man and his wife in a sleek sedan, engine still running, who'd pulled over behind us on the side of the road. They gave us kindly smiles.

"We couldn't help but notice you're having some trouble."

"You and the children," his wife added.

"We wondered if you needed help."

They didn't seem like Nazis, but after so many weeks on the road, I'd become suspicious. "Why would you help us?"

"Well, why wouldn't we?" His smile spread to a grin. "We were visiting my mother-in-law in Ménerbes, bringing her the latest bestsellers. If I could put up with *her* for a week, I'm sure a passel of screaming children would be—"

"*Hé, là*, René," chided his wife good-naturedly.

"We're on our way home to Marseille, if we can be of any use."

"Marseille?" We looked at each other breathlessly. "That's where we're going."

The elderly man looked a little embarrassed, glancing at his back seat. "I don't have room to take you all. I wish I did. But we could perhaps take a few of you?"

"That's very kind," Roger said smoothly. "Perhaps the children, and could you also take *madame*?" He glanced at Helen. "I'm afraid she's just taken a bad turn. If you could take them to our friend's house in Saint-Vincent, you'd be well compensated."

Helen's jaw dropped as Roger so casually offered them John Cleeton's money as a reward. But it didn't matter.

"Compensation?" The old man looked aghast. "Oh, no. We wouldn't dream of accepting payment."

"We live right by the abbey, so it's no trouble at all," his wife added, her eyes sympathetic. "We have six grandchildren of our own." She smiled at Helen. "I've taken a bad turn or two myself."

"We can get them home in an hour, maybe two with the traffic," the elderly man said.

"That's awfully kind." Roger looked at me.

With a quick nod, I took a deep breath and turned to Helen. "You should go," I told her gently.

"No. It's not right," she panted, gripping my arm. Her gaze moved between me and Josette. "I can't—abandon you..."

"You're not abandoning us," I improvised. "You're *helping* us."

"Helping? How?"

I bit my lip. "Once we know you're safe in Marseille, the three of us can walk so much faster." I turned. "Can't we?"

"Yes," said Roger. "It'll be easier."

"So easy." Josette shrugged, as if walking some sixty-odd kilometers was nothing at all.

Helen looked as if she wasn't sure whether to believe us. Noémie cuddled close to her.

"Take the little girls and go. Please. They're all so tired. They need a good night's sleep." I knew she'd resist leaving us for her own safety or comfort. "We'll see you in Marseille tomorrow night at the latest."

Slowly, Helen nodded, and I could see what it cost her.

"What's your name?" Roger asked the man as he tucked Helen's and the little girls' bags into the trunk. "Just in case there's a problem."

"René Destraz, and my wife's Menon. But there won't be. I own the bookstore behind the abbey—anyone can find me if they ask."

We gently assisted first Helen, then the girls, who looked between us wide-eyed, into the back of their sedan.

"Please be careful walking by the road," Helen begged us from the front of the sedan, beside Madame Destraz. "I'll hold on to your documentation. To start working on the visas..." She turned pleadingly to Roger. "I'm counting on you to take care of my girls."

"Nothing to worry about. I have this," Roger said, holding up the map.

She hesitated. "The revolver?"

"In my bag."

"Don't use it!"

"Only if absolutely necessary." He gave a crooked grin. "See you in Marseille."

I had one last view of Helen's agonized eyes and Noémie waving farewell to us with Nounours's ragged paw. Then the sedan disappeared into the traffic, lessening with the deepening night. Soon, even the back lights disappeared, indistinguishable from the rest. I stared down the dark road blankly.

You're my daughter, Margot.

"Was that wise?" Josette sounded tremulous. "To just hand them off to strangers?"

"None of this is wise." Roger's voice was weary. "Everything is a risk."

He looked at me, and something in his gaze made my heart twist. He looked away quickly, and my throat ached.

"Come on," I said thickly. "We'd better get walking."

Shifting our remaining bags on our shoulders, the three of us started down the road, walking in the grass to keep a safe distance from cars going swiftly by us in the dark. I could see the lights of the village ahead. My heart felt numb.

Helen was my mother? How could it be true?

"You're so wonderful, Roger," Josette said as we walked. "We'd never have made it this far without you."

"Asking that old man for help, you mean? Or stealing from Nazis?" His voice was bitter. "Yeah. I'm a real hero."

"You are." Josette was taken aback. "You got the tire—helped carry everything—"

"Forget it."

His long stride got faster. Josette and I had to run to keep up with him. I didn't know why Roger was upset—was he finally tired of Josette's puppy love?—but it felt good to run, to get rid of some of the electric shock coursing through my veins, the jumble of overwhelming emotions I didn't know how to feel.

You're my daughter, Margot.

"Sorry." Slowing down, Roger glanced at me, a half-smile on his lips. He reached into his pocket for his blue box of Gauloises and offered it to me. I took one. Then he offered it to Josette, who shook her head.

"Did I say something wrong?" she panted.

Dark eyebrows lifted as he took a matchbook from his pocket, then lit my cigarette. Our eyes locked above the soft glow of the flame, there in the jasmine-scented Provençal twilight.

"What is it? What did I say?"

"It was nothing you did." Roger looked at her with a wistful smile. "Once we reach Marseille, Josette, we'll see if I'm actually brave. When I find other Frenchmen who want to fight. If we can kick these German dogs out of our country for once and all."

"You must have a low opinion of dogs to compare them to Germans." I inhaled the cigarette with a trembling hand. My lips quirked as I added without thinking, "Choupette would not approve…"

I exhaled, then silently started walking again, tortured by thoughts of Lucie and her little dog. *They're in Marseille*, I told myself. *She's tapping her foot, worried about us, while John Cleeton feeds her dishes of ice cream.* I wanted to believe it so badly.

Josette and Roger swished through the long grass beside me.

"Roger, I've wondered..." Josette licked her lips, then said in a rush: "Do you have a girl waiting for you somewhere?"

"Yes." He flicked ash from his cigarette onto the gravel. "A year ago, I promised myself to one woman for the rest of my life."

"A year ago?" Josette's face fell.

He smiled. "Marianne. La France."

Josette brightened. "Oh."

I rolled my eyes. It was all too cute, having him profess devotion to Marianne, the symbolic personification of France. But Josette was looking at Roger dreamily, as if he, a few years older and once a soldier, was wiser and better than she. It was enraging.

When we reached the village, with squat stone houses, cobblestoned road and only a few windows with electric light, I was too tense to imagine sleeping.

"Let's walk a little longer," I said. "At least until the next town. We could try hitchhiking if we see another car."

"Too dangerous," Josette said automatically.

"Everything is dangerous," Roger said. "I agree with Margot. Let's keep going."

"Good idea," she backtracked, looking at him adoringly.

I was embarrassed for her. As little as I cared for Josette's bossiness, I longed for it now. I hoped she would be able to remember who she was, beneath all that disgusting hero worship, after she left for America.

Josette, unfortunately, was less excited by the idea. She grumbled about it as we walked, saying she had no intention of going. Even Hollywood apparently held little sparkle for her now, compared to the charms of Roger Cochet. Still, as she complained to Roger, I felt a rush of relief that Helen had finally told her. Now I didn't need to worry about accidentally blurting out the secret.

I'd kept my promise to Helen. So there. I'd kept my promise to someone who had lied to me my whole life.

No wonder she'd never let me see my legal birth certificate. Helen always said it was unnecessary, or pretended she didn't know where it was, or that it would be too much trouble to find it. And I'd trusted her.

I walked ahead of Roger and Josette in the deepening night, feeling so much mixed-up rage and grief that I longed to punch something—hard.

You're my daughter, Margot.

I stomped beneath the moonlight, my throat burning, unable to cry. If it was true, and Helen was my birth mother, what did that mean?

It meant she'd abandoned me as a baby. She'd dumped me with some farmer and his wife. She hadn't even intervened when the farmer died and the wife became a prostitute to support us.

All right, so Helen had tracked us down a few years later, after Violette Vashon's death, and stuck around as headmistress. But in all the years she'd raised me, she hadn't acknowledged me as her daughter. If anything, she'd treated me more coldly than the others. What kind of mother was that?

I kicked at a rock and stubbed my toe. I relished the pain. Anything to distract me from the anguish in my heart.

Helen could have told me anytime over the last few years. Instead, she'd waited until she was on the cusp of leaving. Not just leaving—*dying*. She hadn't told me out of love. Not even out of guilt. My hands clenched, my fingernails cutting roughly into my skin.

She'd told me I was her daughter because she hoped to convince me to go with her to America, leaving Lucie behind. It was emotional blackmail—pure selfish manipulation.

Helen wasn't my real mother, whatever she said. A mother

would never ask me to sacrifice everything I believed in—or the person I loved most.

I prayed Lucie was in Marseille right now, safe. I pictured her flinging open the door of John Cleeton's villa, with baby Sophie in her arms and Choupette barking happily at her feet. I saw Lucie's bright blue eyes, her hair around her angelic face like a halo as she beamed. "*Finally!* What took you so long?"

Once we were together, I'd find a job and a home just for us, far from war and orphanages. Somehow. Somewhere.

I didn't need Helen Taylor.

The three of us staggered on along the road in the dark, lit only by moonlight and the headlights of occasional cars, passing the next town and sleeping in an abandoned barn. The fields were fallow, the farmhouse a ruin, and half the wood of the old barn was rotted away. But at least we had a bit of roof over our heads, with soft places to sleep on dried-out hay.

Roger set up a small dinner for us on a blanket, just stale bread and cheese, though I had no appetite. I pushed the end hunk of bread towards Josette amid her constant futile attempts to engage Roger in conversation. It was exhausting.

Finally, I'd had enough. "I'm going to bed."

I went to the far side of the barn, trying to get out of earshot of the two lovebirds. But a moment later, Roger sat down beside me.

"I heard," he said very quietly. "What Helen said to you."

You're my daughter, Margot. I looked up with an intake of breath. "You heard?"

He nodded. "I just wanted you to know I'm here. If you want me."

He only meant to be kind, but the last four words wove around me like a strange whirlwind. *If you want me.*

But what was I thinking? I didn't want Roger. I couldn't. *Wouldn't.*

"You should go back to Josette," I said.

"Why?"

"I'm sure she's been thinking of new compliments for you."

He gave a crooked smile. The dappled moonlight through the broken slats slid over the edges of his face, the hard cheekbones, the five o'clock shadow along his jaw. "Jealous?"

"It's just funny is all." I glanced across the shadowy barn to where Josette was clearly fuming, pretending not to be watching us as she tried to get comfortable, using her bulky bag, with all her clothes and makeup, as a hard, lumpy pillow. For once, she wasn't sleeping in curlers.

Roger touched my shoulder. His dark eyes burned through me in the pale light of the stars shining through the gaps in the ruined roof. "Margot, you have to know—"

I turned away. "I'm tired, Roger. Get some sleep." I called loudly back to Josette, "We're hitting the road at first light. We'll be in Marseille tomorrow."

Dramatically, I flopped over on my side away from him, closing my eyes on the lumpy dried hay, putting my own bag of dirty clothes beneath my cheek.

The next day, my whole body ached from sleeping in that uncomfortable position. We ate a quick, silent breakfast, though Josette kept throwing me inscrutable glances. Well, I told myself, grinding my teeth, if she'd talked herself into being jealous, it was her own stupid fault. I hadn't done anything wrong.

We walked for hours along the dusty, busy road. No one ever picked us up, no matter how many times we stuck a thumb out. The only time we ducked away into the trees was when we saw a Nazi truck roll past. In that moment, I felt every heartbeat in sheer terror, waiting for them to stop and arrest us. But the German truck passed by us in a *whoosh*, just like all the other cars. We kept walking. Trudging up and down the rolling hills, our bags banging against our backs and legs, our shoulders and muscles aching.

We finally reached Marseille after sunset, lit only by the

silvery moon. We smelled the salt and tang of the sea, flowers in bloom, sour, rotting trash, exhaust and smoke.

We were exhausted as we walked wearily through the oldest city in France, second only to Paris in its sprawl and size. The home of "La Marseillaise," the anthem not just of France but of revolution. Or so Josette said, prattling to Roger like she was reading from a Baedeker guidebook.

But she didn't even look like herself anymore. Her blouse and skirt were dusty and wrinkled, and she wasn't wearing any makeup except lipstick and a little powder over her slightly sunburned skin. Even her glorious red hair, normally her best feature, was frizzy and unkempt. No doubt she hadn't wanted Roger to see her in curlers or think she was vain for making an effort.

My striped shirt and trousers were dirty, too, but I didn't look that different than normal because even in Paris I'd rarely tried to look nice. My dark hair was tucked in a braid, my face bare of makeup as always, my cheeks rosy from too much sun.

Even at night, the city seemed awake, swollen with refugees, with government officials, with international travelers camped outside various consulates. There were even a few Nazis, walking the streets with a certain proprietary air, as if eyeing Marseille for future conquest. Would the spider flag of bone and blood triumph over every nation of the world?

Walking wearily through the strange streets, I felt like Dorothy finally reaching Oz, in the much-loved novel Lucie had read to the little girls at bedtime. But this was a darker version. Instead of scarecrows and tin men, monkeys and wicked witches, we saw streetwalkers, drunks, sailors, beggars, in the spice-and-jasmine city stretching languorously and dangerously like a stray cat against the Mediterranean.

"Will you come stay with us at the villa, Roger? Oh, say you will." Josette bounced around him in the shadowy street like a puppy begging for a treat. "I'm sure Monsieur Cleeton has plenty of room."

"I have a friend living on the rue du Panier. I thought I'd look him up." Roger turned his head, his profile angling briefly towards where I followed behind on the sidewalk. "Besides, aren't you all leaving for America?"

"I told you—I'm staying." Josette flashed me a hard glance. "But Margot's going."

"Helen told you that?" I asked, annoyed. After all my struggle to keep America a secret from Josette, Helen had blabbed about me?

"You've always been her favorite," she muttered.

"That's a joke. Anyway, I'm not going."

"Me neither," Josette said. "I'll be eighteen soon. It's my choice how to live my life."

As our footsteps echoed against Marseille's cobblestoned streets, Roger glanced between us. "Don't be too eager to be grown up, you two," he said quietly. "You might look back and miss it someday, having someone who looks after you."

She looked up at him breathlessly. "It's all I want. To look after someone I love."

I rolled my eyes. Even if Roger had liked her, there was no way any man's love could endure such devotion. "Are we almost there? What does the map say?"

Josette looked irritated that I was butting in, but really I was doing her a favor. Roger was fidgeting. She snapped, "It's useless." She waved the map at me like a fan, not even trying to look at it. Was she just trying to prolong her time with Roger?

I held out my hand. "Give it here."

Using the map—which was barely any use, just as she'd said —we wended our way through the smaller, quieter lanes of Marseille, getting lost twice before we found the right street. We were all dirty, weary, weighed down with our bags. Finally,

I saw the glimmer of the sea in the moonlight, the masts filling the old port, the ancient stone abbey of Saint-Victor.

"You should stay with us tonight, Roger," Josette tried again. "It makes more sense now it's so late. Tomorrow if you want, you can go look for your friend—"

"Wait here," he said abruptly. "I'm not sure we're going the right way. Be right back."

After dropping his heavy bags, Roger raced around the corner, leaving us waiting in the dark, empty street. We both set down our bags, too, leaning against the stone wall to rest. All the shops were closed, and we had no money anyhow. My feet were aching, my legs, my whole body. We'd run out of food and water ten kilometers ago. I was hungry, tired. And thirsty. So thirsty.

Turning to me, Josette explained happily, "He went ahead to spare us trouble. He's such a gentleman."

I couldn't take it anymore. "He probably wanted a moment's peace."

"What's that supposed to mean?"

"For heaven's sake, Josette. I've told you. Stop flinging yourself at him. It's embarrassing."

She glared at me. "That's fine, coming from you. You push yourself forward, trying to be everyone's favorite!"

I had the sudden childish desire to yank her hair. But I knew Josette too well to give in to that impulse. The best way to make her angry was to grow cold.

I shrugged, keeping my face blank in the moonlight. Around us, I could hear the distant noise of busier streets, the wail of a siren, the dolorous gong of a church bell. "If I wanted Roger, believe me, I could have him. But I don't."

"Sure," she said sarcastically.

"Men aren't interested in girls who pursue them. A man wants to be the fisherman. Not the gaping fish on a hook."

"Who's being ridiculous now? I'm just encouraging him, that's all. Showing my interest."

"You're doing everything but greasing yourself down and tying yourself like a pig to a spit, twisting yourself in a fire till you're cooked for his dinner."

"Why you—"

"It's humiliating. I'm ashamed for you. Go to America, Josette. Maybe once you're on the other side of the world, you'll stop being such a simpering fool and act like yourself again."

She yanked my wrist so hard I nearly tripped over our bags.

"You're the one who should be ashamed," she hissed. "You're nothing but a nameless love-child."

All the night sounds of the city went quiet. It felt as if the rest of the world disappeared. "What are you talking about?"

"Sister Helen is your *mother*."

I blinked. "You heard her tell me?"

Josette shook her head, her expression ugly. "I saw your birth certificate in La Ravelle. When Sister Helen sent me to look for her sweater."

"You—what?"

"The name was a little different, but the birthday was the same. I immediately knew it was you. I should have seen the resemblance sooner. I kept quiet because I didn't want to hurt your feelings. But you know what? You don't deserve it."

I caught my breath. Josette had known Helen was my mother before I did? I remembered all those days when Josette had seemed strangely distant. Another liar I'd trusted. My eyes stung.

"Shut up," I whispered. "You weren't trying to do me any favors by staying quiet."

"No?"

"You just liked having a secret to lord over me." I rubbed my eyes hard. "If you'd actually cared, you would have told me immediately. But you've been too busy fawning over a man who barely tolerates you."

"I'm sick of you acting like you're better than me! You're

not!" Josette's cheeks were red, her eyes wet with tears of rage. "Sister Helen abandoned you not just once but twice. For all these years, she's been too ashamed to admit you're her daughter. Your father doesn't even know you exist!"

My jaw dropped. "My—my father?"

"You know who he is?" She tossed her frizzy red hair over the shoulders of her wrinkled blouse. "Jean-Luc Ravanel!"

I gaped at her.

Josette pressed her advantage. "Either he doesn't know, or he was too ashamed to admit his *bastard* was in his house. He could hardly wait for you to go away! So he could be with his *real* family!"

I could hear the thrum of blood in my ears. I wanted to slap Josette right across the mouth, until the exultant look left her face and she was sorry—so sorry. But I knew hitting her wouldn't be nearly enough to make her hurt the way I was hurting now. I tightened my hands into fists, trying not to cry, desperate to break her heart, too.

We stared at each other, both of us panting with hatred beneath the moonlight on the quiet street of Marseille.

"Sorry I took so long." Roger came trotting back, a little red-faced from exertion. "I was right. We're on the wrong corner. I think we missed a turn—" He stopped, looking between us. "What happened?"

I didn't let myself think.

Turning with dark purpose, I walked straight to him, wrapped my arms around his shoulders and, standing on tiptoes, kissed him on the mouth.

I felt his surprise, heard his sharp intake of breath before his arms clutched me against his body, close enough that I could feel his warmth, the beat of his heart. Then our lips touched, and for a moment, I was lost. I forgot about Josette, about taking revenge, about my grief and rage. There was only now. This.

Him.

Pulling away, Roger looked down at me beneath the street-light, his dark eyes wide. His voice was almost tender as he breathed, "What was that for?"

Then I heard Josette's low sob, and I remembered everything. I flung her a triumphant glance.

Tears were streaming down her pale cheeks. Wrapping her arms around her body, as if protecting herself, she stared at her feet, her dirty socks in her worn saddle shoes.

Roger looked between us, bewildered. "What's going on?"

I tossed my head. "I just taught her a hard truth."

"What do you mean?"

"That you don't want her, no matter how much she throws herself at you."

Josette grabbed her bag from the sidewalk and blindly started walking down the shadowy street.

Roger stared down at me in horror. Then he picked up his own two bags, turned without a word to me and rushed after her, gently taking her hand. "Ignore her, Josette. The villa's this way."

As he led her down around the corner in the opposite direction, I felt strangely irrelevant, rebuffed. I picked up my own bag and followed them.

Three streets away, down a lane we'd missed, he pointed. "There."

An elegant villa with palm trees, lit up by electric lights.

I glanced at Josette. Her cheeks were streaked with dried tears. She seemed unable to look Roger in the face as she walked past him, and it was as if I didn't exist. Upon reaching the tall wrought-iron gate, she bowed her head, hugging herself again.

Seeing her desolation, I felt the first trickle of shame at what I'd done. And not just to her. I looked at Roger's broad-shouldered shadow. I could still feel the electricity of his lips on mine. The pain and betrayal in his eyes afterward. I'd lost not just his trust but his respect. I hadn't realized until now how much those meant to me.

As Josette lifted her arm and rang the bell, I shook my head hard. I couldn't think about the kiss anymore, or Roger, or Josette. I stared at the villa. When that gate opened, would I see my sister? Or would I be forced to accept the unbearable knowledge that she was lost to me forever?

Lucie. I started to cross the street, my heart in my throat. *Please*, I prayed. *Let it be Lucie who answers. Let it be...*

But Roger grabbed my arm and pulled me aside.

"You're right to despise me, Margot," he said in a low, hoarse voice.

"I don't," I said quickly.

His lips twisted. "Of course you do. Otherwise you never could have..." His jaw tightened, and he looked away. "But you've been right all along. I'm no hero." He handed me one of his bags, the one full of our clothes, and gave a low, bitter laugh. "Before I left St. Agnes's, I overheard the Germans say their commanding officer was looking for Helen Taylor, and there'd be a huge reward to anyone who found her."

"What?" I breathed. "Why would the Nazis be after Helen?"

He shrugged. "No idea. But I came south hoping to find you. To turn her in."

"To—what?"

His dark eyes burned through me. "When I came up with the plan to steal the tire... I brought you and Josette to Caraillon to get you away from her. So you wouldn't fight when I brought the Nazis back to pick her up."

"No! You wouldn't!"

His shoulders sagged. He shook his head. "I couldn't do it. Not to you. Or to Helen and the girls. So I'm leaving you both here, where you'll be safe." He glanced at Josette, still standing across the street, looking wan and pitiful waiting by the villa gate. "Tell her good luck in America. She's better off without me." He gave me a crooked smile. "Convince her, won't you?"

"Roger..." My heart was aching at that smile. "You have to know—I never meant to hurt you..."

"Yeah, sure. I know." He pulled the pack of cigarettes from his shirt pocket and lit one. His fingers shook a little as he inhaled a long drag of smoke. "But you sure didn't mind hurting her, did you? The poor kid."

"Poor kid?" I was flabbergasted. Josette was just a few months younger than I was. "You should have heard the cruel things she said to me—"

"Yeah. The two of you are really good at hurting each other. I expected more of you, Margot. You're strong. A leader. Or you could be. I thought..." He exhaled, shaking his head. "It doesn't matter now. I was in love with a dream."

As he turned away, I heard the sad echo of those last words.

Was in love.

Was.

"Roger—wait."

"I hope Lucie's waiting for you in there right now." Hitching his own bag higher on his shoulder, he tossed aside the cigarette, stubbing it out with his shoe, then glanced back at the villa. A light had been turned on in a second-floor window. His jaw hardened. "In the meantime, you're throwing your other sister away."

"Josette is not my sister." My voice was a little shrill. "She—"

"Whatever you say." He stepped back. I had one last glance of his darkly handsome face before he turned his shoulder. "But from now on, leave me out of it."

26

HELEN

What was that noise?

I sat up in bed, my hands clenched.

The shadowy bedroom around me was quiet, all luxury and peace. Diffuse gray light came through the silk curtains of the high windows, from the city lights of Marseille reaching up into the clouds and the streetlights below.

My heart was pounding, my brain still buzzing with the same worries that had made me toss and turn the previous night. I'd ironically slept less restfully here, in the privacy of this lovely bedroom, with a soft mattress and clean sheets, than in all those nights on the road, sleeping on cots or church pews or even the cold, hard ground. I'd almost taken a sleeping pill, except for my fear of being drugged into stupor when the girls arrived.

If they ever arrived.

Margot. Josette. *Lucie.*

Even tonight, I'd climbed into bed with trepidation, after a long, busy day with John and the girls that had almost kept my worries at bay. Lying in bed, I had no defense against my own churning fears.

Margot and Josette were strong and resourceful, I repeated to myself. Plus they had Roger to help. Though I wasn't entirely sure if Roger's presence meant help or further danger. Why did I still not trust him? He'd been nothing but kind and helpful—to all of us. Perhaps the truth was I'd never trust anyone with my girls. Except the Ravanels, of course.

And John.

I took another deep breath, looking around the dark, pretty bedroom. I had no idea how much it cost John to rent this villa. A fortune. I'd never stayed anywhere so luxurious. Somehow, being here, all the days of dust and grief almost seemed like a bad dream.

The previous night, when the little girls and I had been dropped off by the elderly bookseller and his wife, I'd been exhausted, distraught, ill. The girls were crying with fatigue.

When John had answered his door with a big smile, I'd gasped out, "Lucie? Is she here?"

"Lucie? No." Looking bewildered, he'd shaken his head. And I'd fallen to my knees on the Turkish carpet.

Catching me, he'd called out for his French housekeeper, Madame Paget, to take the girls to their rooms. Then he'd turned to me. "I'm going to take you to your bedroom," he'd said gently. "All right?"

I'd nodded, weeping.

He'd picked me up in his strong arms as if I weighed nothing and carried me up the sweeping staircase without a word, bringing me to this elegant bedroom, with its four-poster oak bed, marble fireplace and big window with a view of the sea.

Against my feeble protestations, he'd lowered me to the bed, then turned away to phone the doctor. While we'd waited for him to arrive, John had sat at the end of the bed until his maid delivered the tea he'd ordered, then poured it himself.

"Helen, I was so worried," he said quietly. "I expected you

weeks ago. What happened? Where's Lucie? And Margot and Josette?"

Maybe it was his kindness; maybe it was that I was so very tired. Or maybe it was that Lucie wasn't here, and I'd left Margot behind, and I had no idea how this would work out, or even if it *would* work out. Whatever the reason, in that moment, I'd finally broken into a million pieces.

Before I'd known what was happening, my entire life story spilled out of me like boiling water from a kettle. The death of my husband and child, which drove me to flee to war. How I'd fallen in love with the doctor I worked with—and the guilt and shame which had caused me to push him away.

And Margot. My guilt and grief about Margot most of all.

By the time the French doctor arrived, I had no words or emotion left. John had listened but said nothing, then avoided my gaze as he let the doctor into the room.

I didn't see John for the rest of that night as the doctor examined me, listening to my lungs with his stethoscope and nodding gravely when I'd told him Jean-Luc's diagnosis. "You must come to the hospital in the morning for tests," he said. "X-rays."

This morning, after a bath, I was almost scared to come downstairs to breakfast. I kept thinking of how I'd spilled my guts to John, and my cheeks burned. Now he knew the truth, he'd despise me as a selfish, fallen woman who'd inadvertently caused my family's deaths, slept with a widower who was not my husband, then given birth to an illegitimate child and pretended she was an orphan.

Would he be cold? Cruel? Tell me he couldn't bear to look at me?

When I crept downstairs, a little stronger after a night of scattered sleep and wretched dreams, I found John waiting at the breakfast table. He was surrounded by the happy, chattering little girls fighting over toast and jam and who got the sweetest fruit or thickest bits of bacon.

Seeing me, John rose from the table, smiling respectfully, as if I were a lady. He told me my hospital visit had been arranged and had the maid bring me a plate filled with delicacies to tempt me—eggs, bacon, croissants, fruit. Over breakfast, he'd shown us all pictures of baby Sophie, now happily ensconced with her family.

"Sophie wasn't sure at first," he told me, "but when her mother gathered her up, suddenly, it was as if she remembered being in those arms. She clung to her mother, almost as much as the woman clung to her."

I could well imagine the feeling, and it caught at my heart. In the brief moment after I'd told Margot I was her mother, I'd seen a flash of something in her eyes. But whatever she'd felt, she hadn't clung to me at all. Perhaps it was too late. I'd ruined any chance for us.

I'd done my best to eat breakfast, after John had gone to such trouble. After I couldn't eat another bite, he rose, hat in hand, and, leaving his housekeeper to mind the girls, he'd had his chauffeur drive us to the best hospital in the city, then sat quietly beside me through my X-rays and tests.

And hours later, when I'd finally been given the diagnosis, he'd comforted me, steadied me, holding my hand. He'd told me he'd pay for treatment—in fact, he must insist on it, or we could no longer be friends.

I'd almost cried with gratitude.

Something was different between us now. Different in *me*.

Was it because I'd finally said goodbye to Jean-Luc, letting my old dream go?

No. It was more.

I realized now that I'd cared about John for a long time. More than I'd let myself admit. More than I'd even let myself feel. I'd kept my heart frozen in ice, scared to love him, because I'd been sure if he ever really knew me, he'd despise me.

But now he knew all my secrets. I'd taken the risk of trusting him with my past, and he hadn't rejected or scorned me. To the contrary, he seemed even more gentle now, more tender. He knew the worst, and he still loved me. I could trust him with my heart.

Sadly, it had all come too late.

I blinked. Closing my eyes, I sank back against my pillow in the quiet of the dark bedroom. I'd been woken by a noise— woken from a dream. But now I heard only seagulls and the noise of the harbor, a distant tugboat. I must have been wrong.

Was that—?

I sat up straight. Yes. A faint bell from downstairs. The gate!

I rose unsteadily from the bed. After turning on a light, I grabbed the silk robe John had provided and pulled it over my nightgown, tying it around my waist as I hurried into the dark hallway.

The girls' doors were still closed; John's bedroom was on the floor below. I rushed down two flights of stairs as best I could, breathing hard, grabbing the railing to make sure I didn't fall. There was no sign of the housekeeper. I unlocked the front door and looked out into the darkness.

Girls' voices. Was that—Margot?

Recklessly, I tripped through the villa's small, manicured garden, past the bougainvillea and water burbling in the stone fountain. As I approached the gate, I heard voices on the other side, quarreling in the night.

"What did you do?" Josette said accusingly.

"Nothing!"

"Roger wouldn't just *leave*. You must have said something!"

Margot's voice, tight and small. "He just said he had to go."

"Nice job, Margot. All this time you've sneered at me,

insisting I'd drive him away, but one kiss from you and he couldn't get away fast enough!"

"You're right." The words were a whisper.

"There must be some message. He wouldn't have left me without saying goodbye!"

"He said... He told me to tell you... good luck in America." My daughter sounded weary and sad. "And that you're better off without him."

"You're lying. I hate you, Margot! You've ruined my life!"

"Girls," I gasped, flinging open the gate. With a joyful sob, I held out my arms. "You're here. You're safe."

Josette dropped her bag and immediately threw herself into my embrace. Margot just looked at me from the open gate. She knew now that she was my daughter. Something shadowed in her eyes, emotion turning flat.

Licking her chapped lips, she whispered, "Lucie?"

Pain returned like an anvil. "I'm sorry. She's not here."

"Oh," she said, and in that one quiet word there was unbearable despair.

"Oh no. Lucie," Josette choked out, wiping her eyes. She looked at Margot, who seemed near tears. The two had always quarreled, growing up—they were both strong characters—but this seemed different. Margot's shoulders slumped.

I said with forced brightness, "But we'll have to hope she's on her way. The other girls are sleeping upstairs. Come in—you must be tired."

"Exhausted," Josette said. "We walked all day."

I looked out at the street before I closed the gate. "No Roger?"

"He left," Margot said.

The redhead glared at her. "We know whose fault that is."

Thank heaven for small favors, at least. "I'm just glad you made it. You must be hungry. Come inside."

They followed me, not meeting my eyes or each other's, and set down their bags in the foyer. When I turned on a small lamp inside the door, they blinked owlishly, looking like dirty and dusty urchins, out of place in the immaculate, gleaming villa.

"This is all Mr. Cleeton's?" Margot said slowly, looking around the foyer.

"He's been so kind to all of us, hasn't he?" I said awkwardly.

Josette's head tilted as she looked up at the chandelier, the gilded railings of the staircase. "I think there's just one of us he's trying to impress."

My cheeks went hot. I wasn't sure how to answer. "I don't think the cook is awake, but if you're hungry, I can take you to the kitchen and make you something..."

There was a rumble of feet from above, a rush of noise like stampeding elephants. Our voices had been overheard, and within a minute, the girls were getting massive hugs and exclamations from Noémie, Estée and Rachel. Behind them, John Cleeton looked darkly handsome, wearing a well-cut robe over pajamas. I blushed as our eyes met.

Smiling, he stood back, then as the hubbub died down asked, "Anyone hungry?"

"We were just talking about that," I said. "But we can make it ourselves if—"

"Nothing better than a midnight feast." He was already ducking back down the hall. "Could you please ask Madame Latour to serve some sandwiches and tea as soon as possible?"

I heard the murmur of the housekeeper's voice in reply.

He turned back, smiling at me. My heart fluttered.

You must know I'd do anything for you, he'd told me in Paris. I'd replied I was too old for romance.

How strange was it that, now I was so deathly ill, my feelings had changed?

Strange, and heartbreaking.

"So how was your train journey with baby Sophie?" Margot asked as we all sat down at the gleaming dining table.

He flinched with a rueful smile. "I've never been around babies much. Afraid I made a hack of it, trying to pretend she was a newborn colt needing care. But we both got through it." He gave a low laugh. "I felt sorry for the other passengers, though."

Margot turned towards the platter of simple sandwiches delivered by John's yawning cook. "Good job catching her through the window."

John shrugged, pouring her and Josette a glass of cool water, which both girls guzzled. "I played football at Texas. Good to know I still have good hands."

"Catching Sophie?" I looked between them, bewildered. "What are you talking about?"

"Nothing for you to worry about now," he said with a wink to Margot.

The girl smiled back at him, then her smile was swept from her face like a pencil mark erased from a page. She hugged herself, looking wan, thin and so young. "There's really been no word from Lucie? Not a word?"

His smile fell in turn. "No. I'm sorry."

"We still could hear from her." I tried to put confidence into my voice. But it was difficult.

Margot set down her half-eaten sandwich and stared at her dirty, scuffed shoes. "We would have heard something by now."

"Don't lose heart. There's always hope."

Margot stared at me, her young face pale with grief and loss. Then she turned away, her shoulders sagging in her wrinkled long-sleeved shirt.

Even Josette seemed subdued, which I could only assume was due to exhaustion, the nasty fight she'd had with Margot or the sudden unexplained departure of Roger Cochet.

He'd left at the perfect time, in my opinion. He'd brought them to me safely, then politely disappeared.

After spending so many hours getting medical tests today, I'd yet to go to the American consulate. I prayed getting the required documentation would be fast and easy. Tomorrow would be my only chance. Our ship to Lisbon would sail the day after.

"So where is baby Sophie now?" asked Josette, stuffing her face with turkey and Brie on freshly baked bread, served with a side of leftover potatoes au gratin and a strawberry tart with fresh cream.

"With her family in Toulouse," John said, pouring himself a glass of wine. He'd chosen a seat beside me at the long dining table. "They wept with joy when they held her."

"Parents." The little girls looked at each other at the word.

"Look." Noémie proudly held out a photograph. Josette and Margot reached for it at the same moment, but Margot snatched it up, looking carefully at baby Sophie being held tenderly by her mother, beaming with tearful joy, with her father and young siblings nearby. Looking away, she set it down on the table in front of Josette, who picked it up, both girls carefully ignoring each other.

"Well"—John stroked his chin, which as it was the middle of the night was whiskery with salt-and-pepper scruff—"it might take a bit of time for Sophie to get used to her new home, but I think she will be happy. The cottage is small and cozy, and she was able to meet her four older brothers."

"I still don't think they deserve her," Margot growled, staring down at her plate. Then she looked up at me. "Any parent who'd abandon a baby is a heartless monster."

Her insult hit its target. I flinched.

"Not heartless. Desperate." John briefly squeezed my hand under the table. "I gather Sophie's father was very ill, and so her mother had to go to work, and they had no way to care for a baby—"

"It doesn't matter *why* they abandoned her. They should be punished, not rewarded."

Her hard words caused a chill in my bones. I started coughing. Glancing at me with concern, John rose and made some hot tea from the nearby kettle, adding honey as I liked it. He placed the china cup in front of me on the dining table.

"Thank you," I murmured, sipping the tea, which helped soothe my throat so I could breathe normally again.

Looking between us, Margot scowled, then rose abruptly. "Where can I sleep?"

John said, "I'd be glad to show you—"

"Just tell me where."

A little taken aback by her rudeness, he said, "Third floor, near Helen and the other girls. Take the last bedroom on the left. There's a bathroom with all modern conveniences. Hot running water if you want a bath. Clean towels and robes."

"Okay," she said, as if she were doing him a big favor by staying here.

He raised his dark eyebrows, then looked at me ruefully.

I'd had enough. I could understand her being rude to me, but John didn't deserve this.

"Margot." I spoke to her directly, and her posture went stiff. "Tomorrow morning, after breakfast, I need you to come with me to the consulate. To get visas for the girls."

She shook her head, refusing to meet my eyes.

"I could come," offered John, ever the peacemaker.

"No. Thank you," I amended. "It must be Margot."

"Forget it," she muttered. "I'm going to look for Lucie tomorrow." She paused, then gave John an apologetic smile. "I'm afraid I'm a little tired. Thank you for your kindness, Mr. Cleeton. Excuse me."

"Of course. If you want to leave your bags, I'll arrange for your clothes to be washed overnight."

"So kind," she murmured. "And thanks for taking care of Sophie."

Margot gave me one last hard glare, then left.

Silence fell in the elegant dining room, the festive midnight feast now crumbs, the little girls watching the drama with big eyes.

Josette rose from the table. "I think I'll go to bed, too, Mr. Cleeton."

"Of course. Your bedroom is the last on the right. Just across from Margot's."

"Lucky me." Her lips twisted down. "After everything she's ruined—"

Her voice broke, and she, too, fled the dining room. Flashing a warning look at John, I followed. I caught up with her in the foyer, just in time to see Margot disappearing up the stairs.

"Josette, I know you're sad to leave Roger behind—"

"I love him." Josette gave me a defiant, tearful smile. "I won't grow out of it. I don't care that I've made a fool of myself. I love him."

Standing in the villa's foyer beneath the dim light of the chandelier, I folded my arms over my silk robe, trying to find the right words. "Even though it hurts now, someday, you'll know leaving was the right thing, so you can escape this awful war. You'll be happy in America. Maybe even a famous movie star someday."

But Josette refused to be mollified. "I'll be acting, all right, but not in movies. I'll be pretending every day that my heart isn't broken and my life destroyed."

"Oh, Josette..." I took her hand. "It feels that way now. But you're so very young. In time—"

"My feelings will never change." She pulled away and went heavily up the stairs.

I watched her go, feeling worried and sad. I told myself she'd grow out of it. But as I returned to the dining room, I wondered if that was true. Sometimes the emotions of youth remained with us throughout our lives.

And sometimes—my eyes sought John's as I entered the room—we were able to start our lives anew.

John's warm gaze lingered. Just having him close, I felt comforted. Until I remembered, and my heart fell.

The little girls had grown fidgety and bored. Now the show was over, they'd started punching each other.

John looked at them. "All right, girls. It's been an exciting evening, but now it's time to head back to bed."

"I'm not tired," said Rachel.

"Don't wanna," said Noémie.

On my last nerve, I opened my mouth to order them sharply upstairs, when John stopped me with a playful glance. He stroked his chin thoughtfully. "I heard a rumor one of the toy shops in Marseille has too many toys. I was going to ask them to drop a few of their extra toys here in the morning..."

Three little faces snapped to attention.

"Toys!"

"What toys?"

He glanced at Noémie's tattered teddy bear, which had now been washed, its arm restuffed and repaired, its missing eye replaced, but it still looked a little tattered and disreputable. "Who knows?" he said airily. "Dolls... jacks... jump ropes. Maybe even a book or two." His expression became mournful. "But if you'll all be too tired in the morning to use them..."

"I won't be tired!"

"I'm going to bed right now!"

"Bed!"

With a joyful cry, the little girls leaped up from their chairs and raced up the stairs as noisily as they'd come down.

John looked at me with a grin. "They've been through a lot

the last few weeks. I thought they deserved a carrot rather than a stick."

"Thank you." I smiled, placing my hand over his. "It seems I never stop thanking you."

His dark eyes met mine. Touching skin to skin felt... intimate. His was rough on the edges, callused from many years on his Texas ranch. He'd hoped to someday leave his ten thousand acres to his son, but he and his wife never had the children they wanted. After she'd died of a long illness, he'd sold it all—sprawling house, cattle, horses, sagebrush-covered land stretching as far as the eye could see.

He'd known heartbreak, too.

His dark gaze fell to my lips. Shivering, I pulled my hand away.

"Right. Well." Smile lines crinkled around his eyes. "I could come with you and Margot to the consulate. If you want some muscle," he added lightly.

"No. Thank you. But... no."

He gave a nod. "I understand. I didn't mean to push."

"I need to talk to Margot—about..."

His handsome face softened. "I know."

Even after so long in Paris, his skin was still tanned from years in the Texas sun. I could easily imagine him in a cowboy hat, astride a horse, riding fast across the horizon, rope in hand. He was strong. Steady. Tough, but tender.

No wonder I'd told him my every secret—well, except South America, but that wasn't my secret to tell, was it?

His dark eyes locked with mine. I caught my breath, and this time it had nothing to do with illness. The two of us were alone in the dining room of his villa, amid the quiet shadows past midnight. We were wearing our night clothes, silk robes over his pajamas, over my nightgown. It felt private. Dangerous. I felt emotionally bare, as if I were naked, standing so close I could almost feel his breath on my skin, the warmth of his body through my silk.

My heart was pounding. Was it wrong of me to pretend we had hope of a future? Selfish beyond measure?

Turning, I went to the window. Pushing the heavy curtains aside, I stared out at the boats in the moonswept harbor and, beyond that, the Mediterranean Sea.

John came closer. "Helen," he said in a low voice behind me. "Won't you tell me I have a chance?"

I looked back at him. The Turkish carpet was soft under my feet, the chandelier's soft light limning the marble fireplace and caressing the sharp planes of his face. "A chance?"

John took a deep breath. "When you never showed up that day at the Gare de Lyon, I left Paris in despair. I could see that you'd only been humoring an old cowboy, being polite to me, while I'd let my feelings run amuck. There was only my wife, you see, and in the years after she died, no one else. I thought that part of my life was over. But since you arrived in Marseille, I've thought... wondered..." His eyes met mine, and he shook his head. "But perhaps I'm only seeing what I want to see."

Lifting my gaze to his, I whispered, "Back in Paris, I was scared."

I heard his intake of breath. Carefully, he brushed a tendril from my cheek. "And now?"

"Now..." For answer, I lifted my gaze, letting love shine from my face.

"Helen..." With a joyful gasp, he cupped my face with those large, calloused hands so tenderly I thought my heart would break. I forced myself to pull away.

"But you heard the doctor's diagnosis. Tuberculosis is no walk in the park. Even if I go to a sanitarium and breathe dry air and do all the treatments—I don't know how long I'll survive." I looked up at him pleadingly. "You could do better than me,

John. Find some young, sweet girl who's healthy, who you know will live a long time."

"None of us know that. Besides." He smiled, his thumb tracing my lower lip. "I only want you."

His touch made me dizzy. A lump rose in my throat. I felt like crying. "Why would you want to waste your time on a dying woman? It's so unfair to you—"

"I'll decide what's fair. I'm coming with you to Arizona, after we get the girls settled."

My lips parted. "But—what business do you have in Arizona?"

He pulled me back into his strong arms, then said softly, "The business of making you better."

"John," I whispered, my heart in my throat.

He lowered his head and kissed my forehead, my cheeks. Even my lips, which I knew wasn't entirely safe, not with my diagnosis, though tuberculosis wasn't as contagious as the flu. I pushed him away breathlessly. "You mustn't."

He smiled, then leaned his forehead against mine. "I must."

I wept, closing my eyes, pressing my cheek against his chest.

All these years, ever since my husband and child had died, I'd thought I didn't deserve love. The one time I'd tried, I'd only ruined lives—my baby's, my own. But I saw now that I'd used the ghost of Jean-Luc to protect myself from ever being hurt again. I'd used my memory of him as an excuse to never take that risk.

Just as I'd pushed Margot away all her life. I'd told myself she was better off without me, that I would only bring her shame. I'd played the role of stern headmistress, hiding my real self away from her, never giving her a chance to really know me at all.

No longer.

From now on, with whatever time I had left, I'd let myself live. I'd be Margot's mother, if she let me.

And how I wanted to be John's woman...

"I would give anything to spend my life with you," I choked out. Anguish twisted my heart, and I pulled away from him, wiping my eyes. "But I can't."

The joy in his eyes trickled away. He said dully, "You can't marry me?"

I shook my head. "Margot will never go to America if it means abandoning Lucie. The only way I'll convince her to board the ship is if I promise to stay in France in her place and find her sister."

John looked incredulous. "But if you stay in this climate, your illness will only get worse... Plus you said Otto Schröder is looking for you. You can't stay in France, Helen. It would be suicide."

I shook my head. "I'll be fine. I'll go back to Boulins and search for clues."

He lifted his chin. "Then I'll stay, too."

"No." My voice was sharper than I intended. I swallowed. "Please, John. If you truly care for me, I need your help."

"Anything."

I looked at him. "Go with Margot and the other girls to America. Keep them safe, get them to their new families. Can you do that, John? For me?"

His expression looked agonized. "But... leave you?"

"Please." My hand trembled as I placed it in his. "I'll never survive if I don't know Margot's safe. That they all are. *Please.*"

He bowed his head in the shadowy room.

"All right." His voice was almost too quiet to hear. "For you."

"Thank you." How wonderful it was, to have someone who cared about me, someone who was willing to help me, even if he didn't understand. "And, John?"

He lifted his head, his dark eyes haunted.

"Once I find Lucie..." I lifted my hand to his rough cheek,

my heart full of love and longing. "I'll come find you. We'll go to Arizona, and I'll do everything I can to get better. I promise you." Tears filled my eyes as I tried to smile. "How could I do otherwise, knowing you're waiting for me?"

He kissed my palm fervently.

But even as I spoke the words, I wept, knowing how unlikely it was that I'd ever reach Arizona.

John had made me feel seen. He'd made me feel wanted. He'd made me feel cherished.

How I wished it wasn't all too late.

27

MARGOT

The American consulate on Place Félix Baret was a madhouse, crowded with refugees speaking French, Dutch, Polish and who knew what else, all desperate to speak to someone, anyone. Even to the fortunate American citizens standing next to them in line.

After three hours waiting in the long queue outside, then another hour sitting beside Helen in the packed waiting area, I was starting to feel desperate myself. It had been hard to sleep last night, in spite of my exhaustion. After a hot bath, I'd put on a new nightgown that had been left on the bed, then slid between the freshly laundered sheets and stared at the ceiling— lost in the eerie quiet and thinking of everything I'd done wrong, everything that had been done wrong to me, and my sixteen-year-old sister lost somewhere with only her ugly little dog to protect her.

I hadn't been able to tell Josette that her Prince Charming was, in fact, even more unscrupulous than I'd imagined. He'd almost given Helen to the Nazis. And yet he'd still had the gall to criticize my treatment of Josette. He'd called her a poor kid.

He'd called her my sister.

*The two of you are really good at hurting each other. I
expected more of you, Margot... It doesn't matter now. I was in
love with a dream.*

A few hours before dawn, I'd come downstairs for a glass of
milk and found John Cleeton sitting alone in the kitchen, in the
dark. I hadn't asked why—I'd assumed it had something to do
with Helen, and she was the last thing I'd wanted to talk about.
I'd asked if he had any packets of sleeping powder, as I'd used
those once or twice while staying with the Lusignys' last
summer. He'd shaken his head apologetically.

In the end, I'd had to settle for warm milk. I knew Helen
had a few sleeping pills in her valise, but I hadn't been willing to
knock on her door and ask.

"Helen loves you, you know," he'd said suddenly, looking up
at me. His voice had caught. "More than anything."

I hadn't known what to say, so I'd just given him a jerky nod
and left.

Now, as I sat beside Helen on hard chairs in the consulate
waiting room, waiting to speak to a diplomatic attaché, I felt
angry, sad. I felt assaulted by all the tears and raised voices
around us. It wasn't just babies crying, either. I had a lump in
my throat myself.

All morning, I'd avoided looking Helen in the eyes or saying
anything but a curt "yes" or "no," in spite of her obvious eagerness to make amends. She thought spending time together today
would make me relent? Fat chance. Sure, she was sorry *now*.
But nothing could make me forgive her. She'd given me away?
Refused to recognize me as her daughter?

Fine. I'd refuse to recognize her as my mother.

"Mrs. Tyler?" A young, harried-looking secretary came up
to where we were packed into the overcrowded waiting area.
"Mr. Moore will see you now."

My legs shook as I rose to my feet, muscles still aching from
our days of walking. My feet hurt in Roger's old clunky shoes,

though my blisters were now covered in plasters. At least my clothes were clean, my knit shirt and trousers washed, along with my red scarf, which tied up my hair. I looked down at my clean socks and knew I owed John Cleeton a debt of gratitude.

I followed Helen and the secretary past stacks of cluttered papers and desks filled with refugees begging weary-looking staffers for visas. As we were escorted past a door to a small back office, I felt the envious gaze of all the other refugees still waiting, waiting without hope. Helen's American accent had been our lucky ticket.

"Everything's going to be fine," she murmured to me now, but I ignored her. I told myself I owed her nothing. I was helping her get visas for the girls, that was all—and to make sure she didn't pull a fast one trying to get me on the ship. After they all set sail tomorrow, I was heading north for Lucie.

"Ernest Moore." A skinny middle-aged man in glasses briefly shook Helen's hand. "Ma'am." He closed the door behind us, pointed with barest courtesy towards two opposite chairs, then returned to sit at his cluttered desk. "You can see we're busy. We normally wouldn't even be open today, but with things as they are..." He harrumphed. "I was told you insisted on speaking with me? Something about French orphans?"

"Yes—"

Looking over Helen in her simple dress, her gray-streaked brown hair in a chignon—and lacking any obvious wealth, like jewels or a fur coat—he gave a perfunctory smile. "I do understand your desire to help, ma'am, but I'm afraid you're wasting your time. As an American citizen, of course we encourage you to repatriate immediately, but for foreign nationals"—his eyes fell on me—"it's a more complicated process." Leaning back in his chair, he added pompously, obviously believing we weren't very bright, "See, you'd also need exit visas from the French government, transit visas, proof of sponsors in America. So sadly—"

"It should all be in order." Leaning forward in her own chair, Helen placed a line of papers on his desk. She pointed. "Affidavits from the American families."

He looked at the documents, nonplussed, then harrumphed. "Well. Half of Europe is clamoring for visas right now, and unfortunately we have very few. So I'm afraid"—he glanced at the earlier note from his secretary—"Estée Lévy, Rachel Lévy, Noémie Bonnet and Josette Dubois must go to the orphanage in Marseille." He frowned, looking up. "I was told five orphans. There are only four."

"My daughter is the other." Helen glanced at me. "But she is an American citizen who merely needs a passport, not a visa."

My daughter. Hearing her call me that so matter-of-factly to a stranger caused a strange thrill through me. I tamped down savagely on my feelings.

"Your daughter?" He lifted an eyebrow. "You have proof of this?"

Reaching into her bag, Helen pushed new documentation towards him, including two tiny copies of my black-and-white school photo taken last year. "As you see."

He looked down at it. His lips twisted in a moue of distaste. "Ah. I see. Your *natural* daughter."

The man said *natural* as if it was something shameful. Illegitimate. Unwanted. I bowed my head, seething, my cheeks burning.

"She's my child, so she's an American," Helen said firmly, her back ramrod straight. "You see there." She pointed. "Margaret Taylor. She was informally adopted for a few years, but her name was never officially changed. She needs a passport."

Margaret Taylor? That was my real name? Not Margot Vashon?

"Ye-ess," the man said reluctantly, as though conferring a great favor. "It is clear she is a citizen, no matter how... irregular her upbringing." He gathered the documents and tapped the bottom edges against his desk. "But we are very busy. It might take a few weeks."

A few weeks! My eyes went wide. Helen and I looked at each other. Her eyes narrowed.

"As for your request to help the four French orphans..." The bureaucrat spread his arms wide, the picture of helpless regret. "Even with sponsors and the proper French visas, I'm afraid it's difficult, impossible, to procure American ones in our current political climate. There's no appetite amongst the public back home to support endless throngs of hungry European refugees, simply because the Germans and French and Brits can't stop picking fights with each other—"

"That's not at all—"

"So I'm afraid there's nothing I can do." He rose to his feet, already gesturing towards the closed office door. "Leave your daughter's birth certificate and other documents with my secretary. We'll have her passport ready sometime next month. Now if you'll excuse me, Mrs. Tyler—"

"Taylor," she corrected politely, still sitting, still smiling. "Helen Taylor."

He slowly looked at her, his eyes wide, as if seeing her for the first time. "Helen—Taylor?"

"Yes."

He looked back at the note his secretary had given him. "Not... Ellen Tyler?"

With a small smile, Helen tilted her head like a quizzical bird. "I believe you were told to expect me, were you not?"

"Why, yes." Circles of red appeared on his pale, thin cheeks. "We had calls about it, from high up. But we expected you weeks ago and started to think—"

"I was unavoidably detained." She lifted a serene eyebrow. "You have what I need?"

"Yes—yes of course," he stammered. He backed away. "I'm

sorry for the confusion, Mrs. Taylor. Your visas should be ready —I'll get them now..."

He fled his office almost at a gallop.

Forgetting my resentment, I turned to stare at Helen in shock. Almost as if I were seeing her for the first time, too.

"Who are you?" I breathed.

Helen looked at me. "You know who I am."

"I don't." I glanced towards the closed door of the small office. "What did you do to earn this kind of treatment? The man hardly looked at us before, but when he heard your name, he almost seemed... afraid. Why?"

She shrugged. "Nothing really. I saved the lives of a few soldiers long ago who are now in politics. And," she added almost as an afterthought, "I've helped the US government a bit here and there. In Germany. In South America."

"What did you do?"

Her eyes gleamed in the sterile office light. "If I knew, I couldn't tell, could I?"

"Were you some kind of *spy*?"

"I wouldn't say I was." She considered, leaning her head. Then she flashed a grin. "And I wouldn't say I wasn't."

Of course she wouldn't tell me. Why would she ever be honest about anything? I set my jaw. "You don't need to get me a passport. I'm staying in France."

Her expression changed. "No, you're not."

"I'll help you get the girls on the ship, but that's it."

Helen grabbed my hand, anguished. "You must go to America, Margot—"

"Don't you mean *Margaret*?" I said acerbically.

Ignoring my outburst, she pleaded, "I need you to help John escort the girls to their new homes in California. And... I wasn't lying when I told you there was a job that would let you attend college. Just—not in Marseille."

I drew back. "What? Where?"

"I've gotten you a scholarship to attend the University of Southern California." She gave a tremulous smile. "You'll live in a dorm. I have a friend in the administration who'll look out for you. I'll pay you a salary for being nanny to the girls on the trip, so you'll have a little money when you arrive. After that, you can work part-time on campus, if you want. But your tuition, room and board are all covered."

She had all my attention now. "You can't be serious."

"Josette will be living with Miss Clarkson not too far away, if you want to see her. But that's your choice. You can study whatever you want for the next four years, get used to being American. Follow your dreams. Become a lawyer." She gripped my hand, her eyes fervent. "Become who you most want to be."

College? In America?

For a moment, I caught my breath. I'd be far from war, able to study in peace, to learn whatever I wanted. In America, unlike France, women were allowed to vote. I'd be living in the new land of California where futures stretched out as wide as the vast Pacific horizon. A woman could be anything there. Not just a lawyer but a hugely successful one, allowed to argue cases in front of any court. Maybe I could even be a judge someday.

I'd earn enough money to buy my own home. I'd be able to protect those I loved. The little girls, if they ever needed help. Josette even. And...

Lucie.

My dream came crashing down. I looked at Helen. "I can't."

"Why?" she cried. "You know it's not safe here. It's only a matter of time before the Nazis decide to take all of France. I need to know you're safe. It'll be the only thing that keeps me going if..." She licked her lips, her voice trembling. "If—"

"I'm not abandoning Lucie," I cut her off.

"That's what I'm trying to tell you." She took a deep breath, releasing the painful grip on my hands. "I'll stay here for Lucie.

While you take the girls on the ship to America, I'll remain in France and find her."

Even as she spoke the words, she wheezed a little. I wondered if it had taken all her effort to repress her weakness in front of the bureaucrat. I stared at the dark hollows beneath her eyes. "But—you're so sick. Dr. Ravanel said…"

Helen shook her head. "I went to the hospital yesterday and got X-rays. I don't have lung cancer. It's tuberculosis."

Relief coursed through me only briefly. Then I bit my lip. "But tuberculosis can be fatal, too. Can't it?"

"Not like lung cancer," she hedged, which seemed putting a bright shine on it, like saying pestilence was highly *géniale* compared to plague. She leaned towards me. "Don't worry. It'll all work out."

I thought of all the famous heroines who'd died of tuberculosis in novels by the Brontës, operas like *La Traviata*, even Greta Garbo on the silver screen. The Victorians had called it consumption. "What is the prognosis? Is there treatment?"

"Yes," she said soothingly. "And as soon as I've brought Lucie safely to America, I'll look into all that."

"But how—"

"I'll be fine." She gave a low laugh. "I could tell you some of the really dodgy things I've dealt with. I've been shot at, bombed, nearly died of multiple diseases, threatened with death in a coup d'état—"

"Threatened with death!"

She stroked her cheek, still in thought. "I once shot a German officer at close range in his own home, helping his wife flee his abuse."

"What if he comes looking for payback? Roger told me…" I hesitated, "back in Paris, he heard—"

"Don't worry. I know how to handle myself." She shrugged. "Whatever happens, I'll handle it."

I stared at her, thinking of all the years I'd classified Sister

Helen as dull, strict, plodding, utterly boring. There was so much more to her than I'd ever imagined.

"Do you really think you can find Lucie if you stay?" I heard myself ask in a small voice.

Helen gave a brisk nod. "I'll go talk to the Lusignys. Dollars to doughnuts, she's stuck in Boulins somewhere. I'll find her, get her visas, then get us both to America quick as we can. Lucie can live with me in Arizona, perhaps, until she graduates high school. Maybe then she'll join you at USC."

I was dazzled by the dream. Safe, at college... and with my sister?

Helen can handle this better than you, a voice whispered in my mind. She had so much more experience. She was older. Tougher. She had all kinds of skills I didn't. She could find Lucie and keep her safe. *Take her offer. Leave France. Go to America.*

My hands shook with the temptation to take the easy way out. I took a deep breath, looking at her in the small, dusty back office of the consulate. "But why? Why would you stay in France and throw yourself back into danger and the Nazi occupation, when you could be safe and free in your home country?"

She looked down at her hands, folded in her lap. "You know why."

"I don't."

"Because I love her." She lifted her gaze, her hazel eyes shining. "And I love you, Margot."

Tears rose in my eyes. I wiped them away savagely. "But you gave me up. Threw me in the trash heap."

"I thought you were better off without me." Her gaze fell. "Especially since I couldn't give you a father."

"Is it Jean-Luc Ravanel?" I whispered.

Her eyes widened. "You guessed?"

I shrugged. I didn't want her to blame Josette. It didn't seem right somehow.

"I loved Jean-Luc, but I didn't think I deserved another family. By the time I changed my mind, he was married to someone else."

"Élisabeth."

"Yes. I couldn't tell him I was having his child. It would have destroyed his peace, his new marriage."

I thought of how hard that sacrifice must have been. "So what did you do?"

She swallowed. "I rented a little house outside Paris, where no one knew me. For several precious weeks after you were born, you were mine, just mine." She reached for my hand. "Just the two of us. You were so beautiful. So unbearably precious." Her eyes glistened with unshed tears. "But I had to let you go."

"Why didn't you just raise me alone?" I said hoarsely over the lump in my throat.

Her lips curved humorlessly. "As my *natural* daughter? Derided and insulted by strangers? While I took you with me through war zones and epidemics?" She shook her head. "I knew you'd have a happier life with the Vashons. They had a lovely farm full of flowers, and they wanted a child so badly."

"And you didn't."

"That's not true. I always wanted you. I've thought of you every single day. But letting you go was the bravest thing I ever did. I did it to give you a better life."

I wouldn't feel sympathy. I *wouldn't*. I set my jaw. "But you could have claimed me as your daughter after my mother—I mean Violette Vashon—after she died. Instead you let me believe my parents were dead and took me to an orphanage."

"I was planning to return to South America and needed to find you and Lucie a home. I was told St. Agnes's was the best in Paris, that St. Agnes girls had done great things for hundreds of years, in art, in literature, in business and law. I knew you'd be proud of where you came from as a St. Agnes girl. But the orphanage needed a temporary headmistress, and money to survive..."

"So you gave both." I swallowed hard. Through the door's window, I could see the man who'd been helping us returning towards the tiny office. "Jean-Luc still doesn't know he's my father, does he?"

Shaking her head, Helen smiled sadly. "Though you're so like him. I kept waiting for him to see it."

"I liked him. I liked his family."

"Yes. Me, too." She paused, then added quietly, "It's why I left them alone."

I felt suddenly sorry for her, looking at her sad face, the wrinkles at her eyes, her gaunt cheekbones, her sagging shoulders. Helen was actually rather pretty, I realized, or she might have been, if she'd taken care of herself, rather than always sacrificing her health for others. A fifty-year-old woman who'd grown up hungry in an orphanage, she'd given her life trying to make up for something, the deaths of her husband and baby, which hadn't even been her fault. She'd loved Jean-Luc but let him go.

Just as she'd done for me.

With a knock, Mr. Moore pushed through the office door, papers filling his hands. "I'm so sorry for the wait, Mrs. Taylor. This should be everything you requested. For your daughter and the other four girls as well."

"Good." Rising to her feet, she took the documentation. As she swiftly looked through it, I rose awkwardly, too. "It seems to be in order."

"Splendid."

Helen gave a charming smile. "I wondered if perhaps I could just ask for one extra last visa."

"Forgive me." He hesitated. "I wish I could, but I've been told to let you know..."

"Yes?"

The man pushed his glasses up nervously. "While those in power remain grateful for your assistance and discretion, I'm supposed to tell you the chit is paid. The debt wiped clean. You must expect no further help of any kind. If you ask for more, there will be consequences."

Helen exhaled with a flare of nostrils. "I understand."

Her face was tranquil, but I felt only fear. No further help from the Americans? Then how would Helen get a visa for Lucie? And what would happen if Helen herself got in a jam—if she was arrested by that Nazi officer, if she was hurt, if she fell gravely ill in France, with no money, alone?

And what if this war didn't end as soon as everyone said it would? What then?

"Oh. And there's one other thing."

"Yes?" Helen said.

Mr. Moore smiled thinly. "We received a telegram for you nearly a week ago. We didn't know where to forward it, but then of course, we expected you soon—"

"A telegram?"

"Concerning"—breathlessly, he consulted the paper in his hand—"Lucie Vashon?"

I almost screamed. "Lucie's safe? She sent a telegram?"

He nodded. "She's been found."

Helen and I gasped, then, without thought, hugged each other. But our joy was short-lived.

"She's in Paris," Mr. Moore said.

Slowly, we turned to face him.

"Paris?" I repeated hoarsely.

He nodded. "The telegram came from a German gentleman. I'll read it." His brow furrowed as he looked at it. "*Lucie and dog found, brought to St. Agnes's. Stop. Tell sister Margot not to worry. Stop. You must come for the exchange. Stop. If you don't, we will come to you in Marseille.* And then the name of the German officer."

Smiling, he proffered the telegram to us. Helen snatched it up, and he continued, sitting back in his chair with a satisfied sigh, "I must admit it's refreshing to have a lost person actually be found." He beamed. "Good news for a change."

"Uh... thank you..." I said when Helen didn't answer. Her cheeks were pale. She seemed to be staring fixedly at the block letters of the telegram, though the number of words on it were so few.

"Well, I'm happy to help. And thank you again, Mrs. Taylor. I hope you'll forgive my earlier confusion if any of your —uh—*contacts* ask. Do you need help finding the way out?"

"No, thank you," I said when Helen still said nothing.

"In that case..." Mr. Moore nodded. "I wish you safe travels."

As Helen and I pushed back through the crowded consulate, she seemed in a daze, still gripping the telegram. I had to lead her through the building and hold the door wide, otherwise it might have hit her in the face.

After drawing her past the long queue of refugees outside the consulate door, I pulled her into a quiet corner of the tree-lined square. "Tell me what's going on. Isn't it good news that Lucie is found? And safe?"

"She's—not safe." She seemed to be having a hard time catching her breath. Staggering back, she rested against a sturdy tree, the crumpled telegram in her hand. I took it from her, looking down at it in the tree's shade.

"Roger told me the Nazi officer who commandeered St. Agnes's offered a big reward for your capture," I said slowly. "He must have somehow tracked down Lucie instead."

"Roger heard that?" Her lips pursed. "I'm surprised he didn't turn me in for the money."

"He was tempted." I gave a humorless smile. "But why does the Nazi officer have such a grudge against you?"

"It's the man I told you about. The one I shot back in 1924."

"Sixteen years ago!" It seemed an eternity. "And he's still mad?"

"I didn't just graze him, Margot. I shot him through the bone, then spirited his wife and child away. He probably still walks with a cane."

"Surely you don't think he'd hurt Lucie?" I looked down at his name, narrowing my eyes. "This... Otto Schröder?"

"No," Helen whispered. "Not if he gets what he wants."

"What does he want?"

She lifted bleak eyes to mine. "Me."

28

MARGOT

This was bad. Very bad. I paced the sidewalk, surrounded by leafy green trees and elegant white buildings of the square. I stopped, facing Helen.

"But how did the man get his hands on Lucie? She can't have walked all the way back to Paris!"

Helen shook her head. "She must have ended up on the wrong side of the demarcation line in Boulins. She didn't have her papers. If she went to the French authorities and mentioned my name..." She rubbed her forehead in the bright, harsh sunlight. "Schröder must have my name on some Gestapo list."

"So what do we do?"

"I need to think." Forehead furrowed, she started walking. Her pace picked up as we returned down the narrow Cours Pierre-Puget with its shops and residences with blue shutters on the pale buildings. Whenever she had to stop to cough, I put my arm beneath her shoulders until the fit passed. She was so thin, so frail. It made me worry.

Then I had a new, scary thought.

"Helen, you don't suppose Lucie told Schröder where we

were—" As I followed her around the corner to John Cleeton's street, she gasped, grabbing my sleeve and yanking me back.

"Soldiers," she breathed. "At the villa gate."

I peeked around her, very slowly, my heart pounding in my throat.

Two young men in bland civilian clothes were lingering casually outside the villa.

I ducked back. "How can you tell they're soldiers?"

"The way they stand," she said crisply. She gave another slow glance around the corner, then sucked in her breath. "They're coming this way. *Run.*"

We turned and ran, back up the street, down the alley, past the Abbaye Saint-Victor. Helen repeatedly stumbled, and once nearly fell. Every time I lifted her up and looked back, hoping we'd lost them, the two men would reappear. As we dodged around a corner, I saw a sign for a bookstore.

"In here," Helen choked out, her face like a ghost's.

"We'll be trapped," I said helplessly, but I knew she couldn't run anymore. And I couldn't carry her. What I wouldn't have given to have Roger with us now!

Monsieur Destraz, the sweet old man who'd given Helen and the girls a ride to Marseille two days before, looked up in surprise from stocking shelves of dusty used books.

"Madame Taylor. I didn't expect to see you so soon—"

"Nazis are chasing us, *monsieur*," she gasped. "Do you have a back door?"

His brow lowered. He asked no questions, just pointed. "The storeroom leads into an alley. I will say nothing."

I nearly wept. "Thank you."

He snapped his book shut and squared his shoulders. "Go."

I helped Helen stagger through the empty shop and out into the alley. With every step, she seemed weaker and sicker. Upon finding a loose gate, we crept through someone's garden. Somehow, we were able to sneak into our rented villa through the back door.

Inside the house, there was pandemonium.

John Cleeton was shouting, "Everyone be calm—everything's fine," while Noémie was crying, and there were open bags all over the floor of the foyer. Josette, Estée and Rachel were frantically tossing in clothes.

Mr. Cleeton stopped when he saw us, relief plain on his face. He raked his hand through his salt-and-pepper hair. "Helen. Thank heaven. I was so worried. You wouldn't believe who just showed up at the door—"

"Nazis?" she inquired with a crooked grin. In spite of her body's weakened state, her spirit was still fire. He stopped.

"How did you know?"

"I saw them lingering in the street. The men chased us, but we got away. I don't think they saw us come back here."

"One of them was Werner," Josette told me in a panic. "I saw his face from the top window."

Werner? The young soldier we'd flirted and drunk pastis with? "Are you sure?"

"Who's Werner?" Helen asked.

"The soldier who let us steal his truck. I'm surprised he's not in some Nazi jail." Josette looked at me. "Did he recognize you?"

Everything had happened so fast. I hadn't had time to look at the soldiers carefully. Hopefully, he'd been too focused on Helen to notice me. "I don't know. I don't think so."

Josette's lips twisted as she looked over my striped Breton shirt and wide-legged trousers. "I'd be surprised if he did. You were pretty then. Dressed like a *girl*."

I rolled my eyes. "Don't start—"

"Four young men rang the bell at the gate and asked for you," Mr. Cleeton told Helen in a low, tense voice. "When I demanded to know their business, they said they were with the police. But only one spoke French—and with the thickest German accent I've ever heard. I wouldn't let them through the gate."

"Oh, John." Helen looked as if she wanted to throw herself in his arms. "Thanks for being on my side."

He looked down at her, brushing a tendril of hair from her face that had escaped her chignon. "I'm always on your side." He took a breath. "But..."

"But?"

"Two of them left and said they'd come back with the police. The real police. They had some wild lie that you're wanted for attempted murder."

Glancing uneasily at the little girls, who were watching with interest, Helen pressed her lips together. "Remember that German officer back in Munich? How I got his wife and child away?"

He sucked in his breath. "So it's not a lie—precisely."

"Margot," Josette said suddenly. "Remember what Werner told us? They were heading south..."

"Looking for an enemy of the Reich," I breathed.

We all turned to look at Helen.

"All right. That's quite enough panic." She clapped her hands briskly, taking charge. "We need to leave the villa. Find someplace to hide until our ship leaves tomorrow." But her strength didn't last. She took a wheezing breath, and Mr. Cleeton held up an arm to support her. She looked up at him in worry. "Unless... unless they already somehow know we're sailing on that ship."

"They might." He set his jaw. "Let me make a phone call." He looked at us. "Be ready to leave in five minutes."

We rushed around the villa, gathering random things. My heart twisted as I looked at the little girls, at Josette. At Helen, who had collapsed pale-faced into a chair. I thought I'd have more time.

"Can I bring you your valise from upstairs?" I asked gently.

Still struggling to catch her breath, she nodded. But as she looked at me, her eyes glowed with love and gratitude.

I felt wretched, thinking of all the mean things I'd said.

John Cleeton came out of the kitchen, beaming. "It's done. I know someone who knows someone, and they found us space on a different ship leaving this afternoon. I paid triple to have our berth registered under a different name."

Helen's face lit up. "John!"

He smiled in pleasure. "If the Nazis saw your name on the manifest for tomorrow, too bad for them—we'll already be gone."

"Thank—you," she gasped.

His worried dark eyes looked down at her. Then he smoothed his face into a smile. "The new ship won't be luxurious, I'm afraid. We'll be packed like sardines."

"H-How?"

He gave a low laugh. "Bribery works, that's how. Ship's taking us to Martinique, not Portugal, but we can easily hop a ship to Florida."

Everyone around me finished packing—only one small bag each to start entirely new lives on the other side of the world, though the little girls also got to keep their favorite new toys, obligingly stuffed in Mr. Cleeton's larger suitcase. I didn't move. My bag was already packed. I just needed to get Helen's.

Could I do this? Could I?

Helen looked up at me. "Don't be—scared," she panted. "You're doing—right thing. I'll go—Paris—tonight."

"Paris?" gasped Josette.

"Lucie's been found," I said dully. "She's back at St. Agnes's."

There was an immediate clamor.

"What!"

"Lucie's found?"

"She's in Paris?"

"Yes," Helen said. "Don't—worry. I'll send her—America."

Send, she'd said. Send. Not bring.

Helen knew that she was going to Paris to die.

I looked at her miserably. This all felt wrong. I didn't like the thought of leaving without Lucie—or...

Or without Helen. My heart twisted. I couldn't hate her. I didn't want her to suffer.

She was my mother.

I took a deep breath. "I don't think I can do this."

I felt her hand on mine. She squeezed weakly, her wan face glowing. "Love you—Margot."

My throat closed. I'd hated her for how badly she'd treated me, how little she'd seemed to care. But now all I could think was how unfair it was, that Helen had sacrificed her life always taking care of others, and her reward for that would be handing herself over to the Nazis to free my sister—and me.

My feelings churned, caught between what I wanted and what I knew was right.

"Helen's not coming with us to America?" Josette's voice was strained.

"No Sister Hewen?" cried Noémie.

"She'll come as soon as she can," Mr. Cleeton said.

I saw a flash of grief in his dark eyes, quickly veiled. He knew. He knew she wasn't coming back.

He knelt in front of Helen. "I won't try to talk you out of staying. You love stronger and harder than anyone I've ever known. Your girls will get to California. I promise you."

She sighed. Closing her eyes, she leaned her forehead against his shoulder. "Love..."

"Forever," he whispered, kissing the top of her hair.

For a moment, they held each other. Then, of one accord, they pulled away. The final moments happened in a whirl of activity. Taxis were called. The housekeeper and staff were paid, undoubtedly with handsome tips. Madame Paget, Madame Latour and the maids quickly fled, their own suitcases in hand. And just like that, it was time to go.

Josette closed her suitcase with a snap, looking at me meaningfully as I came out of my bedroom with my bag. As we went into Helen's room to get her worn leather valise, we spoke quietly, becoming resigned to our fate. We didn't want to leave her, but we knew we had no choice.

We'd be alone, an ocean away from the woman who'd done so much for us, our whole childhoods, expecting no appreciation or praise in return. We felt sad, resigned, guilty. But we could see no other way.

Helen would have to be the one to make the sacrifice.

I spoke quietly to John Cleeton as we followed the others through the back garden, walking furtively towards the two taxis waiting for us two streets over. Helen, walking ahead, climbed slowly into one, helped by Noémie.

"Thank you," I told Mr. Cleeton thickly when we reached our taxi.

The Texan just shook his head, tears in his eyes. Then he placed his suitcase and the valise in the trunk before he climbed in beside Helen and Noémie. I got in the other taxi with Josette and the Lévy sisters, and gripped my own bag in my lap. On the short drive, we looked nervously in every direction. But we made it.

After we arrived at the modern docks to the northwest of the city, Mr. Cleeton paid off the drivers. "Tell no one."

Gaping at the huge tips, they nodded, and I felt a rush of gratitude for John Cleeton being in our lives. How could the trip to America not succeed with him in charge?

The medium-sized ship *Alphonse Dumas* was waiting at the Marseille dock. As Mr. Cleeton had warned, it was no luxury liner but a rusty bucket of bolts that had been refitted to pack paying passengers as their cargo. We joined a stream of passengers far luckier than the *désespérés* back at the consulate, all with visas and a berth booked. But no one looked relaxed, even those who presumably didn't have Nazis hot on their trail. Everyone seemed tense, glancing over their shoulders.

Including us. I tried not to look at the three uniformed members of the *gendarmerie* standing guard on the dock, their hard eyes moving over the crowd, ready to restrain and arrest anyone who tried to rush the ship or start a riot.

With squared shoulders, supported by Mr. Cleeton, Helen led us past them without notice. She stopped for breath at the gangway on the end of the dock. It was crowded with waiting passengers, as the ship's crew double-checked documentation and names on their lists before allowing them to board.

Helen looked at all of us, weighed down with our hastily packed bags. Her lovely face was brave, the kind of brave that breaks your heart.

"I'll say—goodbye here."

"Here?" My back stiffened with panic. No. It was too soon. Too public. People were pushing past us with large parcels. I looked back at the *gendarmes* still not too far away. "Not here!"

"Can't we say goodbye properly on the ship?" Josette begged.

Helen eyed the crew holding the lists. "It's too—risky."

"Don't worry—that's handled," John Cleeton told her firmly. "Come on board."

She blinked. "How—"

Smoothing her hair back from her face, he smiled down at her, his dark eyes sad. "Trust me."

"Stay another minute, Sister Hewen," pleaded Noémie, flinging her small arms around her waist.

Met by such persuasive force, Helen reluctantly bowed her

head. But I saw how painful it was for her to stretch out the goodbye as we crossed towards the two hard-eyed crew members checking names at the gangway.

"Name?" one of the men demanded as we approached.

Mr. Cleeton didn't immediately answer. He was distracted by pulling a bright yellow handkerchief out of his jacket pocket, which seemed caught by the wind.

A different crew member suddenly appeared, nudging the first aside. "I'll handle this, Martin."

"Yes, sir."

"Ah, Monsieur Durand, Madame Durand." He looked from Mr. Cleeton to Helen with shifty eyes. "Welcome. And of course all your lovely children. Your cabin is this way, if you'll please follow me."

We followed him into the old ship, down dark, rusty stairs. In the windowless hold, my heart sank as we walked past a hundred cramped, grimy cots packed together like bags of barley. Fortunately, the crewman kept walking.

"I hope you'll find this comfortable, *monsieur*," he said at last and pushed open a rusted door. Josette and I went in last.

Inside, the cabin was small but private. A porthole window overlooked a water basin on a table with two chairs. Two single beds lined the walls.

"*Monsieur?* It is as I said?"

"Yes." Mr. Cleeton turned back to him. "Thank you."

The crewman left, shutting the door behind him, holding a wad of cash and John Cleeton's gold pocket watch.

Helen stood in the center of the small cabin, looking dazedly between the two single beds and the six of us.

"We'll make it work," John Cleeton said with forced cheer. "The little girls can share the beds. The rest of us will sleep on the floor. It's only for a week, until we reach Martinique."

She hesitated. "Are you sure—?"

He squeezed her hand. "We'll be fine."

Looking up at him, she nodded, then brushed a hand at her eyes. "Come here, girls. One last—big hug. We'll see each other... soon."

I felt an ache in my throat. Helen had kept many secrets in her life, but it was the first and only time I'd ever heard her lie.

Even Noémie seemed to feel the uncertainty of her last statement. The little girls slowly set down their bags. Josette and I had already dropped ours by the door.

We clustered around her, and she threw her arms wide to embrace us, pulling us close. The little girls started sniffling, and my eyes stung as I looked at Josette. Tears were falling unchecked down her cheeks.

"I'm so—proud of you," Helen said unsteadily. "All of you. I know you'll do—wonderfully. Be happy."

"But will *you* be happy, Sister Helen?" wept Estée.

"Why can't you come with us?" cried Noémie.

"Can't we just send Lucie a ticket to follow us?" Rachel pleaded. "Or wait for her until she gets here?"

"We should stay together," Estée said. "We're a family, aren't we?"

"Everything will be... all right. Promise." Helen's eyes met mine. Another lie. My heart twisted with grief.

"Here," sniffled Noémie. With a hiccup, she pressed the tattered Nounours into her hands. "He wants to stay with you. He'll keep you safe."

Helen looked startled, holding the worn teddy bear against her heart. Then her expression crumpled, and tears spilled over her lashes. "Oh, my sweet one." She fell to one knee and hugged the five-year-old. "Thank you... Noémie."

Wiping her eyes, she looked back at John, who helped her to her feet. She looked at us with a tremulous smile. "Will you all do—something for me?"

"Anything," said Estée.

"Look after Margot." Our eyes met as she whispered, "Look after my daughter."

The little girls looked at each other, puzzled.

"Your—daughter?"

"Who?"

"Margot is her daughter," Josette told them gently.

"Really?"

"From your tummy?" said Noémie, looking doubtfully at Helen's slender waist.

"Yes." She wiped her eyes, then smiled. "I kept it—secret. It was silly, wasn't it?"

"Margot's not an orphan like us?" Rachel said slowly.

"A kind lady, Lucie's mother, raised Margot as a baby. After the lady died, I came back to help her." She looked around the girls in the light of the tiny ship cabin. "That's when I met— you. I love you all." Her eyes met mine as she whispered, "So much."

The girls looked at me. "Margot!"

"You have a *maman*," said Noémie.

They hugged me, bringing Helen and Josette into the embrace, too. My heart twisted. I felt the seconds ticking away before I'd leave my mother forever, just when I'd started to really know her. To *love* her.

How could I live without Helen in my life? How?

Josette's tearful eyes met mine. I knew her heart was breaking, too.

Helen finally pulled away from us, wiping her eyes as she gasped, "I should go."

John Cleeton sighed ruefully. "I just wish I'd brought something to toast to our future success. For you in Paris, Helen. And us in America. We could all use the luck."

"Yes." Helen bit her lip. "I had—brandy, but I left it—"

"I brought it." I pulled the silver flask out of my bag. "I kept it to remember you by."

Helen looked at me as if she was about to cry openly.

"Perfect." Mr. Cleeton took the silver flask from me and held it dramatically up in the air. "To our new lives." He looked at each of us in the ship's cabin, even little Noémie. His gaze lingered on Helen's face as he whispered, "To all the things left unsaid and sacrifices made."

Helen gave a trembling smile, her eyes swimming with tears. He put the flask to his lips, then wiped his mouth and handed it to her.

Her lovely face was filled with grief and longing as she took the flask. She paused, hands trembling, then took a long swig. *Really* long. He watched, then gave a crooked grin. "You really know how to take your brandy, *madame*."

"This time I need it," she gasped, wiping her mouth. "For luck. And courage," she added more softly. Her voice trembled as she started to turn. "Now, I really must—"

"Wait, not yet. We have an hour before the ship departs. I'm still a little confused about the girls."

"John…"

"No, really. Where do they each go again? I'd hate to take the wrong kid to the wrong place." His smile faded. "Please," he whispered, taking her hands in his own. "I need just a few last minutes with you. Alone."

Helen blinked fast, swallowing hard.

"Is it really wise, John?" she said in a low voice. Her voice caught. "It might be—easier if I just—go."

But she didn't move away from him. He glanced at Josette and me. "Would you mind taking the little girls up to see the view from the deck?"

"Sure." Josette and I turned to ferry the three little girls towards the cabin door.

"I'm not wittle," Noémie was protesting as we gently pushed them out.

Heart pounding, I looked back one last time. Helen was

sitting beside John, the two of them talking softly at the table. The sunlight from the tiny porthole window illuminated her brown hair like a halo, leaving a reverent trace of golden light as his head bowed to kiss the knuckles of her hand.

With a deep breath, I closed the door.

29

HELEN

The shape and color of sunlight had moved oddly. As my eyes fluttered open, I felt groggy, out of place.

"You're all right." John's voice. "Take it easy."

His larger hand brushed over mine. I felt soft fabric beneath my palms. Forcing my eyes open, I stared up at the swaying ceiling. Something was wrong. I was in bed.

I sat up abruptly, out of breath. Everything in the room started spinning. There was a metallic taste in my mouth. I put my hands to my head. "What—what happened?"

He pulled back his hand. "Please don't be angry with me."

I blinked, and after a few moments, I could focus on his face, the crinkles around his warm dark eyes. Why would I be—?

Then awareness came in a rush. I was in the small cabin of the *Alphonse Dumas*. I was sitting on one of the small beds. The last thing I remembered was sitting at the table, the two of us holding each other and trying not to cry, drinking the last of the brandy as we tried to be brave.

But since then—

The sunlight had moved.

"What time is it?" I sucked in my breath. "The girls—"

"They're fine." He pointed. Estée, Rachel and Noémie were quietly playing checkers on the worn carpet near the door.

I rose from the bed, feeling dizzy. "Did I fall asleep? How long was I out?" Fear went through me. "I need to get off this ship before it leaves dock. Margot would never forgive me if—"

John stood in front of me in the cabin, his head bowed. "Margot's gone. Josette, too."

And I realized for the first time that the ship was moving. I wasn't just dizzy. The ship was swaying beneath my feet.

My mouth fell open. "John, what have you done?"

He lifted his head, and I saw anguish in his dark eyes. "The right thing."

"But Margot, Josette—"

"They departed the ship right after they left the cabin. Estée watched the little girls outside the door. Margot and Josette are staying in France, Helen. To find Lucie."

"But—they can't!" I looked at him, horrified. "They're just children!"

"You're wrong. They planned this. They just asked for my help, and I couldn't turn them down." Coming closer in the tiny cabin, he said, "Margot crushed your sleeping pills into your brandy."

I gasped. "But you drank the brandy too—"

Pressing his sensual lips together, he said quietly, "I only pretended to."

I stared up at him, angry. Betrayed. I said bitterly, "No wonder you insisted on toasting to success."

"That was real. We have to hope for success. For all of us."

"No. I won't accept it!"

"They did it to save your life. They wanted you to go to America. I gave them money and any contacts I thought might help them in France. But they're on their own now."

I backed away. "I'm the adult. I'm the mother. I'm the one who should sacrifice."

"Not this time. They couldn't bear the thought of you going to certain death. And truth be told"—his eyes met mine—"I couldn't either."

I pictured Margot and Josette going into the lion's den, facing down Nazis. Facing *Otto Schröder*. "They're too young to know what they're up against. I can't let this happen."

"It's already done."

Ignoring him, I turned and raced out of the cabin, through the half-empty cots in the hold and up two flights of stairs before I reached the outside deck.

It was crowded with people packed beside the railings. Some refugees were waving at friends and loved ones left behind on the dock, others wept openly as they stared back at the shores of their beloved France one last time.

I pushed past them roughly to the railing and looked down at Marseille's port, rapidly disappearing behind us in the twilight. For a moment, I couldn't see anyone I recognized back on the dock.

Then I saw the flash of red—Josette's hair.

And beside her, my daughter.

"Margot!" I screamed into the wind, waving wildly. "Josette!"

The people around me moved away, looking at me like I was a madwoman, and perhaps I was, swinging my arms like a windmill, screaming loud enough to wake the dead.

On the dock, I saw Margot nudge Josette in the ribs, and then both of them were waving and screaming, too. Whatever they said was lost in the wind, but I suddenly knew what they were trying to tell me.

They'd made this choice as an act of love for me. An act of faith in themselves. They'd done this to protect me, so I'd be safe in America, able to get treatment for my illness. They'd wanted me to live.

They would be the ones to fight.

They were telling me they'd do their best to be strong and brave. If they could learn to trust each other, to take care of each other, they might just win.

Tears streamed down my cheeks as I slowly put down my arms.

"We'll take a ship from Martinique to Miami, then the train," John said quietly beside me. "I'll contact the best sanitarium in Arizona. There will be a room waiting for you. Luckily, I own a home nearby."

I turned accusingly. "You do not."

Glancing back at the three little girls quarreling behind him, he gave a crooked grin. "Well, I will." Following my gaze, he sobered, looking towards the dark blur of the dock. "I'm sorry, Helen. Margot told me their plan as we left the villa. They were going to just run away but decided this was better."

"How?" I demanded, wiping tears from my eyes. "How is it better?"

"If they'd run away, you would have gone after them instead of boarding the ship. Then none of you would have been safe. This way, at least you had a chance to say goodbye."

"You tricked me," I choked out. "All of you."

John lifted his chin. "You raised Margot and Josette to be strong and independent and have a sense of duty—just like you. So why are you so shocked and horrified when they act on that?"

"I know, but..." I swallowed hard, then breathed, "I'm scared."

"Yeah. I'm scared, too." He put his arm around me gently. "We just have to trust everything will work out."

Sniffing, I looked out at the figures on the dock, growing ever smaller.

"John," I whispered, tears spilling down my lashes.

He rubbed a tear off my cheek with the tip of his thumb. "I know." Then he gathered me in his strong arms and exhaled, kissing my hair. "I know."

Noémie looked uncertainly up at us, gripping her teddy against her chest. Estée looked about to cry. Rachel *was* crying. We pulled them closer, all of us in one big embrace. I looked back at Marseille. "I wanted to keep them safe."

"They wanted the same for you." He stroked my hair. "Accept their gift."

I looked up at John, so strong, so fine. For years, he'd waited for me to notice his devotion. But I'd been too afraid, too blinded by past burdens and griefs. Now I knew I'd no longer let my life be ruled by fear. I would follow the example of my girls and be brave—and strong.

Holding each other, we watched the lights of Marseille disappear, blending into the darkening sea. Then, still holding hands, the five of us slowly turned to face west, towards the last fading light on the horizon, towards the future—and America.

John's eyes met mine, and he smiled. "Everything's going to be all right."

And suddenly I knew it would be.

This wasn't the path I'd wanted for them. But Margot and Josette were no longer children. I saw it now. They were strong young women, with minds and wills of their own. They would find Lucie. They would survive. I looked back at Marseille.

It was the Germans who should be afraid.

EPILOGUE

MARGOT

We kept waving, long after the ship was a dark silhouette against the Mediterranean sunset.

"Well," Josette said as the other people on the dock shuffled away in the fading light, their faces downcast, their shoulders heavy with their own worries. "What now?"

"We head for St. Agnes's and get Lucie," I said, as if it were simple.

She shook her head. "We'll need help." She paused. "Roger..."

Remembering his audacity in stealing the Nazi truck, I thought perhaps he could help us, for all that. Assuming he was never tempted again to betray us. I sighed, wondering if I should explain to Josette that he was no hero.

But a small voice told me that Roger hadn't betrayed us. He'd helped us. We'd never have made it to Marseille without him. Maybe he wasn't a hero, but he was at least a friend. Hopefully even now. "You think he'd want to come with us?"

Josette tossed her red hair. "He said he wants to fight Nazis. He's looking for comrades in that battle. Who better than us?

And where better to fight than Paris? His great-aunt is there with Lucie. There's no worthier cause."

I hesitated. As sensible as that all sounded, I knew we had a lot of difficulties ahead of us. I tilted my head. "Did you ever learn why Helen wanted to take you to America?"

Josette shrugged, her gaze evading mine. "Doesn't matter." She set her jaw. "I'm not abandoning Lucie. Besides, this is my home."

I wondered how much of her patriotic fervor came from love for Lucie, and how much came from love for Roger. But what difference did it make? I looked back at the horizon. The ship was a dark smudge against the orange sunset. The choice had been made.

I hoped my mother would forgive us. I hoped she and the girls and John Cleeton would all be happy and safe. I prayed this war would not come to American shores. I wondered if I'd ever find out what happened to them.

"So you agree?" Josette asked, her voice trembling a little.

"About Roger? Yeah. Sure." I hoped he would forgive me, too, and that I could win back his respect. I hoped we could be... friends? Yes. Friends. "But, Josette," I added warningly, "if he comes with us, this time—"

"Don't worry," she said quickly. "I'm not going to throw myself at him again. There's no time for that sort of thing. This is about Lucie."

She held out her hand.

I didn't quite believe her, but I shook it regardless.

"Lucie," I agreed and turned away briskly. "Roger said he was staying with a friend on the rue du Panier, didn't he?"

She nodded. "It shouldn't be hard to track him down." She grinned. "We could hatch plans over a drink."

"As long as it's not pastis."

She snorted. "No." Then she brightened. "Maybe champagne?"

I shook my head. "Champagne is for celebration. For blood oaths and eternal vows." I stroked my chin. "For battle, I'm thinking the proper toast is... whisky."

Josette looked shocked. "Whisky!"

It was strange to think that the two of us were now free to do whatever we wanted, for good or ill: to drink alcohol, to go to a bar with strange men. To steal a dress or work as a spy or shoot Nazis in the street. Or be shot by them. There was no one to tell us what to do anymore. No one to protect us.

Only us.

"Let's get dinner, too," I said recklessly. "I want steak and cheese and red wine. Something that will stick to our ribs."

"Mr. Cleeton's villa is likely crawling with Germans and police by now. Should we find a hotel? Or make tracks out of town?"

"Find a quiet inn near the rue du Panier and make plans over dinner," I said. "We'll leave at first light."

"What then?"

"I don't know." For reassurance, I patted my mother's old service revolver from the Great War, still tucked in its worn leather holster in my bag beside the thick wad of francs from Mr. Cleeton. "We'll figure it out."

"But where do we even start?"

Follow your dreams, my mother had told me. *Become who you most want to be.* She'd taught me everything I needed to be strong. To do what we needed to do.

Tilting my head, I gave Josette a cocky grin. "We managed to get here from Paris, didn't we?" I winked at her. "All we have to do now... is find our way back."

A LETTER FROM JENNA

If you enjoyed *The Home for War Orphans*, I'd love if you could leave a short review. As a new historical author (what wonderful words!), it's lovely to hear from readers and makes a big difference in encouraging others to give my books a try.

If you'd like to keep up to date with my latest Bookouture releases, you can sign up at the following link. Your email address will never be shared, and you can unsubscribe anytime.

www.bookouture.com/jenna-ness

The exodus of refugees escaping the 1940 Nazi invasion of the Low Countries and France was unlike anything ever seen in Europe. As many as ten million people fled the Blitzkrieg. Some families left in a blind, reckless panic, leaving dinners still hot on the table; others carefully stacked their most valuable possessions, from mattresses and cuckoo clocks to pets and grandmothers, and fled in their cars, horse-drawn carts, bicycles or (for the unluckiest) on foot.

My dream of writing historical fiction has also been a long, slow journey over the last fifteen years. Secretly scribbling many attempts at historical novels, I just couldn't get it right. I threw away a thousand pages that didn't work, tried again, failed some more. It hurt so much I kept promising myself I'd give up my dream. Then I kept trying.

Everything changed in 2023 when Maisie Lawrence, an editor at Bookouture who'd just turned down a different historical novel I'd written, asked if I'd ever thought of setting a story in World War II.

I started dreaming about a ragtag group of orphans and their headmistress fleeing Paris, caught in a flood of desperate refugees. A new editor, Ruth Jones, helped me finish their story, which had me caught between tears and hope. The characters of Helen, Margot, Josette and Lucie became dear friends. Their struggles became mine. Thank you for sharing their story.

The drama gets even bigger in the next book in this series, which I'm working on as I write this. You won't believe what Lucie's doing in Paris—or what it will take for Margot and Josette to try to save her.

In the meantime, I'm so happy you're here with me.

Love, Jenna x

www.jennaness.com

facebook.com/JennaNessAuthor
x.com/JennaNessAuthor

PUBLISHING TEAM

Turning a manuscript into a book requires the efforts of many people. The publishing team at Bookouture would like to acknowledge everyone who contributed to this publication.

Commercial
Lauren Morrissette
Hannah Richmond
Imogen Allport

Cover design
Ami Smithson

Data and analysis
Mark Alder
Mohamed Bussuri

Editorial
Ruth Jones
Lizzie Brien

Copyeditor
Laura Kincaid

Proofreader
Liz Hatherell